JOSH HAYES
ENEMY OF
VALOR

D1739082

AETHON
BOOKS

ENEMY OF VALOR

©2020 JOSH HAYES

Print and eBook formatting, and cover design by Steve Beaulieu. Artwork provided by Florent llamas.

Published by Aethon Books LLC. 2019

Dedicated to my kids.

Sara, Sean, Jordynn, and Carter.
I love you and if not for you guys this book would've been finished four months ago.

And to Jamie, who corralled them so I could work.
I love you most of all.

CHAPTER 1

Outskirts of Caldera
Beness System
9 August 2607

Corporal Allen Sheridan dropped to a knee at the end of the alley and peered out into the empty street. Shallow puddles of water and soaked piles of refuse dotted the permacrete in both directions. Several broken-down flyers flanked the street in various stages of disrepair; only a handful looked flightworthy, and Sheridan still wasn't sure he'd chance it.

According to their pre-op briefing, the city of Caldera had been a boomtown when the Beness system had first been settled. Hundreds of developers seized up prime real estate when several surveys had discovered pockets of precious metals in the system, hoping to cash in on the flood of new residents. When it was discovered that the surveys had been wrong, and the pockets contained just under half the ore originally projected, most of the major investors cut their losses and pulled out, leaving less than a quarter of the population holding the bag.

Sheridan edged around the corner of a six-foot stone wall,

putting eyes on the target house: a red brick two-story, badly in need of a paint job and landscaping. The yellow lawn looked like it hadn't been tended to in months. Unlike the majority of the city, this neighborhood hadn't received modern amenities and looked downright ancient. The houses were cheap and packed close together. It was obvious whoever had built them had been trying to create the illusion of wide-open spaces but had failed miserably.

A small flock of birds took off from the stone wall next to him, lifting in the damp air in a flutter of wings and agitated calls. Sheridan winced, watching them fly into the violet and orange sky, and held his breath, listening.

So much for zero footprint, he thought.

He adjusted his MOD27 on his thigh and keyed his taclink. "Seven Alpha, in Position One."

"Roger that. Hold position and stand by," Staff Sergeant Rocha replied. The team leader for Team One had remained with their commandeered vehicles, overseeing their infiltration and making sure the exfil wasn't compromised.

"Copy that." Sheridan shuffled back from the edge of the wall, crouching under the low-hanging branches of a tree on the other side. Water dripped from the wide silver and blue fronds, plinking on his tactical helmet and combat uniform.

His helmet wasn't the full-face tactical helmet they used in void conditions, but the visor that wrapped around the top half of his face still displayed all the pertinent information he needed during the mission. Their "light kit" consisted of body armor and a tactical helmet, combat vest and charcoal gray battle uniform. They all would've preferred to drop in full combat kit, but the need for a low profile and stealth had won out.

The rest of the team was taking up their positions around the perimeter, their names displayed on the bottom left corner of his HUD. But where there should've been seven names, there were only six, a fact that their teammate Stephanie Neal had been more than a little vocal about. She would've been able to hold her own, Sheridan was sure about that, but when it came to medical releases, not even God could overturn her restrictions. She'd taken a hit during their operation to secure a weapons transport more than a week ago, and according to *Legend*'s medical staff, was still recovering.

"Overwatch, in position," Staff Sergeant Hanover, Team One's sniper, advised over the taclink. Sheridan scanned the opposing rooftops for a moment, looking for any sign of the sharpshooter before realizing it would be a futile effort. Hanover was a chameleon, in the truest sense of the word, able to vanish anywhere while still being able to take the necessary shots, and Sheridan had yet to meet anyone who rivaled Hanover's skill behind the trigger.

Corporal Jonathan Reese, the team's electronics specialist, took a knee behind Sheridan, tapping him on the shoulder. "Anything?"

Sheridan tapped his link, looking for the feed from Cole's drones, and shook his head.

"What's taking him so long?" Reese asked.

"Don't know," Sheridan said.

"Haven't seen any lookouts," Reese said.

"I know."

"That's bad."

"Maybe," Sheridan said.

Reese motioned to the house directly across the street. "You know anyone could be watching us, just waiting for us to step out and make ourselves a target. We need eyes."

In the street, a bulky trash hauler slid past, hovering on its counter-grav pads, the air beneath it shimmering. The amount of trash littering the street, however, made the hauler's appearance more than a little ironic. It paused half a block down, floating still for a moment without actually doing anything, then continued on, disappearing around a corner.

"All right," Sergeant Devon Cole said over the taclink, *"drones are up and moving into position."*

"Copy that," Captain Eric Chambers, Valkyrie Team's commander, replied.

Sheridan tapped his link then cycled through its menus until he found the feeds. The fist-sized orbs glided silently through the air on tiny internal counter-grav drives, allowing them to go almost anywhere and observe anything. Their only downside was they weren't well armored, and if located, they could be easily disabled or simply destroyed outright.

As they approached the target house, each cycled through different visual spectrums, giving the team an array of scans to assist their breach. Thermals would identify targets inside the house, IR for electronic countermeasures or internal security defenses, and X-ray to map the internal structure.

Sheridan frowned, pulling up the panel displaying the thermal feed. As far as the drone could pick up, it appeared as though the house was empty. "That's not good."

"Could be interference," Reese suggested.

"That'd make it worse, wouldn't it?"

Reese tapped his link. "Six Alpha, Two, are you seeing what we're seeing?"

"I am," Cole answered. *"They must have some pretty impressive countersurveillance systems running in there. I'm not picking up anything at all."*

"Sheridan," Captain Chambers said, *"you and Reese move up. The rest of us will meet you on the Four Side."*

"Roger that, Captain." Sheridan glanced over his shoulder, nodded at Reese, then stepped out of the alley and quickly crossed the street.

The "Four Side" meant the left-rear of the building, looking at it from the front. "One" being the front-left, Two front-right, and Three right-rear. The terminology wasn't unique to Alliance MARSOC teams, special operators had been using those designations for hundreds of years before the Alliance was even formed, but as the old saying went, if it's not broke…

Sheridan weaved between what had been two flyers parked on the side of the road, now just hollowed-out shells. He had to step over a collection of discarded parts and continued into the walkway between the houses. He crouched low behind a stone retaining wall that matched the one behind him and continued to the service road that ran behind the row of houses. The single lane road was dotted with waste containers and parked vehicles, and like in the main street, one or two looked usable.

He paused at the intersection, then turned right into the alley, keeping low, his MOD27 pulled into his shoulder, sweeping the street ahead. On the far side of the target location, he caught sight of Sergeant Richards, Master Sergeant Kline and Captain Chambers, all moving in his direction, partially concealed by a stripped aircab.

"Closing on the target," Sheridan said, slowing.

"We see you," Kline replied.

Sheridan took a knee behind a small two-door ground car and tapped his link display. The feed from the orbiting drone showed the target location as a translucent red overlay surrounded by grayed-out buildings. Both Saber groups were outlined in green, approaching from the north and south. The target house still appeared empty to the drone's sensors.

"Still nothing on tactical," Sheridan said.

"We're seeing the same," Chambers confirmed. *"Cole, can you get a look inside?"*

"I can try," Cole said. *"But with all the interference inside, there's a fair chance I'll lose the drones once they're in."*

Losing drones wasn't the worst thing that could happen on a

mission, but if you could help it, you wanted to keep as many as you could until the last possible minute. Missions didn't tend to go bad right out of the gate. Usually if things were going to go sideways, they got that way near the end of the mission. If you burned through your stash at the outset, you might not have them later on when you really needed them.

"Understood," Chambers said. *"Send it."*

Sheridan watched on his link's display as one of the drones approached the rear entrance to the target house. As it got close, he could just make out the silver orb floating through the air at eye level. It took another two minutes for the drone to complete its three-hundred-sixty-degree sweep of the target.

"No joy, Captain," Cole said when the drone finished. *"All of the openings are secured. I could probably send one through a window, but…"*

"Negative," Chambers said. *"Stand down. Sheridan, you're up."*

Reese slapped Sheridan on the shoulder. "There you go, Blaster."

Sheridan shook his head and started forward. He pulled a small tube of HX7 from a pouch on his vest and ripped the clear plastic seal free. Ahead, Richards and Kline were moving toward him, eyes and weapons locked on the target house to their left, Sheridan's right. Like Sheridan, they were kitted out in the grays, tac-vests and helmets. Richards had an extra pack on his back containing his medical gear.

Sheridan popped the cap off the tube and started forward, crouching low. The Sabers moved through an open gate at the rear of the property and moved quickly to the back entrance. Holding his rifle one-handed, he pressed the tube against the door's lock and squeezed, forcing explosive foam into the mechanism. After a moment, he tossed the tube aside and pulled a thumbnail-sized explosive capsule from another pouch, pressing it into the hardening pinkish resin before stepping away.

"Ready," Sheridan said, stepping away from the door and activating his link's connection to the cap.

"Do it," Chambers said.

A single tap on his link detonated the explosive foam. The helmet's sound-dampening systems weren't as effective as their fully enclosed rigs, but it helped and reduced what would have been an earsplitting pop to a dull *whoomp.* There was a flash and the door swung violently inward on its hinges, banging against the inside wall.

"Moving," Kline said, moving up the steps and through the dissipating cloud of smoke.

Sheridan followed him in, Richards and Chambers coming in on his heels. Reese stepped in, but held just inside the door, providing the team with rear security. Sheridan toggled his visor's IR filter, turning the dim interior clear as day. A short hallway connected the back room they were standing in to a kitchen, where two separate doorways led to the living area at the front of the house, and a dining area on the side. A set of stairs, in the middle of the main corridor, led up, switchbacking to the second floor.

"Sheridan, Richards, upstairs," Kline said, already pushing through to the front of the house.

Without a word, Sheridan started up, taking the steps one at a time, careful to have sure footing as he ascended, his rifle up and covering the space above him.

Slow is smooth and smooth is fast, he reminded himself, pausing at the top of the stairs, sweeping the small hallway. He knew from the briefing that the closest door was a closet, but he checked it all the same—nothing but some jackets and storage boxes. The latrine was also empty, which left a final door at the end of the hall. If there was someone inside, they would've heard the explosion; there wasn't any reason to be subtle. Without stopping, Sheridan rammed the sole of his boot into the door with a vicious front kick, shattering the frame and sending the door swinging inward with a loud crack. A red outline flashed on his visor's HUD as he entered, a lone figure getting to their feet at the far side of the room.

"Don't move!" Sheridan shouted. "Get your hands up!"

"Please! No!" It was a woman's voice, her figure solidifying as the smoke and dust thinned, her hands waving frantically back and forth as she stepped toward Sheridan.

"GET DOWN!" Sheridan repeated, motioning to the floor with his rifle.

The woman screamed and dropped to her knees, looking away, as if not wanting to see the end coming. "Don't shoot me!"

"Don't move!" Richards shouted, moving around Sheridan, keeping his weapon trained on the woman.

"Please! I don't know where he is!"

She was short, maybe five one, with thinning gray hair and pale skin. Her clothes hung loose on her small frame. The woman looked back at Sheridan with tear-soaked eyes, revealing her terrified expression. She had to be at least sixty.

Sheridan looked at Richards, confused. "What the hell is this?"

CHAPTER 2

Safe House
Outskirts of Caldera
Beness System
9 August 2607

"You have no right to be in my house," the woman said as Richards helped her off the floor. "Get out. I don't want you here."

She pulled away from him, poking him in the chest with a finger. "Don't touch me!"

Sheridan felt a hand tap him on the shoulder and saw Chambers coming up behind him. He moved aside, letting the captain and Master Sergeant Kline into the room. The woman eyed him, anger and confusion burning in her eyes.

"Who the hell do you think you are?" she shouted, her voice cracking slightly. Despite her diminutive frame, she didn't appear as old and frail as Sheridan had assumed when he'd first seen her. She walked toward him, accusatory finger stabbing the air.

Chambers lifted a hand, blocking her repeated pokes. "Ma'am, please, I—"

"Don't you *please* me, young man," the woman said, cutting him off. "I don't give a shit about your please! How dare you barge into my house! What gives you the right to break into my home?"

She certainly didn't appear to have any qualms about stepping up to an armed man half her age wearing full body armor. Sheridan didn't know if she was crazy or just didn't care, but there was something about the woman that reminded him about his own grandmother and how she ran her home. One hundred percent, no questions asked, she was in charge, and everyone knew it. Sheridan couldn't help the smile that spread across his face as the captain struggled to appease her.

"Ma'am, I—"

"And don't give me any local law bullshit, I know Caldera doesn't have anything like this," she continued, backing away. "They wouldn't have the balls to try anything like this on me anyway. Goddamn cowards can't even protect their own." She considered Chambers silently for a long moment. "You're Alliance military."

Obviously caught off guard, Chambers hesitated. Richards raised an eyebrow, giving Sheridan a look that seemed to ask, *"How the hell did she know that?"*

After a moment, Chambers nodded. "Yes."

"Beness isn't part of the Alliance. You have no right to be here."

"I'm not at liberty to discuss our operation, ma'am, but you are coming with us."

Her eyes grew big, hands going to her hips. "Oh, I am, am I? Young man, do you have any idea who you're talking to? It's obvious you don't, because if you did—"

"Listen, ma'am," Chambers said, interrupting her. "We aren't going to stand here arguing. My team and I are here on official orders, and you *are* coming with us, one way or another."

"Heads up," Hanover said over the taclink. *"We've got incoming. Ground transport, moving in from the north. They're moving in slow, like they're looking for something."*

The Sabers in the room exchanged concerned looks with each other.

Her eyes flicked to the rest of the team, seeming to pick up on the fact that something was happening. "What's wrong? What's going on?"

"Redirecting drone three to intercept," Cole advised.

Chambers tapped his link, activating its display. The holographic panel rotated into place around the back of his hand, and the captain turned slightly, shielding the screen from the woman's view. Sheridan leaned forward, watching as the drone flew over several houses, gaining altitude as it went. A targeting reticle tagged the vehicle, outlining it in red. The windows were blacked out, but the drone's thermal sensor identified four individuals inside.

"Maybe they're just out for a nice family outing," Cole suggested. *"Taking in the scenic views?"*

"Unlikely," Kline said. "Not out here."

"They're stopping," Hanover reported. *"Targets exiting."*

Four figures exited the counter-grav transport, their movements coordinated and practiced. Each wore identical black uniforms and tactical vests, their faces covered by black masks. Each had a rifle slung across their chest, and pistols holstered on their thighs. They were most definitely not out looking at the scenery.

"That's not suspicious at all," Richards said. "Who do you think they are?"

"I doubt they're local cops," Sheridan said, giving the woman a sidelong glance, watching her reaction. She seemed worried more than anything, but he didn't think there was any recognition on her face, but he couldn't be sure.

"They're professionals whoever they are," Chambers said. "But it's *what* they're doing *here* that I'm interested in. They didn't just arrive here minutes after we did by chance."

"Well, they can't be after us. No one knows we're here," Richards said. "Maybe they're after her?"

"What are you talking about?" the woman demanded, trying to step around Chambers to see his link. "Who's after me?"

Kline put himself between her and the captain, his arms out to the sides. "Don't."

Richards went to the window and peered down over the street below. "Street's clear."

"All right," Chambers said, "we're out of here. Sheridan, take us out. Richards, don't let her out of your sight."

Richards nodded. "Roger that."

The woman took a nervous step back as Richards approached with his hand out. "Don't touch me!"

"Ma'am, please," Richard said.

"What's going on? I told you, I'm not going anywhere with you. You don't have a—"

"Ma'am, I understand you're scared," Chambers said. "But right now is not the time. We have a ship waiting and—"

She shook her head. "I'm not going anywhere. This is my home. You can't just barge in here and—"

"Listen, you're safe with us, I can promise you that. We're not going to hurt you." Chambers pointed to his link's display. The masked figures were snaking their way down the street, moving with purpose. "I can't, however, say the same about whoever they are."

She considered the display for a moment. "Who are they? What do they want?"

"I don't know, but I can guarantee you, you don't want to find out."

"I need to talk to my son," the woman said. "Where is he?"

12

"Captain, I'm not picking up any identifiers on their uniforms," Cole advised over the taclink. *"I—"*

Cole cut off as Sheridan passed the first landing. He held up briefly, waiting for Cole to finish.

Kline's voice came over the taclink. "What the hell just happened?"

"I just lost contact with all the drones," Cole responded, his voice anxious. *"I can't tell if I've lost the stream or if the units have been destroyed. Trying to reconnect."*

"Figure it out, Sergeant," Kline ordered.

Sheridan reached the ground level and immediately headed for the rear of the house, where Reese was holding the door, covering the approach from the service road.

He turned as Sheridan approached. "What the hell is going on?"

Sheridan shook his head. "Fuck if I know."

"Somebody else decided they wanted to join the party?"

"I guess."

Reese led the two of them away from the house. They paused slightly at the gate, then curled onto the service road, heading back the way they'd come.

"One Alpha Actual, we're en route to your position," Chambers said over the taclink. *"Plus one civilian. Be advised, several unknowns have arrived in the AO. It looks like they may be heading in our direction, and we've lost close-in surveillance."*

"Roger that," Rocha replied. *"Name one, we'll come to you."*

After a brief pause, Chambers said, *"Meet at Razor."*

"Copy Razor, on our way."

Sheridan tapped his link, bringing up the operational map to check his position. Waypoint Razor was three blocks away to the east, a parking lot behind a warehouse. During their pre-mission brief, they'd decided on three extraction methods, zero profile, where the team would exfil exactly how they'd inserted, taking the vehicles they'd confiscated out of town to where the *Doris* was waiting, or have the *Doris* pull them out directly. The last option was for *Legend* to send in a flight of Nemesis IIs and one of her Albatross assault shuttles, but they'd only do that after all other options had failed. The goal was keeping their presence on the planet as clandestine as possible, but if worse came to worst, they weren't going to risk getting caught.

Sheridan checked over his shoulder as he reached the first intersection, caught sight of the rest of the team entering the alley from the target house, then pressed on. He splashed through a puddle as he turned west, heading up a narrow walkway between properties.

"Two blocks out," Rocha said over the taclink.

Sheridan's gaze swept back and forth, across the street, scanning the rows of houses on either side of the street. Empty windows, blinds pulled shut, watching the rooftops, seeking out any sign of ambush. *Where there's one enemy, there's two,* his instructors had drilled into his head during patrol training. The Saber Qualification Course wasn't too unlike regular marine boot camp, just taken up a notch and focused on small-squad tactics instead of large marine mobilizations. There were pros and cons to each, the biggest con being, if shit hit the fan, you didn't have hundreds of other guns to fight off the enemy. No heavy armor to roll in and blast the enemy down to their component atoms, no gunships to clear the way. It was just you and your squad and whatever weapons you brought with you.

The goal of Team Valkyrie was to get in and get out, with as little profile as possible. Big guns weren't high on their priority list, getting out fast was. Getting out without anyone knowing they'd even been there was ideal, but so far in his short time with the Saber Team, that hadn't been something they'd been very successful at.

"I've got eyes on again," Hanover advised, his voice low.

"Looks like they're moving toward the target house from the north."

"Copy that," Chambers said. *"Fall back to the pickup. I think it's safe to say they aren't friendly."*

An updated location marker appeared on Sheridan's visor, showing the new location of the mystery team, the house they'd just vacated marked in red. Either the woman was more popular than she was letting on, or this new team was after the Saber team. No one but *Legend*'s crew knew the team was even on-planet, and they'd left their warship well outside sensor range of the planet and brought the *Doris* in on a fresh transponder. But if they weren't here for the old woman, what were they here for?

Sheridan paused at the end of the walkway, covering the road to the left as Reese moved to cover the right. The two-lane street was identical to the last, flanked by identical houses, and vehicles parked along the street. Though, there was a distinct lack of trash on this section of street, and Sheridan saw no sign of stripped vehicles. It looked like someone was actually taking care of this section of town.

Sheridan was about to call clear when movement at one of the houses caught his attention. A black two-door flyer flared briefly half a block down the street to the south, kicking up several fallen leaves and blowing tiny waves of water across the street as it set down. Its flashing amber and blue emergency lights reflected off the surrounding buildings, and as it settled onto its landing struts, Sheridan read the words on the side.

"What the hell is this?" Reese asked, pressing up behind Sheridan.

Sheridan shook his head and keyed his taclink. "We've got a big problem."

"What you got, Seven?" Chambers asked.

"Cops."

CHAPTER 3

Two blocks from Extraction Point Razor
Outskirts of Caldera
Beness System
9 August 2607

Two uniformed officers stepped out of the flyer, carefully inspecting their surroundings as they crossed to one of the houses. As they neared the front steps, a man dressed in a dark blue robe stepped out, a mug of steaming hot liquid in one hand. He waved at the approaching officers, saying something Sheridan didn't understand. He motioned back at his house, then at the officers again, shaking his head.

One of the officers put up a hand, obviously trying to get the man to calm down. Policing agencies in the URT weren't uncommon. After all, even in the wild west of the galaxy, law and order was still a necessity. Most planets left the security and enforcing duties up to the local municipalities, though some of the larger, more populated worlds employed a planetwide force. CITY was just large enough to support its own agency, and judging from the condition of their uniforms, it was surprisingly well funded.

Which meant their officers were probably well trained and not just a gang of local muscle.

Reese shifted to the other side of the alley. "North side is clear. Think we can just bypass them?"

"I doubt it."

Captain Chambers and the rest of the team came up behind Sheridan, who backed out of the way, allowing Chambers an unobstructed view of the situation. The woman was breathing heavily but no longer arguing about being taken against her will. She slumped against the fence, hands on her knees. Richards stood by her, obviously ready to keep her from collapsing.

"I'm almost to Razor," Rocha said over the taclink.

"Roger," Master Sergeant Kline answered. He was leaning forward, over the captain's shoulder, also trying to get a read on what was going on down the block. "Cole, what's the story on your drones?"

"One through three are off-line. My guess is they were hit with a jamming pulse of some kind. They're gone. I'm prepping my reserves now. Should be airborne in another thirty seconds."

"Roger that."

Chambers turned, looking back down the alley. "Can we redirect?"

Kline shook his head. "If we redirect, we'll run into our friends back there."

Chambers nodded. "Yeah."

"So what if the cops see us," Reese said. "We're going to be off-planet in fifteen minutes anyway. By the time their backup gets here, we'll be long gone. They won't be able to identify us anyway."

"You assume they won't," Chambers said. "But there's always the chance someone can and will, and if they do, the news that a covert Alliance team is operating in the URT and kidnapping civilians… well…"

Reese was silent for a moment, obviously considering that. Sheridan couldn't argue with the captain's logic either, but the problem remained that they still needed to get off-planet, and their ride was straight east, on the other side of the street.

"Okay," Reese said, "then what?"

Sheridan glanced back at the two officers, who appeared to be in some kind of back-and-forth with the caller. He got the impression that they weren't exactly happy about having to deal with the caller. The taller officer said something and made a quick gesture to their flyer, and the man held up his hands apologetically, nodding. Sheridan wondered how many times the officers had been out to this house and dealt with the same complaint time and time again. It definitely looked like they knew him.

He'd known more than a few cops in his lifetime, and while he technically wasn't a street cop, he'd had several conversations with them about "that caller." Knew the officers were probably as annoyed at having to come and talk to this man as Valkyrie was that they were now blocking their escape route. They were probably looking for any excuse to move on to the next call.

"I've got an idea," Sheridan said, pulling his sling over his head and handing this MOD27 to Reese.

Reese took it, frowning. "What are you doing?"

Sheridan ignored him, pulling off his helmet, then immediately undoing his vest and shrugging it off.

"What do you got?" Chambers asked.

"We need them somewhere else, right?" Sheridan asked, nodding toward the officers. "I'm going to give them another call to chase."

Without waiting for permission, Sheridan stepped out of the alley and hurried toward the two officers. Without his tactical gear on, he could've been just another civilian out for a morning stroll. There were no identifiers on the charcoal gray jumpsuit; name, unit, and rank had all been stripped. If anything, he'd pass for a veteran who, after years of serving, hadn't been able to completely separate himself from the uniform.

"… and I thought we told you the last time we were out here that we couldn't keep coming out for these loud-noise calls, Vert," the taller officer was saying as Sheridan came into earshot.

The man stepped back, scoffing. "*All* these calls? That wasn't a loud noise, it was an explosion. I heard it plain as day."

"It was probably just a converter blowing somewhere," the shorter officer said, scratching the stubble on his chin.

"To hell with that," the man said, shaking his head. "I know what I heard."

"Excuse me, officers," Sheridan said as he neared them.

The taller officer turned, holding a hand up to the caller as soon as he caught sight of Sheridan. "Hold on a second, Vert. Can I help you, sir?"

Sheridan raised his hands. "I'm sorry to you both, officers, I don't mean to interrupt, but I think I just saw something really bad, and I was going to call it in, but then I saw you two here, and…"

The shorter officer stepped around his partner, his hand on his holstered pistol, frowning. "What do you mean 'something bad'?"

"I'm not sure, but I saw these men getting out of a car a few blocks away, and the way they were dressed, well, they were wearing masks and had these big guns." Sheridan held out his hands, indicating the size of the guns. "They were walking up the street."

The taller of the two officers stepped forward, frowning. "Masks and guns?"

Sheridan nodded. "That's right, like I said, I'm not sure how you could get any more suspicious."

"Where did you say this was?"

Sheridan pointed north again. "A couple of blocks that way, blue house, I think."

The taller officer started heading for the flyer almost immediately; the second hung back. "How many did you say there were?"

"Four, I think," Sheridan said. "I don't know, man, I just got the hell out of there."

The officer, whose mustache hung past the edges of his mouth, tapped his link. "And what's your address, sir?"

Sheridan hesitated for a moment, his mind racing to find an answer. "I… I'm visiting a friend up the street. I was just out for a run and…"

The officer lifted an eyebrow, and Sheridan could tell by the expression on his face that he wasn't convinced.

"Hey, Masterson, come on, let's go check it out," the taller officer said, already opening the door to the police flyer. "I'll call it in on the way."

"Hang out here for a minute," Masterson told Sheridan before heading after his partner.

Sheridan nodded vigorously. "Of course, officer, whatever you say. Just trying to help. Those guys look like they were up to no good."

"Hey, what about my complaint?" the man said from his porch.

"Yeah, we'll be back as soon as we can," the taller officer said. The tone in his voice, however, suggested otherwise.

Masterson climbed into the passenger side of the flyer as the engines spooled up. The water around the base sprayed away as the counter-grav pads kicked on. Sheridan let out a long, relieved breath as the emergency lights began flashing and the flyer lifted into the air, banking north.

"You've got to be fucking kidding me," the man said, throwing up his arms, splashing brown liquid over his hand. "Well, that's just great, just fucking great." He pointed at Sheridan with his free hand. "You're a real asshole, you know that?"

"Yeah, I know," Sheridan said.

The man gave Sheridan a dismissive wave and climbed back up the stairs to his door. "A real fucking asshole," he said, and slammed the door without looking back.

Sheridan couldn't help but laugh. *I can't believe that worked.*

Sheridan jogged back to where the rest of the team was waiting, all with equally surprised expressions.

"Well, your talent for the unexpected continues to impress," Chambers said.

Reese handed him back his rifle, shaking his head. "I've got to hand it to you, Sheridan, I was expecting to have to come save your ass. How the hell did you know that was gonna work?"

"I didn't." Sheridan pulled his vest back on, then his helmet, the visor's HUD activating as he slid it down in front of his face.

"Next time give us a little bit of a heads-up though, would you?" Chambers asked.

"Roger that, sir," Sheridan said, smiling.

The captain nodded. "Come on, we got a ride to catch."

CHAPTER 4

Officers' Mess
ANS *Legend*
9 August 2607

Fischer pulled at his beard, letting the silence in the small compartment hang. The man at the other end of the table clenched his jaw muscles, nostrils flaring with each breath. He was clearly frustrated, and that was good. Fischer wanted him frustrated, wanted him off guard.

Legend's officers' mess was relatively small compared to others in the same class of warship, with just room enough to feed the eight command staff officers without requiring them to sit on each other's laps. The rectangular table was bolted to the floor, with a bench along the port-side bulkhead and chairs at either end and the starboard side. Fischer and the raider Dennis Larson sat opposite each other, the only ones in the compartment, both vying for the upper hand, though from Fischer's perspective, Larson didn't have a leg to stand on. Upset, angry people weren't generally known for rational thought, and the longer Fischer could keep him uncomfortable, the more likely he was to say something useful.

Which would be an amazing change of pace, Fischer told himself. Despite his calm and collected appearance on the outside, inside he was a jumble of impatience and anxiety. He *knew* this man had information he needed, and he didn't have time to sit around and wait for him to slip up. Fischer needed the information yesterday, not hours or days from now.

They'd been sitting in the room for close to four hours now, and Fischer had already repeated his questions from their previous conversations, all to the same responses: "I don't know anything. I'm a victim. I want a lawyer. You can't hold me like this forever. And where the hell are we anyway?"

"We can," Fischer said, "and we will. I'm not sure you're grasping the dire situation you're actually in, my friend. You're being held as an enemy combatant. Do you know what that means?"

Larson held Fischer's gaze for a long moment, as if trying to read what Fischer was going to say. Larson's link had given them a lot of situational data, information that had led them to Beness, in search of what they hoped would be leverage. It'd been obvious from the beginning that this man wasn't a shot-caller; he was muscle, plain and simple. But sometimes that was enough. Sometimes the muscle was what got you in the door.

"Enemy combatant?" Larson asked, sitting back in his chair. "I ain't at war with nobody."

"Aren't you?" Fischer raised an eyebrow. "Seems to me you and your friends were getting ready to get into a fight with someone."

"You're kidding, right? With all the firepower the Alliance has? Talk about taking a pistol to a railgun fight. We we're just looking to protect what's ours, that's all."

"Protection? And just what exactly are you protecting?"

"Our home, man."

Fischer jerked a thumb over his shoulder. "That rock back there? Huh. Not much there to protect. In fact, it didn't seem like there was anyone really staying there. Looked to me like it was merely a stepping-off point. And if protection is the story you're going with, how can you explain the Pegasi military? You seemed to be having a nice little get-together before we came in and crashed the party."

"I don't know what you're talking about."

"Oh, come on now, you're smarter than that," Fischer said. "You're not going to play the ignorant game on that, are you?"

"I told you, I don't have anything to say to you."

"Okay." Fischer stood and turned for the door. "Beness."

Larson straightened in his seat, eyes locked on Fischer. "What?"

"Caldera specifically," Fischer said, reaching for the handle.

"What the fuck are you talking about?"

"Earlier," Fischer said, "you asked where we were going, it's Caldera. According to the transit data on your link, you come here quite often. We wanted to see what was so interesting about this place."

Larson worked his jaw back and forth, eyes locked on Fischer. "Bullshit."

Got 'im, Fischer thought, turning back to the table. "Is it?"

Larson worked his job back and forth, obviously contemplating Fischer's words. He sniffed. "Fucking mind games. That's all it is. The cops are all the same; liars, every single one of you."

"I'm not a liar," Fischer said. "Not a cop either. You really don't think some city cop is going to come all the way out here to find you, do you? Hell, I wouldn't have come all the way out here to find you if this had been a normal case. But you and I both know there isn't anything normal about this case, don't we?"

Larson didn't answer.

"You might as well help us out, help yourself out too."

Larson sat back in his chair. "I told you, I ain't got nothing to say to you."

"That's fine," Fischer said. "We've got all the time in the world."

"Bullshit, you can't hold me forever. Some point you have to let me go."

Fischer chuckled, shaking his head. "I told you, you're an enemy combatant; that means I can hold you indefinitely. Hell, I could let you rot in a cell and never talk to you again, and no one would ever question it. I don't think you've completely grasped the situation you're in. You have no rights."

Fischer enunciated each word of his final sentence as he stepped away from the door and put both hands down and leaned across the table. He stared into Larson's eyes, watching with practiced ease as the hardness and courage slowly ebbed away. Fischer had the upper hand and Larson knew it.

"I can do whatever the fuck I want to do to you, and there isn't a damn thing you can do about it, so you can sit here and fight it all you want, but the sooner you start helping me, the sooner it will go better for you."

"I told you, I don't know what the plan was. I was just muscle, okay? Most of us were."

Fischer didn't respond, letting the silence of the room do his questioning for him.

After a long, drawn-out moment Larson sighed. "I'm telling the truth, man, okay? I didn't know. All I know is that they were paying a shit-ton of money for the manpower. It wasn't just me either, it was everyone. Hell, man, I made more money than I could have made in four lifetimes raiding commercials."

"Lot of credits for a hired gun."

"Yeah, well, they were real, that's all I give a shit about."

"Ever ask where the money came from?" Fischer asked.

"Fuck no, would you? None of us gave a shit where it came from, just as long as it went in our pocket, know what I mean?"

"And they paid you all this money to do what?"

Larson laughed. "That's the shitty part, man. They paid us four times what we'd been making already, to do exactly what we'd been doing. Only difference was, they told us when and where, you know."

"They chose your targets," Fischer said.

"That's right."

"And you didn't feel the need to ask why?"

"Shit, man, you wanna bite the hand that feeds you?"

A soft chime sounded and the hatch behind Fischer slid open, quietly disappearing into the bulkhead. Eliwood stood in the corridor outside and nodded her head at Fischer, beckoning. He frowned and was about to ask when he decided against it. Whatever it was, Eliwood didn't want Larson hearing what she had to say.

"Give me a minute, would you?" Fischer asked the raider.

Larson sneered at Eliwood, looking her up and down. "Pretty lady friend you got there. She going to ask me the questions now? Wouldn't mind that one bit."

"No," Fischer said, stepping out. "She's going to let me know if you're telling the truth or not."

Command Information Center
ANS *Legend*
9 August 2607

Fischer stood at the edge of *Legend*'s Command Information Center, leaning against the bulkhead, waiting for the briefing to start. Eliwood stood to his right, Sheridan and Master Sergeant Kline next to her. Captain Chambers and the two team leaders, Staff Sergeant Rocha and Staff Sergeant Nguyen, were farther down, all of them silently waiting for *Legend*'s command team to arrive so the briefing could start. Everyone seemed anxious to learn whether or not their detour to Beness had been fruitful or just put them ever more behind schedule.

The crew looked visibly shaken from the events of the last week, both mentally and physically exhausted. They were back en route to Alliance Naval Command after stopping off in Beness to pick up what'd they'd hoped had been one of Cardinal's leaders. Their luck, as it turned out, had not taken a turn for the better. Whatever Dolores Larson was, she was most definitely *not* a dangerous terrorist leader.

The detour hadn't cost them much time, but even so, Fischer couldn't help but think they were behind the eight ball again. Had the operation panned out, it might have proven a worthwhile expenditure, but as it stood, they weren't any better off than they'd been when they'd started, and now they were much further behind.

Captain Ward, *Legend*'s commanding officer, had originally been against the idea of maintaining the blackout, wanting to reach out and alert command as soon as possible, but he'd eventually come around to Fischer's contention that the information needed to stay out of official channels for as long as possible. There just wasn't any other way to maintain a security lock on the information, especially when they didn't have any idea whom they could actually trust.

The events leading up to the battle in Astalt had taken a toll on everyone on board, including Fischer. And even though *Legend* had only taken three casualties, two Nemesis fighter pilots and a mechanic who'd been in the wrong place at the wrong time, the crew had grown incredibly close in their short time together, and the losses hit hard.

Everyone aboard knew it could've been worse, but they also knew they'd been extremely lucky. Fortunately for *Legend* and her warfighters, the enemy had not been prepared for the attack, nor had they been capable of launching an effective counterattack. Most of the raiders had been wiped out; however, some had managed to jump away; and those were loose ends that had haunted Fischer for the better part of the last week.

The hatch at the far end of the compartment opened, and Captain Anderson Ward and the rest of *Legend*'s command staff entered. In his mid-forties, Ward was considered young for his command, but as far as Fischer could tell, more than qualified. If there was one thing Fischer had picked up on during the last week, it was that Ward *listened* to his people. A trait that seemed to be lacking in the majority of commanders Fischer had met.

"Finally," Eliwood muttered, adjusting her position on the station behind her.

Fischer nodded in silent agreement.

"All right, people, listen up," Captain Ward said, stopping in the center of the room. "We'll be arriving in New Tuscany in just under thirty-six hours. From there we're being tasked with tracking down and apprehending all known Cardinal agents and assets we can identify. Unfortunately, that does mean we'll be maintaining blackout conditions aboard ship, and only authorized personnel will be permitted to leave."

Fischer's eyes flicked around the room, trying to catch the reactions of those assembled. To their credit, no one moved, not even so much as an uncomfortable shuffle. They were all professionals and understood the job at hand.

Ward nodded to Fischer and Eliwood before continuing. "We've been instructed to continue liaising with our ASI friends, coordinating our investigation with theirs."

"Are we being assigned to ASI, Captain?" Commander Manchester, *Legend*'s executive officer, asked, crossing his arms.

"Not directly, no," Ward answered. "However, it was made clear to me that our assistance would be available in whatever capacity they require. At this point, Admiral Hunter's only concern is rooting out the traitors. Our orders are to do whatever it takes to find them and bring them to justice. He was extremely clear on that point. Whatever it takes."

Heads nodded in collective agreement.

Ward continued, "Our Saber team will be providing tactical support while our remaining resources will be directed to tracking down leads and other information pertaining to Cardinal. Right now, the knowledge of Cardinal and everything involved with their operation is known only to the crew, Admiral Hunter, and a few key people at ASI. That information is strictly classified.

"As far as the rest of the navy is concerned, we're on prolonged, detached assignment. For the duration of this operation, we've been granted priority access to everything in the Holloman Alliance arsenal, including unlimited access to personnel records, personal history, financials, anything and everything we need to accomplish our mission. Admiral Hunter has briefed the president and received an official declaration of emergency powers to press this investigation wherever it might lead, using any and all means necessary. As of right now, the gloves have come off."

Eliwood leaned close to Fischer and whispered, "Holy shit, that's legit."

Fischer nodded, but didn't answer. The implications of what the captain was saying were far-reaching and, depending on how you looked at it, deeply disturbing. How many other civilizations had gone to extreme lengths to destroy an enemy, only to strip away the rights of the very people they were trying to protect? Having access to that amount of information *would* be extremely useful to their investigation, but if used improperly, it could, and would, cause great harm as well. And, if Fischer was being honest with himself, he wasn't sure he even trusted himself with that kind of access.

"From now on, Cardinal is our only priority. Everything else is secondary," Ward said. "And make no mistake, people, this is the gravest threat our Alliance has ever faced. We're fighting an enemy on two fronts. One we can see and another we cannot. It could mean learning someone we've known for years is one of our worst enemies. Do not let this deter you. This is going to be the most difficult mission we've ever undertaken, but it is quite possibly the most important thing we'll do in our careers."

That last statement seemed to bolster the morale of everyone assembled. The crew stood straighter, shoulders squared, looks of determination covering their faces. The fact that this crew had only just begun their voyage together spoke to their professionalism and absolute trust in their leadership. For Ward to bring them together so quickly was a testament to the reason he'd been selected for the assignment.

It's a good thing he's on our side, Fischer thought.

"I want each of you to personally brief your teams," Ward continued. "Everyone needs to be at the top of their game for this one. Command has handed this mission to us because we're the only team capable. We cannot, *will not*, drop the ball. Failure is not an option." He paused, looking over the faces of his crew, then nodded. "Dismissed."

"Liaise, huh?" Eliwood said, crossing her arms.

"That's what the man said."

"I'm really curious to know what 'whatever capacity they require' actually entails."

Sheridan chuckled. "Me, too."

"Well, first things first," she said. "Dealing with the skeletons in our own closet."

Fischer sighed. He hadn't really had time to process what Gav had said before he'd killed himself. But after they'd left Astalt, he'd had plenty of time to consider the implications, and none of them were good. If there truly was a mole inside the New Tuscany office, their entire investigation could be compromised. He wanted nothing more than to get home and find out, but at the same time, didn't. The thought of one of their own turning against him wasn't something he wanted to entertain.

Despite all that, he hadn't been able to stop playing back every interaction he could remember of the last few months, trying to remember clues from conversations only vaguely recalled. Nothing stood out as strange or insidious, not one. And then another notion had hit him.

"You're assuming it's just the one," Fischer said, giving Eliwood a sidelong glance.

"Come on, Fish, don't do that. I'm already paranoid enough as it is."

Fischer shrugged but didn't respond.

"You really think there could be more than one?"

"Up until a few days ago, I wouldn't have even believed there was one," Fischer said. "Now…"

He trailed off as Captain Ward approached, his expression sympathetic. "Sorry about that back there. I wasn't trying to put you on the spot."

"Not a problem, sir," Fischer said. "Keeps us on our toes."

Ward shook his head. "I have to tell you, Agent Fischer, this whole thing is a little outside my wheelhouse. I'm a warfighter, not an investigator."

"I am interested to know how this liaison thing is going to work. It's the first I'm hearing about it."

"Sorry about that. Given more time, I would've preferred to discuss it with you prior to the briefing, but as it stands…"

"I completely understand, sir. Don't worry about it."

"That being said, I don't think your bosses really understand it either. Of course, they're working on even less information than we are. When we arrive in New Tuscany, *Legend* will hold in the outer system, where a navy sprinter will take you and your partner planetside. I understand your boss has some additional information for you once you arrive. Is there anything you need in the meantime? Have we learned anything from our guests?"

Fischer shook his head. "Absolutely nothing. Continuing the blackout is a start, but I don't think we'll really know anything until we really get into this thing. Unfortunately, I'm afraid once this thing really kicks off, it'll be extremely hard to keep a lid on. Does the president have a plan to deal with the fallout?"

Ward pursed his lips. "Honestly, that is above my pay grade."

Fischer smiled. "I know what you mean."

"But that being said, whatever assistance *Legend* and her crew can provide you, it's yours. I meant what I said back there. I know a lot of guys have mixed feelings about ASI. I have to admit, I was one of them. But you've done nothing but impress me ever since we met back on the *Vision*."

Fischer thought back to his first time meeting Ward, when he'd been the executive officer on the *Vision* under Captain Kimball. Ward had been extremely suspicious of a "spook's" presence aboard his ship, and had their positions been reverse, Fischer wasn't sure his response would've been any different.

"What you did back at the raider outpost really solidified your worth in the eyes of the crew, not to mention the Sabers you pulled out of there," Ward said.

"I was just doing what I could do, sir."

"Yeah, well, if there's ever anything you need, after this whole thing is over I mean, don't hesitate to ask. It's the least I can do."

"Thank you, sir," Fischer said, then had a thought. "Actually, sir, there is something you can do."

CHAPTER 6

Corridor Seven
ANS *Legend*
9 Aug 2607

"So we're going home," Eliwood said, following Fischer out of the briefing room.

"Seems that way," Fischer said. He paused at an intersection, checking the corridor markings on the bulkhead before continuing. Navigating your way through an alliance warship wasn't difficult, but there was definitely an art to it. He found the designation he was looking for and headed in that direction.

"What do you think Carter's going to say?" Eliwood asked.

"He's not going to be happy," Fischer said.

"Not going to be happy? That's the understatement of the century. He's going to lose his shit."

"You're not wrong."

"Yeah," Eliwood said. "I mean, I knew the shit was bad, but I had no idea it was going to be this bad."

Fischer turned another corner and stepped aside as a group of crew members rushed by. "After everything we seen, I'm surprised it's not worse."

"How could it be worse than this?"

"Well, we're not fighting an intergalactic war yet."

"Yet? You don't think it could go another way?"

"Could it? Sure. But I don't think it's going to."

"Well, not unless we can stop it, right?"

Fischer smiled. "Unless we can stop it."

"What are you going to tell Larson?" Eliwood asked with a grin.

"Going to let him sweat it out for a while," Fischer said. "He doesn't know anything."

"You know that for sure?"

"What's to know? Some bad people waved an assload of money in his face, and he jumped in feet-first without asking any questions. Once he found out what he was involved in, he hid his mother away so they, or us, couldn't use her against him."

"It can't be that simple."

"Trust me, it is."

"And that other special ops team?" Eliwood asked.

Fischer thought about that for a moment and shook his head. "That I haven't been able to figure out yet."

"Seems like it's something pretty important."

"Oh, it is," Fischer said. "I just don't know why yet."

They reached the hangar bay and showed their security credentials to the master-at-arms at the entrance. Even on board the most secured, most advanced ship in the fleet, internal security was still paramount, and despite the fact that the crewmen manning the entrance most likely knew who Fischer was, he still did his duty. The guard nodded and tapped the hatch controls, allowing them entry.

Legend's hangar bay was nowhere near the size of a traditional carrier, but for a heavy cruiser it was massive. The Nemesis

II fighters arranged on the flight deck to Fisher's right were being checked and rechecked for combat operations. Two of the canopies were folded back, their pilots sitting in the cockpits, working on internal holodisplays as flight crews loaded munitions. A shower of sparks rained down from under another as crews repaired damage to an aerofoil.

They hadn't lost any fighters in the raid on the outpost in Astalt, but they hadn't gotten away unscathed. Two of the fighters had received significant damage, and while the pilots managed to return to the ship, they wouldn't be spaceworthy for quite some time, if ever.

Three Albatross-class assault shuttles sat opposite the fighters in a diamond formation, their rear cargo ramps folded down, fuel and data cables snaking across the deck. Crew and maintainers moved around the spacecraft, repairing damage, loading munitions, and checking internal components.

The *Doris* sat by herself at the far side of the bay, segregated from the rest of the squadron like a kid in the lunchroom who didn't have any friends. Tensley Jones stood next to a tool cart, tapping on two large holodisplays, shaking his head. Fischer could just see the legs of his engineer, Greg Loomistripoli, under the sprinter's starboard engine nacelle, his upper body hidden inside the spacecraft.

Jones looked up as Fischer approached, his frustrated expression becoming almost accusatory. "You know, for all the credits the Alliance is dumping into this operation, you'd think they'd be able to spare some parts. It was like pulling teeth to get some replacement jump relays and bypass coils. Had to jury-rig my portside thruster control, rerouted it straight through my secondary coolant matrix."

Fischer couldn't help but grin. "You do know nothing you just said means anything to me, right?"

"Do you know what these bastards had the nerve to tell me

when I asked for a phased harmonic array?" Jones asked, seemingly completely oblivious to Fischer's own question. "Told me I wasn't authorized for those systems. Are you fucking kidding me? For everything I've done for those bastards, and they couldn't give me one little array?"

"It is proprietary Alliance military technology," Loomis called out from inside the ship.

"Proprietary, my ass," Jones said, waving a dismissive hand through the air. "They're greedy, all there is to it. Stingy bastards. I guess it's true what they say, no good deed goes unpunished. What about you? You finally finished with your supersecret party?"

"Party wouldn't be the way I'd describe it," Eliwood said.

Fischer crossed his arms. "It's definitely developing."

"Developing, huh? Is that another way of saying everything's going to shit? Because that's the vibes I'm getting."

"Going?" Eliwood asked. "I'd say it's been shitty for a while now."

"Can't argue with that!" Loomis shouted. "Can you hand me the Number Three?"

Jones squatted down by his cart and rummaged through the middle tray. He found what he was looking for and walked it over to Loomis. "Well, at least it can't get any worse."

"Well, I wouldn't say that," Fischer said.

Jones handed the tool up to his engineer and raised an eyebrow at Fischer. "Oh?"

"You know I—ow!" A loud metallic clang echoed out from inside the ship followed by a string of curses from Loomis.

"Take it easy there," Jones said. "You break it, you buy it."

"Yeah, no, I'm okay, thanks," Loomis said.

"All right," Jones said, moving closer to Fischer. "What gives?"

"We've basically been given a blank check for this entire

thing. The military has been ordered to back us with whatever we need."

Jones held both hands up. "Oh, ho! Ho! Mister Big Shot on deck, look out."

"I don't know about that," Fischer said. "I just happened to be in the right place at the right time."

"You didn't happen to be nothing," Jones said, obviously not convinced. "You're on your way up, Fish. I'm telling you. Soon you'll outshine us all and won't be able to fraternize with the likes of us lowlifes. But hey, I don't hate you for it. It'd be a nice change though. Never hurts to have friends in high places, you know?"

Fischer laughed. "High places aren't even on my radar right now. I'm just looking to finish this thing with all my parts still attached."

"Hell, that's what people in my position have been doing for years," Jones said.

"Speaking of your position, I've got another job for you if you're interested."

"A job, huh? Thought you just said the military was supposed to give you everything you needed."

"Yeah, well, I don't think they'll be able to give me this."

"You mean to tell me there's something the all-powerful Holloman Alliance can't handle?"

"I didn't say they couldn't handle it, but I don't think it's something they should handle. It's… delicate."

Jones raised an eyebrow, a grin forming at the corners of his mouth. "Delicate, huh? That sounds shady. I like it."

Fischer hesitated. "Shady's one way to put it."

"In that case, I'm interested."

"I thought you might be," Fischer said, returning his friend's grin. "I've got something I want you to look into. There isn't a whole lot to go on, and it's probably a little risky, but if it pans out, you'll be able to name your price. But unless I miss my guess, you're going to know just the right person to talk to."

"I will, huh?" Jones crossed his arms. "Well, I do know a lot of people. Guess it depends on what you're asking."

Fischer tapped his link. "Let's just say it's something extremely technical." He swiped a finger across his link's holodisplay, sending the file over.

Jones's link flashed to life, appearing over the back of his hand. He spread his fingers over the display and skimmed through the file Fischer had sent. After a moment, his eyes went wide and he looked up. "Okay, and what exactly would you like me to do with this information?"

"I need you to find out who sent it and where they sent it from."

"And this is *all* you have?"

"I know it's thin," Fischer admitted. "But it's all we've got."

"Thin? This is damn near anorexic. Why can't you have your people track this down? I'm sure you could get the paperwork pushed through."

"Because he's already been shut down," Eliwood said.

"I wasn't shut down," Fischer corrected. "I was told I needed more. There's a difference. And not only that, but with everything we've learned over the last week, I'm not sure that we can trust anyone to actually follow through. It was sent through one of Alistair's deep-space comm relays, and their fingerprints are all over this mess."

"Alistair, huh? Shit, Fischer, even without all this other conspiracy bullshit, you'd be hard-pressed to find anyone willing to go up against those guys. They practically own half the galaxy."

"And have bids on the other half," Loomis said, climbing down off the stepladder he'd been standing on and coming up behind Jones. He eyed the data on the holodisplay and whistled. "Now that is something."

"I believe whoever sent that message is part of the command structure of Cardinal, if not *the* Cardinal," Fischer said. "If we can track that message to its origin point, we might be able to get at the very heart of this thing. Get ahead of it for once instead of always picking up the pieces."

"Just having the message and the serial isn't enough," Loomis said. "We're gonna need access to the communication relay's subnet and datacore, and those are things you can't just open up. They've got security systems on top of their security systems. How the hell do you think they got the reputation for being the most secure communications company in the galaxy?"

Fischer tilted his head. "I said it would be interesting, I never said it would be easy."

Jones raised a finger. "Hold up. I know you're not asking me what I think you're asking me."

Fischer had been wondering how long it was going to take his friend to put it together. "She's the best. You know it and I know it."

Jones grimaced. "Fish, no. Absolutely not. There has to be another way."

"If you can think of one, I'm all ears," Fischer said.

Jones turned away, pacing back to the cart, where he stared at the twin holodisplays for several silent moments. "Okay, let's just say she even agrees to see me, and I'm doubtful she will, it's not going to be cheap."

"Cost isn't a factor," Fischer said.

"When you say that, you have to mean it," Jones said. "I'm serious."

"I hear you."

"All right then," Jones said, coming back to Fischer. "But she's not going to do it."

"Convince her."

"Convince her?" Jones laughed. "Have you forgotten what I did to her? Because I guarantee she hasn't."

"It's been a long time," Fischer said. "No one can hold a grudge that long."

"You don't know her at all."

"Aren't you two forgetting something?" Loomis asked. They both turned to look at the engineer. He jabbed a thumb up at the *Doris*'s hull. "Unless we can get the relays up and running, this ol' girl ain't going anywhere."

"I'll talk to the captain and get it squared away," Fischer said. "You should be able to get everything you need."

Jones laughed. "See, Loomis, it pays to have friends in high places."

"And listen," Fischer said, lowering his voice. "When we get back to New Tuscany, there's something I need you to do for me before you head off to Thresh."

Jones raised an eyebrow. "Oh?"

Fischer nodded.

"As long as it keeps me away from Osprey for a little while longer, I'll do anything you want."

CHAPTER 7

Saber Common Room
ANS *Legend*
9 August 2607

"Definitely military," Hanover said, crossing his arms.

Sheridan nodded in agreement. "Definitely."

They were in the Saber's common room, going through the process of breaking down the mission. It was best to do that when everyone was fresh and before they forgot most of the details. Hanover and Sheridan stood behind Cole, who sat in front of three large holodisplays, orchestrating the presentation.

They'd just watched the team stack up on the rear entrance to Larson's mother's house, almost exactly the way Sheridan and the others had. They made entry, disappearing from view as they entered the shielded house, and exiting four minutes later. They stood there for several more minutes, seemingly trying to decide their next move, before one of them looked up and the feed went dark.

"Shit, I'd really like to know what they used to take my

drones out like that," Cole said, backing the footage up and replaying it at half speed.

"They have to be Pegasi," Hanover said.

"But how the hell did they get there so fast?" Sheridan asked. "They were literally on top of us."

As he spoke, the hatch to the common room opened and Captain Chambers entered, Master Sergeant Kline on his heels.

"Who was on top of who?" Kline asked.

"The other team," Sheridan said, pointing to Cole's displays. "It was like they knew exactly where we were going to be."

Chambers and Kline came over to see the footage. "Play it again."

It took less than a second for Cole to cue up the footage, and after it was finished, Chambers agreed with their assessment. "They've definitely received specialized training, but I'm not sure *who* they are matters as much as who they were after."

Sheridan frowned. "You don't think they were after Grandma?"

"She's not exactly a criminal mastermind," Hanover said.

"Maybe they were trying to get leverage on Larson, like us," Cole said.

"Why would they need leverage?" Staff Sergeant Rocha asked from across the compartment. "He was working for them, wasn't he?"

She was adjusting some of the gear on her tactical vest. A diagnostic module sat on the table next to her, running tests on her helmet's SmartHUD. Checking gear, like cleaning weapons, was all part of the Saber training. In fact, it was what most of their time was devoted to, but Luciana Rocha had made it a religion.

Sheridan made a mental note to do the same.

"The same people who implant explosives in your head?" Hanover asked. "They don't sound like the most forgiving organization."

He had a point. If committing suicide was preferred over getting caught and interrogated, Sheridan couldn't imagine what the repercussions for talking were. He thought about the mechanic Fischer had found on Cathcart Station right before they'd met. He couldn't remember the man's name, but he remembered his entire family had been murdered, and none of those deaths had been quick or painless.

"He was protecting her," Sheridan said before he knew he was going to say it.

"Walk it out," Chambers said.

"Well, Larson must have known what kind of people he was getting into bed with, right? Maybe she was the only person he cared about in his life, and he wanted to make sure she was safe from Cardinal's people. I mean, it makes sense, right? Maybe that's why the other team was there, like Cole said."

"No honor among thieves, eh?" Chambers asked.

"It doesn't have anything to do with honor," Hanover said. "It's the simple nature of their business. Fear is what keeps them in power. Fear from the common people, but also from their own people. Besides money, fear is probably the most powerful motivator. When you have both...?" He shrugged, letting the implication hang in the air.

"Talk about a hostile work environment," Cole said.

Sheridan sniffed. "I don't have the least bit of sympathy for them. They made their choices. Think about how many lives they've ruined. They're predators, plain and simple."

"So, we thinking they were Cardinal's people?" Kline asked. "They could be Pegasi."

"Fischer'll figure it out." Sheridan felt his cheeks flush. *Way not to sound like a fangirl,* he thought.

"Maybe," Rocha said. "But I'd say he's got more than his fair share of problems right now."

The common room hatch opened again and Neal appeared, a

wide grin spread across her face. She had changed out of her medbay gown back into her Saber grays, looking like she wanted to take on the galaxy.

"Oh, shit," Cole said, "guess you couldn't milk that scratch forever."

Neal held a small pad above her head. "I'm back, bitches!"

Sheridan couldn't help but laugh and slapped her on the back as she joined them. "It's about time."

"Looks like you guys made some new friends," she said as the drone footage continued to play out on Cole's screens.

"You could say that," Kline said, moving to his locker and dropping onto the chair directly in front of it. He propped his feet up on one of Cole's hard plastic cases and stretched out. "I have to say, I'm about over all this supersecret conspiracy bullshit. Don't like thinking the person serving me at chow might just as soon stick a knife in my back as hand me a sandwich."

"You think there are Cardinal assets on board?" Sheridan asked.

Kline shrugged. "No way of knowing, I guess. Until your boy gets humping on this thing."

Oh, he has been, Sheridan thought, but didn't say. Fischer hadn't been doing anything but "humping" this case from even before they'd met on Stonemeyer, and Sheridan didn't see him taking a break anytime soon.

"We'll be back in Alliance space in about seventy-four hours," Chambers said. "Once in system, we'll transfer all the prisoners to a waiting barge that's been modified to hold them. We're going to have a little bit of downtime while Agent Fischer and his people at ASI work the intel we've collected so far, but after that, my guess is our tempo is about to significantly increase."

"It'll be good to have that sanctimonious bitch out of our hair," Reese said.

It had taken *Legend*'s medical staff six hours of surgery to work out how to extract the explosive charge implanted within her head, but after he'd mastered the procedure, the others didn't take half as long. One by one, the charges had been removed and the prisoners they'd taken from the Astalt raider outpost brought out of their medically induced coma. And for everything they'd learned in the meantime, they might as well have left them in stasis.

Larson had been the only one they'd managed to crack, though after hearing him talk, Sheridan doubted the raider would've had the courage to activate his suicide charge even if he'd had the chance. The Pegasi general, Eliska Karimi, hadn't stopped declaring the end of the Alliance was nigh since she'd regained consciousness. They'd learned her name through the biometric data stored in her link, and aside from proving extremely irritating to listen to, she hadn't said anything useful.

The other prisoners had chosen to simply remain silent, which suited Sheridan just fine, and despite not wanting to look at them any more than he had to, he didn't feel comfortable handing them over to someone else. None of them wanted a repeat of Young's escape, but the fact that they would be housed on a secure Marine barge gave the team some relief.

"Shit, I wouldn't want to inflict that woman on anyone," Cole said. "But I'm glad we don't have to babysit anymore."

"What about Grandma?" Sheridan asked.

"She'll be housed separately," Chambers said. "She's not under arrest per se, but for the time being anyway, she'll be a guest of the Alliance."

"To hell with Karimi," Cole said. "I'd be more scared of Larson's mom than any of the raiders we've met so far. Man, that woman is vicious."

A collective laugh rippled through the compartment. Dolores Larson had definitely given Chambers the third degree when they'd first found her, but she'd laid into Fischer with a vigor and rage that had surprised all of them when he'd tried to question her. It'd taken two guards to get her back to her cell, and she'd screamed bloody murder the entire way back.

"All right," Chambers said. "Study the footage. Keep it fresh. It's hard to say exactly what they were doing on Beness, but it's safe to say they were probably up to no good. Who's got the AAR?"

Across the compartment Richards raised a hand. "Working on it, Captain."

"Let's get it wrapped up and submitted. I want refit completed before we arrive in New Tuscany. And get some rack. The way this thing is shaking out, it might be a while before we get another chance."

CHAPTER 8

Alliance Security and Intelligence
Regional Headquarters
Blue Lake City, New Tuscany
12 August 2607

There hadn't been much to do during the final days of *Legend*'s journey back to Alliance space, leaving Fischer to war-game how he would approach his next important task. Dealing with drug dealers and pirates and murderers was something he did every day without really thinking about it; asking Carissa to pack up the baby and go into hiding was something he really would have preferred not to do. Fortunately for him, their briefing with Carter took precedence, buying him a few precious hours.

"It's going to be okay, Fish," Eliwood had told him on the shuttle ride down from *Legend* to the ASI Regional Headquarters. "I mean, it's not like she's going to kill you or anything."

Fischer laughed. "You don't know Carissa very well at all, do you?"

"It'll be fine. I'm telling you. Just be straight with her."

"Yeah. Right. Just do me a favor, would you?" Fischer asked as they entered the office.

"What's that?"

"Just make sure she doesn't destroy the bike."

Eliwood laughed. "Well, at least you have your priorities straight."

Fischer led the way through the division's lobby and into the bullpen. The staff had been sent home an hour ago to give Fischer and Eliwood access to their boss without anyone knowing they were back. The silence in the office was more than a little unnerving, and Fischer couldn't remember the last time the bullpen had been completely empty.

"Well, you've really done it now, haven't you, Fischer?" Carter asked as they entered his office, shutting the door behind them. The division chief of the New Tuscany field office looked like he'd aged twenty years since Fischer had last seen him only two and a half weeks before.

"Actually, boss, this time it wasn't all his fault," Eliwood said, taking one of the two chairs in front of Carter's desk.

Carter laughed. "Oh, yeah, I'm going to believe that."

"Jones helped a lot," Eliwood offered, and Fischer winced.

The expression on Carter's face shifted from amusement to irritation. "*Tensley* Jones?"

"You're an ass," Fischer muttered.

Carter waved a hand through the air as he sat. "No, you know what, it's fine. Maybe since he's doing all this work for us, I should just toss him a commission, give him an official spot on the team. I'm sure the director would love that."

"Boss, I—"

"Tensley Jones is a loose cannon, Fischer, you know this. I let the whole Stonemeyer slide because, well, the case doesn't happen without it. An isolated incident I can slip past Command without much of an issue, but continuing to enlist his help is only going to put us in muddy waters, something we absolutely do not want in this case."

"Sir, Jones is solid," Fischer said.

"And we haven't even had a chance to talk about Starmaker," Carter said, pointing a finger. "Don't think I've forgotten about that little fiasco."

Fischer hesitated. The disaster that ended the Feringer op had indeed slipped his mind. Defending Jones was a losing proposition; however, he needed to shift perception. "If it hadn't been for Jones, we wouldn't have located the Cardinal outpost, and we'd still be chasing our tails. Not only that, without him we wouldn't have found Gav, and without him…" Fischer trailed off.

"We wouldn't know about the embedded assets," Carter finished for him.

Fischer nodded.

"All right, forget Jones," Carter said. He tapped a data pad on his desk, one of dozens lying scattered over its surface. "What is up with these names?"

"Contact information from General Karimi's link," Eliwood said. "As far as we've been able to figure out, Karimi never contacted them personally. They were more like emergency contacts."

Fischer raised a finger. "Probably."

"I don't like 'probabilities,'" Carter said. "I can't do anything with probabilities. I need definites. Do we know if they are Cardinal assets or not?"

Eliwood sighed. "We're not a hundred percent. But with everything we've seen so far, it's extremely likely."

"I'll be honest," Carter said. "I'm having a hard time with all this. And not just with these three, I'm talking about everything. I personally screened over half the people working in this office, countless more throughout the agency. If the problem is as widespread as you say, then I've vetted some of the very people we're up against, and that scares the hell out of me."

"Understandably so," Fischer said.

"Hell, I don't even know where to start," Carter admitted. "A broad dissemination of the information is definitely the wrong move, we don't want them to know we're onto them, but at the same time, I don't want our loyal people operating in the dark."

"I'm not sure that we've got much of a choice," Fischer said. "We don't have a lot to go on."

Eliwood scoffed. "Now that *is* the understatement of the century."

"Okay, we have nothing to go on," Fischer corrected. "Even more of a reason to hold off taking any drastic measures."

"We know for certain we have a mole?" Carter asked. "You truly believe this Gav person? What makes you think he wasn't just blowing smoke up your ass?"

"He mentioned the Young message. There's only a handful of people who even knew about that message, much less could've gotten the information out. That's a start."

"You, Woody, me, Davis, Campbell." Carter counted the names with his fingers.

"Probably Hoskins too," Eliwood said. "She helped Davis with the decryption."

"Okay, well, I think we can safely check us three off the list," Fischer suggested.

Eliwood raised an eyebrow at him. "Are you sure about that? You've always seemed a little shady to me."

"Davis is solid," Carter said. "I've known her for years. She's never once not come through when I needed her."

"Campbell's been section lead over WRA for, what, four years? I can't see him feeding information to Cardinal."

"Hoskins's got the access, but she's only been with us for, what, two years? My money's on her."

"So what do you want to do?" Carter asked. "Put them in a room?"

Fischer rubbed his chin. Getting each one of them into an interview room was exactly what he would've preferred. But none of their suspects were dumb, and if they were Cardinal assets, they'd know the game was up the moment he asked them in.

"Bringing them in is the last thing we want to do," Fischer said. "Not only do we risk alienating our people if we're wrong, but once we put them in a room, people *are* going to start asking questions. Once it gets out that we've been infiltrated, shit's going to hit the fan."

"We can't just sit around and wait for them to slip up," Eliwood said. "You remember what Gav said; we're in the end game. Whatever they're planning, it's coming sooner rather than later."

"You're not wrong," Fischer said. "But we're jumping into this thing blind and crippled, and this is something we can't afford to screw up."

"What do you suggest?" Carter asked.

"We set up surveillance on everyone we suspect. Watch them for a few days, see if they pop any red flags."

"You really think we can afford the time?" Eliwood asked.

"I don't think we have a choice."

"And you think putting people on our own agents isn't going to raise any flags?"

Fischer shook his head. "We keep our people out of it. We can bring in the Sabers for the legwork, keep the op off the books. They've got some pretty impressive gear themselves."

Carter didn't look convinced.

"I'm telling you, boss, this is the only way we can be sure."

Carter exhaled a long breath. "All right, bring them in. We'll start tomorrow. I want hourly updates."

"Tomorrow?" Fischer asked. "We can start tonight."

"No," Carter said, shaking his head. He held up a hand, silencing Fischer's protest. "You look like shit, Fischer. It's late; you need to get some rest and see your family. Carissa has called me every day for the past week looking for you, and I'm done putting her off."

Fischer leaned back in his chair, rubbing his beard. "I'm going to put hcr in a safe house."

"Probably a good idea."

Eliwood smirked. "God, what I wouldn't do to see the look on her face when you tell her."

"Yeah," Fischer said, the dread he'd felt earlier creeping back in.

"Where you going to send her?" Carter asked.

"Not sure yet," Fisher admitted. "Obviously I'll need to keep it off the books."

Carter nodded. "I'll take care of that. You just let me know what you need." He stood. "Go home, get some sleep, kiss your girls. Get your family settled."

Fischer and Eliwood both stood, following their boss's lead.

"Thanks," Fischer said.

"We're facing a long road ahead," Carter said. "I only see this getting worse before it gets better."

Eliwood gave a humorless laugh. "You know, boss, your morale-building skills are top notch."

"That's what they tell me."

"I'll be here first thing," Fischer said as the office door opened at his approach.

"Be sure to give Carissa my love," Carter said, a knowing grin spreading across his face.

"Oh, yeah," Fischer said, "I'll be sure to do just that. See you in the morning."

Eliwood added, "If he survives that long."

CHAPTER 9

Fischer's Apartment
Blue Lake City, New Tuscany
12 Aug 2607

Fischer swiped his link over the security panel, and the door to his apartment slid silently open. Inside, a single light in the kitchen lit the interior, the living room dark and quiet. He locked the door behind him then surveyed the toy-covered floor and smiled.

"A little baby terrorist," he said under his breath, remembering what his wife had said several weeks before.

He made his way to the kitchen, found a glass, dropped in an ice cube, and poured in two fingers of his Nova Blend, New Tuscan whiskey. The local brew wasn't the most expensive in the galaxy, but it was smooth on the way down, and while it made his gums burn a little, it didn't make it feel like a nuclear bomb had gone off in his mouth. He took a sip, held it for a few seconds, then closed his eyes and swallowed.

"Where in the fuck have you been?"

Fischer opened his eyes to his wife standing a few feet away, bathrobe undone in the front, revealing the tank top and panties she wore to bed. She squinted at him through half-open eyes, her hair matted to one side. She did not look pleased at all.

"Babe, I—"

"Nope," Carissa said, holding up a finger, cutting him off. "You don't get to babe me. Not at all. You said a couple of days. *A couple of days,* Jackson. It's been damn near three fucking weeks. You couldn't call? Carter kept saying you were fine but couldn't tell me anything more than that."

"It was cl—"

"If I have to hear 'it's classified' one more time, I'm going to scream."

Fischer started to explain, then realized that wasn't what she was after. He sighed. "I'm sorry. I wanted to call, truly I did. I couldn't. If I could've, you know I would have. I am sorry, babe."

She held his gaze for several seconds, and slowly the anger plastered across her face began to fade. "You okay?"

Fischer nodded.

"Woody okay?"

"Yeah, we're fine."

"What about Young?"

He shook his head. "We were close. So close."

"What the hell is going on?" She stepped closer to him, now concerned instead of angry. "It's bad, isn't it?"

"Yeah," Fischer said, taking a sip of his whiskey. "It's bad."

"Are you going to be able to fix it?"

"Honestly? I really don't know. How's Maddie?"

"She's been asking about you. As you can see, it's been kind of a madhouse around here."

Fischer laughed. "Little baby terrorist, right?"

Carissa smiled and Fischer's heart ached. He hadn't realized until this moment how much he'd missed his wife.

"Come here," he said, arms wide open.

She wrapped her arms around him and pressed her body

against him. He slipped his free hand under her robe and around the small of her back, her soft skin warm to the touch.

"I love you," he said.

"I love you."

She loosened her grip and leaned back, looking into his eyes. "Tell me."

Fischer sighed and stepped back, sitting on the edge of the counter, the events of the last few weeks running through his mind. "It's bad, babe. I don't even know where to start."

Carissa pulled a glass identical to Fischer's from the cabinet and nodded to the bottle beside him. "Yeah. Well, why don't you start at the beginning?"

It took the better part of an hour to explain what had gone on since he'd left for Cathcart Station. Carissa never touched her drink as Fischer relayed the events of securing the *Firestorm*, the attack on the raider outpost, and finding Grandma Larson on Beness. He saved what they'd learned from Gav for last, almost not telling her, but decided she deserved to know. Especially with what he had planned for her and Maddie.

"Jesus, Jackson," Carissa said, finally taking a sip of her whiskey. "This isn't bad, it's a disaster. You really think you can stop this? Track down all the assets and bring them to justice?"

"I don't know about bringing them all to justice," Fischer said. "My guess is most of them are going to do everything in their power *not* to be taken alive. Almost everyone we've come in contact with has either killed themselves or tried, or simply won't talk, but the majority of them simply turn their brains to mush."

"That's horrible." Carissa grimaced.

"Yeah."

Fischer set his glass down. "Listen, this thing is going to get worse before it gets better. We're fairly confident we have a couple of good leads, but until we can put eyes on, we don't have any idea who we can trust."

"You think Carter?"

"No, Carter's fine. But we do suspect there's at least one mole inside the division, could be more; there's just no way of knowing yet."

"What you're saying is that everyone's a suspect until they're not," Carissa said. "That pretty much sum it up?"

"In a nutshell."

"How the hell can you fight them if you don't even know who they are?"

Fischer chuckled. "Yeah, that's definitely an issue."

"Who do you think it is? The mole, I mean?"

Fischer shrugged. "It could be a few people, really, and none of them I'd've suspected otherwise. We're going to start surveillance tomorrow. No one knows we're back yet, so it should give us a head start. But there's something else."

Carissa narrowed her eyes at him. "Something else?"

Fischer squared his jaw and said, "I want you and Maddie to go somewhere. Away from all this."

"Wait, why? What's wrong?"

"It's just a precaution, babe. Honest."

"The Cardinal you're talking about, you think they'd come after us to get to you, don't you?"

Fischer started to deny it but stopped. His wife was one of the smartest people he'd ever met. She'd seen through his poor attempt to shield her from the reality of their situation. There wasn't any point to pushing the issue now.

"Yes," he said. "It's possible. But I thin—"

"If it's too dangerous for us, it's too dangerous for you, Jackson. That's dumb."

Fischer shook his head. "It's not like that. And it's not like I can just walk away from this either. It's my job, babe."

"Fuck your job. It's not worth your life." She stepped closer to him. "I need you, Jackson. Maddie needs you."

"It's not going to come to that. I promise."

"You can't promise something like that. And if you think it's that bad, it makes me scared for you, too. But I can't just pick up and leave. I have responsibilities. Maddie has school."

"You have vacation saved up," Fischer countered. "And daycare, she's not exactly learning quantum physics. It'll only be for a couple of weeks, I promise."

Carissa didn't respond, only held his gaze for several long, silent moments.

"Look, you want me to be completely honest here? I'm terrified of this thing. It's bigger than anything I've ever worked by far. This isn't a case of some power-hungry crime boss or something. These are people with real power here, power to do practically anything, and when they start feeling the heat, I don't want them to have anything they can use against me."

He set his glass down and cupped her shoulders with both hands. "This isn't what I want, but it's the only thing that makes sense. It's the only thing that will keep you safe until this is over. If I thought there was any other way, I would tell you, but there isn't. Please."

"Okay, Jackson," she said. "We'll go."

Fischer let out a relieved breath, feeling like a huge weight had suddenly been lifted. "Thank you."

"I'll have to pack."

"Sure. We have some time."

"Where are we going?"

Fischer hesitated. "I… I don't know."

"What do you mean, you don't know?"

"Exactly that," Fischer said. "I don't want to give them any leverage. If I don't know where you are, they can't use you against me."

"Who is *they*?"

"Cardinal," Fischer said. "They're what's behind all this."

"You're scaring me, Jackson."

Fischer pulled his wife close again, wrapping his arms around her. "I'm scared too. I won't let anything happen to you." He leaned back, looking into her eyes. "I promise. Come on, I'll help you pack. Jonesy's waiting on you."

Carissa pulled away from him. "Wait, Jonesy?"

"He's going to take you and Maddie off-world until this thing blows over."

"I'm not going with him."

Fischer stopped on his way to the bedroom and turned. "Babe, he's the only one I trust. I can't take you to any of our safe houses. If Cardinal's people are watching me, which I have every reason to believe they are, then as soon as they discover you're gone, the agency safe houses are the first things they'll check."

"But—"

"Listen, Jones knows people, people who don't have any ties to the agency, no ties to the Alliance. People who don't know me. He'll be able to put you someplace no one will ever think to look, and no one will ask any questions."

"Maddie won't understand."

Fischer sighed. "Maddie will be fine. Turn it into an adventure, make it fun. It won't be forever. Jones is going to set you up with a clean credit account with more than enough to last you until this is over."

"How long do you think we'll be gone?"

"Not more than a few weeks," Fischer guessed, though he really had no idea. For all he knew, they could be working this thing for the foreseeable future. But he also knew that wasn't what Carissa needed to hear right now.

"You're lying," Carissa said, canting her head to the side the way she always did when she saw through him.

Fischer didn't answer. There wasn't anything to say.

Carissa watched him for several moments, then finished the

whiskey. She set the glass down on the counter and walked past him, into the bedroom. "What about you?"

"What about me?"

"If we're in danger, you're in danger," she said, entering their walk-in closet and flipping on the light. She rummaged through a pile of blankets and old clothes until she found a light blue duffel and threw it across the room onto their bed.

"Who's going to be watching your back?" she asked, pulling clothes off hangers and tossing them beside the duffel.

"I can take care of myself."

She rolled her eyes, pulling underwear from a drawer. "Yeah, so who? Woody and Carter? You're sure you can trust them?"

"Positive."

"You three against the world, huh? Sounds to me like the odds are stacked against you."

Fischer chuckled. "Aren't they always?"

"You can't take on the entire galaxy by yourself, Jackson."

"Oh, believe me, I know," Fischer said. "I've made some new friends in the last couple of weeks, and anything I can't handle by myself, well, let's just say I'm fairly confident they'll be able to."

CHAPTER 10

Alliance Security and Intelligence
Regional Headquarters
Blue Lake City, New Tuscany
13 Aug 2607

"You look like shit," Eliwood said as Fischer entered the bullpen. The clock on the main holodisplay read 0630 hours.

"Yeah," Fischer said, scratching the back of his head.

"How'd she take it?"

"Better than expected," Fischer said, making a beeline for the coffee cart at the edge of the room.

With the exception of Eliwood and Carter, the office was still empty. It was early, and Fischer had only managed a few hours' sleep before his alarm jolted him awake again. He was having a hard time keeping his eyes open.

He'd fought back tears when Carissa had climbed into the aircab, holding their daughter tight. Jones had arranged the ride, using contacts he'd made over fifteen years of walking the edge between law and outlaw, paid for through a dummy account, and Loomis had come along to escort them all the way to the *Doris*.

There would be no record of the pickup or the flight, and even if someone managed to find something, it would be for a closed account that had only been used the one time.

Sleep had come fitfully, and even though he was glad to be in his own bed and not a bunk on a warship, without Carissa lying next to him, it didn't feel right.

He poured a cup, spooned in creamer and sipped.

"Careful, it's hot," Eliwood warned.

Fischer winced, the liquid burning his lips, and wiped them dry with the back of his hand. "Thanks."

Half a dozen holopanels were floating in the middle of the bullpen, all showing video feeds and personal information from their first three targets. As Fischer looked over them, he still couldn't believe they were actively spying on their own people. Despite the events of the last few weeks, none of this seemed real.

"It's a nightmare," Fischer murmured to himself.

"Huh?" Eliwood asked.

"Nothing." Fischer blew gently on his coffee, then carefully took a sip. "You two are in early."

"Here late, you mean," Eliwood said.

Fischer eyed Carter. "You said we were going to start in the morning."

"Yeah, that's what I said," Carter said. "Had to say something to get you to go home."

"I didn't need to—"

Carter pointed at Fischer. "Yes, you did."

Fischer ground his teeth and looked away, frustrated and embarrassed at the same time. He took another careful sip, then said, "Where are we at?"

"We've been pulling background all morning," Eliwood said. "Personal, banking, family history, past employment, even acquaintance data. Most of it we pulled from their employee files, but we've had to reach out for the other stuff, still waiting on some of it. We're receiving all of Campbell's financials now."

"That's fast," Fischer said, watching the data scroll down one of the screens.

"Yeah, well, when you have presidential authority, that pretty much negates any red tape. We're expecting BLPD's rover feeds and comms access in the next hour or so."

"Too bad we can't pull that card for everything," Fischer said.

"No shit."

"We're going to need help going through all that data," Fischer said. "We're going to need to bring in the rest of the team. Some of them anyway."

"I know," Carter said, crossing his arms. "The question is who and how much access do we give them."

"You're not going to be able to keep them in the dark for long," Eliwood said. "They're going to figure it out, if they haven't already. I'm sure they already think something's up. We don't tend to hire dumb people."

"No," Carter said. "We don't. As much as I hate to say it, regardless of who we recall, we're going to have to keep close tabs on all of them. Most of our time is going to have to be devoted to watching the watchers."

"I'm not a babysitter," Fischer said. "I need to be working this case, boss."

"All things being equal, I'd agree with you. Unfortunately, this thing isn't fucking close to being equal. We're all going to have to do things we don't want until this thing breaks."

"You think it's going to?" Fischer asked.

"Break? Sure it will," Carter said. "They always do."

Eliwood frowned. "What's this? The great Jackson Fischer having doubts? That's not like you."

Fischer sighed and sipped his coffee. "They're not doubts, they're…"

Eliwood raised an eyebrow. "Doubts?"

"It's not that," Fischer said, sitting on the edge of one of the terminals. "It's just… most of the time I feel like I have a handle on it; others… it seems so big, it's too much. And not knowing who to trust, that's the worst part of this whole thing. Smugglers and murderers and raiders, I can deal with that. Not knowing if the person next to you is going to stab you in the back, that's something else entirely."

"Oh, don't worry," Eliwood said. "You'll definitely see me coming."

"Good to know."

"We're cross-checking all three of their histories to see if anything matches up," Carter said. "I'm actually in the middle of running everyone's file. Looking for similar connections."

Fischer shook his head. "These people are smart. They're not going to use the same contacts."

"You assume they're smart," Carter said. "But all criminals are stupid on one level or another. Either they're too confident, or ignorant, or a combination of the two. Hell, everyone makes mistakes. They're bound to have screwed up somewhere along the line."

Carter was right, and Fischer knew he was right, but when it came to Cardinal and their operations, he had a hard time seeing it. Stonemeyer had been a disaster, but Fischer didn't believe that had been a screwup on Young's part; there had been multiple variables that had affected that operation. Primarily the human kind, which, in most cases, was the most unpredictable.

"But do we have the time to wait for that?" Fischer asked. "We can't keep the team at arm's length forever. Hell, I'd say we have another twenty-four hours before they start asking questions."

"If that," Eliwood said.

"I just want to give us enough of a head start before bringing them back in," Carter said. "It's not ideal, but at least we're aware of the threat, and we're not going into this thing blind. And don't forget, not everyone is an asset. Cardinal's reach is wide, but it's not total. This isn't a hopeless endeavor, no matter how bleak it might seem."

Carter's encouraging words surprised Fischer; positive reinforcement wasn't exactly his old friend's go-to motivational tool. But Carter was correct, not everyone was an enemy.

"I put a call into your Marine buddies," Carter said. "They should be transferring down in the next few hours to set up physical surveillance. They seemed eager to get to work."

"They're definitely not the type to sit around and wait," Fischer said. "They want to be working."

"This isn't going to be a guns-blazing, door-kicking assignment," Carter said. "We need stealth and subtlety here if we're going to find anything."

"They're a capable team," Fischer said. "Don't know that I've worked with better. Chambers is as competent as they come, and in their chosen specialty, I don't know that you'd find better. Even in this office."

"High praise," Carter said.

Fischer nodded. "Well deserved."

Carter's link chimed and its panel rotated into position. He tapped the incoming message. "You know if you would've told me a week ago that Blue Lake PD would have been as accommodating as they have been, I wouldn't have…" He trailed off, his face darkening.

Fischer pushed himself off the terminal, stepping closer to his boss. "What is it?"

Carter looked up from his link, eyes hard. "It's Davis."

CHAPTER 11

Outside Davis's Apartment
Blue Lake City, New Tuscany
13 August 2607

The street outside Riley Davis's apartment was shut down for a block in either direction, and orbiting patrols kept the skies clear above. Clusters of reporters on either end of the cordon screamed questions and snapped holos as patrol officers argued with them to stay back.

"It's a cluster already," Fischer said, climbing out of the ASI flyer. "How do they always get here so fast?"

"They're vultures," Eliwood said. "It's what they do."

A man in his early twenties, wearing a gray suit and shoes Fischer could see his reflection in, approached them, hand extended. "Agent Fisher? Detective Cruz, sorry about the cameras. One of the patrol guys got carried away. I hear he's going to have a nice conversation with the chief later."

Fischer shook the man's hand. "No problem."

A wide smile spread across Cruz's face when Eliwood stepped up beside Fischer. "Oh, hi, I'm David Cruz. Nice to meet you."

"Eliwood," she said, not taking the offered hand.

Cruz hesitated for a moment, then straightened and turned back to Fischer. "The body's this way."

Fischer shot Eliwood a look, wondering if there was anything there he needed to know, and she shook her head. He made a mental note to ask her about it later. They followed the detective across the street, between a row of patrol flyers, to the alley just north of Davis's apartment building.

There were several officers standing around exchanging notes, providing security, and just shooting the shit. Fischer knew from experience that the bigger a case or scene was, the more officers would show up to be a part of it. Of course, that also resulted in the majority of those officers standing around with nothing to do once the initial chaos was reined in and the investigators showed up.

A glowing holo-barrier had been set up ten meters into the alley, blocking the view of any onlookers trying to get a view of the corpse. An evidence-processing team was busy collecting evidence and rendering the VR for later examination. A technician standing just in front of the barrier looked up as they approached and nodded at the detective. His white processing overalls were snug around the gut and slightly too short on the arms, exposing the bulky VR manipulation gloves. He pulled his VR goggles off his face, squinting at the new arrivals.

"These the agency guys?" the tech asked.

"That's right," Cruz said. "Eliwood and, I'm sorry I don't remember your name."

"It's Fischer," Eliwood said, moving past the detective without giving him a second look. She moved past the tech, behind the barrier, to get a look at the body.

Fischer stopped next to the tech and extended his hand. "Jackson Fischer, ASI."

"Larry Quade, technical services. We're still working on identifying the body."

Eliwood stood up and shook her head. It wasn't Davis. Fischer peered over the top of the barrier and winced at the scene.

"You know him?" Cruz asked.

Fischer shook his head. The man was in his thirties, average height, average weight, short brown hair, clean shaven. Aside from the single bullet hole in the side of his skull, he looked… "Completely average."

"What's that?" Quade asked.

"Nothing. "We can run him through ours, but my guess we won't have any luck there either."

Detective Cruz frowned. "You're expecting not to find him?"

"I highly doubt it," Fischer said. "How far into the exam are you?"

"Doesn't take an exam to determine cause of death," Cruz said from behind Fischer. "Poor guy was shot in the head. Probably didn't even see it coming."

From the way the body lay, collapsed on itself, the detective was probably right, the man probably hadn't seen it coming, though Fischer wasn't sure if that was a good thing or bad. There was nothing in his hands, which also indicated the man hadn't perceived a threat. So why was he dead?

Fischer looked up to the rover hovering over the scene. "Any video?"

"We're still pulling it from Central," Cruz said. "Should only be a few more minutes. The witnesses ID'd a woman coming from the adjacent building. The security man at the desk gave us the name. Didn't take long to figure out who she was."

One of the technicians moved the head, inspecting the exit wound.

"I wouldn't do that," Fischer said, motioning to the head.

The tech let go and looked up at him, confused. "I've got to get the scans."

"Sure, but if you don't want to lose those hands, you might want to wait until we've neutralized the explosive."

The tech gasped and scrambled away, as did the two near the dead man's feet. Even Cruz, still standing behind the barrier, backed up a step.

"What the hell are you talking about?" Quade demanded.

Fischer crossed his arms, looking down at the gruesome, mangled head. Blood and brain matter were splattered everywhere, and he could see tiny fragments of bone sticking up out of the wound.

"I guess there is a chance the bullet detonated the suicide charge, but I wouldn't bet my hands on it."

"Detonated the… what do you mean?" Cruz asked. "I thought you said you didn't know him."

"I don't," Fischer admitted.

"Then how the hell do you know he has a bomb in his head?"

"That's classified," Eliwood said before Fischer could answer.

"You're kidding," Cruz said.

"Nope." Eliwood gave him a sardonic half-grin.

"What about his link?" Fischer asked. "Did you run a scan?"

"Yeah, first thing," Quade said. "Clean. Whoever killed him either wiped it before they left, or it was clean to begin with."

Fischer tried to visualize Davis erasing the man's link before leaving, but that didn't make much sense. There could've been information about her loaded in, but with all the witnesses who'd said they'd seen her come out of the alley, not to mention the dozens of cameras that would've likely captured her, why go to the trouble? Any evidence on the link wouldn't be any more damning than the rest of it, not collectively, and if she was running and not reporting in, she had to know they were onto her already.

Cruz's link chimed and rotated into place. He looked up at Fischer and pointed to the screen. "Got it."

Fischer stepped closer to see, and Cruz waited for Eliwood to join them before playing the recording. The wide angle was high, a police rover orbiting at least a hundred meters above the ground. The feed was shades of gray and white, thermal. The time stamp at the top left corner read 0515 hours.

Fischer tapped his link; almost two hours had passed. *She could be anywhere,* he thought as the video began.

Five seconds after it started playing, Davis emerged from the front entrance of her apartment building. From the height and angle, the detail wasn't that great, but it was obvious she was in a hurry.

"Can you enhance that?" Fischer asked.

Cruz manipulated the image, enlarging it so they could see her more clearly. Her eyes were sweeping up and down the block as she jogged down the stairs to the sidewalk, heading north. Every few steps she looked behind her, and at one point Fischer thought she'd looked up, directly at the police rover. As she neared the alley, she reached behind her to the small of her back, grabbing something.

"She's already pulling," Eliwood said.

"I don't get it," Cruz said. "She knew the guy was going to be there?"

"He probably called her out?" Fischer said.

"I don't—"

Fischer held up a hand for silence as the footage continued to play. Davis disappeared into the alley, leaving the view of the rover.

"Give us some time in the VR, and we'll be able to reconstruct," Quade said from his side of the barrier.

Fischer didn't think they were going to need it, but it was good to know it would be available.

On the sidewalk a man and woman jumped, obviously startled, and hurried away as Davis reappeared, shoving the pistol back into her pants, and crossed the street, continuing north. She disappeared around a corner, and another shot, this one lower, as if from a car camera, picked her up walking quickly down the sidewalk, still watching her surroundings. The next shot was from another rover, watching her flag down an aircab, get in and take off.

"We've already got Central running down the cab," Cruz said, smiling at Eliwood.

"Yeah, great," Eliwood said, sounding about as unimpressed as Fischer had ever heard her sound.

"You can hold off on that," Fischer said. "We'll take care of it. And our lab team will be here shortly to collect the body."

"Wait, what?" Quade asked. "Now hold on, we were told to cooperate, but—"

"This is now an agency case," Fischer said. "And honestly, I'm not trying to be that guy, but this directly relates to a case we're already working; otherwise, I'd be completely okay with you guys keeping it. We've got enough on our plate."

"Your agent committed a murder in our jurisdiction, and you're going to take the investigation? Don't you think that's a bit of a conflict of interest?" Cruz asked.

"Who said it was murder?" Eliwood asked.

Cruz hesitated for a moment, a nervous grin turning up at the corners of his mouth. "I mean, it's obvious she killed him."

"Could've been self-defense."

"You have no basis for—"

"Listen," Fischer said, cutting him off. "We're not taking the case because we don't think you can handle it, and we're not trying to cover anything up. Whether it was murder or not, *that* really isn't the underlying issue here. This incident is part of an ongoing investigation, and we are going to take it."

"Not really the issue? What the hell does that even mean? What investigation?"

"Unfortunately, I can't tell you that," Fischer said, feeling genuinely sorry for the detective. Had their positions been reversed, Fischer knew how infuriated he'd've been.

"Oh, you can't tell me," Cruz said, giving Eliwood a sidelong glance. "Let me guess, that's classified too, right?"

"That's right," Eliwood said, smiling again.

Cruz scoffed and shook his head. "Well, alright then, I guess that's that."

"We're going to need your people to hold the perimeter until we can get our people here," Fischer said. "Shouldn't be more than an hour."

Cruz looked like he was on the verge of arguing but pursed his lips and said nothing.

"Have you been in the apartment yet?" Fischer asked.

Cruz nodded. "Let me guess, you want my people out of there too?"

"There anything to process?"

"Looks like the place was trashed pretty good," Cruz said.

Fischer frowned. "Like a burglary?"

"That's the way it looks."

"Alright," Fischer said, moving toward the street. "Let's go check it out."

CHAPTER 12

Davis's Apartment
Blue Lake City, New Tuscany
13 Aug 2607

The officer guarding the entrance to Davis's apartment stepped out of the way as Fischer and Eliwood approached. The door had been forced open by the responding officers and left open so they could process the scene. There were several technicians working in the cramped space, documenting evidence and VR mapping the apartment for examination later.

A tall woman with sergeant chevrons on her collar turned as they entered. "Agent Fischer?"

"That's right."

"I've been told this is your baby."

"It certainly seems that way," Fischer said, looking around the apartment. It was small, minimally furnished, and with the exception of the destroyed electronics scattered everywhere, tidy. Multiple holodisplays covered the walls of the living room. Most were flickering error messages or just pixelated images, corrupted by damage to the array they were connected to.

"Looks like somebody went to town." Eliwood pointed to one of the damaged arrays on the table, the metal casing indented in several places.

"Yeah," Fischer said. "Sergeant… Oakridge, would you mind giving as a few minutes?"

The woman eyed him for a second, then nodded. "Sure. Heads up, guys, we're taking a break."

"Thanks."

After the processing team had finished filing out, Fischer moved slowly across the living room, taking everything in.

"She's covering her tracks," Eliwood said, following him.

"Loose ends are bad," Fischer said.

"You don't think the body outside was here just watching, do you?"

Fischer shook his head. "No, I do not."

"So he was here to kill Davis, but she was already on her way out. She surprises him, puts him down, then bolts."

"All the pieces fit."

"I just can't believe it, Fish. I mean, shit, how many years did we work together? She never struck me as the killer type."

"She didn't strike me as the traitor type," Fischer said.

"We're going to have to look at every case she's ever worked," Eliwood said. "Fuck, they can all collapse."

"My guess is she worked those cases just the way she was supposed to," Fischer said, moving into the kitchen. "I doubt Cardinal would've wanted her jeopardizing her position by tampering with random, meaningless cases."

"Probably, but I doubt the lawyers are going to see it that way."

She had a point. Once the news of this broke, any defense attorney worth their salt would be jumping at the opportunity to cast doubt on a state's witness. Especially one with as much case involvement as Davis had. Fischer didn't want to think about how many cases that could turn upside down, or how many criminals could potentially go free on appeal.

"One thing at a time," Fischer said. "If the Alliance doesn't fall apart after this whole thing, we'll worry about case law."

"You think we're going to pull anything off these?"

"I doubt it, but we have to look. Right now, the focus needs to be on finding Davis before Cardinal does."

"You think she's still here?"

"With a two-hour head start? I doubt it. Whether or not she's off-world yet or not, that's the question."

"We can lock down the spaceport and Hypertrans," Eliwood suggested.

Fischer nodded, thinking. "She's going to know we're watching all the main departure points. She'll avoid them like the plague. She's not stupid. She'll have an out."

"We can track the cab."

"Sure. But my guess is it won't tell you anything. She probably used a onetime cred chip. Won't trace to anything."

"So we're screwed."

"She destroyed everything in her apartment for a reason," Fischer said. "There was something here she didn't want us to find."

"Like the fact that she worked for a multinational terrorist group bent on galactic domination?"

Fischer shook his head. "She has to know we already know that. No, she knows we'd be after her regardless. She's covering her tracks so we can't find her. If it was here, I'm betting it's out there too." Fischer motioned above him.

"She's scared of a trail," Eliwood said.

"One that's already getting cold," Fischer said. His link chimed; it was Carter. "Yeah, boss."

"Hoskins is dead."

Fischer sighed. "How?"

"Execution as she was leaving her apartment," Carter said. "Shooter was waiting for her. Two to the back of the skull."

"Sounds a lot like the setup here."

"Except Davis was ready," Eliwood said. "Killed the guy before he had a chance to pull his gun."

"What's her status?"

"She's in the wind, boss."

"Son of a bitch," Carter said. "Do we know where she's heading?"

"Not a clue. She popped a Cardinal asset on her way out and snagged a cab. BLPD is waiting on the logs. She destroyed everything at her place. We're going to need to start a deep dive. What about Campbell?"

"He's fine, just got off the link with him."

"We need to call everyone in for this, boss," Fischer said. "We need to find her before Cardinal does."

CHAPTER 13

The Bullpen
ASI Regional Headquarters
Blue Lake City, New Tuscany
13 August 2607

Agents and techs were just starting to filter into the office when Fischer and Eliwood arrived back at headquarters, powering up their terminals and prepping for the work about to be handed down. They were professionals, they knew even without knowing the particulars that this was as real as it got, and to their credit, they were ready for it.

Fischer and Eliwood met Carter to the middle of the bullpen at the central table. Feeds from the Davis murder scene played on multiple displays around the room.

"You okay?" Carter asked Fischer.

"Yeah."

Nathan Campbell approached the table from the opposite side. His blue shirt was wrinkled, his usually well-manicured hair left unkempt. It didn't look like he'd slept in a few days.

"Jackson, good to see you," he said, leaning against the table.

"You look like shit," Fischer said, grinning.

"Yeah, well, it's been a long couple of weeks."

"It's about to get longer."

"Listen up, everyone," Carter called above the commotion of the room. "Can I get everyone's attention, please?"

It took a few moments for everyone to settle, but when they did, it was obvious Carter had their full and complete attention.

"First, I'd like to say thank you, and apologize for the bit of dramatics we've had over the last couple of days here. I'm sure all of you are equally concerned and wondering what we've had going on. The good news is I'm about to read you all in. The bad news is you're not going to like it."

Throughout the room, colleagues exchanged confused glances.

"I'm sure there's been a lot of rumors going around, and with everything going on, that's to be expected. There's no point in sugarcoating it for you, so I'll just come out and say it. Agent Riley Davis and Technician Hoskins have been confirmed to be double agents, working for a multinational terrorist organization we know only as Cardinal."

A chorus of gasps, muffled conversations and curses filtered through the room.

Carter waited a few seconds before continuing, "I can tell you that Hoskins was murdered this morning, likely by the same people she was working for. Agent Davis, in a similar situation, killed her would-be attacker and has fled the scene." He held up a hand in an effort to quell the growing agitation. "I know you all have a lot of questions, and in the coming days you will get answers, I promise. However, right now, there is a more pressing matter we need to attend to, and I am going to need all of you at the top of your game.

"I know a lot of you were friends with both of them. I'm not blind to the fact that this will be beyond difficult to understand

and cope with, but trust me when I say the very survival of the Alliance could rest on what we do in the next few days."

Carter paused for a long moment, allowing his words to sink in as he looked over the concerned faces of his people. Fischer was sure Carter hadn't meant to sound hyperbolic, but when you chalk something up to those stakes, it tends to sound unbelievable. Not one of the assembled agents looked convinced, and with good reason; had Fischer not experienced everything he had over the last several weeks, he probably would have a hard time believing it too.

"So what do we need to do?" Campbell asked.

"Right now, our first priority is to locate Agent Davis," Carter said. "We believe she has information pertinent to our ongoing investigation into Cardinal. I realize that most of you weren't read into the case originally, and to settle speculation, this does connect to Agent Fischer's investigation into Stonemeyer, Admiral Young's disappearance, and increased joint raider operations along the border.

"I understand you all have your own projects right now, but as of this moment, those are all on hold indefinitely. Our only priority is Cardinal and finding Agent Davis. We have a presidential directive to work this case, which means anything you need, you'll get."

That seemed to better everyone's mood.

"We're going to be burning the midnight oil on this one, folks," Carter said. "Call your spouses, let them know you'll be MIA for the foreseeable future."

In the back, a tech raised his hand. "Sir, what about additional internal threats? Are we satisfied Davis and Hoskins were the only moles?"

"Right now, that does seem to be the case," Carter answered. "We have absolutely no intel on any other inside threat. As I said, right now, we can't afford to focus on anything except tracking down Davis."

"So, we find her, and we find Cardinal?" Campbell asked.

Fischer stepped forward. "Right now, we don't have any information pointing to Cardinal's whereabouts, but we're hoping that Davis does. If we can bring her in and debrief her, the hope is she'll be able to point us in the right direction."

"Which brings us to another point," Carter said as Campbell opened his mouth for an obvious follow-up. "We're on the clock on this one. We know Cardinal is out there hunting loose ends. We need to find Davis before her people do; otherwise…" He left the implication hanging, and by the look on everyone's faces, they all understood what would happen should they fail.

"Do we have any idea where she's gone?" Campbell asked. "What's our starting point?"

"We're going to need quick reaction teams deployed throughout the city," Fischer said. "I doubt she's still on-planet, but if she is, we'll want to be ready to move the second we learn something."

"We've got facial recognition up and running at Hypertrans Blue Lake and the spaceport," Fischer said, "but my guess is she'll avoid those locations, which means private transpo. Contact every snitch, smuggler, dealer, whatever, use up all your favors. Run everything in her files, personal, financial, family, friends, everything. She left the scene in a Starlifter cab. BLPD said they were working with the company to get the flight records, but I want someone to reach out anyway. Let's find out where she went.

"As of this moment, you all have carte blanche to work this case, I don't care what you have to do, but we must find her and find her fast. We're already behind the eight ball here. Are there any questions?"

When there were none, Carter said, "I want updates every thirty minutes. Let's get to work, people."

The room erupted into a flurry of commotion as people began discussing plans of action and making calls, pulling records up on holodisplays, and shouting requests and orders across the room. As Fischer watched the team work, he knew that if anyone was going to find Davis in time, it would be this crew.

"That was inspiring," Eliwood said.

"It was the truth," Fischer said.

Campbell stepped around the table, approaching the trio while giving furtive glances to the agents rushing past.

"What's up?" Fischer asked.

"You said you didn't have any intel pointing to Cardinal."

"That's right."

"What about the message?"

"Message?" Fischer asked a second before he made the connection. "The encrypted message to Young?"

"Unless there's another message I don't know about," Campbell said. "I'm assuming it's that message; otherwise you would-n't've had surveillance on the only other people in the office who knew about it. You were watching to see who the mole was."

Fischer gave Eliwood and Carter a knowing look then sighed. "We had to be sure."

"I get it," Campbell said. "To be honest, I'm not even mad. I would've done the same thing. But my question is, is there more to this investigation than just hunting down Davis? If we can track that relay—"

Fischer held up a hand, cutting Campbell off. "There's a chance that Alistair is behind some or most of what's going on. If not directly, they're definitely bankrolling it."

"You've got to be fucking kidding me."

"I wish I were. But because of that, we can't just go after them with presidential clearance and warrants. We don't want them to know we're onto them."

Campbell nodded. "Smart move. So, what, then? You just going to leave it alone and hope this Davis thing works out?"

"I've got someone working it," Fischer said.

"Who?"

Fischer didn't answer.

Campbell studied him for a moment, then nodded. "All right then. Davis it is."

CHAPTER 14

The Bullpen
ASI Regional Headquarters
Blue Lake City, New Tuscany
13 August 2607

"Do you really think there's going to be anything in there that'll help us?" Eliwood asked. She was leaning back in her chair, feet propped up on the console in front of her, hands manipulating dual holoscreens.

"You don't think there's anything to find?" Fischer asked.

"We've been through her employee file, her financials, her cases, now her personal history. How do we know it's even accurate?"

"She would've had to pass agency screening," Fischer said, "and those are simple surface-level background checks. Hell, they talked to my sixth-grade teacher when they were processing mine. So, unless they dropped the ball somewhere, I'm willing to bet that most of the information should be viable."

"You're assuming the people running the backgrounds aren't

sleepers themselves," Campbell suggested. He stood next to Eliwood, watching the screens and working on his link.

"That's a good point," Fischer said.

Images and data from Davis's file appeared over the central table, flickering slightly, and Campbell immediately began manipulating the panels, configuring them the way he liked. Most of the agency documentation was yearly reviews, a few commendations, a letter of reprimand for an unauthorized absence, nothing that stood out in any way. In fact, it was fairly clean, just the way Fischer expected it to be.

Beside him, Eliwood was manipulating a separate panel, scrolling through the woman's personal history. "Both parents died in a car crash when she was eight. Grandparents were killed in a robbery gone bad on Solomon. One brother, also dead. Damn, she's had a shitty time."

"Makes her a prime target for recruitment," Fischer said.

"Worked a handful of jobs through university," Eliwood continued. "Three years forensics at BLPD before joining the agency eight years ago. Never married, no boyfriends or girlfriends. Lived by herself. Talk about not having a life."

"She didn't want anything to interfere with her work with the agency," Fischer said. "She was always here."

"Not to mention her work *against* the agency," Campbell muttered.

Fischer rubbed his chin. "I doubt she did much work for Cardinal at all until recently. Having the kind of access she had would be essential to their operation. I'm sure she gave them intel occasionally, but I doubt she was ever involved in any active operations against us."

"You mean besides literally everything she was doing," Campbell said. "It doesn't matter whether she gave them one small piece of intel or everything, her betrayal is the same."

"And you don't think she could be redeemed?" Eliwood asked.

"Absolutely not," Campbell said. "If she was looking for redemption, she should've come in."

"Except how could she have known who to trust?" Fischer said.

"Come on, you don't think she knew who the Cardinal assets were and who weren't?" Campbell asked. "I mean, there's no way you're an asset, you're probably the most anti-Cardinal you could get."

"That's a fact," Eliwood said.

"Operational security," Fischer said. "If you don't know who the other assets are, you can't give them up."

"So what do we do?" Eliwood asked.

Fischer sighed. "All right, let's go through her financials again. There has to be something we're missing there."

"We're not missing anything," Eliwood said, obviously frustrated at their lack of progress. "She's a pro, Fish; she covered her tracks like one."

"We've only been at this for a couple of hours," Fischer said. "We're barely scratching the surface. We need to go deep. Let's start pulling everything we have on her friends and acquaintances."

Eliwood laughed. "You mean everyone here?"

"She had to have connections outside the agency," Fischer said. "Run down her travel; look at her most common purchases. There has to be something there."

"And what if there's not?" Eliwood asked.

Fischer squared his jaw. "There is."

Campbell's link chimed. "It's about time." He nodded to the holodisplay above his wrist. "Cab company finally got us that route info."

"Finally," Fischer said. "Where'd she go?"

Campbell frowned. "The middle of the Northside Industrial District."

"Makes sense," Fischer said. "There's hundreds of intraorbital couriers and cargo haulers landing and taking off around the clock. Easy to get lost in the traffic." Fischer pointed to one of the technicians across the bullpen. "Quince, check BLPD's rover network over Northside Industrial, for… what's the time?"

Campbell consulted the report. "Six fifteen."

"Six fifteen," Fischer repeated to Quince. "I want everything they have in the area, ASAP."

"Hmmm," Campbell said, "this is interesting."

"What's that?" Fischer asked.

Campbell scrolled through the data on his link for a moment before answering. "Hold on, I need to make a call."

Fischer frowned as Campbell stepped away, tapping on his link.

"Hi, yes, this is Agent Nathan Campbell, Alliance Security and Intelligence. I have a couple of questions about this biometric data you've included in your documentation."

Fischer and Eliwood exchanged intrigued glances. Fischer sat down on the edge of the console behind him, crossed his arms and waited.

"Yes." Campbell said. "Excellent, okay, thank you." He terminated the link and turned back to Fischer and Eliwood. "You're not going to believe this."

Fischer chuckled. "At this point, I'm sure I'll believe almost anything."

Campbell tapped his link again, then swiped the information on his display to one of the larger projections floating above the main table. A map of the city appeared, showing the pickup and drop-off from Davis's flight that morning.

"You were right about the clean, unregistered cred chip."

"No surprise there," Fischer said. "That's basic tradecraft."

"In fact, she's used a different cred chip *every time* she's flown."

"Every time?" Eliwood asked, taking her feet off the console and leaning forward in her chair. "Doesn't the fact that she used different cred chips each time negate a trail?"

Campbell lifted a finger. "In fact, it would, if Starlifter hadn't installed enhanced biometric scanners in each of their cabs."

"You're kidding?" Fischer asked, his mind already flooding with possibilities.

"So apparently Starlifter has been having a problem with violent passengers and robberies in the last few months, and their higher-ups finally got tired of losing experienced pilots. Six months ago, they started tracking and logging every passenger, including pickup and destination, number of passengers, and conversations. When we submitted our request for the flight record, the system flagged every other trip her biometrics were recorded on."

"She take a lot of flights?"

"A minimum of four flights a month." A map of Blue Lake City appeared above the table as Campbell spoke. Dozens of pulsing yellow dots appeared at different locations across the city, a streaming blue line connecting select dots, indicating the direction of travel.

Campbell stepped closer to the map, pointing to a few of the dots. "Multiple flag locations, which is smart, never uses the same pickup point twice, but they're all within walking distance of her apartment."

"All those drop-offs are centered in the same four-block radius of Blue Lake Plaza," Fischer said. The upscale, bay-front center was home to everything from trendy fashion boutiques to five-star restaurants, to exclusive, member-only nightclubs. Anything the elite of Blue Lake City could think to spend their creds on.

"You really think someone like Davis shopped at the Plaza?" Eliwood asked.

Campbell tapped his link, opening another panel. "According to her accounts, she's never spent a dime anywhere near there."

"Not from her personal account anyway," Fischer said.

"Time stamps suggest she remained in and around the Plaza for about an hour, then left," Eliwood said.

Fischer nodded to the third cluster of dots. "Fairmount district is mostly middle-class commercial businesses, cheap entertainment, that kind of thing. She spent anywhere from fifteen to thirty minutes there before taking a return flight back home."

"No personal account spending there either," Campbell said.

Eliwood crossed her arms. "So she had a high-class meal on Cardinal, then goes window-shopping across town several times a month? I mean, I can see the occasional splurge, but that's a pretty consistent thing."

"I want to pull all the business records for the Plaza and Fairmount," Fischer said. "Run everything for the dates and times she visited, and see if we come up with anything. We might be able to pull facial rec if she visited the right places."

Campbell looked surprised. "You want us to pull *all* the records?"

"That's right," Fischer said. "Everything. Flash the presidential clearance if anyone gives you any trouble."

"And what if it's nothing?" Eliwood asked. "What if she just did all this to throw us off?"

Fischer stared that the dozens of pulsing yellow dots. Randomizing your travel was an essential part of counterintelligence, taught from day one of the academy. It wasn't just to facilitate your own clandestine movements while working a case, but also for everyday life. The threat of attack wasn't extremely high, but on any given day ASI agents throughout the Alliance were put in high-profile positions where their safety was a point of concern. Taking multiple routes to your destination was a very simple way to keep your enemies guessing, preventing them from setting up any kind of ambush.

"It's possible," Fischer said finally. "But she'd had to have known about the biometric scanners in the cabs in the first place to even orchestrate all of this, and if she'd known about them, I doubt she would've continued to use them. Too much of a footprint. I think it's more likely that she didn't know about them, and therefore, that makes whatever she was doing here that much more important."

"I'll start making calls," Campbell said, immediately heading to his desk.

"We're close," Fischer said to Eliwood.

She nodded. "I know."

CHAPTER 15

ASI Regional Headquarters
Blue Lake City, New Tuscany
15 Aug 2607

Fischer leaned back in his chair and rubbed his eyes with the palms of each hand. He set his head back against the back of his chair and let out a long, exhausted sigh. He sat at the edge of the bullpen, half-listening to the conversations going on around him, picking out bits and pieces from each one, but not really paying attention.

He was tired. They'd been pushing nonstop for almost forty-eight hours straight and still had yet to come up with anything solid on Davis's whereabouts. So far, they'd pulled footage from about half of the businesses on the Plaza. Some had been VR compatible, making them easier to sift through. Others had been old simple HD feeds, and running those through the recognition software was tedious and time consuming. And despite everything he'd been telling his crew for the better part of the last two days, Fischer was no longer optimistic about their search.

He closed his eyes and thought about Carissa and Maddie,

wondering how the baby was handling her new environment, wherever that was. Carissa was strong, stronger than Fischer had ever been. The fact that she'd survived so long in the executive world meant she could survive anything. At least, that was what he hoped.

"I miss you," Fischer whispered to himself.

"Hey."

Fischer opened his eyes to see Campbell standing in front of him, holding a mug of steaming coffee.

"I think we've found something."

Fischer accepted the mug and followed Campbell to the central table in the middle of the bullpen. The coffee was old and slightly burnt, but it was caffeine, and right now that was all that mattered.

"We're still coming up short in the Plaza," Campbell said, "but she definitely went here every time she visited Fairmount."

"Voidtronic Investments?" Fischer asked, reading the information panel beside the building's image. "We contact them yet?"

"Fifteen minutes ago. Asked for all the internal feeds and database records for Davis," Campbell said.

"She probably didn't use her real name," Fisher said.

"I sent them her biometrics, along with a copy of the president's authorization letter. They should be getting back to us any minute now."

"Voidtronic doesn't appear in any of her known financials," Eliwood said, stepping around the table, comparing the information on her link to the larger holoscreen above the table.

"Cardinal money," Fischer suggested.

"Could be," Campbell said.

"What else could it be?" Fischer asked, taking another sip of coffee. He eyed the map marked with all the pickups and drop-offs, and suddenly it made sense. "She's meeting her handler."

"At the investment firm?" Campbell asked, skeptical. "Not a very low-key meeting spot."

Fischer set his mug down and pointed at the map. "She's meeting her handler in the Plaza, debriefing and passing on information, likely receiving payment; then she goes all the way out here to stash the creds. She's not co-mingling her funds with her legit income. That's smart."

"Yeah, but, Fish, you saw her apartment," Eliwood said. "She's obviously not spending it. What good is having money if you can't spend it?"

"Maybe she's saving it for a rainy day," Campbell suggested.

"It's definitely raining," Fischer said.

Campbell's link chimed. "Finally." He swiped a finger, sending multiple panels to the main display.

Several identical video feeds, obviously from the same internal camera, showed Davis entering the business, speaking with the receptionist, then having a seat in the lobby to wait. Campbell sped the video up, and soon a man called Davis back to his office, out of visual range.

Eliwood tapped another group of panels, displaying copies of documents, each marked with the Voidtronic logo at the top. "Investment papers."

"Investing?" Campbell asked, leaning closer to the screen. "That's new. Don't know that I've ever seen criminals invest in their future. Should the firm have been running source checks on the creds?"

"Reputable firms should be," Fischer said, scrolling through the documents. "But my guess is Voidtronic is less than reputable."

"That would explain why we got the information so quickly," Eliwood said. "They want us out of their hair as fast as they can manage."

"Could be," Fischer said. He stopped halfway down the third page and pointed. "There. Omnicast Limited."

"Running," Eliwood said.

"She put everything into one stock?" Campbell asked. "Whatever happened to diversification?"

"All right," Eliwood said, tapping her link. "Omnicast Limited, startup out of the Kaiser System. Established seven years ago, but…" Eliwood scrolled down the information, frowning. "There isn't anything listed that shows what they actually do. The site is a simple landing page with contact information, nothing else. No employee list, not product information, nothing."

Campbell flipped through more of the financial documents they'd received from the investment company. "Huh, that's not suspicious at all."

"What's that?" Fischer asked, moving to see what Campbell had found.

"The dividend structure only lists a single payee, a Brice Marks, living in Grey Mount City on Grinas, only habitable world in the Kaidor System."

"She's sending money to someone," Fischer said. "It's a dummy company. Probably doesn't even have a physical address; it's all virtual."

"All right," Eliwood said, "so who's Brice Marks?"

Fischer sniffed and rubbed his chin. "That's the question, isn't it?"

"Not finding a lot on him," Campbell said. "Works for a tech company, in Grey Mount obviously. Single, no other family—no parents, grandparents, aunts, uncles, nothing."

"It's a mask for someone," Fischer said.

"But for who?" Eliwood asked. "Davis doesn't have any family, and we didn't find any intimate connections either, not anyone she'd be sending money to. It doesn't make any sense."

Fischer stared at the data, trying to work it out. Davis had gone to an awful lot of trouble to set this all up. Using unregistered accounts and shell companies to send money to fake people was complicated. Fischer understood doing it for someone close to you, but everything they had suggested Davis had no one in her life who would rate all this trouble.

Unless she did.

"Pull up her family history again," Fischer said.

Eliwood shook her head. "She doesn't have any. They're all dead, remember?"

"Pull it up."

Campbell was already working, swiping through the panels above the table until he found the right one. "Parents died 2587, Solomon. Grandparents a year later, also on Solomon. Brother, Brice, seven years ago."

"How did the brother die?" Fischer asked.

Campbell tapped on the name and frowned. "Hmmm, I'm not showing a cause of death. Just lists him as deceased."

Fischer pointed at Brice Marks's name on the adjacent screen. "Brice Marks is Brice Davis. Davis must have altered the records at some point."

"Could be just a reporting error," Eliwood suggested. "Happens occasionally. Might be the information from Solomon didn't get updated in the Alliance system."

"And if she altered it to begin with, with not listing a cause of death?" Campbell asked. "Wouldn't that make it more believable?"

"Maybe," Fischer said. "Unless someone really started looking into it. But she knew regardless of what she put, it wouldn't hold up under any kind of real scrutiny. Accidental deaths and homicides all generate reports. Hell, even in natural deaths, the coroners generate paperwork. And there would be nothing to back up the entry, so Davis simply changed the status, counting on no one actually taking the time to research it."

"Dead is dead," Eliwood said.

"In most cases, yes," Fischer said. "So, what do we have on the brother before he died?"

"Went to Solomon University, graduated with a degree in Lane Communication Dynamics, worked for a couple of research companies under Alliance contracts. Had a registered address on New Detroit until 2600 when he died." Campbell held up air quotes at the last word.

"So she fakes her brother's death, moves him to Grinas to send him money from Cardinal every month?" Eliwood asked.

"Looks that way," Fischer said.

"Six years ago," Eliwood said. "When she first started working for Cardinal?"

"That'd be my guess."

"So why set all this up?" Campbell asked. "Just to have some place to put the money? That seems like an awful lot of trouble to go through."

Fischer rubbed his chin. "Let's go ask him."

CHAPTER 16

Saber Common Room
ANS *Legend*
En route to Grinas
15 August 2607

"You know," Cole said, picking up the barrel of his MOD27 to inspect it. "You'd think in this day and age, someone would've invented a rifle that didn't require constant maintenance."

"Like what?" Sheridan asked, looking through the inside of his own barrel. He'd just finished wiping it out, ensuring there wasn't any dust or debris inside.

"I don't know, like a blaster or something. Something that's not so... messy."

"The energy requirements for energy weapons are massive," Hanover said from his couch across from Sheridan. He had his HR91 sniper rifle disassembled on a small towel-covered table in front of him, systematically checking and rechecking the dozens of internal components. Operationally, Valkyrie's two snipers put a fraction of the rounds through their weapons than the rest of the team, but during training, they could easily triple those numbers.

"All right, so I'll pack a couple of extra batteries," Cole said, sliding his barrel back into its receiver housing.

"No thanks," Hanover said. "I won't be putting my life into the hands of the lowest bidder. When I pull the trigger, I want to know it's going to fire. I know everything about this weapon system. How she'll fire in the rain, in the wind, hell, in the void. And I know she's going to hit what I'm pointing at."

"Hell, man, I'd put money on you hitting your target regardless of what gun you use," Cole said.

"It's all in the wrist," Hanover said with a grin.

Sheridan chuckled and looked over to where Richards and Reese were getting in a quick workout. One in which Richards, Team One's medic, was smoking Reese and not feeling sorry for it one bit. They were both in the middle of a burnout set of push-ups, going until their muscles gave out. He heard Richard say ninety-five right before Reese said eighty-seven.

At six three, Richards was the tallest member of Team Valkyrie; he was also the strongest. Experience watching the man exercise told Sheridan Richards was about halfway through what he usually did for a set, which meant he was probably good for another eighty or ninety more. Reese didn't have nearly that many in him. Sheridan was surprised he was still going.

At one hundred two Reese called it, collapsing to the deck with an exhausted huff. Richards stopped in the "up" position, grinning as Reese gasped for breath.

"What? You done already? I was just getting warmed up!"

"You can… go to… hell…" Reese panted.

Richards found Sheridan and jerked his head. "Come on, I'll give you the same odds."

Sheridan laughed. "No thanks, I'd like to be able to use my arms tomorrow."

Richards shook his head and went back to pushing.

"So," Cole said, sliding parts of his MOD27 back together, "your boy Fischer is taking us on another rabbit hunt?"

"I don't know why you all think I have some secret connection to Fischer that you all don't," Sheridan said. "I know just as much as you guys do. If that."

Neal walked past, patting him on the shoulder. "It's because of your sparkling personality."

"Yeah, that's it," Cole said. "I was just going to say that."

"Look," Sheridan said. "I don't know where we're headed, but do you guys really think they would have flipped us that fast without a good reason? Hell, we'd barely made it to the surface before we were turned around again. It's got to be something important."

Cole sniffed. "Another clue in the hunt for…" He trailed off. "What the hell are we hunting for anyway?"

"The truth," Sheridan said without thinking. "For Cardinal, to shut them down."

"Yeah, but we still don't really know what the hell Cardinal is, do we? I mean, do we?"

Sheridan thought about it for a moment and sighed, shaking his head. "I don't know."

"Come on, Blaster, tell me where this thing ends," Cole said. "Because I don't think taking down Cardinal is going to be as easy as Fischer makes it sound. Not if they're as big as they seem. That's like toppling-government big."

"I don't know," Sheridan repeated.

"Don't let him get to you," Neal said, settling into the chair to Sheridan's right. She took a long pull on her water bottle then wiped sweat from her forehead with the back of her arm.

Sheridan swallowed and worked his jaw back and forth, focusing on her eyes. It was hard enough to keep his mind right when she was in uniform, but with her sitting there in just a sports bra and training shorts, it was damn near impossible.

You've seen her like this before, he told himself. *Stop it.*

"Yeah," was all he could manage.

"All right, forget Cardinal," Cole said. "What do you want out of this?"

Sheridan knew the answer to that without having to think about it. "I want to see his corpse spinning in the void. I ever get my hands on that motherfucker, he's going straight out an airlock with nothing but his clothes and the names of everyone who died on Stonemeyer."

Cole stared at him for a moment before nodding. "I'm right there with you, man."

"Hey," Neal said, nudging his chair with her foot. "You okay?"

"Yeah," Sheridan said. "I'm fine."

The hatch at the far end of the compartment opened, and Chambers entered, followed by Kline.

Cole lowered his voice and said, "Here we go."

"Carry on, just listen up," Chambers said. "I'm sorry for the quick turnaround time, but I want to commend you on all the nearly perfect refit. There were some hiccups, but we managed to square them away without too many issues, and now we're ready to hit the ground running."

"Excuse me, sir," Cole said, raising his hand. "Do we know yet where we're running to?"

"As a matter of fact, we do. We're currently en route to the Kaidor System, to Grinas, where Agent Fischer and his team are confident we will locate a valuable Cardinal asset."

"Going to be difficult to find one person on an entire planet," Hanover said.

"We have a location on a second VIP who will likely lead to our primary target." Chambers held up a hand, stifling the team's barrage of questions. "You know the drill, people. Command gives us a target package; we take care of it. This is a simple snatch and grab, but I've convinced the captain to allow full kits."

That knowledge immediately elevated the mood in the room. Running missions with anything less than a full Saber combat kit was generally considered less than ideal. The common consensus among the elite operators was that all the advanced gear they trained in wasn't worth its weight in creds if they weren't permitted to utilize it, but all of them understood that subtlety was a necessary requirement for some missions.

"It should be a quick drop," Chambers continued. "Six hours from struts down to dust off. We'll be dropping in approximately ten hours. I want everyone to get some rack and be on the ready line in eight. Any questions?"

There were none.

"All right, carry on."

Cole waited until Chambers had left the room before turning to Sheridan. "Full kit doesn't sound like a simple snatch and grab."

"He's just being overly cautious," Neal said. "I don't blame him." She stood and pulled a towel from her locker. "I'm going to shower and rack out. You boys might want to do the same."

Sheridan watched her leave, thoughts that were definitely not appropriate flooding his mind.

Cole slapped his arm. "Hey."

"What?"

He jerked his head after Neal. "Go after her."

"Get the fuck out of here." Sheridan looked away, hiding the fact that his cheeks were flushing.

"Come on, man, what the hell are you waiting for? You have to know she's into you, right?"

"I… I just don't want to make things awkward for the team."

"You guys keep this up much longer and you won't have to worry about that. Trust me."

Sheridan stared at the hatch to the head, feeling the urge to follow his friend's advice, but knowing simultaneously he shouldn't. "It's not the right time."

Cole laughed. "Well, if not now, I don't know when it would be."

Sheridan sighed. "Neither do I."

CHAPTER 17

**Regional Spaceport
Barcroft's Landing, Thresh
16 August 2607**

A wave of hot, damp air washed over them as the ramp opened, and Jones was sweating before he'd reached the platform. He pulled at his shirt, trying to circulate cooler air.

"Ugh," Jones said, grimacing. "You know, it doesn't matter how many times we come here, I'm never really ready for it, you know?"

The elevated platform was surrounded by tall tropical trees with wide green and purple striped leaves, the branches and thick trucks wrapped in green vines. The shade provided a fair amount of relief from the midday sun, but short of being inside, there was no relief from the constant mugginess of this part of Thresh. Several birds chirped and screeched in the distance, their calls echoing through the jungle.

Loomis walked to the rail and leaned over, looking down at the forest floor some hundred meters below. "Least it's not Olesta. I'd take hot over cold any day."

Olesta, one of the least habitable places inside the URT, was an ice world mined for its crystal-clear water. On any given day, the surface temperature ranged from -250° to -400°.

Jones grunted. "You've got a point there."

Out of all the worlds Jones had visited, Thresh was one of his favorites. Situated along the Alliance's eastern border, Thresh was an independent world that enjoyed all the protections provided by the Protectorate, and none of the regulations. In fact, Thresh's own regulations on privacy rivaled any of the aligned worlds and were paramount to keeping its residents, patrons, and visitors virtually anonymous.

The system maintained a completely neutral governing council, whose only hard and fast rule was not to get involved in Protectorate politics. They maintained a small but effective local navy that never ventured outside the system and provided some of the most secure transit lanes in the entire galaxy. In almost a hundred years since the navy's original inception, there hadn't been a single intrusion or raider attack anywhere in the system. Which, coincidently, made it an ideal location for low-key smugglers like Tensley Jones and his crew to conduct business. As long as they didn't cause a ruckus, the authorities wouldn't give them so much as a second look.

Barcroft's Landing's regional spaceport was no exception. It was rare for pilots to actually interact with the ground crew or maintenance personnel. Everything was handled over a secure local network, and none of the provided services required a name, only payment. He tapped his link, connecting it to the spaceport's network, and once he'd registered as "Short Term Occupant," he sent the required payment and waited for the receipt.

A shuttle appeared from the next pad over, backwash buffeting the trees between them, and rotated away before rising into the air, heading for orbit. The planet was almost forty percent rain forest, all of which was protected. With very few exceptions, cities, towns, and spaceports were restricted to exactly where and how they could build. There was a limit to how many trees you could remove and how much land you could excavate in a certain area. This meant that most settlements were generally hundreds of miles away from each other, largely separated by untamed jungle.

"Come on," Jones said as the shuttle's engines faded into the distance. "Let's get this over with."

After verifying his rental allotment, he swiped to another menu and tapped a finger on the screen. Behind him, *Doris*'s rear cargo ramp folded up and locked into place with a metallic clunk. A message panel appeared above his hand, confirming the ship was secure and her systems locked down.

"You know, one of these trips we should really set up a tour of the Talo Pits," Loomis said as they headed for the stairs at the side of the platform. "Might be able to see one of those trolls."

The massive sinkholes on the Talo continent to the west were some of the largest in known space, each cenote sinking almost fifteen hundred feet beneath the ground. Over a thousand visitors a day visited the landmarks, hoping to see the sentient underground dwellers that were rumored to live there.

"Oh, come on, man, you don't really believe that crap, do you?" Jones jogged down the metal stairs, to a walkway that bisected several other platforms. "There's been people exploring those pits for hundreds of years and no one's ever seen one. It's a myth, nothing more. Someone got spooked by their own shadow and made up a story to save face."

"Yeah, but what if?"

"What if what?" Jones asked. "What if you found some ugly, four-eyed, hairless freak in the bowels of the planet? You want to know what I'd do? I'll tell you what'd I'd do." He stopped and turned to face Loomis. "I'd shoot it right in the face for making me shit my pants. That's what I'd do."

"Well, at least there'd be proof, then," Loomis said.

Jones rolled his eyes and kept walking.

"What about the Glass pools?" Loomis asked. "Oh, wait, aren't those supposed to be haunted?"

"Don't know, don't care. You want to go check them out, do it on your own time, after all of this is done and over with."

"Kind of punchy today, are we?"

"The heat pisses me off."

"That the only thing?"

Jones stopped at the top of another flight of stairs and glared over his shoulder. "You know it's not."

"I don't know why you're all amped up about it," Loomis said. "That was a long time ago. Fischer was right, she's probably forgotten all about it."

"Not a chance."

"I mean, it's not like you stole anything from her," Loomis said, following Jones down the stairs. "And *Doris* was more yours than it ever was hers. Did you leave her all the creds too?"

"Of course I did, but that's not the point."

"Eh, I think you're making a big deal out of nothing. It'll be fine."

Jones blew out a long, frustrated breath. "Fish owes me big time for this."

"Hey, you never know, it might work out better than you'd hoped," Loomis said, slapping Jones on the shoulder. "She's a big-time player now. I'm sure she has dozens of operators like us working for her. Maybe she'll have a job for us. Word on the street is she pays triple market rates for most commissions."

"We're not taking a job from her, regardless of how much it pays," Jones said.

"Could be some big opportunities."

"Even if we wanted to, we've got enough on our plate without taking on any more. The answer is no, even though I highly doubt she'll even ask the question."

Five minutes later they arrived at the spaceport's central tram station, where platforms at various heights serviced multiple lines to different parts of Thresh. Because of the highly restricted ground travel outside metropolitan areas, most of the short-range transportation was conducted by high-speed trams. The extensive network connected almost all the cities on the planet, with the exception of a few remote locations, and like the spaceport they were leaving, it was totally and completely anonymous.

A holomap at the entrance to the station pointed Jones to the correct platform, and soon they were zipping out of the spaceport, over the expansive jungle. The tram was built to fit fifty people comfortably, seventy if you really wanted to load it down, but today only ten others boarded. Jones moved to the rear of the tram and put his back against the wraparound window, keeping an eye on the other passengers.

"You expecting trouble?" Loomis whispered, taking in the scenery behind Jones.

"You aren't?"

Loomis grunted and crossed his arms. "No one knows we're here. If someone was following us, we would've known about it back on Vernog."

"Yeah, well, you know what they say," Jones said. "Complacency kills."

Fourteen hours before, they'd set up Fischer's wife and their daughter in a remote private resort on the ocean world of Vernog. Much like Thresh, Vernog valued privacy and security above all else, but even still it had only been his second choice. If their work hadn't been bringing them here, Jones would've much preferred to leave Carissa and the girl here, but knowing what lay ahead, he didn't want to risk it.

Of all the jobs Jones had taken over the years, whether for Fischer or not, this was by far the most significant. This wasn't avoiding import tariffs on Solomon fire-silk or taxes on Patari nuts, this was something that could and would affect the lives of billions, and it made Jones more than a little uneasy. And considering his payment was probably not going to be on par with the severity of what he was here to do, the risk was most definitely not worth the reward.

Fish is definitely going to owe me for this, Jones thought, even though he was fairly certain Fischer wouldn't ever pay out. But that wasn't really the point, was it? The two men had worked together in one form or another since they first met aboard *Paladin*, helping the other out whenever the opportunity presented itself. The reality of who actually *owed* who wasn't ever really considered.

There was a soft chime as the tram left the station, and a female voice announced the trip into downtown Barcroft would take approximately seven minutes. Jones held onto the handrail above him as the tram weaved its way through the jungle. Sunlight cut through the canopy in sporadic pillars of light, revealing patches of brilliant color from the multitude of fauna below. On any other occasion Jones would have enjoyed the beautiful scenery, but today all of that went virtually ignored, his focus shifting from passenger to passenger, watching for threats.

He'd lived most of his adult life straddling the line between law-abiding citizen and outlaw. He'd worked with a lot of people who were definitely on the wrong side, but he'd helped just as many, if not more, on the right. The thing that mattered above all else was trust. If you didn't have trust, none of it would work. Now, in a world where you really couldn't know whom to trust and who might betray you the first chance they got, things were a lot more complicated. The only thing that remained constant was Fischer. Which, more than anything, was why he was here right now.

"You think it's going to be hard to find her?" Loomis asked, keeping his voice down so no one else could hear.

"We're not going to have to find her," Jones said. "My guess is she already knows we're here."

As if on cue, Jones's link activated, appearing unbidden, the system's home panel glowing above the back of his hand.

"What the hell?"

Loomis leaned close. "Your shit going tits-up?"

He watched as his link began cycling through menus. Screens appeared and vanished as if someone was swiping through them with an invisible hand. He tapped the display repeatedly with a finger without any effect. It was like his link had somehow grown a mind of its own. The security panel opened, and the invisible hand began adjusting settings, changing the lockout protocols.

"No, I don't think so," Jones said.

Almost as abruptly as it had activated, the link's display vanished.

Loomis frowned. "I don't—"

Before he could finish, Jones's link activated a second time, displaying a message panel with the word "FOLLOW" glowing in bright orange letters. Jones and Loomis exchanged glances, and the panel changed to a map of Barcroft with a destination marked with a glowing yellow arrow.

"You've got to be kidding me," Loomis said.

"That's Old Town," Jones said. He laughed, shaking his head. "That's one way to get your message across."

"You think it's a trap?"

Jones shrugged. "Lot of trouble to go through for that."

Loomis hesitated. "You don't… you don't think she works for Cardinal, do you?"

"Not a chance. Osprey's too smart for that."

The tram slowed as the first buildings began to appear through the trees. The capital city, which everyone simply called Barcroft, was home to over three million people, all living in buildings designed to have as little footprint as possible on the local wildlife. Built around and between the massive trees, the city was comprised of multiple levels, above and below the canopy, connected by walkways and the tram system. The older parts of the city had been erected in cleared areas of forest and were the only sections where the city actually appeared to be a city.

Jones's link activated again, advising them to get off at the next stop, then directing them to the appropriate platform for the ride into Old Town. The station was bustling with people heading in all directions, and, at least as far as Jones could tell, none of them seemed the least bit interested in the two outsiders.

Twenty minutes later they stepped off the tram in Old Town and made their way to the iconic promenade, a wide park filled with trees and fauna from all over Thresh. The foliage was in its infancy relative to everything else on the planet, making it at least manageable. A canal weaved its way through the park, flanked by archaic stone walkways. Shops and restaurants followed the canal through the park, enticing passersby with everything from large holographic signs to simple wooden sculptures.

"Doesn't look like much has changed," Loomis said as they made their way down the canal.

"This place never changes," Jones said. "I'm pretty sure there's a regulation against that."

They arrived at their destination fifteen minutes later, a small breakfast and lunch cafe overlooking the canal. Most of the outside tables were full, but that suited Jones just fine. He wasn't particularly hungry, and he didn't want to be sitting out in the open where anyone could take a shot at them.

A young hostess with a brilliant smile and expertly crafted makeup met them at the hostess stand, asked how many, then led them inside.

"Along the back would be great," Jones said.

She nodded and made her way around the tables, leading them to a row of empty tables along the back wall. After seating them, she swiped a menu to their links and told them their server would be right with them, then disappeared back to the front.

"Oh, good, breakfast," Loomis said, tapping his link and scanning the menu. "I'm starving."

"You're always starving," Jones said, not bothering to open his. Instead he scanned the surrounding tables, looking for any sign of her.

"I'm a growing boy," Loomis said.

"It really is a wonder you haven't eaten me out of ship and home."

A server droid appeared, its thin, cylindrical body floating on three counter-grav pads. Four overly long arms were folded up on the side of its chassis, above which a holoprojection of a vaguely human head floated. It wasn't hyperrealistic like some, and as it spoke, the image blinked and flickered. The antique was definitely in need of maintenance.

"May I offer you anything to drink, gentlemen?" The droid's voice was slightly digitized. Its mouth moved slightly out of sync with its words.

"Just coffee," Jones said.

"I'll have coffee too," Loomis said. "And can I get some of your Galaxy Waffles."

"An excellent choice, sir," the droid said. "And which syrup would you prefer? We have a local maple that has won more awards than—"

"That'd be great," Jones said, cutting it off.

The holographic head bowed slightly. "Of course, sir. Excuse me."

Jones glared at Loomis. "Waffles?"

"I told you, I'm hungry."

Jones sighed and shook his head. "I don't know how you can even think about food at a time like this."

"Hey, I'm not the one she hates, remember? I don't have anything to worry about."

"We're in this together," Jones said. "Whatever she does to me, she's going to do to you."

"I'm sure she's more reasonable than that."

"Yeah," Jones said, laughing. "You just wait. You'll see."

CHAPTER 18

Waterside Cafe
Barcroft's Landing, Thresh
16 August 2607

"Ah, finally," Loomis said, rubbing his hands together as the server droid approached their table.

"Your waffles, sir," the droid said, face flickering. A panel in the front of its torso slid up, and one of its lanky arms reached in to produce the meal, a plate-sized fluffy waffle covered in thick brown syrup. It set the plate in front of Loomis and asked if he needed anything else.

"Lots of napkins. I'm a messy eater."

"Of course, sir." The head flickered twice, then completely vanished, the rest of its body floating apparently frozen in midair.

"What the hell?" Jones slid away from the droid.

Two panels above the droid's shoulders opened, and two beam emitters appeared. They extended up from the chassis, angling out to either side. They activated without warning, surrounding their booth in a semitranslucent amber field, cutting them off from the rest of the restaurant.

"You are in no danger," the droid said, but the voice was less digitized now, sounding more human. "The blocking field is shielding us from all optical and audio sensors."

"Blocking field?" Loomis asked. "For coffee and waffles?"

"You always were a little dense, Loomis," the droid said.

"How the hell do you—"

"No, wait," Jones said, holding up a hand. "Osprey?"

"In the flesh," the droid said. "As it were."

"You've got to be kidding me," Jones said.

"What do you want?" Osprey asked.

"Listen, we came here to talk, but not like this, not in the open. We need to meet."

Osprey laughed. "And you think after what you did, I'm going to just let you waltz right in and carry on like nothing happened?"

Jones shook his head. "I'm sorry about leaving. I am, really. I was stupid."

"Go on."

"I was at a bad point in my life, and I made some really dumb mistakes. I never meant to hurt you. Honestly. I've wanted to come see you for years, but…"

"You were busy," Osprey finished for him.

Jones chuckled. "Yeah."

"I see you've made some modifications to my ship."

"She's my ship, and yeah, some upgrades here and there."

"The phased harmonic array is military grade," Osprey said. "How'd you manage that?"

Loomis frowned at Jones and mouthed, "How did she know?"

"You know, just because you have the ability to go anywhere doesn't necessarily mean you should," Jones said.

"That's not ironic at all," Osprey said.

"Can we not do this through a droid, please?" Jones asked.

"I'm curious," Osprey asked, apparently ignoring his question, "how much is Jackson Fischer paying you for this?"

"Jackson—" Jones cut himself off and waited a beat before continuing. "What makes you think I'm working with Fischer?"

"Oh, come on, Tens, do we really have to play this game?"

Jones sighed. "It's enough."

"So you're doing him another favor?"

"Yes, Osprey, I'm doing Fischer a favor. Is there a problem with that?"

"You do know he just abuses your friendship to get what he wants, don't you? How many jobs has he actually paid you for?"

"He does not abuse our friendship," Jones said. "And he's paid me quite a bit over the years, thank you very much."

"You can't lie to me, Tens. The last time your account received any creds from him was four months ago, and that was to cover expenses you incurred dropping into Stonemeyer."

"Do you mind not going through my shit?"

"No, I don't mind at all. Besides, I need to know what I'm working with."

Jones laughed. "Does that mean we're working together."

"No. It means I'm curious. What does Fischer have you out here looking for?"

"I don't want to talk about it in the open."

"The barrier shield is quite safe," Osprey said.

"So you say," Jones replied. "But if you'd seen the shit I've seen in the last few weeks, you'd say different."

"Understandable."

"So can we meet?"

Osprey didn't respond right away, and Jones could imagine her weighing the pros and cons. With Osprey it was always about the ROI. Was it worth it? It was one of the reasons he'd left all those years ago, and while he would never admit it to anyone, there was a part of him that did, in fact, miss her dearly. He'd left her, but he'd never forgotten her. Probably never would.

Finally, she said, "My rates are nonnegotiable."

Jones straightened. "Done."

"If I don't like what I hear, you're out of here. If you ever tell anyone we spoke, I'll deny it. I make no guarantees, and I get paid regardless of whether the job is successfully completed or not."

"You drive a hard bargain."

"That's the beauty of being me," Osprey said.

Jones glanced at Loomis, both eyebrows up, looking for his opinion. He shrugged as if to say, "Your call, boss."

"All right," Jones said.

"All right?" Osprey asked.

"I agree to your terms. Where do we meet?"

Jones's link chimed, the holodisplay rotating into position.

"There will be a cab outside the cafe in sixty seconds. The destination is already loaded in. Make sure you're not followed."

Before Jones could respond, the barrier shield collapsed and the emitters retracted into the server droid at the side of the table. The holographic head reappeared; its flickering face smiling.

"Ah, good," it said, "how are we enjoying our waffles, sir?"

CHAPTER 19

Industrial District
Barcroft's Landing, Thresh
16 August 2607

It had not been a direct flight, something Jones had expected, but after the fifth cab switch, he was beginning to think it might be a little excessive. As the aircab lifted away, he expected his link to activate again with another set of directions, and when it didn't, he began surveying his surroundings.

"We here?" Loomis asked.

"Your guess is as good as mine," Jones said.

Behind them, a large four-story warehouse, a plain gray steel building with no markings whatsoever, stretched the entire length of the block. Dozens of cameras dotted the edge of the roof, and the longer he looked, the more he saw. Clusters of antennas and sensor panels covered the roof, leaving no doubt in Jones's mind.

"We're here," he said.

Loomis scoffed, hands on hips. "About time."

Relieved the trip was over, Jones was now faced with a new problem, one that made his stomach turn in knots. He was minutes away from seeing *her* again, and after so many years, he didn't know if he was prepared for it or not. His link chimed at an incoming call: Osprey.

He accepted the call. "We're here."

"Yes, yes you are," Osprey said. Jones could hear the smile in her voice. She was enjoying making him jump through all these hoops. "Your left. Door's unlocked."

The call terminated before he could respond.

"Was she this paranoid when you were… you know?" Loomis asked.

"When we were together? No, not at all."

The door was unlocked, just like she'd said, and they found themselves inside a small entry room, facing a locked door, like an airlock. Jones pulled the door shut behind him and heard the lock click. The light panel above them flickered slightly as two panels at the sides of the room opened and several scanners appeared on waldo arms. Multiple streams of light passed over them, though Jones didn't feel a thing. The entire procedure took about fifteen seconds; then the arms folded back into their recesses and the interior door unlocked and slid silently open.

They entered a large open warehouse with high ceilings and bare walls. In the center of the space, a square, fully enclosed office sat on a raised platform, five meters from the ground. The plastiglass was one way, mirrored so outsiders would not be able to see in. Underneath the platform there were rows and rows of electronics covered in blinking lights and holodisplays, all connected by what could have been miles of cabling that snaked across the floor in all directions.

Jones ducked as something zipped through the air above him. "What the hell?"

A single fist-sized orb stopped to hover a meter away, just about eye level, rotating slowly. The drone seemed to consider Jones and Loomis for a moment; then as quickly as it'd appeared, it zipped away, disappearing into the darkness of the warehouse.

"Son of a bitch," Jones muttered, straightening as they walked farther into the warehouse.

Another drone appeared in the air ahead, lights dancing around its equator. It began spinning in place; then, in a flash of light, the holoimage of a woman's face appeared, flickering blue and white. The face had aged somewhat since Jones had last seen it, but it was still beautiful.

You're an idiot, Jonesy, he told himself.

"That's far enough," Osprey said, the holoimage a live projection of herself.

Jones put out his arms. "Oh, come on, I told you I wanted to do this in person."

"You're here, I'm here, what more could you possibly need?"

"I don't know," Jones said, "to actually see you."

"Unnecessary. Besides, if I don't like what you say, you're on your way out the door anyway. So what's so important Fischer sends you all the way out here to find me?"

Jones sighed. "We need your help."

"I gathered that."

Jones eyed Loomis out of the corner of his eye, then turned back to Osprey's projection and let out a resigned sigh. "Okay. Where to start? Have you ever heard of a group named Cardinal?"

"Heard rumors, nothing really concrete. Weapons broker mostly, some raiding I hear, never really piqued my interest, to tell you the truth."

"Yeah, well, they should," Jones said. "It's pretty much the biggest thing in the galaxy right now."

"I haven't seen anything on the networks."

"That's because they don't want anyone to know about them yet. But trust me, they're huge."

"Okay, what is it, and what do they want?"

"All I know is what Fischer's told me, but I'll try to explain it so it makes sense."

Osprey listened silently while Jones gave her the rundown, starting with the failed mission on Stonemeyer, which she'd already heard about, to the attack in Astalt, to the raid in Beness. But it wasn't until he brought up Agent Davis that Osprey showed any real interest in what he was saying.

"A double agent, eh? Now that is interesting."

"Right, but that's not why I'm here," Jones said, trying not to let his frustration show. "We need to figure out where this message came from and track it back to its source."

Osprey looked away for a long moment, obviously thinking about what Jones had told her. "It's complicated."

"What do you mean, complicated?" Jones asked. "Like you can't do it complicated or what?"

"It doesn't have anything to do with whether I can do it or not. Of course I can do it, but that doesn't necessary mean I want to. Believe it or not, there are some things that aren't worth the risk, something you should understand better than anyone else."

Jones winced and looked away, wishing he had a snappy comeback for her dig, but knowing anything he said would fall flat. "I said I was sorry."

"Yeah, you did." Osprey sighed. "You do realize the Alistair network is, by far, the most secure system in the galaxy, right? And I'm not being hyperbolic about that. Every single one of the datacores runs on its own internal encryption, each completely separate from each other. As far as I know, there aren't any external connections, and if there are, they're limited to high-level executive personnel, and every entry will be logged and traced."

In truth, Jones hadn't considered any of that and wasn't entirely sure what it all meant. "So you're saying you *won't* do it?"

"Didn't say that either," Osprey said, clearly annoyed. "I said it's complicated. It's going to cost you."

"Price doesn't matter," Jones said, and hoped Fischer had meant what he'd said.

Osprey laughed. "You don't even know how much it is."

"Like I said, price doesn't matter. I'm serious about that, and so are the people paying."

"I'm going to need a special sequence generator to bypass their internal encryption algorithm and mask my node connection ID. Not to mention premium bandwidth. I'm going to need to lease time on one of Thresh's Ultracores; that's not cheap at all."

"Look, I don't need to know how you're going to do it," Jones said, lifting a hand. "I just need to know that you will. And if you are, we need this done ASAP."

"Fast and good are mutually exclusive. I can do one or the other, but something's going to suffer."

Jones sighed. "As quickly as you can manage."

"How fast are we talking about here?"

"Tomorrow?"

Osprey laughed. "Yeah, well, that's not going to happen regardless of how much you pay me. I'm going to need a day at least to set up the proxy nodes and ghost protocols."

"Right, well, as fast as you can, then," Jones said.

"All right. Five million."

If Jones would've eaten breakfast at the cafe, he would have thrown it all up. "Are you fucking kidding me? Five million? That's insane."

"No, this job is insane. And five million is my fee; my expenses are extra. Half up front, half on completion."

Jones shook his head. He could already see Carter losing his mind and wondered if this was how Fischer felt whenever he had to bring the boss bad news. But it wasn't like he had much in the way of alternatives; it was either this or nothing. "I'll have to make a call, but I'm sure it'll be fine."

"Wow, no counteroffer, no haggling on price? You must really want this information."

"I don't want anything," Jones said. "Fischer does. This is his baby. I'm just helping."

"Awfully noble of you."

"Thanks."

"Make your call," Osprey said. "You can use your link again. It'll connect to my network. It's clean. You don't have to worry about any malware or anything."

"You mean any *more* malware."

"I didn't put anything in your link, Tens," Osprey said, her tone feigning injury. "I just borrowed it for a little bit. You should be used to that, right? Borrowing things that are close to people, then disconnecting without so much as a 'see ya later, had a nice time.'"

Jones gritted his teeth and took a deep breath. "I said I was sorry."

"I know," Osprey said. "And I forgave you the first time. I just like to hear you say it."

Loomis laughed and Jones glared at him.

"You always did like a good laugh," Jones said.

"Yeah, well, some things never change. Speaking of which, what'd you do to my ship? She looks a lot different from the last time I saw her."

Jones held up a finger. "First of all, she's my ship. Second of all, she's fine. I've managed to get a few upgrades installed that improve overall performance and stability. She's a much better ship than she was before. She's perfect."

"She was perfect just the way she was," Osprey said.

"Yes," Jones said, not thinking of the *Doris.* "Yes, she was."

CHAPTER 20

Farmland outside Grey Mount City
Planet Grinas, Kaidor System
18 August 2607

Sheridan adjusted his MOD27, moving the weapon so that it hung along the centerline of his chest, resting on the tactical vest he wore over his light blue long-sleeve shirt. He wore his charcoal gray duty pants, mostly because they were comfortable, but also because the fabric allowed for unencumbered movement. Fischer and Eliwood sat at the front of the bay, out of the way, quietly watching the team as the Albatross dropped through Grinas's atmosphere.

"What do you think?" Cole asked, leaning close and speaking under his breath.

"What do I think about what?"

"This whole thing. I mean, tracking down fugitives isn't exactly what we do, right?"

Sheridan grunted. "I think we do whatever we need to do."

"Yeah, I guess."

"This is an important job, Cole. I wouldn't trust anyone else to do it, not with everything else that we've seen over the last couple of weeks. You really think a simple fugitive squad would be able to get this done?"

"Probably not," Cole said.

"I'm hoping Fischer will just be able to talk this Davis person out of doing anything stupid."

"You think he can?"

"I don't know, but if anyone can, he can."

"You guys really connected, didn't you?" Cole asked. "And I'm not giving you shit either, I'm genuinely curious."

Sheridan shrugged. "We went through some shit, and we both have a deep-seated hatred for the same person."

"You think we're ever going to find him?"

"Young?"

"Yeah."

"I don't know," Sheridan said, his chest tightening at the thought. "But I can tell you this, I'm not stopping until I do."

They spent the rest of the flight in silence. Sheridan couldn't get the thought of Young out of his head, the image of him walking out of his cell on the Albatross replaying over and over again in his mind. He'd been having nightmares about it, waking up in cold sweats, and he was grateful that they were back on the hunt again, though he couldn't help thinking they were hunting the wrong person. Fischer had said he hoped Davis would lead them to Cardinal, but in Sheridan's mind, that was almost secondary. He wanted, no, he needed to find Young and bring him to justice. He had trouble thinking of anything else.

At the front of the bay Master Sergeant Kline turned from the cockpit and grabbed the rail on the ceiling with both hands. "All right, eyes up, people! We'll be feet dry in sixty seconds. Team Two, you've got scene security. We're landing ten klicks outside the city and humping it in. Sheridan, Cole, you have point on the ground."

"Roger that, Master Sergeant," they answered in unison.

"Skies are clear, sunny and warm," Master Sergeant Kline said. "Excellent weather for hunting."

"Does he seem unusually happy about this drop, or is it just me?" Cole muttered in Sheridan's ear.

Sheridan wiped away a smile and gave a slight nod.

The ramp at the back of the bay unlocked with a loud, mechanical thunk and immediately began lowering. Green fields stretched out beneath them as far as Sheridan could see, dotted occasionally by rows of trees or small clusters of homes. For the life of him, Sheridan couldn't fathom why someone would want to live all the way out here in the middle of nowhere.

"We're not expecting any immediate contact, and the scopes are clear," Kline said, making his way toward the ramp. "All the same, keep your eyes open and your weapons up."

The Albatross flared slightly, the engines pitching up as it slowed for landing. Sheridan waited as Team Two filed down the ramp, then immediately spread out to secure the landing zone. Sheridan hit the ground a second later, bringing his rifle up and scanning his surroundings.

"Oh, you've got to be kidding me," Cole said, coming up beside him. "What the hell are those?"

They'd landed in the middle of a grass field dotted sporadically with trees and hedges. Fifty meters to the east, a herd of four-legged, tan-skinned reptiles the size of cows stood in the shade of a tall tree, their long, scaled necks erect, glowing yellow eyes locked on the new arrivals. One let out a short, hoarse croak that almost sounded like a dog barking, but otherwise they all stood perfectly still.

Sheridan shook his head. "No idea."

One of the taller creatures stamped a three-toed foot on the ground and lowered its head so it was even with its shoulders. Its eyes locked on Sheridan and the rest of the team. Two more followed the first's lead, lowering their heads as well.

"I'm no expert, but that doesn't look good," Cole said.

"Take it easy," Sheridan muttered, slowly bringing his rifle up, though as he studied the creatures, he wasn't sure how much damage their high-velocity rounds would do. "We're not going to hurt you."

Reese appeared to Sheridan's right, his rifle also up. "Whose bright idea was it to land right next to those things?"

Sheridan shook his head but didn't respond. Whatever they were, they weren't attacking, and he didn't want to provoke any kind of aggressive response. "Pilot probably couldn't see them from the air. Those are some pretty thick leaves."

The branches of the tree stretched out some fifteen meters from the thick main truck, and with twelve feet of clearance from the ground, it was the ideal spot for the creatures to huddle in the shade.

"What's that there?" Cole asked, motioning to the circular trough behind the front row of creatures.

"It's a watering trough," Neal said. She stopped next to Reese and let her rifle hang across her chest. "Haven't you guys ever seen a cattle ranch before?"

"What are you saying?" Cole asked. "Someone's raising those things?"

"Looks like it."

"All right," Master Sergeant Kline called behind them, "enough sightseeing. We've got work to do."

"Hey, Master Sergeant, we're trying not to get eaten over here," Cole said.

"They look harmless," Neal said.

Cole laughed. "Well, why don't you go cuddle up next to one, then?"

"I wouldn't suggest it," Sheridan said. "Might not be carnivorous, but they don't look that friendly."

"Friendly?" Cole asked. "They look downright mean."

"Enough," Kline said. "Can't help where we landed. We've got a mission to complete. Team One, secure the LZ. The rest of you continue on mission. Sheridan, Cole, let's get moving."

"Roger that, Master Sergeant," Sheridan said. He gave the cow-lizards one last look, then moved around the shuttle, heading west toward the city.

The outlines of buildings dotted the horizon, but Sheridan was more concerned with the grass field and trees between. Urban warfare, ship-to-ship operations, station sieges, planetoid incursions—the members of Team Valkyrie trained for it all. But out here, in the wide-open spaces, this was a battlefield for Marines with armor and proper air support. Besides, after spending so much of his life in space, the wide-open spaces unnerved him slightly.

"Movement," Hanover said over the taclink. *"Northwest, four clicks, looks like a gravbike, one rider, coming up fast."*

Sheridan found the bike cresting a small hill, a cloud of dust rising in its wake. He pulled the MOD27's stock into his shoulder, bringing the rifle's optic on target. "What the hell is this?"

"Hold your fire," Captain Chambers ordered.

"Doesn't appear to be hostile," Hanover said. *"Doesn't even look like he's armed. No sign of backup either. Looks like he's alone."*

As the lone figure neared the shuttle, he waved one hand over his head, yelling, but Sheridan couldn't make out what he was saying.

Cole nudged him. "I think he's trying to get your attention, Blaster."

"You think?"

The man brought the gravbike to an abrupt stop twenty meters from the Albatross's nose and hopped off without waiting for it to settle. He spoke with a thick accent that Sheridan couldn't place and strung his words together so quickly it was hard to make out what he was saying. "Wha' da hell y'all pondering ya doin' 'round my babies?"

"Did he just speak English?" Cole asked under his breath.

Sheridan stepped forward, rifle leveled at the new arrival. "Sir, you need to stop right there. Don't come any closer."

"Closer, eh? You're on ma land, aren't ya? Best you start spellin' out your business'n these parts, 'fore things get sideways, yeah!"

Sheridan opened his mouth but shut it again, not really sure how to respond. He gave Cole a sidelong glance, who simply shrugged and shook his head.

"No idea," Cole said.

"Just stop!" Sheridan said. He flicked the safety off with his thumb. *Please don't make me shoot you, guy.*

"Stand down, Corporal." Captain Chambers ducked under the Albatross's port-side wing and approached the man, Master Sergeant Kline close on his heels. He raised a hand. "Sir, can we help you?"

The man laughed, his arms spread wide. "Ya, you canna tell me what inna hell you're landin' here in the middle of me field. Put my keemories into a fit, yeah."

Sheridan looked over his shoulder at the strange creatures still observing them from under the tree. *Kee-more-ies?*

"I'm sorry for disturbing your herd, sir," Chambers said. "I can assure you we meant no harm, Mister…"

The man considered Chambers for a few moments, then finally dropped his arm, the indignant frown fading. "Name's Dippel, folks call me Dips, yeah? Whole plot here's mine, ya understan'? Protected like."

"Again, I apologize for the intrusion, Mr. Dippel," Chambers said. "I can assure you we didn't mean to disturb you, and we won't be staying long."

"Long, eh? Got business here, yeah? Not out here you don't, know that."

"No, not out here."

Dippel's eyebrows went up as he seemed to realize what he was seeing. He glanced around at the other members of the team, to the Albatross, then back to Chambers, a grin slowly appearing at the corners of his mouth.

"Ah, military, yeah? Donna look Pegasi, doh. Bastards donna know their tit from their tat. URT ain't comin' out this way for nothin'. Means you're Alliance, yeah? 'Cept you donna look like any Marine I ever saw."

Chambers cleared his throat. "That's right, we're Alliance Marines."

"Heh, knew it. Still donna 'splain what you're doin' on my land, do it? Less you aren't wantin' nobody to be wise you're here. That the case, makes me a tad keen on why you're here."

"That's classified," Kline said quickly.

"Ha! Canna tell you where to take your *classified* asses, yeah?"

Chambers help up a hand again, trying to calm Dips. "I can't share the details of our mission here, but I can tell you we're only going to be here another six hours max; then we'll be out of your field. I can promise you that. And of course, we'll be more than happy to compensate you for your time and space here."

"Droppin' on the crossers, yeah? 'Bout time someone does, been a pain in my ass for a spell." He smiled and clapped Chambers on the shoulder. "Always knew y'all Alliance shits were above par. Give you a deal. Five thousand."

"I'm sorry?" Chambers asked.

"Five thousand creds," Dips repeated. "Wanna set up here, five thousand what's it cost ya."

Chambers hesitated. "I… uh…"

"Five thousand," Fischer said, appearing behind the captain. He tapped his link as Chambers stepped aside and lifted his chin at the rancher. "Link transfer work for you?"

Dips laughed and opened his link. Fischer tapped in the number then swiped the creds over. A wide grin spread across Dips's face, which quickly turned into laughter.

"Y'all ain't worry 'bout nothin', yeah? Go on, stay however long ya need. Ain't no bother. Gonna be fine right where ya at."

"Thanks," Chambers said, giving Fischer a slightly confused, sidelong look. "I appreciate it."

"No worries, friend."

"You lived on Grinas long?" Fischer asked.

"Whole life. Ma and Pa dropped in when I was knee-high to a hoppa. Been raising keemmis since 'fore I could talk."

Cole leaned close to Sheridan. "And it shows."

"Go into town a lot?" Fischer asked.

Dips shrugged. "Need supplies, make a trip, yeah. Same's the rest."

"If I show you a holo of someone, could you tell me if you've seen them before?"

"Yeah, suppose so."

Fischer tapped his link, bringing up Davis's image. "We're looking for this woman. Have you ever seen her?"

Dips frowned, considering the image. "Eh, she in danger, yeah?"

"That's right," Fischer said.

After several seconds of studying, he shook his head. "No bells, sorry."

"Figured it was a long shot but had to try."

"Mr. Dippel, I do want to thank you for allowing us to use your land," Chambers said. "But we really do have to get moving."

Dips motioned around at the Sabers. "Y'all thinkin' you walkin' all the way to Grey?"

"That's the plan," Kline said.

"Aye, but notta walkin' you're not."

Cole leaned close to Sheridan. "What the hell is he talking about?"

"No clue."

Dips laughed and turned back to his gravbike. "Come on, Alliance. I got ya." Halfway to the bike he stopped and turned. "Ain't got all day now. Donna you fret none, my truck's tip-top, one hundred. Ask anyone. Dips ain't no liar."

Chambers shot Kline and Fischer a questioning look, obviously looking for their thoughts.

Kline shook his head. "I don't like it."

"Well," Fischer said, a grin curling up at the corner of his mouth, "beats walking."

CHAPTER 21

Outskirts of Grey Mount City
Planet Grinas, Kaidor System
18 August 2607

"I have to tell you, Fischer," Sheridan said, "when I woke up this morning, riding in the back of a shit-covered cattle truck was the last thing I thought I'd be doing."

Fischer grunted, tightening his grip on the flat, steel rail behind him, keeping his balance as the truck lurched again. "Could be worse."

"Oh yeah, how?"

"*You* could be covered in shit."

Sheridan laughed. "Good point."

They stood in an oversized truck bed, thirty feet long and ten wide. The rancher had set them up in a counter-grav truck with a wide, covered bed he used to transport his keemories to market, and despite what the rancher had suggested, the truck was in obvious need of an overhaul. The team rocked and swayed with the movement of the truck, zipping over the ground on pads that weren't quite tuned correctly. Instead of a nice, smooth ride, they felt every bump and dip in the road. Every time the truck turned, steel groaned, and Fischer was sure the whole thing was going to rip apart.

The upside, however, was not insignificant. Even in civilian clothing, the team would've likely been spotted by anyone paying attention. Hell, even if you weren't paying attention, it would be hard to miss a group of heavily armed individuals moving tactically through the city. But in full kit, they would have stuck out even worse. With the truck at least they'd be able to get almost anywhere in the city and keep their location and presence hidden until it was absolutely necessary.

He checked his link again. They were a mile outside Grey Mount, named for the mountain range along the western edge of the city. Robalt had tapped into the citywide network, and Fischer had to resist the urge to ask if he'd picked up anything yet. The Saber knew what he was doing, and Fischer didn't want to give him the impression he thought any different. He also didn't want to give the team the idea that he wasn't confident about finding Davis either. They were professionals, no doubt about it, but morale affected everyone, regardless of how highly trained they were. He wanted them watching for threats, not worrying about whether or not their target was here or not. That was his job.

In the cab behind Fischer, Sergeant Richards was driving, with Dips riding shotgun, guiding them on the most optimal route into the city. He picked up bits and pieces of their conversation, but for the most part was glad that he didn't have to pay that close attention. The rancher's dialect was hard to follow, and it was obvious Dips either didn't care or wasn't aware. He just kept right on talking regardless of how confused the Saber looked.

"Donna be trustin' maps," he'd said as the team had been loading up. "Ain't been updated in years. Lots changed since. Dips'll get you there, no worries, yeah?"

Chambers had been slightly apprehensive about the decision

to let the man lead them in, and the captain had been clear that one of his people would do the driving. Not only did he obviously not want to put the lives of the team in the hands of someone they didn't know, he wanted someone who knew evasive driving if things went bad.

"We're entering the city limits now, Captain," Richards said over the taclink. *"Mr. Dips here thinks it's another five to Waypoint Alpha."*

"Roger that," Chambers answered.

Fischer tapped his link and brought up an overlay of the city, swiping to the location of Brice Marks's apartment. The building was in the eastern district, in what looked like the older part of town: several blocks of run-down parkland and entertainment venues, even a half-drained lake. The city's epicenter now had grown in the northern district, where taller, modern office buildings and high-class apartments took center stage. It made sense on a number of levels why Marks had chosen to stay in the older district, especially if he was trying to stay under the radar.

"How's it coming, Robbi?" Chambers asked.

"In the network, Captain. Just working through the local security nodes. Shouldn't be but another minute or so and I'll have complete access. This place isn't exactly Phoenix-level security."

"Now we just hope she's here," Sergeant Kline said.

Fischer rubbed his beard, fighting off a sudden wave of self-doubt. He'd made the right decision in coming here. It'd been the only decision, really, but now facing the possibility that Davis might not be here, he couldn't help at least considering the idea.

"We find Marks, we'll find Davis," he said, while wondering where they would go from here if they didn't.

In truth, he wasn't entirely sure. He was counting on Jones finding something, hoping Osprey would be able to work her magic. The hacker was a known entity throughout ASI, but so far no one had ever been able to put a case on her, and not for lack of trying either. She was extremely good at what she did, to the point of becoming somewhat of a legend or myth within certain circles. But she'd never openly acted against the Alliance, which was probably one of the reasons she wasn't high on ASI's priority list.

I wonder if that will change after this, Fischer thought.

Five minutes later the truck came to a stop and the team filed out of the back. They'd stopped in an alley, flanked by three- and four-story warehouses. Only one of the three visible streetlamps was operational. A few ground transports were parked here and there, interspersed with large cargo containers stacked two and three high. Almost everything looked like it'd been abandoned years ago.

"Looks like this place used to be a hopping spot," Reese said.

"A lot of URT planets are like this," Fischer said. "They boom when they're first set up, and fizzle out as the years go on."

"Everyone wants new opportunities until they figure out they have to work their ass off for them," Sheridan said.

Fischer chuckled. "You're absolutely right."

The Saber team spread out from the truck without orders, clearing side alleys, alcoves and rooftops. Cole unpacked his case and began launching his recon drones. Six silver orbs shot away, disappearing into the early morning darkness, angling for high-orbital surveillance. The team's sniper, Sergeant Hanover, made it to a maintenance ladder on the closest building and started climbing. The rest held various corners and approaches, virtually sealing off the area from intrusion.

Fischer suddenly found himself with nothing to do and didn't like the helpless feeling settling over him. He trusted these people with his life and had no doubts about their competence or abilities, but not being able to contribute was frustrating. He moved around to where Kline and Reese were setting up a makeshift command post; three large holodisplays receiving information from Robalt were working.

The sound of barking dogs echoed in the distance, accompanied by the occasional counter-grav car or flyer on morning commutes. The drone feeds began appearing on the screens one by one, and fortunately it didn't look like there was much foot traffic yet; that was good for them.

"I'm in Marks's building's security network," Robalt advised over the taclink. *"Working through the local node and… hmmm, doesn't look like anyone's home. The internal security alarm is active, but I'm not picking anything up on the sensor network."*

"Any chance the sensors are faulty?" Chambers asked, joining Fischer and Kline.

"It's possible," Robalt said. *"There aren't any video feeds that I can see. Looks like there might have been at one time, but the system's inop now."*

"Any sign of Davis?" Fischer asked before he could stop himself. He'd hoped they'd find them both at the same time. It would've made this whole operation that much easier.

Like your luck is that good, Fischer told himself.

"Nothing yet," Robalt said.

"Rocha, let's get that building secured," Sergeant Kline said.

"Roger that," Team One's leader said. "Neal, Reese, Sheridan, with me."

Without a word, the three Sabers lined up with Rocha and began moving toward the alley, paused briefly, then crossed the street, heading for Marks's building. One of the drones tagged them on the milnet, highlighting their position moving between several parked vehicles.

"Let's hope these babies fare better than the last time," Cole said, fingers dancing over the holodisplay floating in front of him.

"Looks like people are starting to wake up," Cole said as multiple yellow triangles appeared, both inside the building and emerging out onto the sidewalks. The corresponding text boxes labeled each as unknown threat, capturing visual data if possible and sending it back to Robalt's terminal.

"And we'll know if one of those is Marks or not?" Eliwood asked.

Cole nodded. "System's tied in through Robalt's back at the Albatross. It's not enough to identify exactly who they are, but if they're a match for him or Davis, we should get a hit within a second or two."

"I'm into the city's secure storage, which, let me just say, is not that *secure,"* Robalt said. *"I'm going to start running a scrub on the historicals. It's a long shot, but we might be able to peg her off the inbound traffic from the spaceport."*

"Drones on target," Cole said.

Brice Marks's apartment was on the eleventh floor of the high-rise, situated on the northwest corner, facing the mountains. The visual feed from multiple drones showed the location in multiple spectrums—from normal to thermal, X-ray, and infrared —piercing the steel and glass exterior of the building. They watched as the drones moved to get maximum coverage on the apartment, ensuring nothing was missed.

"Empty," Cole said, leaning back from the floating display.

"You sure?" Fischer asked. "No sign of shielding at all? Can he be blocking the sensors?"

"I'm not seeing any sign of shielding," Cole said, tapping on the console. One of the feeds shifted down, scanning the unit directly below the target. A mass of red and orange appeared, body heat registering clearly on the drone's sensor suite. As the drone zoomed in, it became evident that the single mass was actually two, one straddling the other.

"Huh," Eliwood said, crossing her arms. She gave Fischer a sidelong glance. "Looks like it's working, wouldn't you say?"

Fischer couldn't help but chuckle. "I'd say so."

"And working well, I might add," Cole said as the feed moved closer.

"What do you have, Cole?" Sergeant Kline barked.

Cole abruptly straightened, fingers quickly darting across the drone's controls, moving it away from the couple, back to Marks's empty apartment. "Uh, nothing, Master Sergeant. Target location is empty."

"Empty?" Kline asked, moving to see for himself.

Fischer tapped his link, bringing up the information they had on Davis's brother. He scrolled through the data until he found what he was looking for. "Marks works at a company called Aerodine Systems. Could be at work early."

"Or late," Eliwood added.

"Either way." Fischer connected to the city's network and started searching. It didn't take long. "There." He swiped the data to Cole's larger display.

The bottom half of the holopanel became a map of the city, an orange dot pulsing over a location in the southwest corner. A message panel appeared, displaying the address and name of the business as well as a wireframe model of the building, slowly rotating over the map.

Cole touched the display with both hands, then spread them apart, zooming out until a green dot appeared in the northeast corner. "That's us."

Two blue lines drew themselves from the Sabers' position to the Aerodine building, showing the most direct route through the city's streets and the straight-line flight path between the two points.

"That's a hell of a drive," Cole said.

Eliwood looked at Fischer. "You thinking we split up? Some for Marks, some for Davis?"

"We're not splitting the team," Chambers said. He stood on

the far side of Cole's holodisplay, examining the map with his arms crossed.

"Actual, One-Alpha, we're in position," Rocha advised.

"Stand by," Chambers said.

"You don't think they skipped town already?" Eliwood asked.

Fischer didn't want to admit the thought had already crossed his mind. *Always picking up the pieces,* he thought, staring at the empty apartment. "Tap into the local transportation registry. Maybe we can track the vehicles leaving the building."

Eliwood shook her head. "There's got to be hundreds of people living there, Fish. Not counting people coming and going all day long. We're never going to find either of them that way."

"Goddamn it," Fischer growled, turning away from the screens and glaring up at the lightening sky.

"I might be able to tap the network at Aerodine," Robalt said over the taclink. *"If he's there, shouldn't be that hard to find out."*

"Do it," Chambers said. "Rocha, rally on our position."

"Roger."

Chambers stepped toward Fischer. "We're not going to be able to chase these guys all over the city, Fischer. We're too exposed as it is. If local law enforcement—"

"I know." Fischer sighed. "I know."

"So, what, we just sit around and hope either of them show up?" Eliwood asked.

"I—" Fischer's link chimed, cutting him off. He looked down and froze. "Son of a bitch."

"What?" Eliwood asked.

"It's her," Fischer said. "It's Davis."

CHAPTER 22

Pleasant View Estates
Grey Mount City, Grinas
18 August 2607

"You're a hard person to track down," Fischer said, trying to keep his voice steady.

"Apparently not hard enough," Davis said.

"You had to know we'd come after you."

"Oh, I had no doubts. Just figured it would take you a little longer. I'll give you this, Fischer, you don't disappoint."

"You need to come in," Fischer said.

"Not going to happen."

Fischer took a deep breath, giving himself time to think. "Then let's meet. Just you and me."

Davis laughed. *"Right, you and me and your friends with the big guns."*

"Can't do anything about that," Fischer said. "And you know why."

"Yeah, I do."

"Come on. Ten minutes. Let's talk."

There was silence for several moments; then she said, *"Pleasant View Estates, ground-level cafe. Be there in five."*

The connection terminated. Fischer looked at Eliwood, not really sure what to say.

"She's not going to show," Eliwood said. "She's just trying to throw us off."

"Maybe," Fischer said. He tapped his link. "Robbi, Pleasant View Estates, can you get a location?"

"Yeah, one sec."

"You're going to meet her?" Chambers asked.

"It appears that way."

"Our mission is to apprehend her, not talk with her."

Fischer nodded. "And we are going to do just that, after. If she's there, at least we'll know where she is. Your team sets up a perimeter and we'll have her even if she decides to bolt."

Chambers worked his jaw back and forth and leaned in close, keeping this his voice low. "We aren't out here to play games, Agent Fischer. We grab her and we get the hell out of here. That's the mission."

"And if something happens to her during the grab? Or she just decides to blow her brains to mush instead? I need her alive, Captain. Give me ten minutes. Ten minutes and I'll walk her into the shuttle myself."

"Ten minutes, Agent Fischer," Chambers said, the reluctance obvious in his tone. "After that, I'm coming in to get both of you."

It didn't take long to find the building Davis had specified, and after a short drive along the service roads, still mostly deserted, Fischer hopped out of the truck and hurried out to the main streets. Pleasant View Estates.

Fischer was approaching the lobby entrance to Pleasant View Estates, an office/apartment building similar to her brother's building two blocks to the east. He held his breath as he stepped through the automatic glass doors into the expansive lobby, his footsteps echoing across the highly polished marble floor. A ten-meter waterfall was the centerpiece of the space, flowing into an oval pool fifteen meters meter's across. Colorful plants and lush greet shrubs surrounded the entire setup, and ambience noise filtered through the space, making him feel like he'd stepped into the middle of a tropical jungle.

"Seems a big bit high -class for this neighborhood," Eliwood said over the taclink.

Fischer agreed, but remained silent as he moved through the lobby, scanning the shops arranged around the exterior. Shop-workers were in the process of setting up their displays for the day's customers, and what Fischer guessed were residents moved between the lifts at the back of the lobby, to the cafe on his right and the exit behind him. Fischer eyed them all in turn, and he headed for the cafe, watching for any sign they were watching him, but none seemed interested.

"I've got eyes on," Cole said over the taclink. *"Drones in position."*

Fischer nodded and kept moving, wondering how long it would be until the sniper had a bead on Davis. *Please don't do anything stupid,* he thought. Regardless of what she'd done, he didn't want to see her brains sprayed all over the place.

She's not your friend anymore, Fish, another part of his brain reminded him. *She's an enemy of the state.*

He apologized to a couple standing in line outside the cafe and slipped up to the hostess stand. She looked up and smiled as he approached.

"Can I help you, sir?"

"Yeah, they're already inside."

"Sure, go right ahead."

"Turn right," Cole said. *"Four tables in on your right."*

Fischer scanned the tables, spotting Davis right where the

Saber had indicated. She was facing Fischer but was looking down at the menu. He slowed as he approached, and she looked up, meeting Fischer's eyes.

"Jackson," she said, her tone emotionless, almost detached.

"Riley." He slipped into the booth across from her, putting his hands palm down on the table.

She looked around, obviously scanning the cafe for the rest of his team.

"Just me," Fischer said.

Davis finished her scan, then sighed, putting her own hands on the table. "I'm glad it's you."

"Oh?"

"I mean, I figured it would be, but still. How'd you find me?"

"Voidtronic Investments."

Davis sniffed and nodded but said nothing.

"You hid it well," Fischer said. "If we hadn't been looking, no one would've suspected a thing."

"And my brother?"

Fischer shook his head. "We're not here for him."

"We? You mean you and your military friends?"

"That's right," Fischer said. "You've made a few interesting friends yourself."

Davis ground her teeth together, inhaling through her nose. "Yeah."

"What could they have possibly offered you to make you sell your soul like that?"

"Damn," she said, looking away. "They made everything sound so legit, and now, looking back on it, I was such an idiot. I should have known what I was getting into."

"How could you *not?* Conspiracy, espionage, murder? Jesus, Riley, what were you thinking?"

"That's not what I signed up for," she said, unclasping her

hands and leaning forward. "I promise you. That's not at all what they sold me."

"They?"

Davis sighed. "Cardinal."

"What do they want?"

"Right now? Fuck, Jackson, I don't have any idea. All I know is when they first approached me, it was all about cleaning up the Alliance. Getting rid of all the dirty politicians, cleaning up the government, taking out the trash. I swear, it sounded like everything we've all talked about doing. Putting everything right that we'd allowed to crumble over decades of politics and corruption. I mean, the dirt they had on some of these people…"

"So you spied on us?" Fischer said. "Gave them information on our operations?"

"No," Davis said, a little too quickly. "No, I promise. Well, not until recently. They just wanted me watching, documenting. Said when it was time to do the work, they'd let me know. I literally didn't hear from them for another couple of years, and even then, I was to check in and make sure I was still in the agency's good graces. I didn't get activated until after Stonemeyer."

"Activated," Fischer repeated, saying the word like a curse. "You had to know what you were doing wasn't right. You had to know they were playing you."

Davis shook her head. "I was young and naive. Thought I was going to be making a difference. And the money was good. Hell, it was more money than I'd ever seen before, and they were giving it to me for practically nothing. It wasn't until much later that I realized what I was actually doing, and by then it was too late. They had me."

"You could've come to me for help, Davis," Fischer said. "You know that."

She shook her head. "I couldn't. And not only because I didn't know who I could trust, but because of my family. Cardinal had my entire life before they even approached me. I couldn't just stop. I had to protect Brice."

"Okay, then what changed? Why'd you run?"

"I saw the writing on the wall. Once you started putting everything together and the information about Cardinal started spreading, I knew it was only a matter of time before you figured me out or they decided I was too much of a threat. Turned out I was right after all. It just worked out that the guy they sent after me underestimated me. I'm not sorry about that either."

"Don't expect you to be. But I am going to need you to come in."

Davis grimaced as if she'd eaten something sour. "You know I can't do that, Fish. I go back and they'll kill me. I know they're already looking for me. If you found me, they won't be too far behind."

"We can protect you."

"Ha! Come on, Fish. You can't even protect a high-profile person like Young. What can you possibly do to protect people with those kinds of connections? I guarantee you they won't be coming to extract me. A bullet to the head, that's all I rate."

"Does your brother know?"

She looked down at the table and shook her head. "He doesn't know everything, but he knows enough. God bless him, he doesn't ask any questions. Never has. Once I realized what I'd gotten myself into, I knew I needed to get him out of the picture. They already had leverage on me, but I wasn't going to let them go after my family. I set up the investment company and funneled all of Cardinal's money to him. And you know what's funny? I don't think he's touched a single credit."

Fischer leaned forward. "Who is Cardinal, Riley? I mean really. You have to know something."

She laughed. "Fuck, Fischer. Cardinal is everyone, it's everything. They're everywhere—grunts, teachers, spies, government officers, police officers, military—you name it, Cardinal is into it. Throw a fucking rock, you know?"

"They're not everyone."

Davis chewed her bottom lip.

"And I could've helped you," Fischer said. "Still can. Why do you think I came all the way out here?"

"Right. You came all the way out here to help me and not to track down Young?"

Fischer shook his head. "Did that already."

"And?"

"No luck."

"I don't know what you think I can do for you, Fischer," Davis said. "This isn't like anything you've ever dealt with before. This isn't just a case you bring to Judicial. You're not going to win this in the courts. You think they're going to let something like that get in their way? I'd be dead before I even took the stand, and so would you."

"Don't know that," Fischer said. "There are still good people out there, Davis. It's not all doom and gloom."

She shook her head again. "And say it does go to court, what then? You think these people are ever going to step inside a prison?"

"If I can find them, you bet your ass. Who are they? I'm sure you had a handler, right? That's a start. We track these people down one at a time. That's how this works."

"You're never going to be able to track them all down, Fischer. That's what I'm saying. There's too many. And trust me, once this gets out, they *will* turn up the heat."

"I can deal with heat."

Davis leaned close. "But can Clarissa? Can Maddie?"

Fischer's chest tightened, his blood pumping in his ears.

"You see," Davis continued. "These people won't hesitate to use them against you, Jackson. They're evil, evil people. Fuck, I wish I would never have…" She trailed off, looking out the large bay windows on the far side of the cafe.

"We can protect both of you," Fischer said. "You and your brother."

"You can't."

Fischer watched her for several moments. The pain in her eyes was more than a little obvious. She loved her brother and would do anything to protect him, just like he would do for his family. He knew regardless of the consequences, he'd do anything to protect his family, and sitting here seeing the agony on her face, he knew Davis would do the same for hers.

Then a thought occurred to him. "He doesn't know you're here, does he?"

"No," she said. "He doesn't. I haven't seen him in years, Fish. Ever since we faked his death. He's got a wife now; he's got a family. What am I supposed to say to him? How's he going to explain it to them? 'This is my long-lost sister, who's now on the run for her life, and we have to go with her?' I don't think that's the best way to approach this."

"My guess is there won't ever be a good way to approach this," Fischer said.

"You're probably right."

"Say it all worked out, where would you go?"

She chuckled, shaking her head. "I actually have no idea. He never spent the money. Guess he was saving it for a rainy day."

"Well, it's definitely raining."

She looked at him almost longingly, as if she wanted desperately to believe him, but couldn't. She shook her head. "No matter where I go, they're going to catch up with me eventually."

"So why do it on your own?" Fischer asked. "Let me help you. I've got a lot more to offer than you realize. I can protect you and your brother and his family, I promise. But you're going to have to come now. You're going to have to give me what you know. Your handler, all the others you know about. You're going to have to come clean one hundred percent."

"I don't know anything else," Davis said. "They don't work like that. Everything is strictly compartmentalized. We never had group meetings or anything like that."

"I know you better than that. I know you met with your handler once a week. We need to know what happened during those meetings. What'd you talk about? What information did you pass along? War is coming, and you're the only one who can tell us anything about the enemy."

The smile vanished. She held Fischer's gaze for a moment and took a long breath. "My brother and his family, off-planet and safe before I give you anything. I want your personal guarantee, Fischer. Regardless of how useful the information is. I don't care what happens to me, but I need to know they're taken care of."

"You have my word."

CHAPTER 23

Osprey's Compound
Barcroft's Landing, Thresh
18 August 2607

Osprey's base of operations wasn't glamorous; in fact, it was borderline unsanitary. Inside the raised enclosure, the walls were lined with server racks covered with hundreds of blinking status links and connected by dozens of multicolored wires that criss-crossed the floor and ceiling.

As Jones entered her "lair" on the morning of the second day, he had almost gotten over the urge to cover his privates as he passed the rows of electronics. He felt, more than heard, the incessant thrum of the electronics around him, a constant reminder that this woman was one of the most powerful people in the galaxy, and if she really wanted to, she could dismantle his existence one keystroke at a time. If he didn't die of radiation poisoning before then.

She wouldn't be in here if it wasn't safe, he told himself. Then again, she hadn't always been the most reasonable person in the entire galaxy.

"Something wrong?" Osprey asked, as if reading his thoughts.

"No!" Jones said, a little too quickly. "Nothing. I'm fine."

She held her gaze on him for another second, then turned back around to her main displays, six holoscreens filled with data that Jones couldn't begin to comprehend. The setup was impressive, even not knowing what half of it was. Leaps and bounds over what she'd had when they'd been an item.

But as he took his usual spot on the small couch along the side wall just behind her, he couldn't help but hope Fischer was having better luck. Osprey had been at it for almost thirty-six hours straight, stopping only to eat, refill her coffee, and use the restroom. She'd assured him on several occasions that she was making progress, but for the life of him, Jones couldn't see it.

You have to trust her, a voice in his head said. *Yeah,* he argued back, *easy for you to say.*

He sat there for several minutes in silence, watching her work, hands moving across multiple screens with practiced ease and natural determination. Occasionally she'd mutter something to herself, shake her head, or even clap excitedly before returning to her quiet, resolute posture, fingers dutifully tapping away.

Sometime later Loomis entered, carrying three cups of steaming coffee. He handed one to Jones then set one on the console next to Osprey.

"Thanks," she said without looking up.

"Sure thing."

Jones sipped his, impressed. "That's really good, Loomis."

The engineer shrugged. "I just made what she had. Didn't do anything special."

"Double Roasted Del Raycan Special," Osprey said. "Costs a fortune, but it's worth it." She glanced over her shoulder. "That's not included in the price either."

Jones chuckled and took another sip.

Loomis sat down next to him and whispered, "Anything?"

Jones shook his head.

"It's been almost two days."

"I know," Jones replied through clenched teeth. He gave Loomis a look that said, "Drop it," and the engineer shrugged, sitting back to sip his coffee.

As much as he wanted to disagree, Loomis was right, and Jones wasn't sure how much time they'd be able to waste just sitting here waiting. They were on the clock; the problem was that none knew what time it was. It was all relative, but they were still on it. Osprey had been the most skilled programmer he'd ever met, but now he found himself considering the possibility that maybe her skills had diminished in the years since they'd split.

Since you left, the voice corrected him. He sighed.

"You know, that isn't going to help this go any faster," Osprey said without turning around.

"Sorry, that wasn't meant for you," Jones said.

"Yes, it was."

Jones leaned forward, holding his mug in both hands, looking down at the brown liquid swirling inside. "It's just, we've been at this for a couple of days now and…"

"Hey, if you think you can find someone more capable…"

Jones held up a hand, palm out. "That's not what I'm saying. I'm just… are you making any progress at all?"

Finally, she turned, spinning in her chair to face him. There were dark circles under her eyes, and her hair needed brushing. When she put herself to a task, she'd focus on it unrelentingly, oftentimes disregarding simple things like sleep or showers. But she was still beautiful.

"This isn't like slipping into a local traffic control node or a credit company's secure storage," Osprey said. "These guys have more tripwires than…"

Jones raised an eyebrow at her. "Than?"

"It's a lot."

He grinned. "You never were too good at proper analogies."

She held his gaze for a moment, then spun back to her displays. She took a sip, then went back to work. "We're getting there."

"Well, that's better than nothing," Loomis said.

Jones glared at him. Loomis shrugged and went back to sipping his coffee.

After sitting in near silence for almost two hours, Jones stood and began pacing. Admittedly, the room was only big enough for a few strides in either direction, but he couldn't bring himself to sit on the couch any longer.

"Anyone hungry?" he asked, putting his fists into the small of his back and stretching.

"I could go for something," Loomis said.

Osprey didn't answer.

Jones rolled his eyes and tapped his link. "There anything worth ordering in this town?"

She didn't answer.

"Osprey?"

"Hold on!"

Jones sighed. "I get it, you're hard at work, but you need to eat real—"

"Got something." She tapped in several more commands, and several panels appeared with scrolling text and graphical blueprints Jones couldn't identify. Osprey worked through the panels, swiping fingers across the displays, enlarging some, clearing others.

"What is it?" Jones asked, stepping closer, trying to make sense of what he was seeing.

She was working through the information too fast for Jones to keep up. Hundreds of lines of code, circuit schematics and chassis blueprints for what he thought was some kind of communication relay, but he couldn't be sure. As she worked, he felt his chest tightening, frustration building.

He was about to say something when she laughed and clapped her hands. She paused for a moment, double-checking something, then immediately went back to work, fingers dancing over the keys. Jones gave up with a shake of his head and started pacing again.

Five minutes later, he couldn't take it anymore. "Care to enlighten the rest of the class?"

"Hold on." She held up a finger.

"For the love," Jones said, throwing up his hands.

On the couch, Loomis laughed and crossed his legs, smiling at Jones. He was enjoying this.

"Shouldn't you be doing something like, I don't know, checking on my ship or something?" Jones asked.

"Ol' girl ain't going anywhere, boss. She's locked up tighter than an airlock after a breach."

"That," Osprey said, pointing at her far-right holoscreen, "is the interstellar communication database of the largest techno-communications company in the history of human civilization."

"Alistair?" Jones asked, scanning the data. None of it made any sense to him. "You can find the relay we're looking for?"

"Shit, I can find a lot more than that," Osprey said. She tapped a single key, and two new panels appeared, showing camera footage of some ritzy hotel, complete with red carpet, gold accents and bellmen in black tuxedos. An orange line drew itself around what looked like one of the guests just stepping away from the counter, a tall blonde in a long red dress on his arm.

Osprey froze the image. "That's Senator Kramer checking into the Pandora Galactic three days ago, and that pretty young thing there is definitely not his wife."

Loomis pushed himself off the couch and crossed the room to

stand behind Jones. He leaned closer to get a better look at the image. "I'll be damned. Bet you he'd hate to see that getting out."

"No shit," Osprey said.

Loomis put a hand on Jones's shoulder. "Bet we could pull some nice credits off that, eh?"

"Hell, you could probably bank enough creds in one go, you wouldn't have to do it ever again," Osprey said.

"Hold on," Jones said. "First, we're not blackmailing anyone. Second, what the hell does this have to do with finding our comms relay?"

"What? We can't have any fun while we're at it?" Osprey asked.

"I told you, we're on the clock."

"All right, no fun then, maybe later." She closed the window.

"Wait a minute," Loomis said, pointing at the screen. "If you're diving into Alistair's database, why are we looking at security footage from the Pandora Galactic?"

"Ah, fair question." Osprey typed another series of commands, and another panel appeared. "I actually found the information about the comm relay a while ago, but the amount of information contained in there is amazing. Alistair is linked into everything, and I don't mean because they're in business with these places. I mean they left backdoors into everything they've ever manufactured and sold. They literally have access to every piece of technology in the Alliance, not to mention their foreign contracts."

"Okay, well, I don't care about all that," Jones said, feeling slightly annoyed. "I'm here for some very specific information. I don't care about some senator somewhere getting his rocks off with a high-cred hooker. Can you tell me where the message came from or not?"

"Sure." Osprey hit another key. A planetary system appeared above the main screen, four planetoids orbiting a yellow dwarf.

"Saccora. Industrial world smack-dab in the middle of the URT. Independent, home to embassies of the Alliance, Pegasi, URT, hell, even Corwynn has a consulate there. Largest metropolitan area is Ridgecrest, home to about five million, not counting the commercial traffic in and out of the system, of course."

"Saccora?" Loomis asked. "You'd think they'd pick some place out of the way, not surrounded by so many different super-powers. Talk about rolling the dice."

"It makes sense," Jones said. "It's centrally located. The Saccoran Navy doesn't allow foreign military ships within three AUs of the planet. Place is completely neutral. That's why everyone has an embassy there. Great place to hide out if you don't want to be a target of anyone's military."

"Can you narrow it down at all?" Jones asked.

Osprey laughed. "Are you kidding? I just broke into the most secure system ever devised by man, to find a relay node that most governments would kill for, and you're asking me if I can get you a better location?"

"Can you give me something better or not?"

Osprey smiled. "Sure I can. It's just a matter of—"

An alarm sounded and three new holopanels appeared, all showing camera footage from various angles around Osprey's compound. On the first, two figures in body armor, carrying rifles and moving as stealthily as they could, were moving down an alley toward the camera. On the middle, two gravcars touched down across the street from the main entrance, offloading four identically dressed figures, all immediately moving to stack up on the door. Four were covering the rear on the right panel, holding twenty meters from an exterior door.

Osprey spread her fingers across the center panel, enlarging the image, focusing on the figures' clothes. "Well, damn."

"Who?" Jones asked, leaning Osprey's shoulder.

"Well, they're not cops," she said. She looked at him, and he could see the concern on her face. "It's not good."

Another alarm chimed and a fourth panel appeared, this one showing the view of the building's roof, a small shuttle flaring to hover inches from the surface. Six figures dropped from the open side doors, immediately heading for the two roof-access hatches.

"Well, fuck," Osprey said. She tapped in a series of commands, and a message panel displaying the words BLUE FALCON appeared on the central screen. She jammed a finger on the initiate key and the entire terminal blinked off. The incessant humming of the surrounding datacores began winding down one by one, lights winking out in a cascading wave.

She stood and started for the door. "Time to go, boys."

CHAPTER 24

Outside Aerodine Systems
Grey Mount City, Grinas
18 August 2607

"Agent Fischer, we need to be moving," Chambers said over the taclink.

Fischer ignored him and turned to Davis. "Call him again."

"He said he was coming," Davis countered, shifting in the seat next to him.

They were both in the back of the gravcar Davis had rented, two blocks ahead of the rest of the Saber team still hanging back in Dippel's cattle truck. Fischer sat behind the driver, Sheridan, facing Davis, who sat on the far back bench facing front.

"He's not coming," Eliwood said from the front passenger seat.

Davis straightened in her seat, gritting her teeth. "He'll be here."

"Fischer," Chambers said.

"Shit," Fischer muttered, twisting around to see the building ahead of them.

"What?" Davis asked. She wasn't tied into the Sabers' tac-channel.

"Nothing," Fischer said.

"It's not nothing," Eliwood corrected. "The Marine commander wants to get moving. We're exposed, Fischer."

Sheridan nodded, obviously agreeing with Eliwood, but he kept silent.

Fischer turned back around. "You need to call him now, Davis. We're running out of time."

"I said he was coming," Davis said. She tapped her link and tried calling him again. She held up her hands, frustrated. "Maybe he can't answer."

"Something's wrong," Eliwood said.

"Captain's not going to wait forever," Sheridan said.

"I said he's coming!" Davis said, her voice growing louder, more frustrated.

"And if he's not?" Eliwood asked.

Davis glared at Eliwood. "I told you, I'm not leaving without him."

"I'm not really sure you understand the dynamic of this relationship. You don't get a say." Eliwood's tone was level, but Fischer knew it wouldn't stay that way. She was getting anxious, and he couldn't blame her.

The two women held each other's gaze for several moments before Davis finally looked away, turning back to watch the entrance to Aerodine. People were now streaming in and out of the four sets of double doors to the expansive lobby. Several aircabs landed and took off in succession, dropping off, picking up, just like another normal day at the office. Except for one of them, and Fischer was on the verge of cutting bait.

Chambers was right, they couldn't wait forever, but Fischer knew the chances of Davis voluntarily helping them decreased drastically if they left her brother here. Not to mention knowingly leaving behind a family that was sure to be picked up by Cardinal's people. Fischer didn't even want to think about what would happen to them if they were captured. But if they were spotted…

"Look," Fischer said, leaning toward Davis. "I know what you must be feeling right now, but I can't ask these people to put their lives on the line for you or your brother. You *are* the mission, and you gave up your rights when you betrayed your nation." He tapped Sheridan on the shoulder. "Let's—"

"Wait." Davis pointed. "There."

Across the street, Brice Marks stepped out of the far set of double doors and paused on the landing at the top of a short flight of stairs to the sidewalk. He glanced up and down the road, obviously looking for something, then put his hands in his pants pockets and waited.

"What's he doing?" Eliwood asked.

"He's making sure the coast is clear," Davis said.

"Making sure the coast is clear?" Eliwood repeated. "What, is he a secret agent now? We don't have time for this. Let's go."

Davis tapped her link. It rotated into position and her fingers danced across the panel. A second later she was connected. Fischer watched Marks reach down and tap his own link, answering the call.

"Where are you?" Marks asked, his voice quivering.

The car's counter-grav thrummed underneath them as Sheridan maneuvered them into traffic.

"Six cars back, right lane," Davis told her brother. "Black and green four-door."

Marks scanned the street, straightening when he finally saw them. "I see you."

He jogged down the stairs, paused at the street for a line of cars to pass, then jogged across to the far side. Sheridan pulled over again and Eliwood hopped out, opening the rear door.

"Come on, hurry," Eliwood said, flagging him over.

"Where's Riley?" Marks asked, pausing just outside the grav-car's door.

"Brice, get in!" Davis shouted, twisting to face him as he ducked inside.

He paused when he caught sight of Fischer. "What is this?"

"Just get in, Brice."

"Move!" Eliwood pushed him in and shut the door behind him before climbing back into the passenger seat.

"We've got him, Captain," Sheridan said. "We're moving out."

"Riley, what the hell is going on?" Marks pulled himself up on the seat next to Fischer, frowning at him.

"It's going to be okay, Brice, I promise."

Sheridan gunned the throttle and pulled away from the curb, swerving through the stalled morning traffic.

"Okay?" Marks asked. "You've got to be kidding me, *okay?* If everything's okay, then why the hell are you here? Who are these people? You brought the military?"

"I'm not military," Eliwood said.

"Special Agent Jackson Fischer, Alliance Security and Intelligence. I know you probably have a lot of questions, but right now we're in a bit of a time crunch here. Your wife, where is she?"

Confused, Marks looked from Fischer to Davis, obviously looking for help. "What's wrong with Lily? What about Simone?"

"I'm sure they're fine," Davis said. "But please, Brice, we don't have time to waste here. Where are they?"

Marks's nostrils flared and he glared at Fischer, obviously trying to work out what was going on. "If they're hurt..."

"They're not," Fischer said. "Not yet. And I'd like to keep them that way."

Sheridan looked over his shoulder at Fischer. "Chambers is asking for status."

Fischer held up a hand, keeping his gaze locked on Marks.

"Tell us where to go, and we can get everyone off-planet in under an hour. You will all be safe, I promise you."

Marks sighed, shaking his head. "They're heading for our meeting place. Figured something like this would happen eventually. Been setting up our out for a while now."

"Where?" Fischer asked, growing frustrated at having to repeat the question.

"Grinas Station, terminal one," Marks said. "They're booking a flight off-planet."

"You won't need it," Fischer said. "You got that?"

"Got it," Eliwood said, punching the course into the gravcar's navigational system.

"Valkyrie Actual, Seven Alpha, be advised we are en route to Grinas Station. ETA—" Sheridan checked the holodisplay to his right "—thirteen minutes."

"All right," Marks said, "is someone going to tell me what the fuck is going on?"

Fischer looked at Davis, who sighed and said, "It's me."

Marks frowned. "What? The money? They found out?"

Davis nodded.

"Son of a bitch. I knew it wouldn't last forever. So what's the plan now? You get us off planet and she goes to prison, right? What happens to us? The people she works for aren't going to ever leave us alone while she's alive."

"I promise you, we're going to take care of you," Fischer said. "You don't have anything to worry about."

"Yeah, sure, whatever you say," Marks said, unconvinced.

They spent the rest of the ride in silence, watching the city go by around them. Every so often traffic would slow, and Fischer would hold his breath as passengers around them looked in their direction. The rest of them could pass for regular civilians except for the tactical vests Fischer and Eliwood had on, and even though Sheridan didn't have his helmet on, it was hard to hide his black body armor.

Ten minutes later they were pulling into the city's spaceport, merging through several lanes of traffic, moving to the drop-off and pickup lanes. To their right, rows of landing pads for personal shuttles were lined up between the road and pads for large transports farther on. A medium-sized cargo shuttle lifted off, kicking up dust as it rose into the air.

"There they are," Marks said, pointing. His wife's black hair blew in the downdraft of the shuttle, their daughter holding tight to her leg. She couldn't have been more than five or six.

Sheridan slowed and pulled to the side. Marks had the door open and was stepping out before he had completely stopped, jogging to meet his family.

"For fuck's sake," Fischer said, climbing out behind him.

"It's okay," Marks told his wife, embracing her and putting a hand on the child's back. "It's going to be okay."

Fischer stopped a few meters back, giving Marks a little bit of room. Quickly, he scanned the people moving around them, anxious to be back in the car.

"Brice, what the hell is going on?" his wife demanded, seeing Fischer's tactical vest.

"It's fine, Lily. We have to go." Marks ushered them both toward the gravcar.

Eliwood had got out and was now holding the door open, motioning them inside.

"No," Lily pulled out of his grip. "I want to know what the hell is going on. You can't just call a code red and not tell me what it's about. Who are these people? What did you do?"

"He didn't do anything, ma'am," Fischer said, stepping forward. "I'm Agent—"

"I don't give a shit who you are," Lily snapped. "You said your sister was back. What does that mean?"

"Babe, please, I'm—"

"What *does* that mean, Brice? I thought you said we'd never see her again."

"I know what I said," Marks said, obviously more than a little flustered. "Would you please get in the car?"

"I'm not going anywhere until someone tells me exactly what the hell is going—"

The snap of a gunshot rang in the distance, and sparks erupted off the edge of the gravcar's roof with a resounding *twang*. On instinct, Fischer ducked and reached for his pistol. The others ducked as well, Marks moving to shield his family. The girl screamed as another round smacked into the pavement next to Fischer's feet, spraying bits of permacrete and dust.

"Get in!" Eliwood shouted, drawing her pistol.

"Who the hell is shooting at us?" Davis shouted from inside the car.

Fischer backed toward the car, putting himself between their attackers and the Marks family, searching for the threat. Around the landing area, people were just starting to notice something wasn't right, but it was obvious no one had truly figured it out. They all looked lost, as if they were waiting to see if what they'd just heard had been a fluke or not. When the next series of shots rang out, most got the picture.

Screams echoed through the air as more gunshots rang out. People fled in all directions, trying to get to safety while at the same time not knowing where to go. Groups darted in all directions, bumping and tripping over each other, trying to get away.

Something zipped past Fischer's ear, so close he could feel the wind as the bullet sliced through the air. He dropped down, turning to see Marks and his family frozen in obvious shock.

"Get them in the cab!" Fischer shouted, pushing Marks with one hand.

Sheridan's voice came through the taclink. "Valkyrie Seven-

Alpha to all Valkyrie Elements, we are under attack. I say again, we are under attack. Receiving small-arms fire from the west of our position. How copy?"

Sheridan hunched over the hood of the gravcar, using it as a shooting platform. He fired off several rounds, but when Fischer turned, looking for what the Saber had seen, he saw nothing.

"Where?" Fischer shouted, still pushing Marks back.

"There," Sheridan shouted, pointing. "Three o'clock!"

Fischer looked and saw eight figures coming toward them from a matte black Pegasi shuttle. They were all dressed in matching black uniforms, and Fischer knew immediately who they were.

"How the hell did they find us?" Eliwood shouted, moving around the front of the car, taking cover on the back side.

"In!" Fischer shouted. "In! In! In!"

Lily helped their little girl in first, then climbed in after, followed by Marks. Sheridan paused outside the door, tapping his link, activating his connection to their Sabers' taclink again.

Sergeant Rocha's voice came through his cochlear implant. *"Copy that, Seven, we are moving to your position. Sitrep?"*

"Eight hostiles," Sheridan answered. He fired off another burst then said, "Looks like the same team from Caldera."

"The Elites?" Rocha asked.

"Looks that way."

"Evade if possible, Seven," Sergeant Kline said before Sheridan could answer. *"We're coming to you, but this traffic is slowing us down."*

"Roger that!"

"What the hell is going on?" Davis shouted.

"They're going to flank us!" Sheridan shouted.

"Get in!" Fischer slapped the roof. "We need to go! Let's go!"

The gravcar shook as several rounds slammed into the rear, chewing through the steel alloy. Fischer dropped to the ground, covering his head as the barrage continued. The electronics snapped and popped inside as the bullets tore through the vehicle's components. Glass from the back-passenger window blew out in a shower of tiny pieces.

Hands grabbed the back of his tactical vest, lifting him off the ground and around the back of the gravcar. Screams and gunfire became his world as he was dragged away. He struggled to reach back, pry the hands loose, but the grip was too strong.

"Stop!" he shouted, twisting back and forth, trying to wrench himself free.

The hands let go and he dropped to the permacrete. He grunted and pushed himself up to his hands and knees, bringing his pistol up, expecting one of the Elites to shoot him before he ever got on target.

"Stop!" It was Sheridan.

Fischer took a breath, realizing the Saber had pulled him to safety. He pressed his back to the car and saw Eliwood was pulling Marks and his family out, shouting at them to keep their heads down. Sheridan lifted up over the roof and fired off another barrage before ducking back down again as rounds smacked into the far side of the car.

"We can't stay here!" Fischer yelled over the cacophony.

Sheridan squatted next to him, swapping out his magazines. "The team's almost here."

Fischer surveyed the area behind them, looking for any way out. Shuttles and smaller personal flyers were lifting off around them, forcing the fleeing crowds to redirect or slow. The mass panic wasn't confined to the people on the ground either. Two small shuttles almost collided with each other after lifting off, their engines screaming as they narrowly missed sideswiping each other.

Two pads away, the crew of a small shuttle was scrambling to load the remaining cargo crates stacked beside its open ramp.

They all seemed acutely aware of the gunfire raging behind them but were obviously not willing to leave their cargo behind. If they ran…

"There!" Fischer pointed. "The shuttle. Go! Run!"

"Are you insane?" Marks's wife shouted, trying to calm her daughter, whose screaming had turned to sobs. "They're shooting at us!"

"Exactly!" Eliwood yelled, pulling the woman and her child with her. "Come on! We need to get the hell out of here!"

"Goddamn you!" Davis said, grabbing Fischer by his jacket, her eyes blazing with hatred. "You did this! You brought them here! You got us all killed."

CHAPTER 25

Osprey's Compound
Barcroft's Landing, Thresh
18 August 2607

"I thought you said you were untraceable?" Loomis shouted as the trio made their way through the dimly lit, circular tunnel. Osprey ignored him, continuing to press on ahead.

The lights strung above them every ten meters or so occasionally flickered, threatening to go out at any time, and Jones didn't know if he was more afraid of being captured by whoever was chasing them or being trapped down here without light. Neither proposition was intriguing. The gray permacrete was cracked here and there and dotted with green vines and sprouts of foliage. The tunnel looked like it'd been laid down years before but never used. It wasn't quite high enough for Jones to stand up straight, making it hard to keep up with Osprey, already twenty meters ahead.

"Hey!" Loomis shouted. "Goddamn it! You said they wouldn't be able to trace you."

"Just keep moving!" Osprey called back without turning around.

Loomis looked back over his shoulder at Jones, anger and frustration plainly visible. "What the fuck?"

Jones shook his head. "I don't know, just keep going. Can you get a connection to *Doris*?"

The engineer slowed and opened his link, the orange light from the holodisplay glowing off the tunnel around him. He swiped through several screens before finding the one he wanted and tapped in a command. After a few seconds, he looked up, shaking his head. "No dice. It's probably interference from the tunnels. Who knows how deep we are?"

"Damn." If they could connect to the ship, Jones would be able to pilot her remotely, picking them up wherever they were. Of course, doing that would slow them down significantly, as he would have to focus most of his attention on flying and not trying to run, crouched over, through a tunnel.

"It's not the depth," Osprey said. "It's the counter-intrusion field I built around the place. No signals in or out. You know people can track you with these things, right?" She pointed to her wrist.

"I thought that was only the military ones," Loomis said.

Osprey laughed. "Yeah, that's what they want you to think. Come on, man, I know you've seen the shit that's out there. I mean, look at what we just saw with the Alistair surveillance; look what they've done with their networks. They're into everything, and either everyone knows about it or they're willfully ignorant."

"I'm not ignorant," Loomis muttered.

"Out for debate," Jones said. "Okay then, what's your plan? If they've got enough bandwidth to track us down, I'm sure they've got the entire planet on lockdown."

Osprey pulled her pad from a pocket inside her jacket and tapped through a few screens. "Yeah, there's ways around that."

"Like getting all the cops called down on us? The fact that you even have an escape tunnel says a lot. And where the hell are we going, anyway?"

"They weren't cops," Osprey said.

"Okay, who were they, then?" Loomis asked, his breathing becoming labored. He wasn't going to be able to keep this up for much longer.

"I've got a flyer waiting," Osprey said, sliding her pad back into her jacket. "Not too far."

She didn't seem concerned at all that they were being chased by strange people in all black, armed with automatic weapons. Or that she'd wiped out her entire life's work with the press of a button. Jones hadn't even been a tech guy, but he knew Osprey, and he knew she never spent creds on half-ass pieces of gear. He couldn't even imagine how many hundreds of thousands of creds she'd just destroyed.

And it's your fault, the voice told him.

"And you don't think they've found that, too?" Loomis asked.

"It's well hidden."

"Oh, you mean like your whole complex back there?" Loomis jabbed a thumb over his shoulder.

Osprey reached a T-intersection and stopped, turning back to face them, frustrated. A moment later the look was replaced by a half-grin and she nodded. "Yeah."

"Which way?" Jones asked as they finally reached her.

"Couple of hundred meters that way." Osprey nodded to the left.

"What the hell is this place?" Loomis asked, following after her.

"Old waterways built when the first colonists landed. Back then permacrete was the cheapest and fastest way to set up the infrastructure they needed, but when they upgraded to polymer composite, they just sealed off all the old pipes and left them."

"How'd you find them?" Loomis asked.

Jones thought he already knew the answer, which she confirmed by giving Loomis a sardonic look over her shoulder as if to say, "Are you serious?"

"Right," Loomis said, obviously understanding. "Hacker."

"Network infiltration specialist," Osprey corrected, turning back around.

Ten minutes later they'd reached the end of the tunnel, coming to a vertical shaft that stretched up another twenty meters. A small steel ladder stretched up to a ring of lights surrounding the rim of the shaft, now covered by a rust-colored hatch like the one back in her compound.

Osprey pulled out her pad, swiped through a few menus, and a second later the hatch opened. A minute later, they emerged into a small empty room with bare walls and no windows.

"Okay, check your signal now," Osprey said.

Loomis opened his link and went to work. He nodded. "Got her."

Osprey tapped on her pad and showed it to Loomis. "Can you get your ship to those coordinates?"

Loomis gave Jones a questioning look and turned so Jones could see the display. A blinking red dot indicated a position in high Thresh orbit.

"What is it?" Jones asked, looking up from Loomis's display.

"It's an old transfer station," Osprey said. "Hasn't been used in years. I leased it under a shell years ago; use it to stash all my backups. We get there, we can hop on your ship and jet before anyone knows we're there. Can you run dark?"

"Yeah, we can make it," Jones said. "But if they catch us without a transponder running, the navy is more likely to shoot first and ask questions later."

"Thresh's navy is more likely to blow themselves up than actually hit a hostile target. Oh, sure, they have a lot of ships, but their officers are all inept appointees, given their commissions based on how much their families contribute to the system's GDP. Trust me, you don't have to worry about that."

"You know, your track record of what I should and shouldn't worry about isn't very good," Jones said.

"Trust me." Osprey went back to work on her pad, and a moment later a deep rumble echoed up from the tunnel, the ground vibrating under their feet.

"What the hell was that?" Jones asked.

"Don't want anyone following us, do we?" Osprey asked.

"You blew it up?" Loomis looked shocked.

Osprey put her hands on her hips. "Do you think they were coming to ask us to dinner?"

Jones ground his teeth together, but what could he say? It wasn't like they had an abundance of other options.

Loomis looked at Jones, as if expecting him to say something, but Jones didn't know what he could've said. Nothing he said would've made any difference. Osprey was right, they were definitely not there to make friends, they were looking to capture them, or worse, and Jones had a suspicion that it was probably the latter.

They needed to get off-world. He would've rather brought *Doris* straight to them, but with the chances that someone was watching their ship, he couldn't risk that. Sending her up to get lost in the orbital traffic and then vanishing by turning off her transponder wasn't ideal, but right now, there didn't seem to be an overabundance of alternatives.

"Patch me in," Jones said, opening his link.

Loomis paired their links, and Jones's holodisplay appeared, showing him mirrors of the main ship controls from *Doris*'s bridge. He split his attention between the screen and his surroundings as they moved through the small room's only door. They stepped into a vast empty chamber, some kind of processing plant, long abandoned. Sunlight streamed in through dirty windows near the top of the bare walls, illuminating the space; motes of dust sparkled in the stillness. Large machines, which had sat dormant for years, loomed around them, and the sound of unseen critters scampering about the metal catwalks four stories above echoed in the emptiness.

"You know, if they traced back to you, there's a chance they know who you were meeting with," Jones said, watching as *Doris*'s engines warmed up. Additional panels opened as more systems came online.

"It's possible," Osprey said, ducking under a low pipe.

"So they'll be watching my ship."

She paused, looking back at Jones, obviously contemplating the implications. "Right." She pulled her pad out again and tapped away. "There."

"What'd you do?"

"I disabled the spaceport's air traffic control network," Osprey said as if she'd done something as simple as turning off the light in a room.

Jones stopped, his finger hovering above his link. "You did what?"

"You'd better hurry," she said, continuing on through the large warehouse. "Won't take them but a few minutes to get the system back online."

"Wait, you disabled the whole..." Jones trailed off, not even wanting to think about it. Disabling an entire spaceport's ATC network could be devastating in the best of circumstances. At worst, hundreds, if not thousands, of people could be injured or killed.

Osprey moved around a cylindrical pressure tank and ducked

under another cluster of pipes. "My guess is you have about five minutes."

"Son of a bitch," Jones said, turning his attention back to his control array.

As the trio made their way through the building, Jones paused occasionally, focusing on the multiple panels open above his link. He finished preflight just as they reached a door at the far end of the building, and stopped as Osprey went on through, running through the transponder shutdown procedure. Beside him, Loomis worked on his own link, activating *Doris*'s tactical systems and communications.

It took another minute to deactivate the ship's transponder and another thirty seconds to run through takeoff procedures. Another panel appeared above the rest, giving him an optical feed from *Doris*'s nose camera. He slid a finger up the display, increasing power to the engines, and watched as the ground slowly fell away.

"Scopes are clear," Loomis said beside him.

Jones nodded as the information appeared on the bottom left panel. Their course would take *Doris* into orbit and through two of the main inbound/outbound shipping lanes. If anyone was following them, they'd most likely lose them in the dense traffic.

Jones made one last adjustment then stepped through the door, onto an elevated platform that functioned as a loading dock for whatever they'd made here. A steel awning covered the area, stretching out twenty meters from the building, providing most of the area with shade. Ten meters from the edge of the platform a small red and blue flyer sat in the middle of the pad, connected to various pieces of electronic and mechanical equipment by thick cables that snaked in all directions. Occasionally, plumes of steam would shoot out from ports underneath the flyer's forward-swept wings. An elongated oval canopy was open, showing three rows of seats, allowing for nine passengers.

"She's a beauty, isn't she?" Osprey asked, leaving Jones and Loomis at the edge of the loading dock and jogging toward the aircraft.

"*That's* your escape plan?" Jones asked, almost not believing what he was seeing. Sure, the flyer was sleek and could probably outmaneuver anything the local police had, but once they left atmo, things would change. Not to mention that it looked at least twenty years old.

Obviously thinking the same thing, Loomis asked, "Jesus, how old is that thing?"

"She's in pristine condition," Osprey said, ducking under the near-side wing. She reached one of the cables and twisted the coupling free, disconnecting it.

"You're kidding, right?" Loomis asked. "That thing can't have anything bigger than an I-95 or a 90. You'll be lucky to reach orbit, never mind jumping into a lane."

She pulled another connection free. "Well, luckily for us, you've got your ship here."

Jones clenched his teeth, eyeing the flyer with a mixture of contempt and skepticism. Finally, he shook his head and stepped down to the pad, heading for the flyer. "Come on, let's get the hell out of here."

"Good," Osprey said. "You know, this could be a good thing. I've been needing a vacation; no time like the present, I always say."

"You don't always say that," Jones said.

"No? Hmmm, maybe I should."

CHAPTER 26

Grey Mount Spaceport
Grey Mount City, Grinas
18 August 2607

Sheridan switched targets again. He wasn't focusing on kill shots, but rather just trying to keep the Elites from advancing too quickly on their position. He dropped behind cover, swapped magazines again, and looked to the shuttle Fischer had pointed to. There was fifty meters between the two pads—a lot of open space to traverse while under fire.

Another burst of fire ripped into the far side of the car.

"Son of a bitch," Sheridan growled, feeling the impact tremors. He pushed his MOD27 around the rear of the car and fired blind, squeezing off bursts until the magazine ran dry. He ejected the spent mag and slapped in another. Fischer was shouting for the rest of them to head for the shuttle.

They needed to put space between them and the Elites. Sheridan wasn't too keen on boarding a shuttle with people he didn't know. It just opened up too many possibilities that they didn't need to deal with right now. Their only option was to retreat, but as Sheridan surveyed the pads behind them, and the roads beyond, he knew the farther they went, the more they risked putting civilians in danger.

Well, more danger, Sheridan corrected himself.

Screams echoed across the pad as men, women, and children scrambled for cover. He wanted to help them but didn't see any way he could. Three against eight weren't good odds to begin with, but considering only one of them was actually trained in combat, the outcome of this fight was damn near predetermined. Ten minutes didn't sound like a long time, but when you're fighting for your life, ten minutes might as well be an eternity.

"Just get moving," Sheridan said. "Head for the road. Forget the shuttle."

Fischer looked like he was going to argue but seemed to think better of it.

"The team is coming," Sheridan said. "We need to be where they can get to us. Get to that flyer first. We're going to have to leapfrog out of here."

Just to the left of the shuttle, a sleek red and white flyer sat on its landing struts, surrounded by what looked like part containers. Sections of the fuselage were exposed, obviously in a state of system-wide repairs or refits. It was by no means flightworthy, but the containers would give them some cover at least.

Sheridan fired blindly again. "Fischer, go! Get them out of here."

Fischer didn't hesitate. He grabbed Davis by the arm and pulled her up. "Come on! There! We're moving!"

Marks and his wife grabbed their daughter, and all four ran, weaving through the thinning mass of people all scrambling for safety. A man and woman tripped over each other, rolling across the tarmac before helping each other up to keep going.

"Go," Sheridan said to Eliwood. "I'll cover you."

Eliwood hesitated for a moment, then nodded and ran.

Sheridan rose and fired, this time sending aimed shots down-range. The enemy team had slowed their assault now that they were receiving fire as well, but they were still coming. Two ducked as Sheridan fired, disappearing behind a maintenance truck parked just behind a medium-lift cargo shuttle.

"What I wouldn't give for a Ramsey right now," Sheridan muttered to himself. A single round from the multipurpose rocket launcher would've turned that truck to scrap, not to mention the two Elites using it for cover.

Three were shifting to the right, angling for another small shuttle two pads away. The two behind the maintenance truck popped out occasionally to fire. He'd counted eight when he'd first seen them approaching, but now he couldn't see the final three. He quickly scanned the grounds again, then decided it didn't matter. He couldn't stay here.

He pushed himself to his feet and ran, bullets chewing into the permacrete behind him. He could hear and feel the impacts through his boots, but he didn't turn to look. He ran harder, waving at the two agents to press on. Several people screamed and yelled and pushed their way across the tarmac, making it hard for Sheridan to track Fischer's movements. The crowds ducked and flinched with every shot, creating an almost comical scene as they ran for safety.

"Move!" Sheridan shouted, pulling one man out of the way as he angled for Eliwood's position behind one of the closest containers.

A woman to his left gasped and folded over, collapsing to the ground, unmoving. Another screamed as her leg was knocked out from under her. A man spun from an impact to his shoulder, throwing him into two others, sending all three to the ground. It was obvious the Elites weren't particular about their targets.

Eliwood leaned out from behind the container, her pistol leveled at something behind Sheridan. He forced himself not to look as she fired. Two shots were all she could get off before she had to pull up as another group of screaming people ran past, almost colliding with Sheridan.

"Son of a bitch!" Eliwood shouted, waving. "Get the hell out of the way!"

Sheridan reached the container and pulled himself close, pressing against Eliwood. "Need to move." He brought his rifle up, searching for a target.

"You think?"

"Go!" Sheridan nodded back toward the others. "Help Fischer! I'll hold them off!"

"You can't hold them off by yourself!" Eliwood said, leaning out and firing another burst.

"No choice. Go. I'll slow them down so you can get away. The rest of the team will be here any minute."

Eliwood held his gaze for a moment, flinching briefly as several rounds slammed into the far side of the container. "Don't get too far behind."

"I won't."

She nodded, then ran after her partner, keeping low and weaving through the thinning crowd. Fischer had paused behind the row of waist-high crates, waiting as Eliwood approached, the frustration and confusion on his face as clear as crystal.

Fischer tapped his link, and a moment later his voice came through Sheridan's cochlear implant. *"What the hell are you doing, Allen?"*

"Just get them out of here," Sheridan said, turning his attention back to the Elites. "I'll slow these bastards down."

"Not the plan," Fischer barked. *"Move your ass, Marine. We're all getting out of here together."*

"Yeah!" Sheridan shouted. "Get them out of here! Head for the road. Use the traffic for cover." When Fischer didn't respond, Sheridan looked over his shoulder. "GO!"

"Son of a bitch!" Fischer shouted. "Come on, go! Go! Go!"

Sheridan fired another burst at the Elites creeping on the right. The two Elites emerged from behind the maintenance truck, running full speed for a refueling cart behind them and Sheridan. He brought his rifle up, found a target and fired. His first rounds hit home, knocking one of the Elites clean off his feet, sending him flying. His partner barely even seemed to notice; taking only a second to glance at his fallen comrade before turning his attention back to the fight, bringing up his rifle. The Elite fired and Sheridan immediately ducked behind the container.

This was a great idea, Sheridan told himself.

"Seven Alpha, Actual, what's your status?" Captain Chambers asked over the taclink.

We're fucked, that's our status, Sheridan thought, putting his back to the crates. "One target down, seven more still up and closing. We're heading to the road just east of the landing area. Going to try to lose them in the traffic."

"Roger that. We're still five minutes out."

Fucking traffic, Sheridan thought, then said, "I understand, sir." He twisted around the edge of the container, found the Elite who'd just shot at him, and fired. Two meters away from the refueling cart, the Elite fell unceremoniously to the permacrete. "Two down."

"Six-One is inbound," Chambers continued. *"ETA three and a half minutes."*

Well, that's something.

Two more Elites appeared to Sheridan's right, emerging from a group of civilians as they ran for cover; both had rifles up. Sheridan dropped to the ground, pressing his entire body as far down as it would go, trying to become one with the permacrete. Bullets chewed into the container above him.

He shifted and fired, sending several quick bursts at the enemy, forcing them apart. Sheridan found the right one in his sights and squeezed. His shots knocked the man's feet out from under him, and he landed hard on his chest, his face bouncing off the ground with a wet smack. He didn't get up. The other disappeared behind the rear strut of a shuttle before leaning around it to fire, the bullets smacking harmlessly into the crates beside Sheridan.

We're not going to last another three minutes, Sheridan thought.

CHAPTER 27

Grey Mount Spaceport
Grey Mount City, Grinas
18 August 2607

"Get down," Fischer shouted, pushing Marks and his wife down behind one of the only remaining aircabs still parked along the roadway in front of the spaceport. The girl screamed, and Marks pulled her to the ground with them.

Eliwood rounded the front of the cab and stopped with her hands on her knees. "Need to keep moving."

"Yeah," Fischer said. "I know."

Screams and shouts continued to rip through the air around them as people spread out through the stalled traffic. Angry drivers shouted at the fleeing crowds without realizing the danger they were in. People punched and kicked cars that tried to cut them off.

Movement near the spaceport's entrance caught Fischer's attention: a group of uniformed security guards spilling out of the sliding glass doors. Three men and two women, dressed in dark blue utilities and gun belts, shouted for people to clear out and get down. Fischer couldn't tell if they knew where the threat was coming from or not, but they clearly didn't have any idea what they were up against. Their weapons were still holstered on their hips.

"We need to stop them," Fischer said, stepping around Eliwood. "No! Stop!"

He might have been mute for all the good his warning did. The guard at the head of the group, a short woman with long black hair, took the first round, the impact spinning her like a top. She hit the ground before the rest of them had even realized what had happened.

"Son of a bitch," Fischer growled through clenched teeth.

Two Elites had made it past the flyer but didn't have a shot on Sheridan. They'd left him for their comrades and were pressing on for Fischer and his group. They were outside Fischer's range, but he knew he had to do something. He leaned over the aircab's roof and fired. All but one of his shots missed. The Elite he'd hit stumbled sideways but didn't fall. He brought his rifle up.

"Get down!" Fischer shouted, ducking down.

"Give me a gun!" Davis shouted.

"No, get out of here!" Fischer shouted back. "Get across the road!"

The aircab's windshield exploded in a shower of blinking shards of glass and shook with the impact of several rounds slamming into the far side. Fischer covered his head with his arms, flinching as multiple impacts shook the vehicle.

"Come on!" Marks yelled.

Fischer opened his eyes to see the man pulling his wife and daughter after him, running for a line of cars ten meters away. Davis was behind them, shielding the family as they retreated.

Fischer stood, found a target and fired, unloading the entire magazine. Beside him, Eliwood did the same, then ejected the empty with one hand while reaching for another with the other. To his left, the security guards were pulling their downed comrade to safety, the woman's body lifeless and limp.

We're not going to make it, Fischer told himself.

He glanced back at Davis and her brother. They'd reached the first gravcar and were starting to weave through the traffic. The fleeing crowds were starting to thin, and he could finally hear the sound of approaching sirens.

"Hear that? The cavalry's on its way," Eliwood said before sending a three-round volley downrange.

"Yeah, I—"

"Fischer!" Davis shouted, cutting him off. She was pointing at something above them. "Loo—"

Her body jerked suddenly, her expression turning from excitement to confusion and pain as she stumbled back. A second round hit, knocking her down, behind one of the gravcars.

"No!" Fischer shouted, getting to his feet.

"Fish!" Eliwood yelled, grabbing his wrist and pulling him back down. A string of bullets slammed into the aircab, shaking it. "What the hell is wrong with you?"

A loud roar drowned out his answer as a shadow played across their position. A long *thwwwwwwrp* ripped through the air.

"I know that sound," Fischer said, getting to his knees.

Eliwood looked up and laughed. "Aha, you bastards! Now what!"

"Valkyrie Six-One to all ground elements, we are on station and engaging hostile targets."

Fischer twisted to see an Albatross make a low pass across the string of landing pads, the Viper III autocannons mounted on either side of the fuselage chewing through the permacrete, leaving identical paths of destruction in their wakes. On the ground the Elites scrambled, separating and racing for cover with seemingly no regard for the well-being of their compatriots.

Two were cut in half by the devastating fire, their bodies

shredding apart. The refueling cart exploded as Viper fire chewed through it. The blast sent one of the Elites spinning through the air. He landed five meters away and rolled to his chest and immediately scrambled to his hands and knees.

Still behind the container, Sheridan was focused on something else and didn't see the enemy getting up.

He tapped his link. "Sheridan, your left!"

The Saber didn't answer, but immediately shifted fire, hitting the Elite just as he'd gotten to his feet. Three rounds knocked him on his back, and this time he didn't get up.

In the air, the Albatross came around for another pass. Its Vipers spit out long bursts of fire, ripping through the flyer where the last two Elites were hiding, turning into so much burning slag. It flew through the smoke from the wreckage, engines flaring as it turned, its autocannons going quiet.

Almost as quickly as it'd started, the fighting was over, leaving only cries of pain and fear. One of the flyer's engines exploded in a massive fireball that curled into the sky and sent flaming debris arching in all directions.

Fischer slowly straightened, looking over the devastation. The fight had only lasted a few minutes, but the destruction was profound. Dozens of bodies littered the ground, either unmoving or reaching for help from anyone who would give it. Slowly, people began returning to help the injured and check on loved ones. As some found their loved ones dead or dying, the crying and screams of anguish filled the air again.

Eliwood stood beside him, breathing heavily. "Where's Davis?"

"Shit," Fischer said, turning to where he'd seen her fall. "Come on."

CHAPTER 28

Grey Mount Spaceport
Grey Mount City, Grinas
18 August 2607

Fischer felt like he'd been punched square in the gut as he rounded the front of the gravcar and saw Davis lying in her brother's arms, blood soaking her clothes. He looked up as Fischer approached, tears streaking his face, his arms and hands covered in glistening red.

"No, no, no," Fischer said, dropping down next to them. He reached to check for a pulse, but Marks pulled her away.

"Don't touch her!" Marks snapped. "Don't you dare touch her!"

"I just need to—"

"She's dead! You don't need to do anything, you bastard. You got her killed. It's your fault!"

Looking over Davis's body, Fischer knew Marks was right. There wasn't anything he could do. Even after everything she'd done, he felt sick, gut punched. He hadn't wanted this. "I'm sorry."

"Sorry?" Marks asked. "I don't give a fuck about your 'sorry.' You did this. You brought those bastards here. You killed her."

Marks's wife and daughter huddled next to him, sobbing, eyes wet with tears. Fischer's stomach turned as he looked over their dirty smudged faces, wondering if Marks was correct. Would Davis be alive if they hadn't come here?

No, he told himself, *that's not going to help you right now.*

Boots pounding on the permacrete drew his attention away from the grieving family. Sheridan jogged toward them, rifle hanging across his chest, barrel down. He took a knee beside them and pulled his helmet off. His face and hair glistened with sweat, his cheeks lined from the helmet's padding. At the sight of Davis, his shoulders dropped and he shook his head.

"Goddamn it," Sheridan muttered, running a hand through his matted hair.

Fischer stood and turned away, not wanting to look at Davis any more than he had to, but the sight of the devastated landing area littered with even more dead bodies wasn't a better alternative. Sirens were growing louder, and flashing emergency lights coming over the spaceport announced the arrival of the local police.

"We need to get to the Albatross," Sheridan said.

Fischer pushed his pistol back into its holster. "Yeah."

Eliwood leaned down to help Marks. "Come on, we're not out of this yet."

"Get away!" Marks yelled. "We're not going anywhere with you."

"Listen," Fischer said, squatting on the balls of his feet. "I know you don't know me. You don't have any reason to trust me, I get it. But you have to believe me when I say I have nothing but the best intentions for you and your family, I promise."

"Like you did for my sister?"

Fischer opened his mouth to respond but couldn't find the

words. He knew instantly that nothing he could say would assuage this man's grief, and anything he did say would likely only make the situation worse.

Eliwood took a knee beside him. "Listen, I knew Riley; she deserved better. But staying here isn't safe. They'll come for you and your family."

"You don't know anything about her," Marks said through gritted teeth.

"I know she cared about you and your family very much," Eliwood said. "I know she wanted the best for you all. Still does. Believe it or not, I'll be grieving her loss right along with you when the time comes, but right now, we need to get on that shuttle back there and get off-world before those badges get here."

"But we don't know anything," Lily said. "If those men were after Riley, why would they come after us?"

"Because they'll think you do know something," Fischer said. "Whatever Davis knew anyway. They can't afford loose ends."

Marks held her gaze but didn't respond. After a long moment, he nodded. "Okay."

Eliwood stood and held out a hand. "Come on, let's get your family someplace safe."

Tires squealed and Fischer turned to see the rest of the Saber team dismounting Dips's transport truck. Bystanders backed away from the team as they weaved through the traffic. The onlookers pointed and spoke in low tones as the Sabers reached Fischer, and the bigger their little group got, the louder and more heated the onlookers became.

"Murderers!"

"Alliance bastards!"

"Richards!" Captain Chambers shouted, seeing Davis.

Fischer locked eyes with Chambers and shook his head. As the medic passed, Chambers put a hand on the Saber's shoulder, stopping him before he reached Davis. She was gone; there wasn't any reason to aggravate the situation. For a moment it looked like Richards was on the verge of protesting, but when he saw Davis's condition, he seemed to understand.

Someone in the crowd shouted, "They killed them! Look!"

"Fucking killers!"

"We need to go," Chambers said.

"Come on," Eliwood said, offering her hand again.

"We're bringing her with us," Marks said, nodding at his sister.

"Of course." Eliwood gave Chambers a knowing look.

"We can take care of her, sir," the captain said, motioning to Neal and Richards.

The medic pulled an expandable stretcher from off his pack and laid it down next to Davis's body. Fischer helped Marks extricate himself from her, then helped Neal and Richards move the body, covering it with a black blanket.

"Sir, please," Chambers said to Marks, motioning to the waiting Albatross.

Marks reluctantly headed for the shuttle, never taking his arms from around his family. Fischer and Eliwood fell into step behind them as the Sabers moved to provide security for the small procession.

Behind them, the crowd grew, becoming more infuriated as it did, and as the team reached the bottom of the ramp, they'd begun cursing them and throwing anything they could get their hands on. The first two local police flyers landed thirty meters away from the Albatross and were almost immediately swarmed by angry citizens, all pointing toward the Sabers.

"Stop them!"

"They killed all these people!"

"Don't let them get away!"

At the top of the ramp, Fischer turned and waited for the rest of the team to board. Chambers notified the pilot when he stepped off the tarmac, and the engines started spinning up. Fischer grabbed the rail above him as the Albatross lifted off the perma-crete, watching as the police tried desperately to push through the crowd to get at the Sabers.

Sheridan stopped next to him, shaking his head. "Sorry about Davis. I know she was… a friend."

Fischer clenched his jaw. Davis had been a friend; had turning her back on her nation changed that? As the shuttle lifted away, his mind suggested it had, but the nauseous feeling in his stomach and ache in his heart told him otherwise. Whatever else she'd done, she'd always been a good investigator; he couldn't count the number of times she'd broken a case wide open when he'd been stuck.

But, try as he might, he couldn't shake the feeling that it had been their fault after all; if they hadn't followed her trail all the way out here, she might still be alive. The innocent lives lost today could have been prevented if he'd done his job better.

No, he thought. *Don't do that to yourself.* It was her decisions that had brought them all to this point. Davis, not them, had put herself in danger the moment she'd started working with Cardi-nal, and regardless of any extenuating circumstances, Fischer knew he had to remember that. With a case like this, there would always be collateral damage.

But at what point does it become too much? Fischer asked himself.

"You okay?" Sheridan asked.

Fischer turned away from the ramp as it sealed shut. "Yeah."

"You sure?"

"I'm sure."

Sheridan nodded, but his expression suggested he wasn't quite convinced. After a moment, he said, "We're going to make it right."

Fischer managed a half-smile and put a hand on the man's shoulder. "Thanks. I appreciate that."

"I'm not saying that just to say it," Sheridan said. "We're going to find the bastards responsible for this and make them pay."

"Yes," Fischer said. "We will."

CHAPTER 29

Saber Common Room
ANS *Legend*
18 August 2607

"All right, let's break this shitshow down," Chambers said when they were back aboard *Legend* and in their common room. He'd invited both Fischer and Eliwood to attend the after-action briefing, specifically excluding the ship's command staff to allow the team to deconstruct what had happened without command influence. He would brief Captain Ward and his staff later.

Fischer sat with Eliwood at the back of the room, still trying to come to grips with what had happened. There were so many questions running through his mind that he was having trouble isolating legitimate concerns as his mind ran wild with conspiracies and suppositions. What he really needed was time to sit and think and work it all out, but he also understood the importance of this briefing and was grateful to have been included.

Around the compartment, the Sabers were busy doffing their gear or breaking down their weapons. The only one who'd actually fired his rifle was Sheridan, but it didn't appear to be a

JOSH HAYES

consideration for the others as they broke their weapons down to inspect and reassemble them.

A clean weapon is a functional weapon. The words of Fischer's range instructors resonated in his mind.

"First," Chambers continued, "I know we had some issues on the ground. Present company excluded, this op did not play out as planned; however, I don't think it could've gone much differently. We were up shit creek on this one, and considering the outcome, it could have been much worse."

The comment hit Fischer like a gut punch. His chest tightened and he could feel his face start to flush. It had been his investigation that had led them all here. Everything that had happened ultimately rested on his shoulders. It was his fault. He was in charge of every step in this case; everything attached to it was his responsibility. The fact that this entire ship was, in effect, an extension of his investigation meant he'd become responsible for every soul on board. That thought hit him like a truck.

"Take it easy, Fish," Eliwood whispered, putting a hand on his arm.

Fischer let out a long breath and nodded. "Right."

"And not to point out the elephant in the room," Chambers said, "but, Sheridan, you did a hell of a job down there. Those Pegasi bastards will think twice before fucking with Valkyrie again."

"If there's any left," Neal added, grinning. "Just like Blaster to hog all the action."

A chorus of cheers and applause rippled through the compartment. Several slapped Sheridan on the back or raised their drinks to praise his efforts. Considering what they'd just been through, the mood was surprisingly light. But, Fischer knew, these were professional warfighters. This was what they were paid to do.

"Maybe next time save some for the rest of us, okay?" Sergeant Cole said.

"Right, 'cause you'll do more than take pictures of them," Richards chided.

Cole held up one of his fist-size orbs. "Hey! They have feelings, you know!"

"Sure they do."

"All right," Chambers said, obviously trying to rein the conversation back in. "What could we have done better?"

"Not ride in a shit-covered livestock truck," Neal said, hanging her vest in her locker.

"I second that," Reese said. "I'll be cleaning shit out of my kit for weeks."

"Next time we'll let you walk, Reese," Sergeant Kline said. "God knows you need the help on your fitness scores."

"Ahh, Master Sergeant, that hurts my feelings."

"That's not all that'll be hurting, you don't take your next eval up a notch."

Chambers laughed and held up a hand. "Let's talk takeaways."

"Maintaining team cohesion is nonnegotiable," Hanover said without a hint of levity. The rest of the team turned to him, and Chambers invited him to explain. The sniper pushed the bolt on his rifle forward. "We introduced too many outside elements into our operational dynamic without fully vetting them before doing so. No offense." He looked at Fischer.

"None taken," Fischer answered.

"Walk it out," Chambers said, nodding to Hanover.

"Our teams are designed and constructed to fit our operational doctrine, and we train to a certain standard. We all know what's expected of us, and we know the capabilities of the team and its individual members. In this case, we allowed an outside agency to determine the course our mission took, which drastically changed the manner in which we would've normally approached the operation otherwise, and it resulted in a failed mission. Not only did we lose the primary objective, but we are now responsible for the lives of her brother and his family. Not to mention the civilian collateral damage."

The sniper's words seem to resonate with everyone in the room, and the mood immediately became somber. Fischer wanted to say something, but knew it wouldn't make anything better. Hanover had said "we" not "he," putting the outcome of the mission on everyone's shoulders, not just his. Fischer wondered if the sniper truly believed that regardless of outcome it was a team effort, or if he was just trying not to put him on the spot.

Either way, Fischer was grateful for the breakdown. Hanover was right, Fischer had introduced an unfamiliar element into their unit, and not only that, he had allowed Davis to control how the mission played out. That was his fault. He'd let his personal feelings cloud his judgment, and that had led to the mission's failure.

That's not going to happen again, Fischer thought.

After letting the silence hang for a moment, Chambers nodded. "Can't say I disagree. Anyone else have a different take?"

"The mission went to shit, yes," Sheridan said. "I just want to say I don't believe that was Agent Fischer's fault."

"No one is blaming Agent Fischer for anything," Chambers said. "Kirk is right, there were several elements that led to the mission's ultimate failure that need to be addressed."

"Like the fact that the Pegasi knew where we were going to be?" Sheridan asked. "I mean, I think that's the real question here. Granted, the mission could've been handled differently, but I think regardless of team composition or unplanned objectives, we need to work out how this PKE team tracked us down."

"Again," Neal added. "How they tracked us down *again.*"

"We don't have any indication that they were actually tracking us," Sergeant Kline said. "It's entirely possible they were there looking for Marks and his family, just like we were."

"And they just happened to show up at the same time we did?" Sheridan asked. "I find that hard to believe."

"Once is a coincidence," Hanover said. "Twice is a pattern."

"Could they have been tracking Davis?" Sergeant Rocha asked. "She was the asset, right? If this whole Cardinal thing is a Pegasi-led operation, it makes sense they would have ways of keeping tabs on their people."

Fischer listened to the discussion, his mind racing. It was like trying to put together a puzzle without knowing what the overall picture looked like; any of the pieces could go anywhere. Davis had been extremely careful with every aspect of her plan. If she'd thought Cardinal had been tracking her, she would've said something.

"What if they were just after Marks?" Robalt suggested. "Like Larson's mother on Caldera."

"You're supposing they were after his mom in the first place," Kline said.

"Which doesn't make a lot of sense, considering they already knew who Larson was, and they wouldn't have known he hadn't suicided like all the rest of them," Reese said.

"Everything we've seen so far suggested that Larson was nothing more than a soldier," Chambers said. "He didn't give us anything we didn't already know."

"If they were here for Davis, why wait until she was at the spaceport?" Eliwood asked, obviously playing the devil's advocate. "Why not take her at the diner like we did?"

"Maybe they'd just arrived," Rocha said. "They were behind the curve on Caldera too."

"They're obviously not Valkyrie level," Cole said with a grin.

"No, they're not," Sergeant Kline said. "But they're damn close."

"And they weren't *that* far behind us," Chambers added.

"Come to think of it, if you consider the distances and travel times involved, they were literally on our heels."

"You think they were following us?" Fischer asked.

"Ordinarily I would say the possibility of that would be zero," Chambers said. "But these are most definitely not ordinary times."

"Can we determine if they were the same team?" Fischer asked.

"The Albatross sensors probably picked them up when they engaged," Robalt said. "I might be able to extract the footage and compare."

"Get on it," Chambers said.

"But if there are following us, how the hell do they know where we are?" Sheridan asked. "We've been under full blackout conditions since before the Astalt raid."

Cole nodded. "And besides, didn't Hunter say when this whole thing started that no one knew about *Legend* but a few key people?"

"Hard to track a ship that no one knows about," Robalt said. "Especially when most of the people who know about it are on board."

"Not everyone," Hanover said. He nodded to Fischer. "Your friend knows about us."

"Jones is solid," Fischer said.

Hanover pulled the bolt out of his rifle and began wiping it down with a rag. "Except that he wasn't vetted by anyone on the *Legend*'s command staff before coming on board."

"He was vetted by me," Fischer said, a little too harshly. "If there is a leak, there's not a chance in hell it's Jones."

"So says you," Hanover said.

Fischer straightened. "Jones has saved my ass more times than I can count. He might not be the cleanest person around, but he's a patriot. I guarantee you if he were here, he'd punch you right in the mouth for even suggesting anything different."

"So where is he?"

Fischer hesitated for a moment. The last time he'd spoken with Jones had been on *Legend*'s hangar deck before dropping into the New Tuscan system. He knew where Jones had been going, but he also knew that the very nature of what Jones was doing meant he could be anywhere by now. But telling them he didn't know where Jones was would not foster confidence in his investigation, and there was already enough doubt going around to deal with any more.

Finally, Fischer said, "Working."

Hanover set the barrel aside. "And you don't think he's off soaking up the rays on some beach somewhere?"

It was everything Fischer could do to keep his voice level. "No, I don't. And if you want to argue about it more—"

Chambers lifted a hand. "All right. Let's keep it civil."

"But what if they are?" Sheridan said, sitting forward on the edge of his seat.

"What if they are what?" Chambers asked.

"Following us?"

"I think we've established—"

"Right, logic suggests they don't have any way to track us." Sheridan stood up and started pacing. "But what's the simplest answer here? They've turned up at two different locations, in two very different parts of the URT, hours after we arrive, and managed to track us down almost immediately. No one's that lucky."

"Okay, so how are they finding us?" Reese asked. "If you're thinking they put a tracking device on board, you're crazy. Any routine diagnostic would find it and disable it."

Sheridan shrugged. "I'm just spitballing here."

"What about someone feeding them the information?" Eliwood asked.

"Impossible," Kline said. "Everyone on board has been vetted."

"Yeah, but vetted by who?" Eliwood asked.

"Fleet Command vetted and approved every single member of the crew," Chambers answered. "Some were personally cleared by Hunter himself."

"Yeah, but didn't he vet Young too?" Sheridan asked, immediately turning red. "Sorry, sir."

Chambers shook his head. "This is an open discussion. Speak your mind. And you're right, that is something we need to consider."

"You think Hunter's working for Cardinal?" Reese asked. "That's crazy."

Eliwood leaned forward in her seat. "No, crazy is a middle-aged man flipping out because he thinks the birds outside his window are plotting to kill him, so he burns the tree down. Only the flames don't just destroy the tree, they jump to the adjacent house and kill everyone inside, including the kids who fed those birds every day after school. *That's* crazy. This is fucking insane."

"The fact that Hunter commissioned this ship and enabled her crew to carry out our mission completely autonomously suggests he's not working for Cardinal."

"I agree," Fischer said, rubbing his beard. "Okay, let's run with it though. If someone were giving the Pegasi information on our operations, how would they do it?"

"You'd need a communication node and the clearance access to use it," Reese said.

"And pretty much everyone on board has that authority," Cole said.

"And not only that, those nodes are used for onboard communication as well," Reese said.

"So even if we watch them, we wouldn't be able to pinpoint who's talking to who?" Fischer asked.

Robalt shook his head. "Not unless we were watching all the nodes one hundred percent of the time, and even then, it'd be really easy to miss."

"They're all logged, but we'd need command-level clearance for that." Reese added.

Fischer thought about the months he'd spent combing through the *New Washington*'s comm logs, looking for anything that would give them something on Young. He'd found the message from Cardinal, sure, but how long had that taken, and what did they really know about it? Almost nothing. And if Jones was having anywhere near the luck Fischer was, they might all be right back where they started—zero.

"How many logs are we talking about?" Kline asked.

"Daily?" Reese asked. "Thousands at least."

"Like finding a needle in a stack of needles," Neal said.

"Unless we knew when the message was sent," Robalt said. "That would cut down on the number of logs we'd need to work through."

"And how would we determine that?" Fischer asked.

The electronic technician shrugged. "Well, if it were me, I'd only send information I knew was going to be valuable, and I'd immediately delete the file."

"If he's deleting the file after sending it, then how are we going to find him?" Eliwood asked.

"Deleting it doesn't change the usage information," Robalt explained. "There will still be a log entry in the node, there just won't be any data associated with it."

"How does the type of information help us narrow down the search?" Sheridan asked.

Robalt sat back. "Well, if this Elite team is actually following us through space, I can think of something they'd have to have no matter what."

"Our location?" Sheridan asked.

"Where we're *going* to be," Fischer said.

"Exactamundo," Robalt said, snapping his fingers.

"The only people who would know what our destinations are going to be are on board this ship," Reese said.

"All right, listen up," Chambers said, walking to the middle of the compartment. "We're treading in some very dangerous waters here. We're talking treason. This isn't something we can just run into blind. There are a couple of things we need to consider before moving forward."

The answers hit Fischer almost immediately. "The clearance to look and who is actually sending the information."

"Correct," Chambers answered.

"We don't want to run the risk of asking the wrong person," Fischer said. "Might tip them off."

"You think it's someone on the command team?" Eliwood said.

"Who else would have the clearance to access and use the system like that?" Fischer asked.

"You think Captain Ward's involved?" Eliwood said.

Fischer shook his head. "No. But I don't have a solid explanation as to why. It just doesn't feel right. He's had multiple opportunities to sabotage our investigation and he hasn't. But honestly, we could probably say the same about the rest of the command staff as well."

"Well, we can't very well lock them all in a room until they crack," Eliwood said.

"I don't think it's Ward either," Sheridan said.

Cole laughed. "Because you're such a good judge of character."

Fischer turned to Robalt. "Can you do this without command clearance? I mean, can you physically do it?"

"It'd take me a few hours to get set up, but probably, yeah."

Fischer gave Captain Chambers an expectant look, and the Saber commander sighed, his expression pensive. "If we do this and we're wrong, we'll be violating at least a dozen regulations, not the least of which is treason. Hell, it's tantamount to mutiny, something that hasn't happened aboard an Alliance warship in the history of the navy."

The mood in the room had gone from reluctant excitement to somber reflection. They all knew what it meant if they were court-martialed for mutiny: a long walk out a short airlock.

"We don't do this unless everyone is on board," Chambers said. "I won't think any less of you if you do. If any one of you disagrees with what's being proposed right now, let's hear it."

No one spoke.

Chambers nodded. "All right. Robalt, Reese, set it up. I want updates every thirty minutes, and we don't act on anything until we've all had a chance to review whatever we find. Got it? All right, let's get to work."

CHAPTER 30

Saber Common Room
ANS *Legend*
19 August 2607

"Now, that's interesting," Robalt said, leaning forward in his seat. The orange hue of the holodisplay in front of him reflected off his face.

Fischer pushed himself up from the couch he'd been lying on and winced. He pressed his thumbs into his back, trying to relieve the tightness, and groaned as he stood. Carissa always teased him about being an old man, his beard had contained streaks of gray for a number of years, but now he was actually starting to feel it. He worked his elbows back and forth, trying to pop his back as he crossed the compartment to look over Robalt's shoulder.

"Moving kind of slow there, boss," Robalt said without looking up, half a grin on his face.

"Shut the hell up."

They were three hours into their second day of searching and finding nothing. Eliwood had gone to her cabin around 0100 hours, but Fischer had decided to stay close, opting to sleep on one of the couches in the common room. It had not been the best idea he'd ever had.

Most of the team were training in *Legend*'s main hangar bay, with Robalt and Reese left behind to help the investigation along. The Sabers had set up twin terminals at one end of the compartment, tying directly into the ship's main systems.

"What'd you find?" Fischer asked.

"Well, I've spent most of the time looking through the alpha nodes and coming up short," Robalt explained, his fingers swiping through menus. "Which, when you think about it, makes sense; if you don't want anyone to know you're up to no good, you don't use the most commonly accessed communication nodes on the ship. We already know if they're deleting the records, they have command-level clearance, right?"

"Right," Fischer said. "Makes sense."

"And if you have that level of clearance, you'd be able to access this." Robalt tapped his screen. A new panel appeared. "Every ship has an extremely redundant communication system in case primary and secondary systems go off-line or are damaged in combat. But a lesser known fact is that every ship has an emergency node that is completely separate from the main system. It's not even supposed to be online during normal operations. Hell, I don't think I've ever heard of one being used before. They're basically a redundancy to the redundancy to the redundancy, used only as a last resort."

"Okay?" Fischer said.

Robalt pointed. "So why is it being used?"

Fischer stepped closer. "Who's using it?"

"I don't know," Robalt said. "But I can tell you it's been accessed twice. Once when we detoured to Caldera after our attack on the Astalt outpost, and again when we set course for Grinas."

"That's how the Elites knew where we were going to be,"

Fischer said, feeling anger swell in his chest. There was a spy on board.

Robalt nodded.

"And you can't tell who accessed the node?" Fischer asked.

"No. And whatever they sent has been erased."

"But they couldn't erase the fact that they'd used the node?" Fischer asked.

"The only way you can delete that data is to physically destroy the node," Robalt said. "And…"

"And whoever is using it isn't done yet," Fischer said.

Fischer's mind raced with possibilities, mainly trying to picture who on *Legend*'s command crew could be working for Cardinal. He was almost sure it wasn't Ward, but it was only a hunch, and right now he couldn't afford the luxury of disqualifying anyone simply based on a hunch. But now that they knew, what could they do with the information? They couldn't take it to the captain, not without knowing for sure.

"Now that we know about it, can we monitor it?" Fischer asked.

Robalt tapped a bottom on the display and grinned. "My own personal trace program is already running."

"Good." Fischer pointed at the screen. "The next time the bastard makes a call, it will be his last."

A part of Fischer was excited to have something, anything to work on, but another part of him was reluctant to feel any hope, not with everything he'd experienced thus far. He tried to convince himself this was like any case: when one piece of evidence falls apart, you find something else until you've exhausted that until there's nothing left; then you move on to the next one. But with Cardinal, it never felt like he was making any progress, that the cause led nowhere and this entire thing was on the verge of collapsing around him.

Fischer's link chimed, the caller ID appearing on the holodisplay as it rotated around his wrist. Commander Manchester. Fischer accepted the call. "Yes, Commander?"

"Agent Fischer, the captain wanted to inform you that the *Doris* has just passed the outer beacon and will be landing shortly. Mr. Jones is requesting to speak with you ASAP. He'll be arriving in the main bay in five minutes."

Fischer noted the contempt in Manchester's voice and the decision to use the "mister" moniker in lieu of his rightful "captain" title, wondering what Manchester had against Jones.

"It's about time," Eliwood said under her breath.

"Thank you, Commander," Fischer said, ignoring his partner. "I'm on my way." He terminated the call and nodded at Robalt. "Stay on it. We need to let Chambers know."

The tech gave him a mock salute. "Already on it, boss."

"Come on," Fischer said to Eliwood and Sheridan. "Let's find out if our dice roll paid off."

CHAPTER 31

Hangar Bay One
ANS *Legend*
19 August 2607

Doris's rear cargo ramp was already folding down when Fischer entered the bay. The sprinter's designated landing zone on the far side of the bay was segregated from the rows of fighters and assault shuttles guarded by three masters-at-arms. Fischer led them through the ever-changing obstacle course of maintenance carts, deckhands and ordnance loaders, and couldn't help but feel apprehension at what Jones would say. If what they'd learned about the emergency comm node didn't pan out, the ultimate success of their investigation might rest on what Jones had found.

The pilot appeared at the top of the ramp, followed by Loomis and a woman Fischer didn't recognize at first.

"Oh, shit," Fischer said as they neared and he realized who it was.

"Looks like your buddy picked up a new friend," Eliwood said under her breath.

Fischer laughed. "Yeah."

"Who is that?"

"That's Jonesy's ex."

Fischer stopped at the bottom of the ramp and motioned to the hacker. "Osprey, didn't figure I'd see you here."

"You're not the only one."

"Went well, then?" Fischer asked Jones, struggling to keep the amusement off his face.

"Well, I doubt I'll be making any trips back to Thresh in the near future, I can tell you that much."

"That bad?"

"That bad?" Jones repeated, putting his arms out to his sides. "That bad? You know, the more work I do for you, the shorter my list of vocational opportunities becomes. First Stonemeyer, now Thresh. Before you know it, I'll be banned from the entire URT, and that, my friend, is extremely bad for business, if you know what I mean."

"Did you get anything?" Fischer asked. Jones was obviously worked up about something, and Fischer had no doubt he'd hear about it in due course, but right now, the only thing on his mind was Cardinal.

"Your compassion is overwhelming," Jones said. "*Yes*, we got something. Probably."

"Probably?" Fischer asked.

"That's right. We were kind of in a hurry," Jones said. "Didn't have a lot of time to vet the information."

"Who's your friend?" Eliwood asked, a curious grin on her face.

A flash of confusion spread across Jones's face as he turned to Osprey. "This is, uh…"

The woman smiled, extending a hand as she stepped off the ramp. "Call me Osprey."

"Eliwood." She took the hand. "You the hacker they're talking about?"

Osprey sniffed and gave Jones a sidelong look. "I prefer network infiltration specialist. Sounds a lot less…" She trailed off.

"Like a criminal?" Eliwood finished for her.

She smiled. "Exactly."

"Excuse me!" a voice called from behind them.

Fischer turned to see Lieutenant Commander Stinson, *Legend*'s flight operations officer, and a small entourage coming toward them.

"We'll talk about it later," Fischer told Jones.

Jones gave the military men a cursory glance and nodded.

"Mr. Jones," Stinson said, coming to a stop a few meters away from the group, "it seems like you've found a friend."

"That's the rumor." Jones crossed his arms.

"Any new arrivals must be cleared by the captain before they're allowed to board the ship. And I'm going to need a linkID."

"Yeah," Osprey said, drawing the word out. "That's not going to happen."

The FOO gave her a curious smile. "I'm sorry to burst your bubble, ma'am, but either you allow these men to scan you, or you will not be allowed on board."

"Commander Stinson," Fischer said, "under the circumstances, I think—"

"The circumstances are clear. No one will be permitted on board this ship without the express authorization of the captain. No exceptions. That is true under the most common of circumstances. LinkID, please."

"I'd love to oblige you, Commander," Osprey said. "But that's just not possible."

"I'm not asking."

Jones sighed. "She doesn't have a link."

"What do you mean she doesn't have a link?" Stinson asked, obviously still processing what he'd said.

Osprey held out her hand. "Not wired. I have this though." She produced a data pad from inside her jacket.

The lieutenant commander took the pad and handed it to one of his subordinates without taking his eyes off the hacker. "You're one of those, eh?"

"I'm not sure if I should be offended by that or not, Commander."

"I can vouch for her," Jones said. "She's not going to cause any trouble. She's here to help."

"You?" Stinson asked with a sardonic grin. "And what makes you think you're in a position to vouch for anyone?"

"My stunning good looks and positive attitude?"

"Commander Stinson," Fischer said, "I understand there's protocol we need to go through here, but they have information that is critical to our mission, and the longer we stand here debating whether or not they're worthy of entry puts us that much more behind."

The crewman handed Stinson Osprey's pad and whispered something into the commander's ear.

"It seems you've got quite the extensive record," Stinson said. "Wanted in multiple systems, including Solomon, for a list of charges that would take too long to recite here."

Osprey shrugged. "What can I say, rookies make silly mistakes." She held up a finger. "But I can honestly say I'm a reformed individual now. Completely different person."

"Oh?" Stinson raised an eyebrow.

"Oh, yeah. I cover my tracks a lot better now."

Fischer stepped between them before Stinson could respond. "Commander Stinson, regardless of this woman's background, she is integral to our case."

"Agent Fischer, I know this might come as somewhat of a

surprise to you," Stinson said, "but your investigation doesn't have anything to do with the security aboard this ship, and considering the current situation in the Alliance right now, that should be something all of us should be more alert to."

"Yes, and this investigation is pivotal to the Alliance's continued existence," Fischer said.

Stinson turned and nodded to the two masters-at-arms waiting behind him. They stepped forward, one pulling a pair of electrocuffs from a pouch on his belt.

"This woman is a wanted criminal," Stinson continued as the men secured Osprey. "She will be remanded into custody and held until such time as the captain can decide what will be done with her. End of discussion."

"I gotta say, Jonesy, this isn't the kind of vacation I had in mind," Osprey said. She didn't resist as the cuffs were secured around her wrists.

"This is bullshit, Fish," Jones said.

"I know," Fischer said, eyeing Stinson. The FOO showed no sign of hesitation or second-guessing his decision. "You're wrong."

"Any more surprise guests we should be worried about?" Stinson asked, his hands clasped behind his back.

Fischer looked at Jones, who shook his head.

"Very well," Stinson said. "Should I reiterate the shipboard rules and restrictions you're subject to while on board?"

"Oh, I'm pretty sure I remember," Jones said.

"Good."

The lieutenant commander turned without another word and followed his entourage across the hangar deck.

When he was out of earshot, Jones said, "That guy can kiss my ass."

"Well, to be fair, you did bring a wanted criminal on board the most advanced, and secret, ship in the fleet," Eliwood said.

"Didn't have too much of a choice," Jones said. "Hell, we're lucky we got off Thresh to begin with."

"Lucky?" Fischer frowned. "What do you mean? What happened?"

"Let's just say the operation didn't go as smoothly as I'd anticipated," Jones said, walking past Fischer as if that cleared it all up.

"Jonesy," Fischer said, following on his heels, "what happened?"

Jones laid out what had happened on Thresh as they made their way back to the Saber's common room. The fact that Alistair was so extensively embedded within their own networks didn't surprise Fischer in the least, not after everything he'd seen over the last few weeks. Jones was just wrapping up his story when they reached the common room hatch.

"Yeah, well, we've got some pretty major problems of our own." Fischer swiped his hand over the security panel, and the hatch slid open. He led them into the Saber common room, where Valkyrie team had spread throughout the compartment, attending to their gear or helping Robalt and Reese with their research of the rest of *Legend*'s nodes.

"You know, Fish," Jones said, "if Alistair is involved in this thing, they know what we were looking for, and they're going to be trying to clean it up as fast as they can."

Fischer nodded. "Doesn't give us a lot of time."

"What doesn't give us a lot of time?" Chambers asked. He set a pad down he'd been reading and leaned forward on the couch at the side of the compartment. "Did you find the information you were looking for?"

"Yes," Fischer said before Jones could answer. "But we've got a problem."

CHAPTER 32

Saber Common Room
ANS *Legend*
19 August 2607

"Ugh," Neal said, making a face and returning her sandwich to her plate, minus one bite from the corner. "You'd think on the most advanced warship in the fleet they'd be able to make you a decent turkey and cheese."

Sheridan turned his own identical sandwich over in his hands, chewing. "I don't know, I don't think it's that bad."

"That's because you're a primitive cave-dweller with absolutely no taste in modern cuisine."

Sheridan swallowed. "It's a little dry, but…"

"My point is it shouldn't be dry at all," Neal said and took a long pull from her water bottle. "I bet you're the kind of guy who likes e-rats, aren't you?"

"Steak and mushrooms isn't bad."

Neal shook her head. "Caveman."

Sheridan chuckled and finish his turkey and cheese. By the

last bite he'd decided that Neal had actually been correct in her assessment but decided against disclosing that particular realization lest she hold it over his head for the foreseeable future. They shared a couch along the rear bulkhead of Valkyrie's common room. The rest of the team was spread around the compartment, each passing the time in their own way while Fischer and Chambers briefed *Legend*'s command staff on what Jones had discovered on Thresh. They'd been gone for over an hour, and Sheridan didn't know whether that was a good or bad thing.

"What's this about that Jones guy bringing back a criminal?" Cole asked, coming up behind Sheridan, opening a meal packet from the galley.

"Hell if I know," Sheridan said, taking another bite. "Stinson was all kinds of pissed off though. Looked like he wanted to throw her right out the airlock."

"She cute?"

"What the hell does that matter?" Neal asked.

Cole shrugged. "Well, if she's hot, we don't want to throw her out the airlock."

"You're an asshole, Cole," Neal said.

"Eh, can't really argue that," Cole said. He ripped open the plastic-wrapped sandwich and took a bite of turkey and cheese. "Hey, not bad."

"Ugh," Neal said, looking away.

Sheridan laughed.

The hatch opened and Chambers entered, followed by Kline, Fischer, Eliwood and Jones. None of them looked especially pleased.

"Eyes up, Valkyrie," Chambers said, moving to the forward bulkhead and turning to face the room.

Around the compartment, the team set aside what they'd been doing, to focus on the captain. Though Robalt and Reese stayed at their stations, still watching the nodes.

"Sarge looks pissed," Neal whispered in Sheridan's ear, dropping onto the couch next to him.

"Yeah."

Valkyrie Team's senior noncom moved to the far side of the compartment, where he put his back against the bulkhead and crossed his arms. For a moment, Sheridan got the impression that Kline might have been pouting, but immediately disregarded the thought. Kline was many things, but a pouter was not one of them. He wasn't happy, that was obvious, but he looked like he was on the verge of ripping someone's head off, not going to his bunk to sulk.

Sheridan caught Fischer's gaze as the agent moved to one of the empty chairs along the port side, but his expression gave nothing away.

"All right," Chambers said as the rest found their seats. "I'm not going to sugarcoat it. You all know what's at stake here. The importance of this mission cannot be overstated. I know we've been coming up on some roadblocks here recently, and I know you're all ready to start seeing this thing go our way for a change. Well, the information Mr. Jones here has brought points us in the right direction. The captain has given the go-ahead for a Saccora mission, full assault protocol. There's only one problem."

The answer hit Sheridan almost immediately. "We still don't know who the spy is."

"Exactly right," Chambers said.

"This actually might be a good thing," Fischer said.

Chambers folded his arms across his chest. "Oh?"

"Like Robalt said, if there is someone passing on our whereabouts to Cardinal, they're only doing it when they have something solid. If the spy really is part of the command team, my guess would be we're going to be seeing a message flash here very soon."

Chambers nodded. "We are dropping in unannounced and in

full kit. Our priority will be to secure the Alliance embassy on the ground then go from there."

"All due respect, sir," Hanover said. "That's not much of a plan."

"It's *not* a plan," Kline muttered. "We're going into an unknown situation blind and deaf and dumb."

"Once we're in range, I can tap into the local network," Robalt said. "If our onboard friend sends a message out, I might be able to pull the destination IP and map the location."

"If we had access to Osprey, we might be able to track the original message to its source," Fischer suggested.

Chambers shook his head. "It's going to be a hard sell getting the captain to sign off on that."

"It's a risk," Fischer said. "I'll grant you that, but in this situation, I think we should be making use of every advantage we have."

"I'll work on it," Chambers said.

"According to this," Reese said from behind his holodisplays, "an Ambassador Wantanabe has been stationed on Saccora for eighteen months; no security protocol violations, the embassy hasn't reported any local problems or deficiencies."

"Doesn't mean we can trust him," Eliwood said.

"His file's pretty clean," Reese said. "One derog for unprofessional conduct during his second year for shagging up with an aide, but other than that…"

Sitting on the couch beside him, Neal muttered, "What's that? An asshole, horndog politician? Say it ain't so."

"They're all assholes," Sheridan said so only she could hear. "Professional liars."

Tobias Delaney was the only member of the Diplomatic Corps Sheridan had ever met, and if that encounter was anything to go on, he didn't have much hope for any ambassador he was likely to meet. He knew it was probably unreasonable to label all diplomats as untrustworthy shitheads, but try as he might, Sheridan just couldn't get past what had happened on Stonemeyer. Special operations was a dirty business, but at least you only had to worry about the enemy in front of you. When it came to politics, you had to be just as cautious about your allies. Perhaps even more so.

"It's ironic, don't you think?"

Sheridan frowned at her. "What?"

"That in a profession where trust and partnership are portrayed as the most important aspects of a person's character, they're actually the least common."

"Don't know that I've ever seen anything good come out of politics. It's all bullshit. None of those people live in the real world. Tobias Delaney was a grade A, class 1 piece of shit, and you know what's even more disturbing than that? They let him keep affecting lives even knowing he was dirty. When you don't even have the balls to call a rotten egg a rotten egg, I have no use for you at all. The Corps' leadership are just as responsible for what happened on Stonemeyer, if not more so. They knew, and they let it happen anyway. And we're the ones who paid the price."

"I'm sorry about that."

"Not your fault."

At the front of the room, Chambers cleared his throat. Sheridan looked up, realizing that the others were all looking at him and Neal now. Apparently he'd gotten a little carried away.

"I'm sorry, sir," Sheridan said.

"It's all right," Chambers said. "As I was saying—"

"Whoa, heads up!" Robalt shouted from his station. "I got something."

Sheridan jumped off the couch and joined the rest of the team as they grouped around Robalt's station. The electronics specialist was locked onto the displays, swiping panels and typing in commands.

"The node?" Fischer asked.

"Yeah," he said, nodding. "We got 'em."

CHAPTER 33

Corridor 1B
ANS *Legend*
19 August 2607

"Make a hole!" Sheridan growled, twisting sideways and pushing past two crewmen. He barely heard their angry responses as he moved on, sidestepping a surprised woman coming out of a side passage.

"Sorry," Fischer said as he passed the woman behind Sheridan.

"We should've put everyone on lockdown," Sheridan said, turning left into another corridor. He looked over his shoulder as Fischer followed. "Wouldn't that make it easier to find this guy?"

"Possibly," Fischer answered. "But it's also just as likely that we'd push whoever it is further underground. He might not surface again, compounding our problem. We need to catch him in the act."

"Can't you just shut it down?" Sheridan asked, swiping his link across the security pad for a hatch marked LADDER FOUR-TEEN. "Terminate his access?"

He ducked through the hatch into the aft ladder, one of two switchback ladders that stretched the entire height of the ship. There were several other ladders placed in key locations throughout the ship, but only two that touched every single deck. The design facilitated ease of access between multiple sections, but also relieved congestion through the most heavily traveled areas.

"No," Fischer said, following Sheridan through. "Don't shut it down; let it keep running. We shut it down and he'll know he's caught. Don't do anything that'll alert him we know anything. Can you monitor the call?"

"Probably," Robalt said, *"but if he's watching for that…"*

Fischer was silent for a moment, obviously considering the implications of what he was asking. Finally, he said, "Don't do anything."

"What about security?" Sheridan asked Fischer, turning to descend the ladder.

The investigator shook his head. "No. We do this ourselves."

Part of Sheridan was relieved at that. Not only was he looking forward to apprehending the spy, but they'd run the risk of exposing themselves early if the spy wasn't working alone. Not knowing whom they could trust was starting to weigh on him; it felt like the entire galaxy was against him.

"Who do you think it is?" Sheridan asked, already reaching for the next ladder as Fischer joined him on the landing one deck down.

"It's either someone with command-level access, or someone who's got the skill to bypass the security."

"Military encryption is some of the best stuff in the galaxy," Sheridan said, sliding down to the next landing.

"You're right," Fischer said. "But when the people who built the system are working against you…"

Sheridan gritted his teeth, trying to come to terms with the thought that someone he knew was actively working against the Alliance. Somewhere in the back of his mind he hoped that it wasn't anyone he knew well or, at the very least, hadn't done anything nice for. He didn't have any qualms about what needed to be done though. This was war, and whoever the spy turned out to be, they were working to kill him and his friends. He would not hesitate.

I'm not going to let any more of my friends fall to a gutless traitor, Sheridan told himself. *I'm not.*

"Hey," Fischer said, stepping off the ladder, his expression concerned. "You okay?"

"Fine," Sheridan said. "Let's get this son of a bitch."

Sheridan led them down three more ladders to deck six, then pushed the hatch open and took a second to orient himself. "This way." He started forward, dodging crew and watching the corridor markings. He knew *Legend*'s layout reasonably well but hadn't had the time to memorize it yet. He didn't want to lose his way on something this important.

They reached the compartment five minutes later, and each took up a position on either side of the hatch, pistols drawn. The words ELECTRONIC UTILITY 2B – AUTHORIZED PERSONNEL ONLY and the compartment number were stenciled on the bulkhead beside the hatch.

Several crew had stopped, stunned at what they were seeing, obviously conflicted on what to do. The sight of armed Marines and special agents wasn't exactly something you saw every day on board ship.

"Get back," Fischer hissed, waving them away.

A few hesitated, but finally the crowd dispersed, ducking behind corners only to peek out again to watch.

Sheridan looked at Fischer, making sure he was ready before swiping his link across the hatch's security panel. It didn't open. Frowning, Sheridan checked again. "Locked."

"Shit," Fischer said. "Robbi, we have a locked hatch here."

"Working."

"I'll go left," Sheridan said. "You go right."

Fischer nodded.

The security panel next to the hatch blinked to life, its glowing screen changing as if being operated by an invisible hand. The red LOCKED panel flashed to green.

"Open," Robalt said.

Sheridan took a long breath and looked at Fischer. The investigator nodded and Sheridan tapped the panel. The hatch slid open with a barely audible *shhhh*, and Sheridan rolled in, his pistol up at eye level, sweeping ahead for targets. The compartment was dark save for a row of holoscreens floating over the forward bulkhead. Two racks of electronics stretched away from the hatch, creating three identical walkways to the back of the compartment, where another hatch led into a smaller secondary room.

Sheridan saw all of it and none of it, focusing his attention downrange, scanning for things that could shoot at him. He slowed at the end of the rack and peered through the hatch into the back room. Orange light glowed from the compartment. A shadow moved, and Sheridan steeled himself for an attack, his finger pressing ever so slightly on the trigger.

He stepped forward, inching around the edge of the open hatch and pointing his pistol at the man's back. "Don't move!"

"You don't have a choice," a familiar voice said. "You have to shoot."

"Turn around!" Sheridan shouted, feeling Fischer come up beside him. "Hands up! I will kill you."

Slowly, the man turned, and Sheridan's blood ran cold. Commander Manchester gave him a weak, almost apologetic smile.

"Why?" Fischer asked.

"We all have our callings, Corporal," Manchester said.

"And yours was to, what? Betray everything you stood for?"

Legend's executive officer sighed; then his head twitched sideways, eyes bulging, blood spraying from his mouth.

"No!" Fischer shouted.

Manchester's body fell forward, his face smacking against the bulkhead with a wet crunch; then his body collapsed to the floor.

"Son of a bitch," Sheridan growled, rage burning in his stomach. "The charge. Fuck! I didn't—"

"Sheridan, what's your status?" Chambers asked.

Sheridan didn't answer. Couldn't find the words to say. He just stood there, watching the blood slowly spread across the deck. The vision of Hastings lying on the basement floor flashed in his mind.

"Agent Fischer?" Chambers asked. *"Are you okay? What happened?"*

"We're fine," Fischer said.

Sheridan swallowed hard, pushing away the memory of Hastings. "Target down."

CHAPTER 34

Electronic Utility Compartment 2B
ANS *Legend*
19 August 2607

"I don't believe it," Captain Ward said, looking down at Manchester's corpse, hands on his hips, shaking his head, the look of utter shock and dismay plain on his face. On everyone's face for that matter.

Fischer couldn't blame him; a betrayal on this level was likely to hit the entire crew, and it would hit hard. *I'd feel the same way if Eliwood turned out to be...* He didn't finish the thought. He couldn't. With the galaxy falling apart around him, he would not even entertain that possibility.

She's not.

"Excuse me, sir," Robalt said. Ward stepped out of the way as the electronic tech squeezed by to kneel next to the body.

Fischer watched as he began cloning the dead man's link, hoping he hadn't had time to wipe it. Muffled voices from the corridor behind him drew his attention as Kline instructed his team to set up a cordon. Ordinarily that would've been handled by the ship's security team, but these were not ordinary circumstances, and Ward didn't want to take any chances.

Reese stood awkwardly next to the terminal Manchester had been using. Fortunately, the commander hadn't had time to wipe what he'd been doing, and the electronic tech was confident he'd be able to retrieve whatever Manchester had been working on.

"This should only take about five minutes, sir," Robalt said.

"Will you be able to identify any co-conspirators?" Ward asked Chambers.

"To be honest, sir, we've barely touched this," Chambers said. "That is the first thing we're going to look into once we have all the data pulled from the XO's…" He trailed off, expression hardening. "From the dead man's link."

The fact that Chambers refused to say Manchester's name, even his rank or title, said a lot about the Saber's feelings about the man's betrayal.

Fischer cleared his throat. "Captain Ward, I'd suggest locking down ship personnel until we can confirm if there are additional threats. A shelter-in-place scenario. We can slow the spread of information, and if there are other sleepers on board, we can keep them stationary while we hunt."

"If you would've come to me with this earlier, we might've have saved a lot of time."

"Yes, sir," Fischer said. "But, no offense, we weren't entirely sure who we could trust with the information. Still aren't."

Ward glared at Fischer. "I'm not a spy, Agent Fischer."

"No, sir," Fischer said.

"Unless they take it as a threat to their mission," Ward said. "They might very well start a counterattack if they think we're onto them. There are a lot of critical systems aboard, and fouling any one of them could have disastrous consequences."

"So we need a situation that requires a lockdown but won't arouse any suspicion," Fischer said.

"Mechanical failure somewhere?" Eliwood suggested. She stood just inside the hatch, arms crossed, leaning against the bulkhead. "Containment failure in engineering? Life-support systems?"

"Those scenarios require a ship-wide response from multiple sections performing any number of duties."

"Okay, is there any scenario that doesn't?"

"This is a warship, Agent Eliwood," Captain Ward said. "Everything that happens on board requires a ship-wide response."

"What about a prisoner escape?" Fischer asked.

"I'm sorry?"

"A prisoner escape," Fischer repeated. "The appropriate response to that would be to lock down every compartment and conduct a room-by-room search. We use the Saber team to sweep the ship while we search Manchester's link."

"A prisoner escape?" Ward asked. His tone suggested he couldn't believe Fischer had even mentioned it.

"It would give you a legitimate reason for keeping everyone locked in place."

"Internal sensors would be able to determine if anyone was someplace they shouldn't be," Robalt said, without looking up from his link's display. He seemed to realize he'd spoken aloud and looked up sheepishly. "Sorry, sir."

"I can position my people at either end of the ship," Captain Chambers said. "We can sweep inward from both directions."

"That's all well and good, Captain," Ward said, "but we don't know who we're looking for, and even if we did, is there any guarantee whoever they find won't end up the same way?" He nodded to Manchester's corpse.

"The ship has a nonlethal arsenal in the armory," Chambers suggested. "Stun first; ask questions later."

"We'd need to completely incapacitate," Fischer said. "If they're conscious at all, they can trigger the device."

"Stunners pack a pretty nasty punch," Robalt offered. "Hit the right setting and whoever they hit will be out for a couple of hours."

"How many people are we talking about here?" Ward asked. "Do you think they'd be in communication with each other?"

"Does it matter?" Eliwood said. They all looked at her, equally curious to where she was going. "Why are we even talking nonlethal? We have our destination already."

Sheridan nodded. "Right."

"What matters is the safety and security of this crew," Ward said. "These sleepers may have information we need."

"They're not going to give you anything," Eliwood said. "If we do manage to track them down, they're just going to kill themselves like they all do. They're true believers."

She was right, Fischer knew. There was no question about it. But he didn't like it.

"Your objection is noted, Agent Eliwood," Ward said, tapping his link. He waited a second for it to connect. "Commander Stinson, report to electronic utility 2B immediately."

"Yes, sir," Stinson said.

"And, Stinson…"

"Yes, sir."

Ward eyed Fischer as he spoke. "Do it quietly."

"Aye, sir."

Ward terminated the call. "You realize what we're about to do is unprecedented."

"There's a first time for everything, sir," Fischer said.

"And if Manchester was the only one?" Ward asked. "Then I'll be putting my entire crew into confinement without cause."

"It's not like they're going anywhere," Eliwood said.

"It's not without cause," Fischer said before Ward could

respond. "In fact, we have more than enough cause. You don't lose that because we find out we were wrong. In my world that's called probable cause. As long as you meet that standard, your investigation is righteous."

"An officer in this man's navy is held to a higher standard, Agent Fischer."

"Morally? Yes. Procedurally, no. In a court of law, you are held to the same exact standard as any other citizen. You aren't in any danger of criminal prosecution for wrongful imprisonment or confinement, if that's what you're worried about."

"I wasn't worried about that at all," Ward said. "I'm worried about maintaining the loyalty of my crew, not to mention their readiness. I do not take my position as captain lightly. It is a grave responsibility, and the men and women who serve under me must trust me, to say nothing of their respect. Locking down the ship and detaining those who've done no wrong is trending very close to a line I don't wish to cross."

Fischer held the captain's gaze for a long moment, then nodded. "I understand, sir."

"Got something," Corporal Reese said, the glow of the holo-screens along the bulkhead silhouetting him in the dimly lit space. "The message was short, but I've got a destination code. He was definitely sending it to someone on Saccora."

Fischer felt a surge of hope. "Can you trace it?"

"Sure, but we have to be connected to the Saccora network; otherwise it's just a meaningless number."

"It's a start," Fischer said.

"Sir," Chambers said to Ward, "Stinson's here."

Ward nodded and Chambers relayed the order through his taclink. A moment later Stinson stepped through the hatch, confusion and worry etched across his face. His eyes swept the compartment, moving from person to person before finally landing on the corpse in the back.

"Oh my god! What the hell happened?" Stinson asked.

"Commander Stinson," Ward said, "there is a situation on board that you need to be aware of; however, I have to advise you that under no circumstances will you speak about it to anyone else. Is that understood?"

"Absolutely, sir."

"Agent Fischer."

Fischer nodded and relayed what they'd learned since returning from Thresh. As he spoke, Stinson's expression grew steadily darker. When he learned about Manchester, he turned so pale Fischer was worried he was going to be sick.

"I don't believe it," Stinson said. "And you think there are more spies on board?"

"There's no way to be certain," Fischer said. "But we're hoping the data contained in his link will shed some more light on that."

"But you're not sure?"

"No."

"Captain, I have to say, I'm not comfortable with this at all. If there are more sleeper agents embedded in the crew, what's to keep them from turning on the crew confined with them if they realize we're onto them? Those men and women would have no way of knowing their lives were in danger until it was too late."

"Their lives are already in danger, Commander," Fischer said. "Standing here, right now, our lives are in danger. The fact that we already know there are sleepers throughout the military and government should tell you there are likely more on board that we don't know about."

Stinson took a long breath then turned to the captain. "What do you need me to do?"

"Relieve the security team in the brig with two from Captain Chambers's team. Initiate a ship-wide combat-readiness exercise. There will be a power surge in relay junction seventeen, at which time the brig's security containment field will fail. You will then initiate a ship-wide lockdown while we sweep for the escaped prisoner. No one but the Saber team will be permitted to leave their stations."

"Aye, sir," Stinson said. "And how will we know who to apprehend, sir?"

Ward shot Chambers a questioning glance.

"Robbi?" Chambers asked.

"Just… about… there… Got it." Robalt stood, his fingers tapping away at his link's display. "Going through the commander's comm logs and message archive. I've got a couple of personal programs I'm running to help scrub through the data, a few keywords and sequence designations that—"

"Robbi," Chambers said, cutting the tech off.

"Yes, sir?"

"We don't need the play-by-play."

"Roger that, sir."

"I would never have thought in a million years that Manchester could've been a double agent," Stinson said, slipping his hands into his pant pockets, shaking his head. "Not in a million years. I mean, I've known him my entire career, and the whole time he was just waiting for the right time to slip a knife into my back."

"Right now we need to focus on what's right in front of us," Captain Ward said. "Commander Stinson, I'm designating you as executive officer. You'll need to appoint a replacement for flight ops."

Stinson's expression turned from thoughtful consideration to one hundred percent business in the blink of an eye. "Aye, sir. Lieutenant Wainwright has been putting in the time. She'd make a great flight commander."

A thought hit Fischer as he stood listening to the two men, something he hadn't considered before and probably should have.

He thought about all the rest of the bodies he'd picked up over the last few months, thinking about what they all had in common: they'd all had their links wiped before they'd been able to process them, and most had been living with the suicide charge in their heads.

What was the old saying? Two birds, one stone.

"Excuse me, sir," Fischer said. "We might be able to stack our deck a little."

"What do you mean?"

"Say there's a chance that Manchester and the other sleepers knew each other. Wouldn't they want to figure out if something happened to him, right? Or if he'd blown their cover."

Ward frowned. "Where are you going with this?"

"If he was incapacitated somehow, not dead, say in some kind of accident, and they knew we were going to examine him, they might want to check and see if we'd discovered the charge in his head, or at the very least wipe his link. Make sure if we haven't figured it out yet, that we won't. Instead of ripping this ship apart looking for them…"

"We make them come to us," Ward finished.

Fischer nodded.

The captain folded his arms across his chest. "What exactly did you have in mind, Agent Fischer?"

CHAPTER 35

Medical Bay
ANS *Legend*
19 August 2607

Fischer adjusted the charcoal gray jumpsuit for the tenth time and sighed. The fabric was a little too tight around the crotch; the arms and legs a little too short. He wondered if the hiccup in sizing had been a deliberate move by Stinson—payback for what had happened on the flight deck when Jones had returned.

Beside him, Sheridan grinned. "Been a while, huh?"

"The enjoyment you're getting from my discomfort is noted and will be remembered," Fischer said. "I know it's been a few years since I've been in uniform, but I don't remember the grays being this restrictive."

"You got the right size, right?"

"Stinson said it was an extra-large," Fischer said, pulling on the collar, trying to get a look at the label. "It's the same size I've worn for years. I swear, they make everything smaller now."

In his cochlear implant, Eliwood said, *"Have you considered the possibility that it might not be the uniform?"*

"You're supposed to be watching my back, Aniyah, not commenting on my wardrobe."

"Oh, I'm confident I can do both."

Fischer and Sheridan were standing at the back of one of the half-dozen semiprivate medical beds in *Legend*'s medical bay, the curtains drawn around them, the rest of the team waiting in an adjacent compartment. They would function as a quick response team for them, just in case things went south. Though, Fischer was sure that if this thing took a turn for the worse, a quick response team wouldn't be all that helpful.

It took two hours to set up the "accident"; a negligent discharge in the Sabers' private training area in cargo bay four, and Neal had volunteered to be the sacrificial lamb. Manchester had been in the wrong place at the wrong time. Cole had started the rumor of a court-martial and confinement, and the investigation was still ongoing. It'd taken some extensive coordination with Commander Stinson, but they'd managed to move Manchester's body without much trouble. After enough crew had arrived to try to get a look at the scene, they'd moved the body to medical, allowing more rumors to spread that he was dead, and the ship's doctor was set to perform an autopsy.

The speed at which the members of Team Valkyrie had taken to their assignments in putting this thing together impressed Fischer. If it had been up to ASI to set something like this in motion, it would've taken days, not to mention kilometers of red tape. Now, standing in the dark, surrounded by the soft hum of the medical machines, Fischer prayed it would work. In the last ten minutes alone he'd thought of at least a dozen ways this operation could go wrong, and he was sure he wasn't even scratching the surface.

It's going to work, he reassured himself.

"Eyes up," Corporal Reese said over the taclink. "I've got movement."

Fischer and Sheridan exchanged knowing glances, and Fischer slowly wrapped his fingers around the pistol's grip. In all likelihood Sheridan would have the faster reaction and put bullets downrange long before he could, but he was not going to be caught flatfooted.

"Two bodies," Reese said. "They're approaching the forward hatch. Getting them ID'd now."

"It's Haskins and Lodge," Captain Ward said, an edge of disgust in his voice. "Engineering and communications techs. They were assigned to *Legend* during the first wave of recruitment, before the command staff had been appointed."

Fischer thought he heard some relief in the captain's voice.

"It doesn't look like they're armed," Reese said.

"It's the little things," Fischer said.

"Ten seconds to the hatch."

Fischer gave Sheridan a sidelong glance. "We take them hard and fast. Don't give them time to react."

Sheridan nodded, adjusting his grip on the stunner. The compact pistol shot a subsonic incapacitating round that would shock its target into immediate unconsciousness. Theoretically. Having witnessed, firsthand, the lack of effect the weapon had on people amped on stims, Fischer was more than a little apprehensive about its deployment. He'd seen one man walk through five rounds without breaking a sweat before putting the officer firing the pistol in the hospital in critical condition.

The sound of the hatch opening was barely audible across the compartment. Fischer held his breath, visualizing the two men entering ten meters to his left.

"Come on," a male voice said.

"Where is everyone?" a second male asked.

"Doesn't matter," the first said. "We have work to do. Seal the hatch. I'll get the link."

"Right."

Fischer nodded at Sheridan, who raised his stunner to his chest, the muzzle pointing straight out. Fischer reached for the edge of the curtain and waited for Sheridan's nod. At the signal he ripped the curtain back, and the Saber advanced, firing his weapon before his arms had fully extended. The first round hit his target in the clavicle, a deep thump followed by the snap of the stunning charge. The man's cry of surprise was abruptly cut off as his legs gave out under him and he collapsed to the deck.

Sheridan was moving to the second target before the first hit the ground, leveling on his chest, and fired. The pistol jumped slightly and the stunner hit dead center. The man's hand had been reaching for the zipper on his flight suit, and as the charge went off, his entire body spasmed. He fell to his knees, then toppled forward, landing face-first on the deck.

"Targets down," Sheridan said.

Fischer pulled two pairs of electrocuffs from his hip pocket and went to work securing both men. "Nice shots."

"Yeah," Sheridan said, squatting down next to the first man, performing a quick pat down. "Nothing."

Fischer finished his search and shook his head. "Same."

"No weapons, no equipment," Sheridan said. "What the hell were they doing?"

Five seconds later Chambers entered along with Captain Ward and Commander Stinson. The ship's doctor, Commander Moore, followed, directing her accompanying nurses to prep their operating area.

"Excuse me," Dr. Moore said, squeezing past Fischer to get at the first man. She knelt down beside him and pressed a thumb-sized injector against the man's neck. There was a hiss and she immediately repeated the procedure on the second.

Moore slipped the injector into one of her many coat pockets, then tapped her link and produced a small handheld scanner. After two quick scans, she stood, nodding. "Well, I'm not sure if I'm relieved or terrified. Positive for micro explosive devices. Both are still live and active."

"Can you extract them?" Captain Ward asked.

Moore laughed, though Fischer couldn't tell if it was a comedic laugh or nervous. "Sir, I'm sure this might come as a shock to you, but I'm a medical doctor, as in internal human medicine. Improvised micro explosive devices aren't actually my field of expertise. In fact, I know little to nothing about bombs of any kind."

"I can have my explosive ordnance techs assist in the procedure, Doctor," Chambers said.

Moore sighed, obviously apprehensive about the prospect of operating on a live explosive.

"Doctor, I understand your reluctance," Fischer said. "But these men could have critical information to my case and our mission out here."

"I can't make any promises," Moore said finally. "And there is a very real chance they could die during the procedure."

"Nice work," Sheridan told Fischer under his breath.

"It's too bad they can't all be that easy."

Sheridan smiled. "You got that right."

CHAPTER 36

Saber Common Room
ANS *Legend*
20 August 2607

"Answer me this, Fish," Eliwood said, leaning against the star-board bulkhead near the back of the compartment.

Fischer sipped his coffee and winced. Too hot and slightly burnt. "Why are we on the most advanced warship in modern history and they can't find a way to brew a decent cup of coffee?"

It wasn't horrible, far from the worst he'd ever had, but it wasn't great either. At the risk of being called a snob, he hadn't mentioned it to anyone, but he longed for his Del Raycan Special Blend. Its light, crisp aroma and smooth taste had ruined him for any other brew.

"Well, yes, obviously that," she said. "But something's really been bothering me. How do you think they've managed to radi-calize so many people?"

"There's a lot of people out there looking for something to believe in," Fischer said. "You find the right type of person and it doesn't take much. Just look at all the gangs and raiders operating locally throughout most systems. They provide safety and security and membership to people who otherwise might not have anything at all."

"You're saying that all these people turned against their nations because they wanted to be in a club?"

"I'm saying it's not as difficult to indoctrinate as you think."

"I've been rolling it around in my head for days, and I can't work it out."

Fischer took another sip of the not-bad coffee. "Work what out?"

"Davis."

"What about her?"

Eliwood blew out a frustrated breath. "I mean, she'd been doing *good* work for so many years, putting bad people in cells, *helping* good people. I can't begin to count how many cases she was instrumental in solving. And to throw all that away? She had to have known she was working for the wrong side, right? I mean, she had to."

"I think she eventually worked it out," Fischer said. "But by the time she did, it was too late. There was nothing she could do. She was in too deep. She had her family to think about. And maybe that's why she tried to do so much good. Trying to outweigh the bad."

Eliwood turned, scoffing. "Her family. We were her family, Fish. How can a person just turn their back on the people closest to them?"

Fischer sighed. "I don't know."

Eliwood's shoulders slumped. When their eyes met a moment later, they were filled with resolve. "I want to crush these bastards, Fish."

"So do I."

"Not just whatever's on Saccora, I mean everywhere."

"We will," Fischer said. He glanced across the compartment,

where both electronics specialists were scrubbing the data they'd collected from the links of the three shipboard spies.

Engineering Mate Sean Haskins was out of surgery, recovering in a locked-down cabin, guarded by three armed masters-at-arms and two Sabers. Communications Mate Eric Lodge was still in surgery, having the charge rendered safe by Sergeant Neal and removed by Dr. Moore. It'd taken several hours for Moore to work out exactly how to remove the charge, and the procedure had taken about six.

"You think they're going to find anything?" Eliwood asked, nodding to the focused specialists.

"If there's anything to find, they'll find it," Fischer said with a little more confidence than he felt.

The custom equipment Robalt had built rivaled some of the most advanced setups Fischer had ever seen. The legal implications of having the gear on board a navy warship notwithstanding, the equipment had definitely come in handy, and on this point at least, the ends *did* justify the means.

Robalt's hands worked faster than Fischer could track, tapping buttons, swiping across holodisplay panels, flicking information away and bringing it closer. It was like a well-choreographed dance that only he knew the moves to. Corporal Reese, Team One's specialist, stood behind him, occasionally pointing out various items on the screens and serving as a sounding board for his partner. Together they rivaled the best computer techs Fischer had ever known.

"Now this is interesting," Robalt said, leaning closer to the multiple holodisplays arranged in front of him.

"What you got?" Reese asked, looking up from his link.

"Hold on," Robalt said, focused on his work. He shifted panels around, rearranging the information and highlighting specific lines of data.

Fischer gave Eliwood a knowing look, and they both crossed

the compartment to get a look at what Robalt had found. Fischer stood, hands in his pockets, waiting as Robalt's eyes flicked from screen to screen, his expression never changing. It was as if his entire body had melded with his equipment; he was one with the data. Fischer was sure if the Alliance Navy Marching Band was playing right next to him, the specialist wouldn't've heard a note.

Reese patted his partner's shoulder and pointed to the screen without saying a word. Robalt nodded and tapped the area Reese had indicated.

Fischer said, "You know, if either of you are interested in work after Valkyrie, ASI would snatch both of you up in a heartbeat."

Robalt paused for a moment, looking over his displays at Fischer. "Intelligence, huh? Well, I can't say that I've ever seen myself as a pad-pushing desk jockey, but the idea has merit."

"Isn't military intelligence kind of a contradiction in terms?" Reese asked, grinning.

"Lot of pads need pushing," Fischer said, laughing. "But I'm serious, we're always looking for talented techs."

"I'll hold you to that, sir," Robalt said.

Fischer groaned. "How many times do I have to say…?"

"I know, I know." Robalt turned his attention back to his screens. "Don't call you 'sir,' got it. Well, I think when you hear what I'm about to tell you, you might even spring for a promotion or two."

Intrigued, Fischer moved behind the specialist. "Find something interesting?"

"Interesting might not be the right word." Robalt tapped a final sequence and leaned back from the displays. "I've been running comparisons on the links we've managed to clone, and while most of the information is stuff you'd expect to find, there are some things that are unique."

"Such as?" Fischer asked.

"Well, I'm not one hundred percent sure, but it looks like I've stumbled across a partitioned node of passwords or security phrases hidden in several files on all three links we recovered. I'm running a search now on the one we got from Gav."

Fischer leaned closer, reading the data on the screens. "Cardinal passwords?"

"That's the way it's looking," Robalt said. "They're not in any particular order, and there isn't any reference material to explain their use, but they're there."

"They were probably given instructions beforehand," Fischer said.

Eliwood appeared on the other side of the displays, shaking her head. "And here I thought the number one rule of tradecraft is not to write your passwords down."

"Typically speaking, that's correct," Reese said, "but in this case, I think there is something else."

"What's that?" Fischer asked.

"It's like a sign/countersign system, only for links," Reese explained. "The assets sync links, and if they have the proper code sequence, it will trigger a specific response. If they want to transmit data to a link with the correct decryption protocols, it would likely initiate a coded response between the devices and identify themselves to each other."

Robalt looked up. "It's a friend or foe sequence, to let other Cardinal operatives know who they are."

"You said there are multiple sequences?" Fischer asked, nodding to Sheridan as the corporal approached.

"It's likely that there are different sequences for different scenarios."

"So without knowing the proper scenario, we wouldn't know which sequence is the correct one?"

Reese nodded. "That's right."

"So they're worthless," Sheridan said.

"No," Robalt said. "We know they exist now; that's valuable information. And given enough time, we might be able to deconstruct their communications logs and pinpoint which sequence is used for what."

"How much time?" Fischer asked.

"A couple of weeks," Robalt said. He gave Fischer an apologetic look.

"A couple of weeks," Fischer repeated. "We don't have that kind of time."

"I know."

"Any way we can speed that up?" Eliwood asked.

"Sure," Reese said, shrugging. "Give us about twenty more guys and mainframe access."

"Might be able to swing the access," Fischer said. "Unfortunately, we're a little light on personnel."

"There is someone," Eliwood said, giving Fischer a knowing look.

He knew immediately what she was implying and held up a finger. "Absolutely not. No way."

"I'm just saying," Eliwood said, putting her hands up. "It's an option."

"Even if I wanted to give her access, the captain would never allow it, and I can't say that I blame him. The number of regulations he'd be ignoring…" Fischer shook his head. "Not a chance."

Eliwood put her hands on her hips. "Look, all I'm saying is that we're up against a wall here, and at this point in the game, I'd think we want to use everything at our disposal to end this thing. It's not like we have a lot of other options."

"Do you have any idea how much classified information we'd risk exposing if we allowed her access?" Fischer asked. "I can't even begin to imagine the shitstorm that would start back home."

"Normally I'd agree with you," Eliwood said. "And under normal circumstances, you'd be absolutely right, but nothing about what we're doing is normal, is it? You have to admit, Fish, this whole thing is just one big cluster that we're just barely holding together. And even then, not really."

Fischer ground his teeth and shook his head. He knew she was right, but he didn't want to admit it. Even the little bit of information Osprey had already potentially been exposed to would bring them under the scrutiny from the Intelligence Oversight Committee, and the fact that he'd entrusted Jones with classified ASI intelligence with the sole intention of handing that intelligence off to a known criminal would be more than a little difficult to explain away. The current situation notwithstanding, the act itself was a clear violation of ASI regulations and could be considered by some to be treasonous.

Of course, if they failed and the Alliance collapsed because of Cardinal, none of that would matter. None of this would. It'd be a footnote in a history book, if that.

And taking risks is part of the game, Fischer told himself.

Robalt looked up from his screens. "I'm not going to lie, Osprey would probably cut our search time in half; she's a legend in the community. No pun intended."

"Legend or not, the captain's not going to give her unfettered access to the ship's network. If anything happened…"

"Won't know unless you ask," Eliwood said, smiling.

"It wouldn't be unfettered," Reese said. "We'd be sitting next to her the whole time."

"I can watch her," Eliwood offered.

Fischer laughed. "Because you'd know what to look for if she started doing something she wasn't supposed to."

Eliwood straightened, frowning. "What are you trying to say?"

"I'm not trying to say anything," Fischer said. "You're an investigator, not a tech. The kind of skills Osprey has are way beyond what I think anyone could realistically comprehend."

"Okay," she said. "But still…"

"Fischer," Sheridan said, his voice low, "I'm not sure we can be too picky about how we work this case. You said it yourself, if Cardinal is heading toward the endgame, we need to do everything we can to stop it."

Fischer sighed. They were right. Their logic was sound, and though he hated to admit it, he agreed with them. So why was he so reluctant?

Because giving a wanted criminal access to the most secure networks in the Alliance isn't exactly on your top ten list, Fischer thought. His mind raced to find an alternative, but he already knew there wasn't one. *It's the lesser of two evils.*

"All right," he said finally. "I'll talk to the captain." He held up a finger. "But don't get your hopes up."

CHAPTER 37

Command Staff Briefing Room
ANS *Legend*
20 August 2607

The hatch to *Legend*'s briefing room opened, and Captain Ward entered, followed by Stinson. Fischer, Eliwood, the Valkyrie command team, and *Legend*'s command crew all pushed back from the table to stand. The rest of *Legend*'s staff officers had been brought up to speed during the surgeries of Haskins and Lodge, all of whom had had the same reaction as Stinson had: shocked, betrayed, disappointed, and angry. And now that everyone was on the same page, it was time to work out how they wanted to bring this operation to a close.

"Sit." Ward patted the air as everyone stood, beckoning them back into their seats. He took his seat and put both hands on the table. "All right, where are we?"

"We've got all our pilots on alert, sir," Stinson reported, taking his seat next to Ward. "We're doing hourly rotations in Ready Five, and the assault birds are standing by."

"All our gun batteries have been cycled and are synced with

fire control," Lieutenant Commander Ivan Nesset said. "Target designation protocols have been uploaded, and fire sequences have been set."

"All drives are operating with full redundancies, and containment crews are in place and ready," Lieutenant Commander Adelina Tavares, *Legend*'s chief engineer, reported. "Shield nodes are running at eighty percent right now. I'm diverting power to the standby nodes. We'll be able to push to one hundred and fifteen percent no problem."

Lieutenant Hano Sadao, the ship's operations officer, straightened in his chair. "I have emergency response crews stationed through the ship, and they're coordinating with Dr. Moore's medical teams to provide immediate care."

Fischer listened as the command crew continued to give Captain Ward updates on their critical items and procedures for the coming operation. They were as professional as they came; even with the knowledge of Manchester's betrayal, they continued to perform as if that was merely an afterthought.

"What about your team, Captain?" Ward asked Chambers.

"We're looking at several different options, sir, but the situation on the ground will ultimately dictate our response. At the moment, our plan is to drop in full kit; from there we'll determine whether to downgrade or not. Obviously, my preference would be to not. It'll be early morning local time when we drop, so we'll have a few hours of darkness working for us."

Ward nodded. "Understood."

"Dropping into an embassy with a platoon of fully armored Sabers isn't exactly subtle," Stinson said.

"I don't think subtle is what you want here, Commander," Fischer said. "Considering our Marines haven't had that much luck with embassies in recent history."

"I agree," Chambers said.

"Stonemeyer was an isolated incident," Stinson said before

Ward could respond. "And not everyone who works for the Diplomatic Corps is dirty."

"Never said they were," Fischer said, "but given what we know, I'd say the chances of Cardinal's people infiltrating more than one Alliance installation in the system is fairly high. Just look at the landscape; you've got Alliance military, Pegasi military, the Saccora Navy, all stationed in the same system? We know Cardinal has people in both navies. I don't think it would be unreasonable to assume the embassy is controlled by them as well. In fact, I'd bet on it."

"It's your team, Captain Chambers," Ward said, seeming to ignore Stinson's and Fischer's brief aside. "I'll leave its operational and logistical details to you and your staff."

"Thank you, sir."

"What's your plan once you're on the ground?" Ward asked.

"Securing the embassy is first thing on the list. Once that's done, we can use it as a forward operation base. I'd like to detail some augmentees. My team is good, but the chances of a multiphase operation are high, and we can only do so much. We'll need additional manpower for security, and we're going to need some additional tech people."

"Let's put together a list." Ward nodded to Stinson; then to Chambers he asked, "What kind of opposition are we looking at here?"

"At the embassy? It's hard to say, sir," Chambers said. "If they follow standard Corps procedure, they'll have at least a platoon strength for internal security. Most likely ex-military, though probably not tier one operators. Most security forces I've run into are former Marines."

"And if you face resistance?"

"I think it's doubtful they'd attack first," Chambers said. "If they do, we'll either pacify them or exfil. But with the high likelihood of surprise on our side, I think it's unlikely the former will be necessary. I'm sure we can get the drop on them, sir."

"And we know that for sure?" Ward asked. "They won't know we're coming."

"We know he didn't get his message off," Chambers said.

"That specific message, yes, but there could have been others."

Fischer leaned forward. "It's possible, sir, but the information about Saccora wasn't known beforehand, so Manchester wouldn't have had any reason to suspect our going there. And Haskins and Lodge didn't have the opportunity to access any of *Legend*'s communications nodes. We were monitoring them."

"There's one thing that bothers me about all this," Stinson said. "If Manchester was working for Cardinal, why didn't he warn the outpost in Astalt we were coming?"

"It's possible he wasn't aware of the outpost beforehand," Fischer said. "It could be that the message didn't get to them in time or that he'd been ordered to strict radio silence unless absolutely necessary. Could be a number of things. It's my impression that the majority of Cardinal's operations are compartmentalized much like ours are. In an operation like that, it'd be impossible to keep the lid on without heavy need-to-know restrictions. We'll know more once we've given the data a thorough examination."

"Makes sense," Ward said, nodding. "Back to the embassy, I'm concerned about friendly fire here. I don't want to be shooting at our own people if we can help it."

"Yes, sir," Chambers said. "I'm confident it won't come to that. We'll have superior numbers, surprise, and confusion on our side. My guess is they'll be as reluctant to engage, but if they do, we'll do our best to minimize casualties."

"And what's the timeline we're looking at?"

"We'll have the embassy secured in under ten minutes," Chambers said. "After that, it's hard to say. Without knowing the true extent of the enemy's capabilities, there's no way I can say for sure, but we're hoping four to six hours."

Fischer leaned forward. "Once we're tied into the planet's network, we'll be able to start narrowing the focus of our search. It shouldn't take very long at all after that."

"And what exactly *is* our mission here, Agent Fischer?" Ward asked.

"Sir?"

"I want to know the endgame."

Fischer took a minute to consider the question. If someone would've asked him the same question three months ago, he would've said capturing Young, but now, after seeing everything involved with the Cardinal agenda, he knew Young was only a small part of that.

"The destruction of Cardinal, sir," Fischer finally answered. "We need to dismantle their infrastructure."

"And have we come to a conclusion on who Cardinal is?"

"I don't believe Cardinal is a person," Fischer said. "I think Cardinal is an idea. As to their underlying theology, or what exactly their endgame is, I don't know, but I know we're no longer just talking about one person here. But everything I've seen suggests whatever force is behind Cardinal is here on Saccora. This is where all the evidence leads."

"And what happens when we find it?"

"We destroy it, sir."

Stinson laughed. "Easier said than done. We can't just launch orbit strikes and call it a day. We're going to have to positively identify our targets, regardless of where they are."

Ward nodded. "We're not going to be charging in guns blazing here. There still could be a chance you're wrong about all of this. I want solid intel before we authorize any direct action."

Fischer felt like the conversation was slipping away. He'd been so focused on finding this place that he hadn't taken the time to consider what they'd do once they found it. "So we identify them."

"That will take time," Stinson said. "And without knowing exactly what we're up against, it's impossible to say how long it will take. There are any number of variables in play to estimate that."

"Understood, Captain," Ward said.

"We hold that embassy any longer than a day and people are going to start asking questions," Stinson said.

Fischer wanted to object but didn't. Stinson was right. They couldn't just occupy the place for days on end. Eventually someone would get wise, either figuring out the embassy was under lockdown, or some random patrol would locate *Legend* in the outer system. Any number of things could hinder the mission, and the longer they spent on the ground, the more likely it was that something would go wrong.

"As soon as we drop, we're going to be on the clock," Ward said. "I'll allow Valkyrie leeway operationally, but we're in no position for a prolonged engagement. I want solid intel before you move. Be sure of your targets. I don't have to tell you what's riding on this, and what happens if we get it wrong."

"Yes, sir," Chambers said.

"If we're not seeing progress in twelve hours, I'll pull the plug."

"Understood, sir."

"What about our local units?" Ward asked Stinson.

"I've been going over the fleet records, and it doesn't look like many ships are moved in or out of the system."

"They have the people they want," Eliwood said.

Fischer nodded. "Let me guess, Second Fleet?"

"Got it in one," Stinson said.

Fischer shook his head; he wasn't surprised. Second Fleet had, until three months ago, been commanded by Marcus Young, the disgraced admiral behind the Stonemeyer disaster. While some felt that had been the extent of his involvement, Fischer had always known it had gone deeper. Young had too much ego to be relegated to a simple errand boy. He needed to be involved on a far deeper level, and knowing what he did now, it didn't surprise Fischer at all.

"Are we saying the Alliance ships are going to be involved?" Ward asked.

"I think until we know for sure, it'd be negligent to think otherwise," Fischer said. "At the very least the command crews. But we can't discount the enlisted either, especially from what we've seen here on *Legend*."

"This is a nightmare," Lieutenant Sadao said. "They can't all be Cardinal's people, can they?"

Fischer shook his head. "I don't think we can completely rule out the idea. But even if they aren't, the true Alliance ranks don't know what we know, and what's to stop the command crews from telling them we're some kind of rogue operation and they have orders to shoot us down?"

"We have a verified order package from Admiral Hunter," Ward said.

"That may be the case, sir, but again, the command crew can say whatever they want to say, and it's doubtful the crew would even second-guess it. It's not like they're going to rise up and mutiny just because we say so."

"So what? We drop in-system and pray they don't shoot us as we launch a mission to destroy their headquarters?" Stinson leaned forward, his forearms on the table. "Sir, I'm just playing devil's advocate here, but to me, that doesn't sound like the best scenario. I know we're under blackout conditions, sir, but in this case, I think we need to request additional support."

Fischer's chest tightened at the thought of waiting even a minute longer. They were in a sprint to the finish now. If they let up, even a little, they'd lose the race; he was convinced of that. The longer they waited, the harder it would be to take Cardinal down. He started to say as much when Captain Ward shook his head.

"It would take at least a week for backup units to arrive, and that's assuming they're dispatched immediately." Stinson started to argue, but Ward lifted a hand. "In any other scenario, I would agree with you one hundred percent, Commander, but here, I don't think we have the luxury of time."

Fischer blew out a relieved breath.

"And backup units notwithstanding, there are additional considerations to take into account," Ward said.

Stinson frowned. "Sir?"

"With the exception of *Legend*'s crew, we have no idea who we can trust."

"Trust-ish," Eliwood muttered at the side of the table.

Fischer winced. The comment was, at best, ill-advised, but he couldn't say it was unwarranted. Of all the worst-case scenarios he'd imagined over the years, this was by far the worst: taking the fight to an unknown enemy, with unknown strength, where even his allies could very well turn out to be his enemy.

But do we have another choice? Fischer asked himself. The thought of pulling back and assessing the situation sickened him, but so did pushing forward without backup. They were, well and truly, between a rock and a hard place, and both were deadly. If they didn't go forward with the attack, Cardinal would grow closer to its endgame, whatever that was, and Fischer would not allow that to happen.

"We have to assume they'll know our ship signature from the attack in Astalt," Ward said, bringing Fischer's attention back to the meeting.

"That might be a good thing, sir," Chambers said. Ward raised an eyebrow, and the Saber captain continued, "Well, sir, if they start shooting at us as soon as we drop in, at least we'll know whose side they're on. We wouldn't have to worry about them shooting us in the back when we're least expecting it."

"If they start shooting at us, we'll evade and retreat," Ward said, then raised a hand as Fischer started to object. "We might have the firepower to take on a ragtag fleet of raiders, but we can't take on multiple Alliance warships and hope to come out on top. That's just basic math, and as much as I want to see this thing through to the end, I will not force the issue if it comes to that. We'll retreat and contact Admiral Hunter for further instructions."

"One option would be a ballistic approach," Stinson said. "We make our translation in the outer system, set course and burn until we reach speed, then go dark. Drift in right under their noses. Set a best speed, fly by, launch the birds as we pass by."

Fischer was surprised at the suggestion, especially coming from Stinson, who'd been the voice of opposition throughout much of the briefing.

"We'd have to maintain the run until we were outside sensor range to correct our trajectory," Ward said. "Doesn't put us in a very good position to react should our forces need assistance."

"If the shit hits the fan and our people need help, it won't matter whether we're stealth or not," Stinson countered.

Ward rubbed the tip of his nose with a finger and sighed. "And spin-up time would be about ten minutes. With the engines running at minimum, we'd have to power down our weapons and shield. We'd be defenseless and powerless to shoot back if someone spotted us."

"It's an option, sir. Didn't say it was ideal."

"It's doubtful anyone would see our birds launching," Chambers said. "As long as we can penetrate the embassy's network and shut down their link to the planetary network, we should be able to keep the news of our arrival quiet. At least for a little while."

Ward sat quietly for several minutes, obviously running the scenario through his mind, considering their points and counter-points. It wasn't an easy decision, regardless of what anyone thought. And while Fischer preferred to think of this whole thing as his case, the ultimate responsibility rested on Ward's shoulders alone. What he decided here would not only affect the lives of his crew, but those on the ground and in the ships orbiting the planet. Not to mention the civilians living on the surface, or throughout the Alliance and the Pegasi Empire, who weren't even aware of the conflict.

"All right," Ward said, "let's get our assault teams assembled and prepped. We'll play possum as long as we can, but once we're outed, we'll give them a fight they'll never forget."

CHAPTER 38

Valkyrie Six-One
Inbound to the Holloman Embassy
Ridgecrest City, Saccoran System
22 August 2607

Sheridan sat silently, listening to the hum of the Albatross's engines as they dropped through Saccora's stratosphere, trying his damnedest not to think about the last time he'd dropped onto an Alliance embassy under less than ideal circumstances. But try as he might, images of Hastings and Biagini and Prof, even Wallace and Thomas flooded his mind, an endless stream of memories from the Stonemeyer mission Darkstar. Memories that made him heartbroken and furious at the same time.

His chest tightened; Darkstar Six-One lurching violently around him and as it dropped out of the sky. The blazing fireball of Six-Two as it smashed into the building and rained fire and twisted steel onto the street below. Watching as Ford's body snapped back, a bullet smashing through his helmet, knocking him to the ground. The SUV flipping out from under them, the militia soldiers ripping them from the wreckage.

He gritted his teeth at Biagini's screams, remembering how they'd brutalized her. His stomach turned, her battered face smiling up at him, asking why they were doing this. None of them had understood why the militia had attacked them, not at the time anyway. Now, knowing everything he knew, rage burned in Sheridan's chest, rage he wasn't sure he could contain. Rage he didn't *want* to contain.

I'm going to kill him, Sheridan thought as the face of Marcus Young appeared.

"Hey," Cole said, nudging Sheridan from his thoughts. "You okay?"

Sheridan shook himself. "Fine."

"You don't look it."

"Bad memories."

"Stonemeyer?"

Sheridan nodded. "Seems like every time I get in one of these…"

"That's not going to happen this time," Cole said. "We're ready for it this time."

"I know."

"These assholes aren't going to know what hit them."

Sheridan smiled, wishing he had the confidence his friend did. "Damn straight."

He looked up and down the length of the Albatross's bay. The members of Team Valkyrie were spread throughout, silently preparing themselves for what was coming. They all knew a fight was waiting for them at the end of the flight, all knew the stakes, and all were ready to bring the pain.

Two more assault shuttles and the *Doris* were dropping with them, each shuttle carrying thirty armed augmentees, the *Doris* bringing Fischer, Eliwood and the hacker, Osprey. Chambers hadn't been keen on allowing her access to any of the ship's systems, but using *Doris*'s systems, that was another story and one that didn't expose classified Alliance technology or intelligence.

The team had spent two days training the augmentees on the basics of marksmanship and close-quarters combat, though ideally, their contribution to the mission would be limited to providing rear security once Valkyrie had secured the embassy. To their credit, the crew had taken to the extra duties with a vigor that spoke to their commitment to *Legend*'s mission. And though two days wasn't nearly enough time to properly train and equip the augmentees, the *Legend*'s crew had come through in exemplary fashion. Trainers and trainees alike would have preferred more time to train, but unfortunately that wasn't in the cards for this mission. They all had to work with what they had, and they all had to step up and do what they needed to do.

Including you, Sheridan told himself. *Eyes up. Focus.*

"Time on target, twelve minutes," the Albatross's pilot said over the team's taclink.

"Eyes up, Valkyrie," Master Sergeant Kline said after acknowledging the pilot. "We all know what's riding on this drop. Keep your head in the game. We don't have any way of knowing whether the troops down there are friendly or not, so until we know for sure, we treat everyone, and I do mean everyone, as hostile. Standard ROEs apply—don't shoot unless they present a threat, understood?"

Throughout the bay, the Sabers nodded.

Chambers rose from his seat at the front. "First priority is security for the LZ. Team Two will organize inner and outer perimeters with the augmentation force while Team One secures the interior of the compound. Second priority is the network and communications center. Robbi, how we looking?"

Robalt looked up from his link display. He and Reese were working in tandem, along with Osprey, to infiltrate the embassy's network prior to their landing, but Sheridan could tell from the frustrated look on Robalt's face, they weren't having much luck.

"Working through the DC security is a little tricky, sir," Robalt said. "Especially if we don't want them to know."

"In a few minutes it's not going to matter anyway," Chambers said. "Give it another five minutes; if you can't pick the lock, kick the door in."

Robalt smiled. "That I can do, sir."

"This is kind of messed up, don't you think?" Cole asked Sheridan under his breath.

"What's that?"

"Flying down to engage our own guys."

Sheridan gave Cole a sidelong glance. "Yeah, well, they might not be our guys."

Cole nodded and inhaled a long breath. "Yeah. I guess. Still, doesn't feel right."

"I'm more worried about what we're going to find at this Cardinal outpost," Sheridan said. "We don't have any idea what we're facing down there; could be dozens or hundreds."

"Or thousands," Cole said.

"Exactly."

"We deal with what's right in front of us," Cole said, interrupting Sheridan. "One thing at a time. We're on step one; you're thinking about step one hundred and two. Eyes up, sight picture, target acquisition. That's all we have to worry about."

Sheridan nodded slowly. The problem was that he couldn't just focus on what was in front of him anymore. He knew too much. Knew how much this operation meant, not just for Valkyrie or *Legend*'s crew, but for the entire Alliance, and the thought of failing them weighed heavily on him. But more than that, he feared not fulfilling his promise to his friends from Stonemeyer.

After a moment, Cole slapped Sheridan's arm. "Hey, relax.

Stick with me. I got your back, man. All you need to worry about is having mine, yeah?"

"Yeah," Sheridan said, staring at the deck.

Cole smiled. "That's the look of a stone-cold killer if I've ever seen one. Come on, Blaster, you got this."

"God, I hate that name."

"It's a great name," Cole said, laughing. "It's a badge of honor. You need to wear that shit with pride, my friend. You don't want anyone to forget about it."

"Oh no, we wouldn't want that."

"Hey! We're in," Robalt called from across the bay. "Accessing main security network now."

Reese looked up from his display. "We should have their comms in about thirty seconds. I can either lock them down completely or monitor."

"Monitor for now," Chambers said. "If they start saying anything we don't like, turn them off."

"Roger that, sir."

"That's good for us," Cole told Sheridan.

"Yeah," Sheridan said. "It's about time the good guys win one for once."

CHAPTER 39

Holloman Alliance Embassy
Ridgecrest City, Saccora
22 August 2607

The Albatross's deck shifted under Sheridan's feet, the nose lifting as the engines pitched up, drowning out the whine of the landing struts folding out of the fuselage below him. Ahead of him, the ramp had already lowered into place, and the city lights of Ridgecrest stretched away from them. With almost three hours before dawn, the blinking lights of distant aircraft dotted the darkness.

A panel opened on the left side of this visor, showing him a bird's-eye view of the embassy compound from Cole's drones circling above, the thermal scope highlighting heated areas in varying levels of grays and white. Orange outlines identified nine figures stationed around the compound's security wall. A row of Diplomatic Corps gravcars and flyers were arranged in two rows along the rear of the main building in the center of the complex. A mixture of security and embassy staff filed out of the exit, moving through the collection of vehicles, toward the open area where the Sabers' assault shuttle would touch down.

"Remember," Kline said, moving to the top of the ramp with Chambers. "They're friendlies. Until they're not."

Sheridan tapped his link, minimizing the drone's feed, and followed the rest of Team One down the ramp as the shuttle settled. They kept their weapons at port arms, barrels down, trying to move as unthreateningly as possible. Though Sheridan was doubtful a team of heavily armed MARSOC Marines would look anything *but* threatening, even to those on their side.

Chambers led the team toward the embassy, slowing as three staffers in black suits, flanked by four security guards in charcoal gray uniforms and body armor, approached. The male staffer leading the procession didn't look pleased, his eyes locked on Chambers, the backwash from the shuttle's engines blowing his long brown hair across his face.

"So much for a warm welcome," Cole muttered behind Sheridan. He tapped his link and made adjustments to the drones' flightpaths above them.

"Yeah," Sheridan said, eyes scanning the complex around them. Guards positioned at the two overwatch positions he could see came out of stations, watching the Sabers with keen interest.

"What is the meaning of this?" the staffer demanded, pointing a finger at Captain Chambers. "And whose idea was it to make an unscheduled landing without prior Corps authorization? You're damn lucky our targeting sensors registered your IFF signal before we blew you out of the sky!"

"I'm Captain Eric Chambers, Alliance Special Operations Command. We're here on official fleet orders. Where is the ambassador?"

The staffer frowned and hesitated. "My name is Alexander Clemons, I'm the ambassador's executive assistant. What is the purpose of your visit?"

"That is between me and Ambassador Wantanabe."

"The ambassador is not on site at the moment."

"Then we'll wait for him inside," Chambers said.

"I can't permit you to enter without prior authorization," Clemons said. "And of course, you will not be permitted to bring your weapons inside the compound."

"He can't be serious," Cole whispered.

Sheridan shook his head but didn't answer.

"I'm afraid that will not be possible, Mr. Clemons," Chambers said. "My orders come straight from Fleet Command, which come straight from the president of the Alliance. They supersede any other orders or mandates. You will let us pass and provide us access to your facility. We are hunting a wanted fugitive and require this facility as a base of operations."

"Fleet Command has no authority over the Diplomatic Corps or its resources. You can't just walk in here and commandeer whatever you want at will. Even if such an order exists, this is not my call to make. I will notify the ambassador of your request. You can wait back on your shuttle, Captain." Clemons tapped his link before Chambers could answer, and began working through his menus.

"I'm afraid I can't allow you to make any outgoing calls, Mr. Clemons," Chambers said, taking a step forward.

"You can't *allow* me? I don't know who you think you are, but as I've already explained, you don't have any authority here and—"

"Kill it, Robbi," Chambers said over the taclink.

"Roger," Robalt answered.

Clemons's expression changed from indignation to confusion as his link's holodisplay went blank. He glared at Chambers. "What—? Are you out of your mind, Captain? Interfering with official Diplomatic Corps communications? Captain, you will

273

cease and desist and vacate these premises immediately, before I have you arrested and confined."

"I'm afraid I can't do that, sir," Chambers said. "Now, I need you and your staff to stand down and—"

Behind the group, the two additional shuttles were touching down, kicking up warm gusts of wind. The embassy security guards exchanged worried looks, as if they were starting to understand the hopelessness of their position.

Chambers continued, louder, "My forces are going to secure this compound. No one is allowed to enter or leave. All communications are prohibited until further notice, and you will comply with all our orders or you will be detained."

"Lieutenant Grady," Clemons said.

One of the security guards stepped closer to the staffer, hand on the pistol still holstered at his waist. He was in his thirties, well built, with a military-style high-and-tight haircut and square jaw. Probably only a year or two out from the regular Marine Corps. Unlike the other guards, he wasn't wearing a tactical vest, and his uniform looked neatly pressed and fresh.

Without taking his eyes from Chambers, he said, "Yes, sir."

"These men are trespassing on Diplomatic Corps property in violation of DCR twenty-one dash three. You will place them under arrest and confiscate their weapons."

The order seemed to surprise the lieutenant. He opened his mouth to respond, but no words came out as the dozens of additional troops came streaming out of the shuttles.

"He's got to be shitting his pants right about now," Cole whispered.

"Yeah," Sheridan replied, forgetting for a moment that the man might well have been a Cardinal asset, and sympathizing with the impossible position Clemons had just put him in.

Clemons frowned and turned. "Lieutenant Grady, did you hear me?"

"Uh, yes... yes, sir, I did." He sighed, frowning. "Sir, I don't thin—"

"It is not your job to think, Lieutenant," Clemons snapped. "I have given you an order. You and your men will comply immediately."

Grady straightened, his expression shifting from uncertainty to determination, but Sheridan thought there was still some hesitation there. *Are you one of them or not?* he thought.

"Walker, Daschner, on me." Grady stepped forward, eyes locked on Chambers. "Captain Chambers, you're in violation of—"

Chambers lifted an open hand. "Son, you really need to stand down."

"... of regulation twenty-one dash three, unlawful entry into a restricted Corps facility or structure," the lieutenant continued, ignoring Chambers. "You are hereby ordered to relinquish your weapons and surrender."

The guards behind Grady lifted their rifles, the base model of Sheridan's own MOD27, but kept their muzzles pointing at the ground.

Blood pumped in Sheridan's ears and he adjusted his grip on his own rifle. *Please,* he thought, *don't do this.*

The image of Thomas holding Hastings at gunpoint flashed through his mind, and he squeezed his eyes shut, trying to push away the memory. *No.* He swallowed hard, eyes flicking between Grady and Chambers.

Chambers spoke with a relaxed, confident tone. "Whatever you may be thinking, Lieutenant, this is not going to go down the way you think it is. We have orders from Fleet Admiral Hunter, and we are authorized to be here. There are things going on here that you cannot understand. You are outgunned and overmatched, and despite what you may think, you do not have legal standing.

Please lower your weapon. No one wants to shoot anyone here today."

Grady didn't move.

"Lieutenant?" Clemons snapped again. "Arrest those men!"

"Sir, I—" Grady said.

"Do it!"

"Okay, we need to bring it down a notch before this thing gets out of hand," Chambers said. "I can show you the orders from Fleet Command. See for yourself."

Grady chewed on his lower lip, obviously considering the captain's offer.

Do it, Sheridan thought, mentally willing the man to comply. There really wasn't any other option. Grady and his small team were no match for the Saber team, not to mention their augmentees filling in behind Valkyrie.

"Sir?" one of Grady's men asked.

"Stand by," Grady said. "All right, Captain, let's see those orders."

Sheridan let out a relieved breath.

"What are you doing?" Clemons demanded, grabbing Grady's arm. The lieutenant glared at Clemons, shrugging off the man's hold and stepping toward Chambers.

The captain punched his link, swiped through to the data he wanted, then sent the packet to Grady. It took less than a minute for the security guard to read through the document on this own link, and when he was done, he closed it and turned to his team.

"Stand down."

The guards immediately lowered their weapons, obviously as relieved as Sheridan felt.

"What? No!" Clemons shouted.

Ignoring him, Chambers motioned to Sheridan's team. "Let's get moving. Neal, Reese, secure our friend here. Let's secure those weapons."

"Stop!" a staffer shouted. "You are violating... Stop! You have no authority to—"

"You can't do this!" Clemons shouted as Neal and Reese worked to secure him.

Neal put a hand on his shoulder and said, "If it were me, I'd shut the hell up. Trust me."

Sheridan approached Grady and tapped his visor open. "I'm sorry to do this, but I'm going to need your weapon."

Grady's eyes narrowed for a moment, then widened in recognition. "You're Sheridan. *The* Sheridan. From Stonemeyer, right?"

"That's right," Sheridan said. He wasn't completely surprised by the man's recognition. His face had been plastered on all the news feeds for weeks after he'd returned. The way the man spoke, it was almost reverent.

Grady unslung his rifle and held it out. "My last assignment was the 307th. Hastings was my lieutenant before he got transferred. He was a good man."

Sheridan took the rifle and slung it over one shoulder. "He was."

"It was horrible what happened to him, what happened to everyone. I'm glad you made it out of there."

"Thanks."

Grady gave Clemons a sidelong glance and lowered his voice. "Listen, he's an asshole; everyone knows it. I should've known the money the DC was offering for this posting was too good, but once you start seeing those creds..."

"I hear you."

"What can I do to help?"

The sound of engines pitching up drew their attention to the landing area, where the *Doris* was flaring for landing just behind the assault shuttles. The rhythmic thumping of the sprinter's drive cut through the air, vibrating Sheridan's chest as she slowed, her landing structs folding out from recesses along her underbelly.

Several of the augmentees ducked away from the torrent of wind kicked up before settling onto the ground.

"One of yours?" Grady asked.

"That's right."

"Kind of a piece of shit."

Sheridan chuckled. "Yeah."

"Holy shit, is that who I think it is?"

Sheridan smiled as Fischer stepped off the ramp, Eliwood in tow. "It most definitely is."

Grady shook his head. "You guys really aren't playing around."

"No," Sheridan said. "No, we're not."

CHAPTER 40

Holloman Alliance Embassy
Ridgecrest City, Saccora
22 August 2607

"What do you think about him?" Fischer asked Sheridan. He lifted a chin to Lieutenant Grady, who was leading them through the embassy's main lobby. The remaining guards had been secured along with the staff and were being escorted into the building by a squad of augmentees behind the Valkyrie Team.

"I don't know," Sheridan said. "Said he knew Hastings from back in the day and knew who we were. Didn't seem upset about our being here at all. Comes off as a straight-up guy, offered to help, but if you're asking if he's a Cardinal asset or not, I just don't know."

Their footsteps echoed off the polished marble floor as they made their way through the lobby. The glow of the surrounding city and the embassy's exterior lights shown through a four-story-high wall of glass at the front of the building. Two more guards at the security desk near the back of the room were relieved of their weapons, and augmentees were assigned to control access.

"We'll use this as the main holding area," Chambers said, scanning the lobby. "I want a detail in the guard post outside and a team to provide security for the prisoners. Sergeant Kline, I want two of our people stationed here at all times."

"Roger that, sir. Kennedy, Oliver, you're up."

Both Sabers nodded and moved to either side of the space, splitting their areas of responsibility. The embassy staff were herded into the center of the room and made to sit silently.

"No one has anything to worry about as long as they follow our instructions," Chambers said.

A few of the staffers hurled curses in response, but no one put up a real fight. There was no way of knowing who was a Cardinal asset and who wasn't, so everyone was detained. No exceptions. Once they were able to sort everything out, those not involved would be released, though Fisher didn't think that number would be many. Not this close to Cardinal.

"Where is the ambassador?" Chambers asked when the commotion had settled.

No one answered.

Finally, Lieutenant Grady said, "He's off site, sir. Left about an hour ago with the security chief and an escort. They were scheduled for a meeting with the governor."

"Kind of early for a meeting."

Grady shrugged. "They're not that uncommon, sir. In fact, they've been growing more frequent over the last few weeks."

I'm sure they have, Sheridan thought. If the ambassador was, in fact, a Cardinal asset and was having a clandestine meeting with another Cardinal asset, they'd want to keep that as private as possible.

"Do you know when he's supposed to return?"

"Meeting was scheduled for a couple of hours, but they always run over. The ambo and Governor Adrouin are pretty close."

"That doesn't play well for us," Fischer said. "If he doesn't know already, he'll figure out he's lost contact with the embassy. He'll definitely call in for help from the destroyers. Maybe even the planetary defense forces."

"Doesn't change our mission," Chambers said. "We're still against the clock. This just gives us more incentive. Let's move."

Five minutes later they arrived at the compound's communication center, where they found ten more staffers and two more guards, who were immediately escorted out and detained with the rest. The center was located on the third floor and filled with multiple terminals, the walls covered with holodisplays showing feeds from interior and exterior security cameras, local news channels, and maps of the city, system and sector.

Reese and Robalt immediately began syncing their equipment with the embassy's off-line network, and soon both were swiping through data faster than Fischer could follow.

"Jesus, there's a lot of data to sort through here," Robalt said, shaking his head. He'd taken his helmet off, and light from the screens in front of him reflected off his face. "We're talking thousands of entries a day, comm logs, security reports, reports from all over the sector, status logs. It's going to take a minute to go through all of this."

"Focus on the local comm logs first," Fischer said.

"Tap into the emergency response band too," Chambers said. "And can we run a network sweep for the ambo? We should be able to get his linkID from the embassy's records."

"Already on top of it," Reese said. "Setting up the tracker protocol now."

Robalt looked up at Fischer. "You know, it'd be helpful to have a starting point. Following these logs across the city could literally take days."

Fischer nodded and tapped his link. "Osprey, any luck on the trace?"

The decision to leave the hacker with Jones on the *Doris* had been Chambers's, and the point had been nonnegotiable. Regardless of whether the embassy staff were Cardinal assets or not, they all knew there was information stored there that was not only critical to the Alliance but to other nations as well. They'd been able to contain what she'd seen and been allowed access to aboard the *Legend,* but they all agreed allowing her access to the embassy's systems would be grossly negligent, regardless of whose side she claimed to be on.

"I've narrowed it down to the northeast sector," Osprey said. *"Working through several security partitions to get a better location now."*

"Send me the network links to those local nodes," Fischer said. "That should speed things up on our end."

"Coming at you."

"Here," he told Robalt, forwarding the data to the Saber's terminal. "Focus your search on those nodes."

"Northeast, eh?" Robalt said. "That checks out."

Behind him, Reese worked his hands over the city map, enlarging that area of the city. The nodes appeared as yellow pulsing dots with streaming yellow lines interconnecting them.

"It could be anywhere," Reese said, panning across the top-down view of the city. He zoomed in occasionally, getting better looks at buildings or complexes, but none stood out.

"All right, I got it," Osprey said over the taclink.

A surge of anticipation flowed through Fischer as he reached for his link. "What is it?"

"Relay seven-four-two-eight," Osprey said. *"That's the node Young's message came through. Working on an origination point now."*

A node near the top left corner of the map flashed red, and Reese immediately shifted his focus, centering it. The node was surrounded by several high-rises and blocks of office buildings and commercial spaces, as well as several residential towers interspersed among them.

"Filtering out other traffic," Robalt said. "Oh, yeah, there's been a shit-ton of traffic through that node."

"To or from," Fischer asked.

"Both. The last message to go through there was sent this morning. Give me a second, I can give you the sender ID. Okay, and now, the address."

A new pulsing dot appeared on the holomap.

"Pulling location data now," Reese said. "It'll take just a second to render the layout."

Chambers joined Fischer in front of the map, watching as the electronics specialist worked. "Cole, let's get eyes on."

"Already on it," the drone pilot said. "Coordinating with Guerrero. Time on target three minutes."

"Where are we?" Fischer asked.

"One sec," Reese said. The map zoomed out again, and a green square appeared over the embassy.

Fischer traced a path through the city streets and frowned. "What's that, about eight klicks?"

Reese tapped a command into his link and a blue line began to draw itself across the city, connecting the two locations. "Flight time for the Albatrosses: six minutes."

"Six minutes," Fischer repeated, eyes locked on the pulsing dot marking the Cardinal's compound. Three months ago he'd all but convinced himself they'd never get to this point. That the case was just going to fade away into obscurity and Young's victims would never get the justice they deserved.

But this isn't about them, is it? Fischer asked himself, not really wanting to know the answer. His desire to find Young went deeper than some simple pursuit of justice. Desire didn't encapsulate the drive he felt, and it didn't have anything to do with bringing justice to Young's victims.

Fischer needed to see him at the end. *Needed* Young to know it was him that brought this thing to a close. Anything less would be a failure.

"What about security?" Chambers asked, bringing Fischer's thoughts back to the map in front of him.

"Preliminary data coming in now," Cole called from across the room.

Reese went to work importing the information. He turned and frowned at Fischer. "Uh, sir, can you back up just a bit? That's fine, thanks."

A flash of blue appeared in the air where Fischer had been standing, and multiple blue lines grew out from the epicenter. Within seconds they'd formed the outline of a building and were branching off and splitting in additional lines as the scans from Cole's drones acquired more information. The team gathered around as the render progressed, watching the lines crisscross and form additional buildings complete with internal layouts.

Three identical towers were arranged around a central octagonal building, each with multiple landing pads at various levels. The center building was half the height of the twenty-story outer towers, but twice as wide. A series of tubular walkways crisscrossed between the towers, connecting the outer towers to each other and the central building.

As the buildings continued to render, the interior layouts became more distinct, and heat signatures from individuals inside began to populate the outer spaces. A running tab appeared above the projection, counting the number of targets as the drones acquired them.

"Whoa, hold up," Cole said, tapping a series of commands into his terminal. Red icons appeared, highlighting ten locations around the perimeter of the compound and on top of the three outer towers. "I've got multiple anti-aircraft and missile batteries, autocannon turrets, and sensors most ships would be lucky to have. We're definitely not dealing with amateurs here."

"I could've told you that," Sheridan muttered.

"Pulling the drones back," Guerrero said. "They're stealthy, but if those bastards pick them up, they'll definitely know someone's looking at them."

"Agreed." Chambers crossed his arms. "Firepower like that rules out an airborne infil, not to mention exfil. The birds definitely aren't landing in that."

"Does anyone else think that complex looks a little strange?" Eliwood asked, crossing her arms, frowning.

Fischer took a fresh look, trying to see what his partner was picking up. "What?"

"Doesn't look like any raider outpost I've ever seen. Those look like office spaces. Hell, if not for the amount of firepower they're packing, it'd look like just another commercial office complex."

"Maybe it was at one point," Sheridan suggested.

Fischer looked to Robalt. "Do we have any developer or owner information?"

"Yeah, hold on." The tech specialist tapped a few commands into his terminal, then shook his head, chuckling. "I'll give you one guess who built it."

"Alistair Holdings," Fischer said, not surprised.

"Got it in one."

"Well, at least we know we're looking at the right place," Sheridan said.

"Yeah, but how do we get there? That's the issue," Eliwood said.

"We've got the Ramseys," Sheridan suggested, stepping closer to the projection.

"But only four launchers," Kline said. "Hitting multiple

targets at once is out of the question, and I guarantee once we start shooting, someone's going to get wise. Even if we managed to take out their defenses, we'd be landing in a hot LZ, under fire and outgunned."

"I'm getting a massive EM signal coming from that southeast tower," Robalt said. The building in question grew to fill the entire projection, the electromagnetic field glowing yellow against the blue wireframe render.

"What is it?" Chambers asked.

Robalt shrugged. "Hard to say, sir. There's multiple signatures, and the energy reading's through the roof. Looks like a dozen relay nodes. I'd say you're looking at their central command and control facility. The processing power they have their rivals *Legend*'s for sure."

"Can you tap into it?" Fischer asked. "See what we're dealing with?"

"Everything's self-contained and off-line," Robalt said, shaking his head. "Makes sense though, it's the same thing we do for ours. Local access only. Keeps everything nice and tidy."

"Looks like the central building there is where most of the comm traffic is coming from," Reese said.

"Geographically separated, off-line systems, protected by anti-air and who knows how many anti-intrusion measures and security forces," Robalt said. "That's your target right there, sir. Any information worth going to that extent to protect is information you'll want to have."

Fischer pointed to the landing pad two levels above the data center. "We can land here."

"If it weren't for the anti-air, I'd agree with you," Chambers said.

"Assaulting from the ground and ascending sixteen stories isn't ideal," Kline said.

"No, it's not," Chambers agreed.

"What about a HALO jump?" Sheridan suggested.

"A HALO jump onto a roof isn't as easy as it sounds," Kline said. "Not to mention a roof with the kind of defenses we're talking about here. Besides, once we're on the ground, there's still the issue of air support. We get into a fight, no one's coming to pull us out of that."

"So we have two objectives," Chambers said. "The intel and the defenses. Regardless of how we get in, we're going to need the birds to get out. Exfilling through the city is out of the question considering all the unknown variables."

"To take out their weapons, we're going to need to be tied directly into their systems," Robalt said. "Either that or standing in front of the controls."

"The problem is we don't know where those controls are," Kline said. "And turning that place upside down looking for them isn't a feasible option."

Chambers nodded. "Agreed. Okay, let's work the problem. Priorities?"

"We have to take out that security hub," Robalt said. "As long as that's up and running, nothing else matters."

"Okay, how do we locate the hub?"

"Monitor their personnel for patrol patterns," Cole suggested. "At some point they'll probably have to report to the office, yeah? I can map their routes with the drone's IR. Should be able to work it out from that."

"How long?" Chambers asked.

Cole blew out a long breath. "A couple of hours."

"We don't have that kind of time."

"We could use a tick," a new voice said, the words echoing across the room.

Everyone in the room paused, exchanging confused glances with each other.

"Who the hell was that?" Chambers asked.

"Oh no," Fischer groaned, knowing instantly.

"Oh, just your friendly network intrusion specialist is all," Osprey said. *"Sounds like you guys need a hand."*

CHAPTER 41

The *Doris*
Holloman Alliance Embassy
Ridgecrest City, Saccora
22 August 2607

"Do you have any idea how many laws you've broken?" Chambers demanded, striding up the cargo ramp into *Doris*'s cargo bay.

Osprey sat back from the holodisplay she'd been working on and leaned back against the bulkhead. She propped her feet up on the crate next to the display and said, "Oh, I don't know, at least twenty."

"How did you bypass the embassy's security protocols?" Chambers asked.

Osprey lifted both eyebrows. "Uh, hacker…"

"You were given strict instructions on what you could and could not access."

"Hey, I'm sorry, I got curious," she said. "Plus, I figured eventually you guys were going to ask for my help anyway, so I just got a head start. You *do* need my help, don't you?"

Chambers hesitated, his jaw muscles clenching, obviously conflicted. He sighed, looking up at the bay's ceiling and shaking his head. Finally, he asked, "Okay, what's a tick?"

Osprey smiled and leaned forward, clapping her hands once, then rubbing them together. "You're wanting to tap into a secure network, right? Not tied into the planetary network?"

"That's right."

"Okay, so we use a tick." The way she said it implied Chambers should've known what she was talking about, but the captain just shook his head, obviously as confused as the rest of them.

Osprey sighed. She held up her thumb and index finger a centimeter apart. "Tiny microbots that physically attach to their network nodes, giving us outside access."

"And when the counter-intrusion systems fry the connection?" Robalt asked. "I've heard of those things before, and they're not as useful as you might think. Once the network security routines discover the breach, they'll automatically fry the connection, severing the link and alerting them to the fact that someone is trying to subvert their security measures. That's sure to get someone's attention."

"Ah, true. But that's what the Chameleon is for."

"Chameleon?" Chambers asked.

"It masks itself using the same resonance frequency and internal code. The network security routines won't even know it's there."

"Are you saying you can infiltrate their security network without being discovered?" Chambers asked.

Osprey rocked her head back and forth, as if she were rolling the idea around in her head before answering. "It's possible. Course, I can't make any guarantees with the equipment I have here."

"And what exactly would you need to make it work?"

"Not a lot. A couple of multi-connection links with quantum

network access, a high-resolution VR input and firmware, with redundant backup cores and modulated I/O stream."

Chambers laughed. "Is that all?"

"Oh, and a couple of your surveillance drones and a double mocha espresso, no foam."

Chambers turned to Robalt and Reese, who were standing near the back of the bay, just behind Fischer, looking like he wanted to strangle her. He spoke through clenched teeth. "I take it one of you understood what the hell she just said."

Robalt cleared his throat. "Yes, sir."

"And do we have any of that equipment?"

"No, sir, we don't," Reese said. "But the embassy does."

"Of course it does." Chambers gave the ceiling of the bay a look as if to ask, "Why me?"

"Get me the gear and thirty minutes and you'll be good for your little attack mission," Osprey said, smiling. "Cardinal won't ever see it coming."

Chambers glared at Fischer.

"What kind of access will you have?" Fischer asked. "I expect even with a physical connection, someone's going to notice if you start turning off their security protocols. And they're definitely going to notice when their sensor network goes off-line."

"Incremental, intermittent network failure," Osprey said. "Happens sometimes to larger networks, especially one as big as we're talking about. Just with the information I pulled from your drones, I could tell they're pushing a lot of high-bandwidth data through their network. It's fairly common, actually. You set up a network for the size of operation you have, not the one you might have in the future. Before too long your network has tripled in size and you start running into bandwidth issues and lag."

"Incremental, intermittent network failure," Robalt said, rubbing his chin. "It could work."

"See, told ya," Osprey said.

"Robbi?" Chambers asked.

"You only kill the systems you need at the time you need them," Robbi explained. "Instead of taking the entire system off-line, you just drop them temporarily. Most security networks are set up in zones, so we can just shut down the particular zone we need as we need it; then once we're done, we switch it back on."

"And no one will be suspicious about their security zones dropping off-line all of a sudden?" Chambers asked.

"Oh, they'll eventually get wise, sir," Robalt said. "But it should at least give us enough time to infiltrate the compound."

"How much time are we talking about here?"

"That really depends on how good their people are," Osprey said. "If it were me, I'd start running a broad-spectrum network diagnostic as soon as the network started dropping. The Chameleon isn't foolproof, and once they start tracing the command input origin, odds are they'll figure out what's going on and shut down the node."

"How much time?" Chambers repeated.

"For a pro? Five, maybe ten minutes. For your average tech? Fifteen. Probably."

"Fifteen minutes," Chambers said. "Not a lot of time."

Osprey pursed her lips and nodded, agreeing with the captain's sentiment.

"How long would it take to locate the security center once you're tied into it?" Chambers asked.

"Shit, fifteen, twenty seconds. If that."

"As soon as we hit the security center, they're going to know something's wrong," Kline said.

"But they won't know what they're up against," Chambers said. "All right, what's our priority here, Agent Fischer?"

"Sir?"

"We're operating under two different, but not mutually exclusive, mandates: destroy and disrupt the raider's ability to make war against the Alliance, and locate Admiral Young. As we've already seen from the Astalt raid and the intel collected from the raiders, there is a lot more going on with this Cardinal agenda than previously thought. Besides Young's capture, what do you need to accomplish your mission?"

"Well, sir, and as much as it pains me to say it, I don't think Admiral Young is a priority anymore. Not with everything we've learned about Cardinal and their operation."

"What the hell are you talking about?" Sheridan snapped. "Young *is* the target. He's the only thing that matters. All those people who died on Stonemeyer—"

Fischer held up a hand. "I didn't mean to imply that he wasn't a target. Believe me, I want to catch the son of a bitch too, but Cardinal, as a whole, represents a much larger threat to the Alliance than Young ever did. Even if he is alive, we *know* who he is; we don't know who else may be working for them."

Sheridan looked like he wanted to argue, but he kept silent.

"Look, Allen—" Fischer broke off as Sheridan turned away from him, a mask of rage and disgust plastered across his face. A knot twisted in Fischer's gut. He needed to bring Sheridan back. "Young is still a priority, but there are still hundreds—if not thousands—of people working for Cardinal that we haven't identified, and if everyone involved is getting their orders from this place, it stands to reason that the identities of those people could be somewhere in those cores."

"It's a big 'if,'" Chambers said.

"It is," Fischer said. "But it's the best thing we've got, and it's potentially the break we've been looking for. If the identities of Cardinal's assets are stored in there, that's the only thing that matters. Nothing else. Not Young, not the Pegasi, nothing."

"And what if they're not?" Chambers asked.

"Then we'll have to cross that bridge when we come to it," Fischer said. "Right now, that's our best option. The fact that the whole of the Alliance has been infiltrated by Cardinal will eventually get out, and once it does, all hell will break loose. If we're going to have any chance at containing the fallout, we're going to need that information."

Chambers was silent for several moments, looking over the projection of Cardinal's compound. He sighed and shook his head. "I don't like it."

Fischer stepped forward. "Captain, I—"

"I don't like it," Chambers repeated, cutting Fischer off, "but I don't see that there's any other options. Rocha, your team has the security center. Nguyen, you're on intel retrieval. Plan accordingly." He turned to Kline. "Let's get the team kitted out for a double HALO, Sergeant."

"Roger that, sir."

"Robbi, help our network intrusion specialist into the embassy. Get her whatever she needs."

"Roger that, sir," Robalt said.

"Let's move, people!" Kline shouted, already descending *Doris*'s ramp. "Eyes up!"

Sheridan moved past Fischer, refusing to make eye contact. Fischer reached out, grabbing his arm. "Young is still on the list, Allen."

The corporal glared at Fischer, grinding his teeth. Finally, he said, "Yeah." He pulled his arm free and followed the rest of the Sabers out of the bay.

"He'll be all right," Robalt said, coming up beside Fischer. "Just a little butt hurt is all. He'll get over it."

"Yeah," Fischer said. What he'd said had been true, but he couldn't help thinking he'd betrayed the Saber somehow. He desperately wanted to take it back, phrase it differently, hell, not even say it at all. Sheridan had survived one of the most horrible events Fischer had ever investigated; he'd been shot, beaten, betrayed and left for dead. He'd lost friends, watched them get killed, brutalized, and tortured. And Fischer had just implied the man responsible for all of that no longer mattered.

Nice move, Fish. Nice move, he thought, looking away from the projection. "Shit."

CHAPTER 42

Valkyrie Six-One
Skies over Ridgecrest City
Saccora
22 August 2607

Sheridan rolled his shoulders, trying to shift the weight of the thruster pack on his back, more than a little glad he only had to carry it for the duration of the jump. The exosuit he wore over his combat fatigues was too bulky to make precise movements while standing, but once in the air, it turned him into an aerodynamic threat from above.

He flexed his hands, watching the control readouts on his visor. Small thrusters mounted below his wrists would allow him to control his course, and larger thrusters on his ankles would slow his descent when he neared the surface, bringing him to a gentle twenty miles per hour before touching down. Though before today, his target had been an open field at MARSOC Training Command, not the roof of a twenty-story skyscraper, and from this high, that target was minuscule to say the least.

He'd done dozens of high-altitude-low-opening jumps

throughout training, but this was his first combat jump. True, the navigational systems took care of most of the hard work, but Sheridan still had to make the flight adjustments, and as much as he thought of himself as a warfighter, he was no pilot.

They'd already completed one extended orbit of the compound, waiting for Osprey to work her magic and find them a target. Sheridan didn't like the idea of relying on a criminal for the operational intel, but it wasn't like he, or any of them for that matter, had a choice. He couldn't believe Fischer trusted her at all. Still couldn't believe what he'd said about Young.

"What happens if she doesn't find it?"

"Don't know," Sheridan said.

"I guess our definition of expedient and hers are different."

"Yeah," Sheridan said.

He blew out a long breath and flexed his hands, watching the icons for his aerofins move on his HUD, trying to clear his head. How did Young *not* matter? Fischer knew better than anyone what the bastard had done on Stonemeyer; how could he say he didn't matter? Young was *everything*!

"Hey, you okay? Sheridan?"

"Yeah," Sheridan said through clenched teeth. "Fine."

"You still thinking about what Fischer said about Young?"

Sheridan didn't answer.

"We're going to get that bastard," Cole said. "You know that, right?"

Sheridan nodded.

"I swear to God, Blaster, the confidence you're exuding right now is ridiculous. Come on, man, get your head in the game."

Sheridan took a long breath and pushed everything but the mission out of his mind.

Eyes up, Saber, he told himself, watching the mission time slowly tick higher. Going into battle preoccupied was something his MARSOC instructors had repeatedly warned him against.

Settle your business before you go downrange. Don't take anything with you; leave it all on the field.

"I'm good," Sheridan said. "Eyes up."

Cole held Sheridan's gaze through their visors, obviously gauging his friend's sincerity. Sheridan grinned and gave him a friendly shove. "I'm good, for shit's sake. What are you, my mother, all of a sudden?"

"Just making sure you're a hundred percent. I know what this means to you."

Sheridan tapped the side of his helmet with a finger. "I'm here."

"Good. Because I don't want to have to explain to Neal why you aren't buying her a beer after this whole thing is over."

"Wait, what's that—"

Captain Chambers's icon appeared on Sheridan's HUD, followed by his voice through Valkyrie's taclink. *"Valkyrie Actual to all Valkyrie elements, be advised, locational data being uploaded to the milnet at this time. One-Alpha, we found you guys a target."*

Sheridan's pulse quickened as Rocha acknowledged, and a second later a series of waypoints and GPS data appeared on his HUD. A miniature version of the compound projection in the embassy's control room appeared center screen on his visor, a red outline drawing itself around a corner section of the east tower.

Chambers continued, *"The security center is located here, on the twenty-second floor. There's no direct access, but Osprey is confident she'll be able to disrupt the building's internal network long enough for you to make your way down from the roof. Team Two will be assaulting the data center in the west tower."*

"How much time do we have?" Rocha asked.

"She'll wait until you're in position, then kill the network. By then, we'll have worked out a best-speed route down to the center," Chambers said.

Sheridan and Cole exchanged glances, both sharing the same confused expression.

Cole mouthed, "How long?"

"Roger that, Actual," Rocha said. "How much time will we have after touchdown?"

"Five, maybe six minutes. You're going to have to move fast."

"Roger that, sir," Rocha said.

"We'll monitor your descent from here and keep you advised of any issues. Actual clear."

When the channel closed, Cole said, "What the hell? Five minutes? There's no way we can clear down eight levels in five minutes."

Rocha shook her head. "We're going to have to double-time it."

"Sarge, I—" Cole started.

"I don't want to hear it, Cole," Rocha snapped, cutting him off. "We've got our orders. We will carry them out to the best of our ability. We're going to take out that hub, understood? What-ever it takes."

"Roger that," Cole said.

The Albatross's internal comms chimed. *"Heads up back there. We'll be at the updated drop zone in about two minutes."*

"All right, Team," Rocha said, standing. Her movements weren't smooth. The exosuits used for HALO jumps weren't built for walking, they were built for flying. Or more accurately, falling with style.

The light at the end of the bay flashed orange as the ramp unlocked and began folding open. Cold air washed over them as they stepped toward the top of the ramp. Occasionally Sheridan caught sight of Ridgecrest's night lights through breaks in the clouds. Waypoints appeared on his HUD, giving him coordinates to follow for the jump that would bring him right down on the roof of the target building.

"Thirty seconds."

It's bigger than it looks, Sheridan told himself, staring at the glowing mass of the city. Standing on the ground, looking up at the tall buildings, it was hard to think of them as small, but up here, looking down, even the largest skyscraper looked like a toy.

"All right, people," Staff Sergeant Rocha said over the taclink. "This is it. No fuckups. Watch your altitude and stay on course. HALO jumps are tricky in the best of circumstances, but hitting a target as small as we're talking is... well, if you don't make it, you're going to be on your own. And you all know what we're up against here. Eyes up, Team."

"Eyes up," the team chorused back.

The orange strobe above them flashed to green.

"Go! Go! Go!" Rocha shouted.

Hanover and Vega were out first, followed by Neal and Cole, then Sheridan. He stepped off the edge of the ramp and became weightless, buffeted by cold wind as he plummeted toward the surface. The three Sabers below him appeared on his HUD as green triangles, all following the same heading. An altimeter ticked down in the center of his vision, rapidly decreasing.

He passed through the cloud layer ten seconds later, the city stretching out dozens of kilometers below him. Cardinal's compound was in the northwestern quadrant, marked with a yellow triangle. Occasionally a directional arrow would appear, advising Sheridan to adjust his course, keeping him on target. If he missed, there would be no rejoining his team, he'd either have to find a way rejoin his team or hotstep it back to the embassy, and considering what they were up against, neither proposition was appealing.

"Valkyrie Six-one, One Alpha, Team is clear. Proceed to over-watch position," Sergeant Rocha said over the taclink.

"Roger that, One, proceeding to overwatch. Good luck down there."

The altimeter flashed below five thousand feet, the lines of streets and outlines of buildings becoming more and more distinct as he fell. His flight computer alerted him to a number of aircraft in his vicinity and began calculating adjustments to his course should any of them veer into his path. Crashing through an unsuspecting shuttle would cut his trip short really quick.

If not for the wind buffeting against him and the ground growing steadily closer below him, the night might have been peaceful. His helmet's sound dampening reduced the roaring wind to a minor whistle, and the aerothrusters on his back kept him from tumbling uncontrollably through the night sky. But knowing what waited for him and his team at the end of this drop made enjoying the serene descent more than a little difficult.

An alert sounded as he passed three thousand feet, and a secondary timer appeared, giving him the countdown to when he would have to activate his boots' retro thrusters and his wrists' stability controls.

"Five-Alpha and Five-Bravo are feet dry," Hanover said over the taclink. His icon on Sheridan's HUD put the two snipers on the north tower of Cardinal's compound, from where he'd provide overwatch support for both teams. *"Primary LZ clear. Doesn't look like anyone's minding the store."*

"Roger that, Five," Chambers said.

At five hundred feet, Sheridan's altimeter alarm sounded. He flipped over, locking his legs out under him, and activated his boot thrusters. The exosuit locked into place automatically, keeping his legs from buckling under the force of the blast. He put his hands out, firing his wrist thrusters to keep himself upright and on course, following the instructions from his onboard flight computer.

The thrusters kicked up a cloud of dust seconds before he landed, the thrusters automatically deactivating as his boots touched down. He dropped to a knee, his exosuit flexing to absorb the impact, then stood, the exosuit disengaging around him. Latches and bolts unlocked, and the frame opened, allowing the suit to fall away as Sheridan stepped out of it. The exosuit folded up onto itself, becoming a small bundle the Sabers could either carry with them or leave depending on the situation. Sheridan stashed his with the others and joined Cole and Neal at the far side of the roof.

Cole motioned to one of the autocannons a meter away. The twin-barreled guns pointed down at the roof. The internal electronics were quiet, that was a good sign, but just being so close to the thing gave Sheridan pause. Even wearing full kit, his armor would do nothing against the thirty-millimeter solid tungsten projectiles they fired at over a thousand rounds a minute.

"So far, so good," Cole said.

Sheridan nodded. "For now."

"It'll be fine. If they knew we were here, I think we'd know."

Neal took a knee on the far side of the turret. "Eyes on the door."

"Valkyrie Actual, One-Alpha, we are on target and requesting infil route to target," Rocha said, stepping out of her exosuit, moving out of the way for Richards to land.

"Uploading now, One-Alpha," Chambers said.

"Don't forget," Rocha said to her team. "This is a sprint, not a marathon. If it's a threat, take it out. We're not taking prisoners here. Make your shots count. They lie where they drop."

"Be advised," Chambers said, *"Bravo team is on target as well and standing by."*

"Roger."

A new panel appeared on Sheridan's HUD, showing him the fastest route through the building to their destination six floors down. The maintenance access would take them down through two levels of mechanical spaces, to the top-level offices, to another stairwell that would lead them down to the security office.

"Section security will be down in ten seconds, stand by," Chambers said.

"Sheridan, once it's down, you go," Rocha said.

"Roger that, Sarge." Sheridan pulled his MOD27 into his shoulder and blew out a long breath. Bouncing slightly on the balls of his feet, he readied himself to charge forward. There were no friendlies ahead. Everyone he saw with a gun would get three center mass, no matter what. There would be no orders to drop weapons or put hands in the air. He gritted his teeth.

Something mechanical whirred behind them, followed by a chorus of electronic beeps.

"Oh shit," Cole said.

Sheridan turned just in time to see the autocannon turret rise off its bracket, pointing up into the dark, early morning sky. Across the roof, two panels on a raised platform opened, and a missile launcher appeared, spinning up and around, mirroring the autocannon's movements.

"Back up," Cole said.

"What the fuck is happening?" Neal asked.

"They're tracking something," Cole said.

"Valkyrie Actual, One-Alpha, the enemy weapon systems up here are activating," Rocha said. "Please advise."

"Stand by, One, we're working through an issue back here," Chambers said.

"An issue?" Cole asked. "What the hell kind of—"

Rocha raised a hand, silencing any further comment. "Actual, One-Alpha, do we abort?"

The autocannon turret's twin barrels spun briefly before stopping. They rotated one hundred and eighty degrees, spinning, then stopped again.

"If those systems are coming back online, what about the intrusion countermeasures?" Sheridan asked.

"Lock it up," Rocha snapped. "Actual, what's the call?"

"We lost control over the compound's active defenses," Chambers explained. "We're having trouble keeping the systems locked down. We just lost internal security."

"We need to get the hell out of here," Cole said. "They're going to know we're here, if they don't already."

The idea of aborting terrified Sheridan, and his mind raced, trying to come up with another option. If they didn't have control of the building's internal security systems, any move they made would set off the alarms and bring the cavalry in. If they couldn't make it to the security office and shut down the system…

Sheridan moved to the edge of the roof, looking over the waist-high retaining wall. "Hanover, can you see the security office from your location?"

"Affirmative, but I don't have a clear shot through the plastiglass."

"Sheridan, what the hell are you doing?" Cole asked.

Sheridan eyed the collection of exosuits, a plan forming in his mind. "If we don't get the system shut down quick, it's mission over."

"Yeah," Cole said, obviously confused.

"The security center is six floors down." Sheridan pointed over the side. "If they're already looking for targets, they've got to be at least a little suspicious, which means the element of surprise is quickly going away. We need to get in there and shut the entire system down for good."

Rocha stepped up to them. "What's on your mind, Sheridan?"

Sheridan put a hand on Cole's shoulder. "Come on, we're going to go for another fall."

CHAPTER 43

East Tower, Cardinal Compound
Ridgecrest City, Saccora
22 August 2607

"I want to go on the record here and say that this is a horrible idea," Cole said, sliding his arms through the frame of his exosuit.

Beside him, Sheridan had just finished donning his and was waiting for the suit to sync back up with his link and tactical helmet. After a second, his remaining fuel and the suit's integrity popped onto his HUD. "Thirty-five percent."

"Not a lot of room for error," Rocha said. "You hard stop and it's going to empty quick. You'll only have about ten seconds."

"It'll be more than enough," Sheridan said, flexing his hands, watching the aero controls respond on his HUD. He turned to Cole. "You wait ten seconds and come right after me, okay?"

Cole flexed his hands, and the aerofins on the back of his suit folded out from their recesses, then retracted. "Yeah."

"Once we're in, we can clear the route for the rest of you to come down and shut the system down at the same time."

"You sure about this, Corporal?" Rocha asked.

Sheridan nodded. "Positive. It'll be fine."

"Here's the bang," Neal said, holding out a palm-sized block of explosive. "Slap it on and get the hell out of the way."

"Thanks," Sheridan said, taking the explosive and slipping it inside a pouch and securing the cover.

"One-Alpha, Actual, be advised, we just lost our connection to the tick," Chambers said. *"Their security systems will be coming back online in a matter of seconds. Recommend you abort mission."*

"Negative, Actual," Rocha answered. "We are deviating from the mission parameters. Stand by. Hanover, you have the count?"

"Roger that," the sniper replied.

She nodded at Sheridan. "Go."

Sheridan walked to the retaining wall and looked over the edge. He clenched his jaw and said, "Eyes up." Then he jumped over the wall.

As soon as he cleared the roof, he jammed his thumb on his boot thruster controls. The exosuit's frame locked around his legs as the rockets fired, reflecting orange and red from the glass facade of the building that was nothing more than a blur.

"Five," Hanover said.

Sheridan barely heard him, trying to ignore the suit's proximity warning alarm and focus on his flight controls.

"Four."

A wind gust pushed him sideways and he bumped into the side of the building, cracking the glass and knocking him slightly off course. He grunted, gritting his teeth as he reached out, using his wrist thrusters to correct his trajectory.

"Three. Correct right."

I know, Sheridan thought, feeding more power to the wrist thrusters.

An alarm sounded and a warning flashed on his HUD: thirty percent fuel.

"Two."

He pushed the boots to max power. His stomach turned as they fired, and his body lurched as if he'd just landed in a pool of water after falling from the high-dive. He had just enough presence of mind to pull the explosive block from his pouch just as Hanover announced, "One," over the taclink, and he slapped it against the plastiglass.

He used his thrusters to "fly" sideways, away from the window, and shouted, "Now!"

The window exploded in a shower of glass and flame. The blast wave slammed against Sheridan, pushing him farther away as additional impact and proximity warnings rang in his helmet. He twisted around, aiming his body at the now open window, and fired all his thrusters at full power. There was a slight delay before the power hit maximum, but when it did, it was like someone had shot Sheridan out of a railgun. As soon as he cleared the window, he killed the thrusters, but his momentum carried him over a row of computer terminals, legs smacking against metal, and he spun into two technicians who'd never had a chance to move.

The exosuit absorbed most of the impact, and Sheridan landed in a heap, tangled with the two other men. He pushed one off and slammed his hand against the suit release. Angry and confused shouts echoed throughout the center as Sheridan lunged forward, out of the still-opening suit, pulling his pistol from its holster and searching for the closest target.

Cole shouted something over the taclink Sheridan didn't quite catch as he fired two rounds into a security guard coming around the end of the row. The guard hadn't had time to pull his sidearm and never made a sound as he hit the floor. Sheridan turned, found another target, and put three rounds into a second guard as more screams and shouts filled the room.

Two unarmed technicians at the far side of the room put their hands in the air as Sheridan turned on them, both sharing the same terrified expression.

"Everybody, face down on the ground now!" Sheridan shouted.

"Sheridan, the door!" It was Hanover.

Two more guards appeared to Sheridan's right, their weapons already up. Sheridan ducked back, firing from the hip as he sidestepped to the right, getting himself off the "X." The first rounds went wide, sparking off the electronics mounted on the wall. A single bullet caught the first guard in the hip, spinning him into the second, but gave Sheridan enough time to push out to full extension. He fired again, putting another round into the guard he'd just shot, then two more into the next.

"The window!" Hanover said. *"Get Cole!"*

Sheridan looked and saw two gloved hands holding onto the bottom of the window frame, Cole's helmet just coming up into view. He pushed a chair out of the way and lunged forward, reaching the window a second later and grabbing his friend's arm.

"I got you!" he shouted. He pulled with everything he had, putting a boot against the wall, pushing hard. For a moment it didn't feel like he was going to be able to lift him. Cole's body weight and kit alone put him at over two hundred and twenty pounds, but add the exosuit, and he was closer to two fifty. He put his other boot against the wall and heaved, muscles straining; a moment later he felt movement.

"Come on!" he shouted. Cole put an arm over the edge and pulled himself up. Sheridan, still holding one arm, stepped back to give him room to come in.

"Got it!" Cole grunted, getting a leg over. "That was clo—"

Sheridan didn't hear the shots, but felt Cole's body jerk as the bullets hit his chest. The impact knocked Cole back, and Sheridan could feel him slipping from his grasp. Something slammed into the back of Sheridan's shoulder, sending him stumbling forward. Stars danced in his vision as pain lashed through his back. A second impact at his side dropped Sheridan to one knee, and Cole's arm slipped free.

"No!" Sheridan shouted, falling forward, reaching. He missed Cole's hand by inches and could only watch as his friend fell away. "Cole!"

A round zipped past his head, then another and another. Instincts and training forced Sheridan to the floor. He rolled away from the window, gritting his teeth at the pain radiating through him as he pushed himself back to his feet.

"Move left," Hanover said. *"Now!"*

Sheridan dove to the side, and several high-powered rounds from Hanover's rifle tore through the air behind him. He caught himself on a terminal, managed to keep his footing and draw his pistol, searching for more targets. A guard at the back of the room slumped against the wall, sliding to the floor, leaving a streak of red behind him on the pastel green wall.

"Target down," Hanover advised.

"Seven Alpha, what's your status?" Sergeant Rocha called through the taclink.

Sheridan scanned the room, looking for additional threats, then turned back to the broken window.

"Seven, are you all right?" Rocha asked.

"I've got eyes on," Hanover said. *"Sheridan, sound off."*

"Cole? What about Cole?" Sheridan asked, leaning out, searching the ground below for his friend. It was too dark; he couldn't make anything out. He switched to thermals but still had no luck. "Can you see him? Is he okay? Cole!"

"Sheridan, you need to disable the system," Rocha said.

"Devon, are you there? Do you read me?" Sheridan asked, fury burning in his chest.

There was no response.

"Sheridan! The system! Now!" Rocha shouted. *"Shut it down!"*

"Son of a bitch!" Sheridan turned away from the window, sweeping the room.

With the threats neutralized, he finally took in the space: several rows of holo-terminals and a main station in the center of the room, four large screens floating in the air just above a six-foot oval table. Multiple screens showed feeds from countless security cameras, internal and external. Three screens along the left wall were flashing red, all looked like they were part of an aiming and targeting system for the rooftop defenses.

They're searching for targets, Sheridan thought, stepping closer.

He turned to the central system, barely able to concentrate on what he was looking for; the image of Cole's hand slipping from his grasp frozen in his mind.

If you don't shut this down, none of you will make it home, Cole's voice in his head. *Make the bastards pay.*

Sheridan tapped the display, frowning as information and message panels populated the holoscreen.

"We're seeing a lot of activity down here," Chambers said over the taclink. *"They know you're there; you need to move. Looks like two groups for your position, Sheridan."*

"Confirmed," Hanover said. *"I've got movement on the northwest stairwell, three floors down."*

"We're going to breach," Rocha said.

"You've got another team moving to cut you off," Hanover said. *"I don't have a shot."*

"Roger that."

Sheridan swiped through several more screens, trying to find the shutdown controls. "Come on, come on. I'm not finding anything. I can't shut it down."

Fischer's icon appeared on Sheridan's HUD. *"You don't want* to shut it down; you want to route the operational access through to us here. You're going to need to run a remote proxy switch and allow the system to connect to the outside network."

"Yeah, sure," Sheridan said, holding both hands out, "and just how the hell do I do that?"

"I'm going to bring Osprey on the taclink. She'll walk you through it."

"Fantastic," Sheridan said, glancing around the room at the different holodisplays.

"Whatever you're going to do, you're going to need to do it soon," Chambers said. "Bravo breaching, pushing to the data center."

Sheridan swiped through more message panels, looking for something, anything, remotely close to what Fischer was looking for. Cole would've known.

No, Sheridan thought. Don't do that. Focus.

Fischer's icon flashed again, but instead of the investigator's voice coming through the taclink, it was Osprey's. "Okay, guns, listen up. This is going to be tricky."

CHAPTER 44

Holloman Alliance Embassy
Ridgecrest City, Saccora
22 August 2607

Fischer listened as Osprey walked Sheridan through the procedure, only understanding about half of what the hacker was saying, hoping that Sheridan understood it better than he did. Fortunately, it sounded like they were making progress, which was about all the positive he could say about the mission so far.

Team One had been stopped halfway to the security office by two groups of armed guards, slowing their progress. Team Two had just reached the outer offices of the data center and were engaged with guards there as well, but they were making better progress than Team One.

Hearing Sheridan scream as his friend fell had turned Fischer's stomach, and as much as he wanted to feel differently, he couldn't help but feel responsible, not to mention guilty, that he'd brought these people here, and now he wasn't even out there with them. He should be out there fighting, not stuck inside a secure embassy, looking at holoscreens. He should be *doing* something.

And what are you going to do that those trained warfighters aren't doing? Fischer flexed his fingers, making a fist, then releasing it. *Nothing.*

"This is taking too long," Chambers said, pacing behind Osprey.

The hacker straightened and put both arms out. "You wanna give this a try? I'd be happy to let you have a shot! This shit ain't as easy as I make it look."

The expression on Chambers's face suggested he didn't appreciate the hacker's sense of humor. "Just get it done!"

"Augmentees are in the air," Kline said. "ETA seven minutes."

"Won't do us any good if the defenses are still up," Chambers said. "One Alpha, what's your status?"

"Still engaged," Rocha said. *"They're packed in pretty tight down here."*

Kline moved to the screens showing the drone feeds and shook his head. "They've got two birds warming up on the north tower. Looks like somebody's planning to make a run for it."

Chambers joined him, accessing the screens for himself. "Five Alpha, can you confirm we have rabbits below you?"

"Stand by," Hanover replied. *"Confirmed, Actual, I've got eyes on two CLASS shuttles. They're definitely warming up their engines, but I'm not seeing any rabbits yet."*

"Roger that," Chambers said. "Keep an eye on them."

"Valkyrie Actual, One Bravo, we have made entry into the data center," Sergeant Nguyen said. *"Setting up relay now."*

Frustrated at not being able to contribute, Fischer moved to where Robalt and Eliwood would be coordinating the data transfer. "What can I do?"

"Ain't nothing *to* do," Robalt said, watching his screens. A message panel appeared, warning of a pending connection, and he accepted it. Several new panels appeared, displaying information Fischer didn't understand. "We're linked up."

"How much time do you need?" Chambers asked.

"Hard to say, sir," Robalt said without looking up. "Stand by."

"These are comm records and logistic reports," Robalt said, pointing to one of the panels. "And those are the names and linkIDs of the people assigned to the building. We're getting somewhere, but, Jesus, there's a lot of data here. This is going to take a bit."

"I'm in!" Osprey shouted.

"What do you have?" Chambers asked.

"Launch control, internal security network, targeting, damn near everything."

"Can you isolate our teams?" Kline asked, stepping close to Osprey, pointing a finger in her face, then to the displays around her. "Push the enemy back?"

Osprey held both hands up in surrender and backed away from the Saber. "Hey, shit, yeah, man, just give me half a second."

"Do you hear what's going on out there?" Kline asked. "They don't have half a second. Now get to work and make something happen."

"All right, all right, for shit's sake. No need to get all up in my face about it. Okay, bringing up internal security feeds and weapons control now."

Six additional holodisplays appeared, showing high angles from inside multiple corridors inside the complex. On each, the Sabers of both teams were engaging the enemy; Rocha's team was proceeding down the stairs, toward the security center; and Bravo was holding the data center, fighting off two separate groups of hostiles.

One of the feeds shook, the image filling with static briefly after a fragmentation grenade blew through one of the walls to the data center. Sergeant Nguyen fired several shots through the smoking hole, not hitting anything, but keeping the enemy back.

Another grenade detonated behind the north wall, the blast sending Sergeant Oliver flipping over one of the terminals as dust and debris sprayed into the room. Guerrero ducked, crouching down, protecting herself from raining plaster and fragmentation.

"They're really taking a beating in there," Fischer said.

"Get those birds in now," Kline said to someone over his taclink. "One team to the west tower, the other to the east. We're not going to be able to hold out much longer, Captain."

"Understood." Chambers leaned close to Osprey. "Lock down every door in that place and scramble their comms. The more confused and confined we can make them, the better."

"I'm working on it. I'm working on it."

Eliwood looked up from her panel. "Holy shit, Fish, look at this."

Fischer moved around to look at the data streaming down his partner's holodisplay and felt a surge of excitement as he read the names populating the screen. He couldn't help the grin spreading across his face.

"This is it," Fischer said, putting a hand on Eliwood's shoulder.

"It's a fucking goldmine," Eliwood said, sharing his expression.

"What do you got?" Chambers asked.

Fischer didn't answer right away, watching lines of names appear. There were hundreds of names, four columns continuously scrolling down the display. Fischer reached over Eliwood's shoulder and tapped one. Another panel appeared, listing the person's location, employer, last known contact and trigger event, biometric data and linkID.

"Agent Fischer?" Chambers said, coming up behind him.

Fischer looked up. "This is what we came for."

"What the hell is a trigger event?" Eliwood asked.

Fischer shook his head. "Probably a predetermined event meant to move the sleeper from inactive to active without direct contact from their handler."

"Maybe that explains what happened to Manchester and the others."

"Maybe."

"Valkyrie Actual, Five Bravo," the Bravo Team sniper said, *"I've got eyes on multiple rabbits heading for those shuttles."*

"Roger that, Five, stand by." Chambers moved back to Osprey's station. "Get me eyes on those shuttles."

"I can do better than that. I'm tapped directly into the building's security suite now. I've got access to all the internal and external—"

"Just get me a visual," Chambers said, cutting her off.

Fischer nodded to Eliwood's screen. "Good work."

He joined Chambers just as four panels appeared, showing multiple angles of the shuttles. A small stream of people exited onto the platform behind the shuttles. Several armed security guards escorted them, watching the skies around and above them as they made their way to the ramps.

"Those are Pegasi uniforms," Osprey said, pointing at a group of four officers dressed in Pegasi Elite black.

"We need to keep those shuttles grounded," Fischer said.

"Autocannons could do it," Osprey said. "But we'd probably lose a couple in the process."

"Collateral damage is always a risk," Chambers said. "Keep those birds out of the air."

A fifth display appeared, showing the angle from Valkyrie's orbiting drones. Red outlines appeared around each individual, tagging them on the team's milnet.

Fischer leaned closer to the display, watching the people move across the landing pad. "What about facial recognition? Can you ID any of them?"

"Yeah, should be able to." Osprey tapped in a few commands, and the computer began pulling facial profiles.

"Holy fuck," Sheridan said over the taclink.

Chambers and Fischer shared a confused glance.

"Seven-Alpha, Actual, status?"

"He's here," Sheridan said.

"Seven, say again," Chambers said. "Who's here? Sheridan?"

Hanover came over the link. *"Actual, Overwatch, be advised, Seven Alpha is on the move. I've got him leaving the security center for the northwest stairwell."*

"Sheridan, what the hell is going on?" Chambers asked, sounding more than a little frustrated. He pointed to the screen. "What the hell did he see?"

Osprey threw up her hands. "How the hell should I know?"

"Enhance it," Chambers said. "I want to see what he saw."

The drone feed zoomed in on the group, and a second later, Fischer saw it. His blood ran cold. "Holy fuck."

At the bottom of the ramp of one of the shuttles, waiting as several others were ushered on, was Marcus Young.

Fischer bolted for the exit, tapping his link as he ran.

"Fischer, wait!" Chambers shouted.

But Fischer didn't have time to wait. He cleared the door and sprinted down the hall to the lift at the far end. His link connected a second later.

"Yeah?" Jones asked.

"Start her up, Jonesy," Fischer said. "We've got a rabbit to catch."

CHAPTER 45

East Tower, Cardinal Compound
Ridgecrest City, Saccora
22 August 2607

Sheridan took the stairs four and five at a time, pushing hard and praying he didn't land wrong. He hit the landing, skidded into the wall, righted himself and continued down the next flight.

"Corporal Sheridan, report," Chambers shouted through the taclink. *"Young is not the mission here."*

"He *is* the mission!"

At the next landing, Sheridan shouldered through the door, snapping it from the frame, bursting into the main hallway. He stumbled into the wall, dropping his MOD27 briefly to keep himself upright, then sprinted down the hall, bringing his rifle back up. He was two floors below the security center now and halfway from the skywalk that connected the east tower to the north.

You can make it, he told himself.

Ahead, two armed guards came out of a side hall, weapons in hand. But they weren't up and ready like Sheridan's was, and the surprised expressions on their faces told him they hadn't been expecting anyone. It took less than a second to get his first three-round burst off, even less time to shift between targets and fire again. His shots echoed in the empty hall, muted by his helmet's dampeners, and both men dropped before they'd even had a chance.

Sheridan didn't stop. He couldn't stop.

Hanover's name appeared on his HUD. *"Seven Alpha, Five Alpha, you're not going to make it. They're already loading up."*

"I'm going to make it," Sheridan shouted. He reached the skywalk entrance and shouldered through the door. Inside, the plastiglass-enclosed walkway spanned the two hundred meters to the north tower, crossing over one of the large landing pads extending off the side of the building. Sheridan could just see the tops of the shuttles as he started across.

"Which shuttle is he on?" Sheridan asked.

"Young is not the mission!" Chambers repeated.

Sheridan never stopped running, a plan already forming in his mind. The ramp to the closest shuttle began folding up, and he cursed silently, pushing harder. The building's exterior lights illuminated the shuttle as it lifted off the pad, turning away and slowly moving away.

"One of them is taking off!" he shouted. "Which is it?"

"The second one," Fischer said. *"It's the second one! It's still on the pad."*

Sheridan pulled his MOD27 into his shoulder and held the trigger back. The magazine emptied three seconds later, every round punching through the plastiglass at the other end of the skywalk. He ejected the magazine, slapped in another, and went back to work. He crossed the halfway mark just as his second magazine went dry. He reloaded.

"Sheridan, that's a bad idea," Hanover warned.

The captain's icon flashed on his HUD. *"Sheridan, stand down!"*

Sheridan ignored him, knowing he was disobeying orders, knowing he could face discipline, and knowing he didn't care. Young was the only thing that mattered, the only thing that made sense. If he got away today, now when he was so close.

He's not getting away this time, Sheridan told himself as Chambers continued to order him back. Not this time. He would pay for what he'd done. He'd taken so much from so many, not just the members of his old unit, but their families as well. The members of the Stonemeyer embassy, all those civilians. Someone needed to pay for those lives, and today, it would be Marcus Young.

"The ramp's closing!" Hanover shouted.

The top of the shuttle's fuselage came into view, the red and green marker lights reflecting off the matte gray exterior. The sound of the engines pitching up for takeoff. His mind raced for options, but none came. He aimed and fired, sending a stream of rounds into the shuttle's starboard engine, and sparks erupted in the darkness. The bullets had no effect.

He ran dry twenty meters away from the window, let his MOD27 hang from its sling, and pulled a frag from his vest. He tapped the arming switch with his thumb, counted two, and threw. The grenade sailed through the air, bounced off the top of the wing and exploded. The blast tore through the fuselage, ripping through steel and internal systems. Fire belched from the opening in the hull as flaming debris arched into the air.

The shuttle slammed back down to the pad, its starboard-side landing strut snapping under the force of the impact. It listed to port, the tip of the wing grinding against the pad as the shuttle spun around, its engines screaming. The starboard wing broke off, bounced and toppled over the side, disappearing into the darkness. The shuttle skipped to a stop half a meter away from the skywalk, facing Sheridan. He could just make out the pilots behind the wraparound plastiglass viewport.

He drew his pistol, aimed and fired. His rounds smashed through the viewport, hitting the pilot center mass. The pilot, still strapped into his flight couch, spasmed violently as the rounds hit home. To his left, the copilot was struggling to remove his own harness even as Sheridan shifted targets and fired. He shook twice, then went limp.

Sheridan reached the end of the skywalk, stopping in the frame of the plastiglass he'd shattered. It was nine meters to the pad, six to the shuttle. It wasn't an easy jump by any means, but what else could he do?

"Whatever it takes," Sheridan said. He stepped back and jumped.

He landed hard. His feet shot out from under him, slipping down the curved fuselage, off the shuttle. He hit the platform and heard a sharp crack, pain coursed through his left leg, and he cried out as he fell to the deck. Stars and tears blurred his vision. He had to suppress the urge to vomit. He groaned and pushed himself up to all fours, squeezing his eyes shut hard, trying to clear them.

Get up!

"Valkyrie Actual, Five Bravo, Sheridan is down!" Hanover's voice was distant on the taclink, like he was underwater.

He grunted, gritting his teeth against the pain. His left leg felt like it was on fire. Every time he moved it, flashes of pain shot through his body. A part of his mind was screaming at him to get up; the other was telling him to get off the injured leg. The throbbing brought him back to Stonemeyer, falling out of the van, hitting the street, the bullet slamming into his thigh.

You have to keep going, he told himself. *Young is right there.*

Biagini flashed in his mind, her bruised and battered face looking up at him from the floor of their cell back on Stonemeyer.

Their captors had just thrown her in after having their way with her again; he could feel her legs quivering against him.

"It's going to be okay," Sheridan had told her. "I'm going to get you out of here."

"I know," she said. And she smiled at him. "I know you will."

"Seven Alpha, what's your status?" Chambers asked.

But Chambers hadn't been on Stonemeyer.

"Sheridan, report status now, damn it!" Chambers demanded.

A resounding metallic clang brought Sheridan back as smoke filled the air in front of him. A chorus of screams and coughing filtered out from the shuttle's bay as the occupants streamed out, running down the ramp to the pad below. A man in a Pegasi uniform emerged, hand over his mouth. Two men in civilian suits followed, helping a crying woman wearing a gray blouse and pants. Another Pegasi military officer came out next, a gun belt around his waist, pistol still in the holster. He coughed into one hand; the other held a bleeding wound on his forehead.

He got to his feet, pushing the pain down, putting it somewhere it wouldn't bother him. He had to ignore it now, deal with it later. The only thing that mattered was Young. Chambers continued to yell through the taclink, but Sheridan couldn't make out the words. Nothing else mattered. Just Young.

He leaned against the shuttle's fuselage, using it to take the pressure off his leg and let his empty MOD27 hang across his chest. He drew his pistol, taking a mental inventory of his remaining ammunition. Two magazines for his pistol, one in the weapon, the other in its pouch—forty rounds.

I won't need half that, Sheridan told himself, holding the pistol close to his chest and inching his way down the length of the shuttle. He paused a meter from the tail, watching the group sit and help each other, scanning the crowd for threats. Only two actually had weapons in hand, Pegasi H72s, not the most reliable weapon, but it wouldn't take more than one round to put down a threat. The guards searched the darkness for signs of their attackers, ignoring the pained cries of the other passengers. Three others had pistols holstered on hips, though they seemed more concerned with helping the injured than providing security.

A few stragglers made their way down the ramp. The final person hit the platform and turned slightly, and Sheridan recognized the face immediately. Marcus Young stumbled forward, weaving around two people who'd collapsed as soon as they'd exited the crashed shuttle, one crying, propped up on her shoulder, the other lying completely still, probably dead. Young cradled his right arm across his chest, walking with a limp, favoring his right leg.

Sheridan's heart pounded in his chest. The entire world around him faded away. The only thing he saw was Young standing in a sea of blackness. He brought his pistol up, hands trembling uncontrollably. He gritted his teeth, trying to will his hands to be still. His finger moved to the trigger, but he didn't squeeze. Something like vindication washed over him, knowing there wasn't any way Young would get away from him this time.

This time he would pay.

He straightened, took a deep breath and stepped forward, away from the shuttle. "Marcus Young!"

Young jumped and turned, his face streaked with blood from a wound on his head. The two guards with rifles turned as well, both several meters behind him on either side. The guard on the left said something that might have been a curse and lifted his rifle. Sheridan aimed and fired on instinct, hitting the guard square in the chest, then immediately shifted to the second and fired without waiting to see the first one drop.

Screams of pain and surprise filled the air as the people backed away from the sudden blasts. Young stumbled back as Sheridan moved forward, bringing his pistol back on target, the former admiral's chest filling his sights.

"You're not getting away this time, asshole," Sheridan growled.

To his right, one of the Pegasi military officers reached for his holstered pistol.

"Don't!" Sheridan yelled, shifting targets, his eyes scanning everyone, watching for additional threats. The other two froze as Sheridan's gaze fell on them in turn.

"Fucking Alliance," the first said, pulling his pistol.

It was a dumb move. Sheridan was already on target; there wasn't any chance of the officer beating him to the punch. He fired twice, both rounds hitting home, knocking the officer on his back. Several people screamed, ducking and backing away from the gunfire. One of the other guards shouted and pulled his pistol, firing as soon as the barrel cleared his holster. Sparks shot off the pad several meters in front of him as Sheridan shifted targets and fired.

Sheridan moved right, "getting off the 'X'" as they called it in training, grimacing as he put weight on his bad leg. The stars returned, dancing at the edges of his vision as tears of agony began to flow again. The Pegasi fired again; the bullet zipped through the air next to Sheridan's head. He dropped to his good knee, leveled his pistol, and fired.

The round missed.

Sheridan adjusted his aim, but before he could get the next round off, the man jolted upright, spinning to the side, blood spraying from a gaping wound in his upper back. His pistol went flying and he fell to the deck, hitting with a wet smack.

"What?" Sheridan asked, stunned.

"Tango down," Hanover advised over the taclink.

There's one more, Sheridan's mind warned him, and he immediately twisted around, searching for the final target. The Pegasi, a lieutenant from the rank device on his collar, froze when Sheridan's gun found him, his hand hovering over the holstered pistol.

"Don't fucking do it," Sheridan told him, finger already squeezing gently on his trigger.

"Don't shoot," the lieutenant said, his voice almost a whimper.

Sheridan motioned to the pistol. "On the deck. Get rid of it."

Cautiously, he reached down and pulled his weapon from his holster and tossed it away. The pistol bounced and slid across the platform, stopping some three meters away.

"On your knees," Sheridan ordered.

The lieutenant nodded and complied. "Please don't kill me."

"Don't do anything stupid and you won't have anything to worry about."

Sheridan's gaze fell on Young, a pit forming in his stomach. Finally, after all these months of searching, he'd found him. The man who'd caused him so much pain. The man responsible for the lives of all his friends and so many others. The man Sheridan had vowed to end. But now, meters away from him, Young wasn't as intimidating as Sheridan had built him up to be.

He wore a plain gray jacket over a blue shirt, stained with spots of blood from his head wound, and his gray trousers were smudged with dirt and grime. One hand still pressed against his head; streaks of red lined the side of his face. He didn't look much like the pompous ass from the briefings he'd seen, much less the confident military commander he'd envisioned. Standing there, bleeding and battered, Marcus Young looked like a defeated shell of a man. He almost didn't look capable of the things he'd done.

But he did do them, Sheridan reminded himself. He put more weight on his good leg and blew out a long breath before leveling his pistol at Young's chest. Young's expression changed from confusion to terror as he realized what was coming next.

"Please," Young begged. "Please don't."

"I've got you covered, Seven," Hanover advised over the taclink. *"Don't do anything stupid."*

Young's face was a mask of desperation. "Please, I'll do whatever you want. Don't kill me. I know things. I know where the moles—"

"Shut the fuck up," Sheridan shouted, taking an agonizing step forward.

Young cowered, holding up a hand in front of his face. "No!"

The MP10's sight wobbled as his leg throbbed. He blinked away tears, gritting his teeth as he tried to push the pain back down. "You're going to pay for what you've done."

"Please!" Young screamed, his voice cracking under the strain. "Tell me what you want. I'll do anything. Please, whatever it is, it's yours."

"What I want?" Sheridan limped toward him, reaching back with one hand to hit the visor release. It folded back into his helmet, revealing his face for the first time. "You know who I am?"

Young hesitated for a moment, his mouth hanging open. He frowned, trying to understand; then his eyes widened in recognition. "You?"

"Say my name, you piece of shit."

"I don't—"

"You fucking know!" Sheridan screamed. "You know Biagini! You know Ford! You know Hastings! You fucking know!"

"Sh-Sheridan," Young said, "you're Sheridan."

"Say their goddamn names!"

Young flinched, backing away again.

Sheridan limped after him. "You killed my friends. You killed Hastings. You killed Biagini. You killed Cole."

"Sheridan, take it easy," Hanover said.

"I didn't!" Young wailed. "Please, it was a mistake. It should never have happened. I swear! It was a mistake, that's all!"

"The only mistake was not killing you when I had the chance," Sheridan said, his finger rubbing his own trigger. "You killed them. Their blood is on your hands. And you will pay for what you've done."

Motion to his right caught his attention, one of the civilians standing next to one of the dead guards, lifting the rifle off the platform. Sheridan shifted his pistol over to shoot, and a hole exploded in the man's chest. The impact from Hanover's shot sent him flying, the rifle spinning out of his hands.

"You son of a bitch!" Young crossed the distance between them before Sheridan could react, slamming into his chest and sending them both reeling.

Sheridan wrapped his arms around Young as they fell, tensing for the impact. Agony flashed through his body when they landed, Sheridan on his back, Young on top of him. Young pushed himself up, straddling Sheridan, and before he could react, a fist connected with the bridge of Sheridan's nose with a loud crack. Hot blood sprayed across Sheridan's face. Sheridan put his hands up, trying to block the next punch, but all he could see was Young's face skewed into a hateful sneer.

Sheridan thrust his hips up, trying to throw Young off. His leg erupted in agony as Young dropped his weight down on Sheridan's pelvis, ramming it back down to the deck. Sheridan's MOD27 dug into his stomach, pinned between the two men. His mind went to his pistol, but his hand was empty. He lashed out, batting away Young's attack, looking for an opportunity to land a punch of his own.

"You want to fucking finish this?" Young screamed, both hands wrapping around Sheridan's neck. "I'll fucking finish it."

Sheridan opened his mouth, and warm blood streamed in, gagging him. He thrust his hips up again, twisting this time. He kicked off as hard as he could, launching Young over his head, then rolled over, pushing himself up to his knees. He sucked in precious air as Young caught himself and lunged back, reaching for the rifle slung across Sheridan's chest.

He grabbed Young with one hand, pulling him off balance. With the other, he pulled his tac-knife from its sheath at the small of his back and slammed it into Young's stomach. His eyes bulged, gasping with pain as the blade pierced flesh and muscle. Sheridan pushed it in as far as it would go, then ripped it free to plunge it in again. Warm blood poured over his gloved hand.

Young cried out, hands desperately trying to fend off Sheridan's attack while trying to back away. Sheridan held firm, not letting him retreat, and rammed the knife home a third time. Young fell back and Sheridan went with him, and this time he was on top, he had the advantage. Blood streamed from Sheridan's nose, running over his clenched teeth and onto Sheridan's chest, staining his shirt. Rage swelled in his chest; he saw red.

Blood pumped from Young's wound, and slowly, his strength ebbed away, putting up less and less of a fight. The hatred that had blazed in his eyes only moments before became pain and finally acceptance as his hands fell limp to the deck. Sheridan straddled Young's waist, holding the knife firm, never taking his eyes away from his enemy. He watched the life drain from Young's face as his head collapsed to the deck, then leaned to the side, eyes open in an eternal death stare.

Sheridan didn't move for several moments, some illogical part of his mind fearful that Young might wake and return from the dead. But he didn't, and as he sat back, his vision began to clear. The stark silence that had enveloped him gave way to the crackling fire in the shuttle behind him and the comms chatter coming through the taclink, the cries and screams of the people around him on the platform.

"Sheridan, report status!" Chambers demanded.

Sheridan looked down at Young's dead body, his breath coming in ragged gasps. He left the knife in the man's chest and pushed himself to his feet, grimacing as he hobbled back. He spit blood and wiped his mouth with the back of his hand.

"I'm fine," he croaked.

"Say again, Seven, you're unreadable."

Sheridan cleared his throat and spit another wad of blood onto the deck beside Young's corpse. "I'm fine, sir. Mission accomplished."

CHAPTER 46

The *Doris*
Skies over Ridgecrest City, Saccora
22 August 2607

"I really don't know how I let you talk me into this shit all the time," Jones said from his flight couch.

Fischer held onto the base of the pilot's couch, grunting as Jones banked his ship hard to port. "Because I'm the one who finds you all the fun jobs."

"Fun?" Jones scoffed. "Well, if this is your idea of fun, I think I'll pass on the next *fun* adventure, if you don't mind. I think I've had about as much of that shit as I can take."

"Come on, you like it," Fischer said.

Jones laughed. "Eh, I can't say I hate it."

"Can you link me into the drones' feeds?" Fischer asked.

"Loomis, do something useful, would you?" Jones called to his engineer at the front of the cockpit. "Can't you see our guest needs something."

"Guest? Fish ain't no guest. He's like a distant cousin who visits all the time and never leaves," Loomis countered.

A moment later a bank of holodisplays appeared in front of Fischer, giving him multiple angles of Cardinal's compound. Now that the enemy knew they were there, Guerrero had moved the drones in closer, picking up groups of fighters advancing on the two teams from multiple angles. One of the drones was following Sheridan as he plowed through the doors onto the skywalk and started shooting at something Fischer couldn't see.

"What the hell is he doing?" Jones asked.

"What's he thinking? He's going to take on those shuttles with just his rifle?" Loomis asked. "That's insane."

"No way," Jones said.

Fischer watched as Sheridan ran dry and changed magazines. A second drone moved to cover the platform and shuttles, illuminated from lights mounted on the building above. The far shuttle lifted off the deck, banked away and disappeared from view. A moment later an explosion ripped through one of the shuttle's wings, sending flaming debris streaming through the air.

"What the hell was that?" Loomis asked as the shuttle crashed and spun across the platform.

"I don't—oh, son of a bitch," Fischer muttered as Sheridan jumped through the shattered opening he'd created and onto the damaged shuttle, grimacing when Sheridan hit and slid to the platform below.

"Goddamn," Loomis said. "That looked like it hurt."

"I'll give your boy this," Jones said. "He's got about the biggest set of balls I've seen this side of the URT. No shit."

Fischer shook his head and repeated, "No shit."

An alarm sounded and Fischer looked over his shoulder to Jones. The pilot frowned, tapping at the wraparound holodisplay floating in front of his couch. Multiple targets were appearing on his screens, red flashing icons indicating hostile ships closing.

"Looks like we're going to have company," Jones said. "Multiple bogies incoming."

"Who?" Fischer asked.

Jones laughed and tapped the screen. "I'll give you three guesses, and the first two don't count."

The outlines of three Pegasi Gryphon assault shuttles and two Wraith-class fighters appeared in the darkness, all racing across the city toward Cardinal's compound. As they neared, the two Wraiths pulled away from the shuttles, pushing to attack first. Several additional panels opened, identifying their armament: racks under each wing carrying ten air-to-ground missiles, and a nose-mounted multibarrel autocannon.

"Are they targeting us?" Fischer asked.

"Wraiths are fast, but their maneuvering and electronics are shit," Jones said, tapping on his display. "Loomis?"

"Yeah, yeah, I'm doing it."

A steady tone went off and Jones killed it almost immediately.

"What's happening?" Fischer asked.

"Hold on," Jones said. "Loomis?"

"Almost... there!"

"What?" Fischer asked.

"It's about time." Jones banked the ship hard right and gunned the engines, charging toward the Pegasi.

Fischer grunted, holding on tight. "Wait, you're attacking?"

"Both of those bastards just painted us hostile," Jones said. "And I don't play that hit-me-first bullshit."

"They can't know who we are," Fischer said, more a statement than a question.

"I don't think they care," Jones said.

"Weapons away!" Loomis shouted, and Fischer heard the whoosh of missiles leaving their tubes.

"Since when did you get missiles?" Fischer asked.

"Since you had me neck-deep in pirates for months, that's when."

Fischer watched as the missiles streaked toward their target.

Saccora's sun was just starting to breach the horizon, turning the black sky shades of purple and orange. The Wraiths peeled away, climbing to evade, *Doris*'s missiles arching up to follow, leaving trails of white smoke in their wakes.

"Boom!" Jones shouted, clapping his hands.

The first Pegasi fighter exploded in a brilliant fireball, sending pieces of fuselage streaking through the early morning sky. The second fighter pulled up and away, launching flares out of recesses on the underside of his wings. The missiles ignored the countermeasures and slammed home, ripping the Wraith apart.

"Told you," Jones said. "Their tech ain't shit."

As he spoke, a stream of orange tracers cut through the darkness, barely missing the back end of the Pegasi shuttles. A second stream ripped through its portside wing, ripping it clean off in an explosion that lit up the sky.

"Oh, shit!" Loomis cried out. "Looks like Osprey's got the autocannons working."

"I've got more fighters incoming," Jones said, turning his ship back toward Cardinal's compound as additional target alerts chimed through the bridge.

"And this time they know who we are," Fischer said. He tapped his link. "Captain Chambers, it's Fischer. Be advised, we've engaged Pegasi fighters above the city. We've scrapped two, but six more are incoming."

"You engaged?"

"Didn't have much of a choice," Fischer said. "They were coming for a fight."

There was silence for a moment; then Chambers said, *"We're running out of time, then. Sergeant Kline, let's start moving our teams to exfil."*

"Wait!" Fischer said, a little too loudly. "We're not done with the data transfer."

"It'll have to be enough," Chambers said. *"We stay here any longer, we risk getting pinned down. If that happens, none of the intel we find will make any difference if we can't get it to the people who matter. You need to RTS right now, Fischer. That's an order. We're pulling out."*

Fischer looked at the holopanel showing Sheridan holding a gun on Young. "What about Sheridan?"

"We've got a team en route to his position right now. I say again, fall back."

On the display, Young charged Sheridan, knocking him to the deck.

Fischer terminated the link and looked up at Jones. "Get us there. Now."

"You got it."

Fischer's grip on the couch support beneath Jones tightened as they raced toward Cardinal's compound. The steady thumping of *Doris*'s autocannons reverberated through the hull. Another one of the Gryphons exploded under anti-air fire from Cardinal's captured turrets, sending the wreckage plummeting to the city below.

"Oh shit!" Jones shouted. "Hold on!"

The deck under Fischer's feet abruptly dropped and his stomach turned. He fell forward, almost losing his grip, and swung into the ladder mounted on the front of Jones's flight couch. He wrapped his free arm around one of the rungs, keeping himself upright, and glared at Jones.

"What the hell, Jonesy!"

Jones didn't answer, all of his attention focused on his screens as he twisted the flight controls, sending the *Doris* into a steep dive, banking left. Another alarm rang out, but Fischer couldn't read the warnings populating the screens.

"Loomis!" Jones shouted.

"Yeah?"

"Flip and fire in three, yeah?"

"Yeah, okay, hold up. Let me tighten this… okay, good to go!"

"You'd better hold on tight, Fish," Jones said, giving no further explanation before he started counting. "Three… two… one."

Jones pulled back hard on the controls. *Doris*'s engines screamed and the entire ship shook around Fischer as her nose shot up, flipping over. Fischer squeezed his eyes shut and held on as the world around him turned upside down. A second later they were inverted, and he heard the whooping of missiles leaving their launch tubes as alarms shrilled throughout the bridge.

"What the hell is going on?" Fischer asked through gritted teeth, muscles straining to keep himself from flying across the compartment.

"Just hold on!" Jones shouted.

"Got one!" Loomis shouted. "Got two!"

The ship rolled left, righting itself, and Fischer was sure he was going to lose his breakfast. Another barrage of missiles fired as *Doris*'s autocannons laid down an almost constant stream of fire. On the screens above, Fischer watched as twin explosions ripped through two more Wraiths, blowing them right out of the middle of a Pegasi attack formation.

"That'll piss 'em off," Jones said, laughing. "Ope, hold on."

The *Doris* dipped suddenly, accelerating between a line of high-rises. The Cardinal's compound lay head, the three towers rising out of the surrounding buildings like mysterious obelisks. Lines of autocannon fire streaked through the lightening sky, chasing unseen targets in all directions. The horizon angled up as Jones put the ship into a hard left turn, the city becoming nothing more than a blur.

"Got two on us," Loomis shouted. "Bearing one-seven-five and coming in fast."

"Yeah," Jones said, almost disinterested. His fingers moved

over his holodisplay with practiced grace, killing the alarms and closing panels while maneuvering the ship through the cityscape.

Another hard turn brought them around a triangular tower with several sensor clusters atop its spire. Cannon fire from one of the Pegasi fighters blew apart one of the clusters, sending flaming wreckage tumbling down the side of the building, to the street below.

They leveled out again, holding fifty meters above a six-lane highway, charging for a gap between two identical buildings. Tracer fire zipped past the *Doris*'s nose, stitching a line through the street and punching holes in the surrounding buildings. The view shifted as Jones rocked the *Doris* left, then right, and back again, obviously not wanting to give their pursuers a clean shot.

"They're gaining!" Loomis called back.

"I know! I know!" Jones shouted.

"Rocket! Rocket! Rocket!"

A single rocket shot past, trailing smoke and curling through the air, arching toward the taller building on the right. It slammed into the upper floors and exploded, ripping a massive hole in the steel and plastiglass. *Doris* flew through the growing cloud of smoke and flame. Fischer ducked instinctively as chunks of debris bounced off the ship's hull.

"Too close, boss!" Loomis said. "A little too close!"

Fischer looked up at Jones through his holodisplay. "We get hit by one of those things…"

"Would both of you just shut the hell up!"

He pushed his flight controls forward and jerked them right. The engines flared, screaming as the ship slowed abruptly, flying around the flaming building, using it for cover. Fischer pulled tight against the ladder again, promising himself to never fly with Jones again.

"I've got six more incoming!" Loomis shouted. "Nine-seven-mark-two-three."

"There's too many, Jones!" Fischer shouted.

"You don't say!"

The autocannon fired, sweeping between multiple targets. Red boxes drew themselves around the first three fighters as warning icons appeared on Jones's display. Six warnings flashed as each fighter launched missiles. They curled through the air, streaking after the *Doris*.

The ship shook, her engines screaming as Jones pushed them to their limits. He banked left, pulling up hard, skimming the roofs of three tenement buildings, blowing dust and debris in their wake. Flares shot from recesses in *Doris*'s hull, filling the air with hundreds of brilliant flashing points of light.

Two of the missiles veered off, smashing into separate buildings. Another exploded inside the cloud of flares, sending out a sparkling blast wave in all directions. Two slammed into each other, creating a brilliant fireball, setting fire to the buildings below. The final missile cleared the flares, racing after *Doris* and her crew.

"Brace for impact!" Jones shouted.

Fischer clenched his teeth, squeezed his eyes together and waited for the end. He'd always considered the fact that he'd meet a violent end, but getting blown apart aboard his friend's ship hadn't been one of the scenarios he'd envisioned.

Nothing happened.

"What the shit was that?" Jones shouted.

Fischer opened his eyes. The holopanel showed an expanding ball of flame, pieces of debris streaking through the air away from it.

It exploded? Fischer thought.

"We've got more incoming!" Loomis shouted. "Dead ahead, multiple bogeys on an intercept!"

Jones reached forward and enhanced the image, waiting for

the computer to identify the new arrivals. A panel appeared that Fischer couldn't read.

"Holy shit!" Jones laughed. "It's about time the cavalry showed up!"

Five Nemesis II fighters dropped out of the cloud cover ahead, silhouetted against the brightening orange sky, guns blazing. They spread apart, each firing clusters of missiles that curled through the air, racing to meet their targets.

CHAPTER 47

North Tower, Cardinal Compound
Ridgecrest City, Saccora
22 August 2607

The crowd watched Sheridan in stunned silence, obviously shocked at the viciousness of his attack. He spit another wad of blood and phlegm onto the platform and gritted his teeth at the pain shooting up his leg as he stepped toward the MP10 he'd dropped when Young had attacked. He picked it up, ejecting the magazine to check the load. With a round still in the chamber, he had almost half a magazine in the pistol and another full one on his vest. It probably wouldn't be enough to fend off the entire crowd if they decided to charge him, but he would definitely take the majority of them with him.

"Don't even think about it," Sheridan warned them, slapping the magazine back in. "Just back away and don't do anything stupid. We're all just going to hang out here for a bit. There's no reason any more of you have to die."

A woman laughed. "Are you serious? You can barely stand." She pushed herself to her feet and dusted off her pants. Her brown hair was matted and disheveled from sweat and smoke. "What are you going to do, shoot us all? I doubt it."

"I will if I have to." He blew out blood and snot from his nose, wiping off the excess with the back of a hand.

A series of explosions echoed in the darkness behind Sheridan, accompanied by autocannon fire and screaming engines. Several of the people in the group looked past him, and he followed their gaze as two fireballs vanished above the city several kilometers away.

He turned back as two more stood. "Get down!"

Both flinched, dropping to their knees, their hands up. The woman, however, didn't. She adjusted her jacket and took a step forward. "This isn't going to solve anything, you know that, don't you? You have to know that."

"Shut up and get on the ground." Sheridan leveled his pistol. "I mean it."

The woman stopped but remained standing. She squared her shoulders and lifted her chin in silent defiance.

"I will kill you," Sheridan said, moving his finger from the frame to the trigger.

More explosions sounded in the distance. Autocannons above him belched out streams of anti-aircraft rounds, drawing lines of orange across the lightening sky. What looked like missiles slammed into a row of buildings several blocks away, sending flaming wreckage raining down. A flight of Pegasi Wraiths appeared briefly, veering away from each other as autocannon fire tore through the air where'd they'd just been.

But who had the Pegasi been shooting at?

A lone ship appeared, shooting up from between two highrises, flares filling the air behind it. Sheridan couldn't help but laugh at the sight of the familiar ship. *Doris*'s autocannon fired off a burst behind them, then cut off abruptly, shifting to attack something ahead of them. Sheridan followed the stream of fire to another flight of Wraiths, all lining up for attacks on the *Doris*.

Sheridan's gut twisted, knowing there wasn't any way the sprinter could fight off so many, no matter how many modifications Jones had installed. It was just simple math.

"Get out of there," Sheridan whispered to the ascending ship.

Flashes at the corner of his vision caught his attention, and suddenly a cluster of missiles were racing through the air. He traced their tails of smoke back and felt a lump turn in his throat.

"Way to go, *Legend*!" Sheridan pumped a fist into the air as the Nemesis IIs engaged the Pegasi. He turned to the brunette, giving her an I-told-you-so smile. "Today Cardinal ends, you sanctimonious bitch."

"It won't make any difference," she said, her expression stone-faced and voice flat. She glared at him with a burning hatred, and Sheridan knew he couldn't give her an opening. If she had the chance, she'd kill him, he had no doubt about that.

Sheridan sneered. "You don't have any idea who you're fucking with."

She opened her mouth to answer but hesitated, her eyes flicking to something above and behind him. Hairs on the back of his neck stood on end, and he turned, bringing his pistol up in anticipation. A gunshot rang out before he could get his own on target, and sparks erupted from the deck by his feet. Three figures appeared in the opening over the skywalk above him, one holding a rifle, the other two, pistols. All three firing.

He lunged right, forgetting his injured leg for a split second, diving for cover behind the shuttle. He hit the deck and almost threw up as agonizing pain shot through his leg. Behind him, bullets slammed into the deck, the impacts vibrating through the platform. Sheridan scrambled behind the nose of the shuttle just as more rounds hit the fuselage on the far side.

"Son of a bitch!" he grunted through gritted teeth.

To his left, the woman was trying to pull a rifle free from one of the dead guards. Sheridan groaned, fighting off waves of nausea as he shifted position, lifting his pistol in one hand and firing. His rounds found her upper chest and side, dropping her without so much as a pained cry. Her corpse fell across the guard's, pinning the rifle between them.

"Stay down," Sheridan shouted to the remaining people. He wiped more blood and snot from his nose and shook his head. "Son of a bitch."

Sheridan never heard the shot, but the impact and painful cry weren't hard to miss. The gunfire ceased, and a fraction of a second later something heavy thudded against the deck. There was a collective gasp from the shuttle's passengers, then silence for a few seconds before the next round of gunfire started up again.

"Valkyrie Actual, Five Alpha, be advised Seven has been pinned down by enemy fire. I've engaged one but don't have a shot on the others."

"I appreciate that, Five," Sheridan said.

"Don't appreciate it too much," Hanover replied. *"You've got more incoming, above and below, and I'm not going to be able to stop them all."*

"Valkyrie Actual, One Alpha, the augmentation force has secured our route to the LZ," Sergeant Rocha said. *"We're going to push to Seven's position. How copy?"*

"Don't know that I'd recommend that," Hanover said. *"I'm picking up a lot of hostiles massing between you and the skywalk."*

"Confirmed," Chambers said. *"We're seeing the same thing on the drone feeds. There is no way you're going to reach Sheridan without a prolonged engagement. We've got air support on station, but our time on target is rapidly running out."*

Sheridan looked up as another flight of Nemesis IIs shot over the compound, their autocannons blazing. Missiles blasted free from their launchers, streaking out of sight toward the enemy. The orange and purple sky was giving way to a clear, azure morning, which might have been a beautiful sight had it not been for the gunfire and explosions ripping the city apart.

"Sir, Seven is pinned down and surrounded by hostile enemy forces," Sergeant Rocha said.

"I understand the situation, Sergeant," Chambers countered. *"I'm looking at the feeds right now, and there is absolutely no way your team will make it there. Exfil with the augmentees. I'll direct air support to cover a pickup."*

There was silence on the channel for a moment, and Sheridan new Rocha was biting her tongue. The captain was right, there wasn't any other way they'd be able to pull it off, and now, sitting with his back to the shuttle he'd destroyed, Sheridan couldn't help but feel more than a little guilty. If he would've listened to Chambers before leaving his post and chasing after Young, his team wouldn't've been put in the position of coming after him.

"Go, One," Sheridan said. "Get out of here."

"We're not leaving you behind," Rocha argued.

"Go!" Sheridan repeated. "Come and pick me up in the bird."

"Roger that," Rocha said after a few moments of silence. *"Moving to exfil."*

"Seven, what's your status?" Chambers asked.

Sheridan adjusted his position, grimacing as he moved his leg to the side. He gave the passengers a sidelong glance and said, "Just perfect, sir."

"Good to hear." Despite Sheridan disobeying his order, Chambers didn't sound angry, he sounded concerned. *"Eyes up, Corporal, we're coming to get you."*

"Roger that, sir."

"Careful, Seven," Hanover said. *"Watch—"*

There was a thud and a grunt to Sheridan's left, followed by a chorus of startled screams. One of the passengers, who'd obviously been going to one of the dropped weapons, fell on his back, a hole ripped through his chest. Those nearby spread away from the fallen man as his blood spread out over the deck.

"Stay down!" Sheridan shouted.

Gunfire chewed through the shuttle, ripping steel. The hull at Sheridan's back vibrated with every impact. He ducked instinctively as the rounds hit, praying the shuttle's hull would hold up against the onslaught.

"You're going to die, asshole," a man shouted, aiming a pistol and firing before Sheridan could react. The first round punched into his shoulder, throwing him against the shuttle's fuselage. A second slammed into his upper thigh.

Sheridan screamed in pain, grabbing the leg, covering the wound. He brought his pistol up and fired, hitting the man in the stomach and chest. He collapsed to the deck, pistol spinning away.

"Get him!" another man shouted.

"Go!" another woman yelled.

The Pegasi officer he'd disarmed was getting to his feet, already lunging toward the pistol he'd discarded. Sheridan lifted the pistol, grunting in pain from the effort, his movements sluggish. He fired and missed. A second later the man's head exploded before he could get another shot off. Hanover was still at it.

"He can't shoot us all!" another man at the back shouted, getting to his feet.

This seemed to bolster the rest, and they all started to get up. Sheridan aimed and fired at the nearest target, a woman in a blue skirt. Everything around him seemed to be slowing down, the world suddenly becoming smaller. Two rounds smacked into her stomach, doubling her over, tripping the man behind her.

He fired again and again, but now they were spreading out,

making it harder for him to get off quick shots. He dropped another and Hanover decapitated another, but they still came. The slide on his pistol locked back on an empty magazine, and he struggled to get his last magazine out of its pouch, his hand slick with blood.

As he slapped his last magazine in, a part of his mind wondered where all the blood had come from. He glanced at his leg and saw a dark stain spreading across his pants, saw blood spilling onto the deck.

An artery, he thought. *They hit my fucking artery.*

He really was going to die here. He fired again, but he was only vaguely aware of the shots. The pistol bucked wildly in his hand every time he fired. Faces of hatred and rage charged him. Two men were pulling the rifle free from the guard's body.

But it was all a dream.

And, strangely, it was a peaceful dream.

You got that son of a bitch, he told himself, his arm dropping to the deck, losing strength to hold it. Young was gone, and it was the only justice he could give his friends.

"Leave me," he said, his voice only barely audible, even to him. He didn't want the others to risk themselves for him. He'd completed his mission; that was all that mattered. He'd proven himself worthy of Valkyrie. Worthy of Cole. Worthy of Biagini. Worthy of them all.

The platform erupted under a hail of autocannon fire, filling the air with smoke and twisted steel, blood and gore. A barrage of high-velocity rounds ripped through the charging crowd, severing limbs and punching massive wounds. A handful of agonized screams were cut short as the attack continued, dropping them all in a matter of seconds.

Sheridan barely had enough time to comprehend what was happening before the howl of *Doris*'s engines cut thought the air, the ship flaring above the platform, turning its cannons to the attackers on the skywalk above. Plastiglass and steel were shredded as the sound of enemy gunfire was drowned out and eventually silenced altogether.

The autocannon went quiet and the *Doris* rotated to land, struts already extending underneath her chassis. The rear cargo ramp opened, Sheridan's friend standing at the top, one hand holding onto the rail above him. Without waiting for the ship to settle, Fischer made his way down the ramp, onto the platform, then around the dozens of dead to kneel in front of Sheridan.

"You know, this is becoming a trend," Fischer said, grinning.

Sheridan tried to laugh, but a flash of agony cut it short. Specks of gray danced in his vision, and he could feel his eyes getting heavy. He swallowed, tasting blood. His stomach turned.

"Fish…"

Fischer grabbed his shoulder. "Hey, you okay?"

"Yeah…"

Fischer said something, but Sheridan couldn't make out the words. He was so tired.

He closed his eyes and let the blackness take him.

CHAPTER 48

Medical Bay
ANS *Legend*
22 August 2607

Muffled voices echoed in the darkness; a soft, rhythmic chime played on a loop. He opened his eyes, looking at a flat gray ceiling. An array of medical equipment surrounded him, and he could just see the bottom edge of a holodisplay above his head. His body throbbed with a dull ache; his mouth was dry.

"Hey," a familiar voice said, "he's awake."

Neal appeared next to him, hair pulled back, face almost glowing. She smiled at him and the dull ache vanished, replaced by something else, something far more distinct.

"How are you feeling?" she asked, her hands grabbing hold of his.

Sheridan tried to speak, but his throat was parched. He licked his lips, trying to work moisture back into his throat. "Hey," was all he could manage.

"Hey yourself," Neal said.

Hanover appeared opposite Neal.

"Where… what happened?" Sheridan asked.

"You lost a lot of blood," Neal said, nodding to his leg. "Trying to upstage me, huh?"

Sheridan felt his leg, wincing at the tender flesh. "Trust me, wasn't trying. What happened? Where's Fischer?"

"We're on our way back to New Tuscany," Hanover said.

"Cardinal?"

"We fucking trashed their shit," Neal said, crossing her arms. "After we pulled out, Ward authorized air-to-grounds. The Nemesis IIs wrecked those bastards. Tore 'em a new asshole."

Sheridan adjusted his position on the bed, trying to get a little more comfortable, and groaned as the dull ache returned, his left leg and shoulder throbbing. He grunted, squeezing his eyes against the pain.

"Son of a bitch," he groaned through clenched teeth.

He opened his eyes to see Neal's face screwed up, sympathetic to his suffering. "Doc said to let her know if you need more meds."

Sheridan let out a long breath. "Whooo. Yeah."

"Been out a few days," Hanover said. "We'll be at New Tuscany in about fourteen hours."

"What about the other shuttle?" Sheridan asked. "The one that got away."

"The *Montgomery* and *Void Hawk* detained it as it left orbit," Neal said.

Sheridan frowned, trying to put the names together. "What?"

"Alliance cruisers in the Saccora task force," Neal explained. "There was a lot of confusion there for a while, but as soon as Ward transmitted Hunter's orders, they came over pretty quick. Pushed the Pegasi cruisers outside *Legend*'s engagement envelope and held them there while we exfilled, and the Nemesis guys took care of Cardinal's compound."

"'Bout time something went our way," Sheridan said, repeating what Cole had said.

"Captain's still not too sure why they didn't turn and attack," Hanover said. "They had more than enough opportunity, and *Legend* was occupied with the extraction effort. It would've been close to a fair fight."

"That's probably why they didn't," Sheridan said. "Those assholes aren't interested in a fair fight. Never have been."

The curtain behind Neal was pulled back and Dr. Moore appeared. She checked the holodisplay above Sheridan's head and smiled down at him. "How you feeling?"

"Like shit," Sheridan said.

"Well, considering what your body's been through in the past forty-eight hours, I'd say that's about par for the course."

"That bad, huh?"

"That bad?" Neal repeated, as if he'd said something stupid.

"Corporal Sheridan," Moore said, flicking her wrist, opening her link, "it is not an overstatement to say that if not for your friend, you would not be lying here today."

Sheridan frowned. "Fischer?"

"Injected the biosynth and stopped the bleeding," Moore said. "And not a moment too soon. Another thirty seconds, I doubt you would've made it back to the ship."

"Starting a trend."

"I'm sorry?"

"Nothing," Sheridan said. "Don't suppose you could up the meds a little, could you, Doc? I'm starting to feel it."

Moore tapped her link and swiped a finger up the screen. Almost immediately, Sheridan felt warmth flow into his body. His head settled back onto the pillow and he let out a long, relieved breath.

"That's it." He closed his eyes, immediately seeing the faces of his team from Stonemeyer. Ford. Biagini. Henderson. Hastings.

Faces he didn't ever want to forget. Then he saw one he didn't want to remember: Young. His chest tightened at the image, and the rhythmic beeping sped up.

"Corporal?" Moore asked.

"I'm fine."

Neal squeezed his hand. "You don't have to act tough. You've already impressed the shit out of me."

Sheridan let out a pained breath. Not physical, he could already feel the meds starting to work their magic. Cole's hand slipping from his. His friend falling into the darkness.

He opened his eyes, seeing Neal's face looking down at him. "Cole?"

She sniffed and closed her eyes, pursing her lips. She too was fighting back a wave of emotions. She nodded.

"I couldn't save him," Sheridan muttered.

"There wasn't anything you could have done," Neal countered.

Cole's hand slipping out of his. "I could have held on. I could have pulled him back inside."

"You did what you could," Hanover said. "You might not think so, but there wasn't anything else you could've done."

"Fucking bastards."

"They got what they deserved," Neal said.

"No," Sheridan said, trying to push their faces away. "They deserved better."

Neal frowned, obviously confused, but didn't say anything.

"I'd like to be there when they tell his parents," Sheridan said.

"I'm sure that won't be a problem," Neal said. "Chambers said they'll likely give him the Alliance Cross, with honors."

"He wouldn't have cared about medals," Sheridan said.

"Maybe," Hanover said. "But sometimes medals and awards aren't for the person they're given to. Sometimes they're for everyone else. A way to show their appreciation and admiration."

"Rumor is Chambers is going to put you in for the Silver Star," Neal said.

"For what?"

"For what?" Neal asked, surprised. "I don't know, a double HALO through the window of a building, going after those shuttles, getting the security system down so we could get our people out of there. Fischer said the data we pulled out of the data center is going to bring down a shit-ton of people."

"Going after those shuttles was stupid," Sheridan said.

Neal laughed. "You're goddamn right it was."

"I guess that means Chambers isn't pissed at me?"

"What, that you went off mission, put yourself and everyone else in jeopardy to chase down a target who may or may not have been mission critical? Hell yeah, he was pissed. Can you blame him?"

Sheridan wanted to argue it had been the right thing to do, considering the circumstances, but when put that way, he could immediately see it'd been the wrong move. He'd let his emotions and hatred for Young override every thought and push him to act rashly, without considering the implications his actions would have on the rest of the team. But still…

"I couldn't just let him get away," Sheridan said, though his confidence had waned slightly. If given the chance, he'd knew he'd make the same choice again. Without a doubt.

"I know. And I think the captain does too."

"But…"

"No buts," Hanover said. "You did what you had to do. I think most of us would've made the same decision."

"Even Chambers," Neal added.

"So he's not going to boot me off the team?"

Neal laughed. "Boot you off? Are you kidding? He told me to tell you to get your ass out of bed and back to training; there's a lot of work to do."

"What work?"

"What, you think everything's finished just because we destroyed their base?" Neal asked. "Hunter's putting together a taskforce to go after every Cardinal asset we get our hands on. Leading it himself is the rumor."

"I thought he was retiring," Sheridan said.

"Who knows," Neal said, shrugging. "Rumor is the president asked him personally to stay on until this thing was wrapped up. I don't know, all I know is he's added a full company of Marines to our ground combat element, as well as a handful of battleships and a flotilla of destroyers. We're going to have our own little fleet."

"That's crazy."

"There's a lot of work to do," Hanover said. "With all the information we pulled off Cardinal's network, we'll be busy for a while."

"Yeah." Neal squeezed Sheridan's hand again. "So you need to stop being lazy and get back to work."

"Well, not right away," Dr. Moore said, moving to the end of the bed. "You'll be up and around here in a few days."

"We've got a few weeks' turnaround anyway," Neal said. "Captain is giving everyone a week's liberty before we need to report back to *Legend*."

Sheridan shifted position again. He couldn't seem to find a good position on the bed. "Can I sit?"

"Sure." The doctor tapped a control on the side of the bed, and it slowly lifted.

"That's much better." He took another breath, trying to calm the nausea. "I wonder how many people are going to be dropping dead now. You know, because of their suicide charges."

"Probably not as many as you think," Hanover said. "Historically they've only been triggered when the threat of capture and questions was imminent, but if there's a way out…"

"Bastards had better not ever stop running, then," Sheridan said. "I won't stop chasing them. Not ever. Not 'til they're all dead or locked up."

"That's the plan," Neal said. "According to Fischer anyway."

"What's he doing?"

"Trying to parse as much of the intel as possible before we get back to Alliance space," Neal said. "It'll probably be another twenty-four to thirty-six hours before anyone in the Alliance knows about the attack on Saccora. He wants to have as many targets identified as possible before we get back."

Sheridan frowned. "We're not going?"

Neal shook her head. "They're putting together several local strike teams to hit as many of them as they can at the same time. Captain Ward stood us down because we've been up-tempo so long. Doesn't want us burnt out before we start the second phase of this thing."

It made sense, but Sheridan couldn't help feeling left out, almost cast aside. He didn't like the idea of others going out to do the work that he should be doing, especially when he was able to do the work.

Well, he thought, *eventually.*

Hanover's link chimed and it rotated into position. He read the message. "Vega needs a spotter. Training never stops. I'll catch you later, Sheridan."

"Sure, brother."

The doctor waited until Hanover had gone before tapping her own link closed. "Everything is tracking fine, Corporal. If you need anything, the nurse is just a link away."

"Thanks, Doc," Sheridan said. "I appreciate it."

Moore smiled, tapped the end of the bed and disappeared behind the curtain, leaving only Sheridan and Neal.

"So," Sheridan said, immediately feeling self-conscious, "a week liberty?"

Neal smiled. "That's right."

"Got any big plans? Going to see parents or friends or anything?"

Neal lifted her chin. "Are you asking if I'm going to see a *man*? Maybe a woman?"

Sheridan chuckled and scratched his chin. "I guess it really wasn't that slick."

"Not at all."

"Well, do you?"

"Do I what, have plans?"

"Yeah."

"Sure do."

"Like what?"

Neal sniffed, grinning. "Like this."

She leaned over and kissed him.

CHAPTER 49

ASI Regional Headquarters
Blue Lake City, New Tuscany
26 August 2607

"You don't have to be here, you know?" Eliwood said.

Fischer straightened, his back aching, and glared at his partner. "I told you. Yes. I do."

"You need to go see her."

"I will," Fischer said. "When this is done."

The bullpen was full, every station manned, every agent and technician working on the exact same thing: Cardinal. They'd managed to copy about ninety percent of the information stored in the Cardinal data center before they'd been forced to retreat, but despite that, they still had more data here than anyone knew what to do with. Fischer and Robalt had worked to narrow down their data pool during the jump back to Alliance space, but they'd barely scratched the surface.

"You do realize that this isn't going to be done for months, probably years," Eliwood said.

"I don't mean the entire thing," Fischer said. "I just mean this

359

part here. I want to make sure there aren't any more assets within the agency."

"No one else has gone missing. Seems to me, if there were more traitors in our midst, we'd've known about it by now."

"Maybe, but that doesn't mean they're not here. They're in the data somewhere; we just need to know where to look."

Eliwood crossed her arms and leaned back against a console behind her. "I bet Nathan can write a really cool shortcut application for that."

"I told you, I'm working on it," Campbell called from the other side of the central table.

"Oh, right." Eliwood winked at Fischer, who shook his head. "You've got the hard job."

"I'll tell you who has the hard job," Fischer said. "Whoever they're sending to try and fix things with the Pegasi. I wouldn't want that job, wouldn't wish it on anyone."

An entire battlegroup had been dispatched to Pegasi space, bringing with them an entire team of diplomatic envoys, personally vetted by the President and cleared through an extensive search of the Saccora database. With only ninety percent of the available data to compare to, there was still a chance an asset might slip through, but everyone involved in the process considered it unlikely.

"Not like it's going to make any difference," Eliwood said. "Those bastards have been looking for a reason to fight us for years. Now that they have one, I doubt they'd give it up easily."

"Their leaders might want conflict, but I doubt their people do." Fischer scratched his beard. It was in bad need of a trim.

"Those people believe everything their damned Most High tells them. Eat it up with a damn spoon."

"Maybe some of them do," Fischer said. "But not all."

"I guess we'll know in a couple weeks when they get back," Eliwood said, turning back to the holoscreens.

Fischer took a long breath, surveying the bullpen. Data scrolled down every holoscreen in the place and had been for the last two days. The office had been working around the clock ever since they'd returned, with most of them simply crashing at their desks and sneaking a snack here and there. Fischer had stolen a couple of hours sleep in one of the interview rooms, but it had left him tight and sore all over.

"Got another one," Campbell said, looking up from his terminal.

The image of an older man, with long graying hair hanging over his ears, appeared on the holoscreen in front of Fischer, his name and title appearing in a message panel underneath.

"Communications director, Hypertrans Blue Lake," Eliwood read.

"Not surprised," Fischer said. "Puts him in a position to see the movements of almost the entire city and then some. The team moving?"

Campbell nodded. "Deploying now."

As soon as Fischer had briefed Carter about what they'd found, the division chief had established multiple strike teams consisting of agents from ASI's tactical response operators and local law enforcement officers. They were stationed at key locations around New Tuscany, ready to move as soon as the headquarters team identified a person as a Cardinal asset.

There were hundreds of names included in the data they'd recovered from the Saccora compound, but as they started to parse it out, they realized that some of the names weren't actually assets. Targets of opportunity, uninitiated sources of intel, people they'd approached but weren't sure they could turn—those names were all logged, and they had to physically check every file to determine if the suspect was a true asset or not.

Fischer would've preferred they'd held off until they'd identified all of the local assets, but there wasn't any way they could be sure they'd get them all anyway. Not to mention the fact that they'd already identified over fifteen people and were quickly running out of response teams to respond and apprehend them. Only three had triggered their suicide charges, but surprisingly, the others hadn't had any implanted.

Equally surprising was that two who'd had charges implanted hadn't detonated them, choosing instead to surrender when the strike teams took them into custody. They'd been interviewed, but as Fischer had anticipated, they hadn't uncovered anything useful. But it seemed that, like with Davis, there were varying levels of commitment to the Cardinal cause.

Case in point was the shuttle *Montgomery* and *Void Hawk* had detained leaving Saccora with twenty high-level Cardinal executives, Ambassador Wantanabe and Saccora's governor among them. The communication officer from *Void Hawk*, Lieutenant Commander Jennings, had been the only other Alliance member of the group, but he'd triggered his charge after an unsuccessful attempt to overload the shuttle's engines. He'd died minutes before the security team took them all into custody. The fact that the rest of the passengers, the ambassador and governor included, didn't have suicide devices was both confusing and more than a little telling. The people seemingly in charge of Cardinal hadn't seen fit to commit their lives to the cause, which in and of itself spoke volumes.

Behind him, Carter's office door slid open. "Who is it this time?"

"Louis Culbrough, Hypertrans Blue Lake," Eliwood called over her shoulder.

Carter grunted. "Not surprised."

Eliwood gave Fischer a sardonic, sidelong glance. He ignored her. "Strike Team Eleven is deploying as we speak."

"Good," Carter said, joining them at the center of the bullpen. "I hope he resists."

Eliwood laughed. "Shit, boss, tell us what you really think."

"They can all burn in hell," Carter said, sweeping his hand around the office. "The lot of them. What are you still doing here?"

Fischer frowned. "What are you talking about? This is my case. I need to be here. I need to work it."

"Oh, bullshit," Carter said. "It's an agency case. *We* are working it. But most of this is running on autopilot anyway. We can do without you for a couple of days."

Multiple video feeds began populating the main screens, showing the raid in real time. Most of the apprehensions had occurred at the suspects' homes, usually catching them in various stages of packing. Some they'd had to track down using BLPD's surveillance and enforcement drones, and so far, they'd only lost two.

The feeds from the team's helmet cams showed them descending on Hypertrans corporate offices next to the expansive terminal building. Memories of his showdown with Sergeant Thomas flooded into Fischer's mind as he watched the first group deploy as the shuttle touched down right outside the main entrance. The first members out ordered the corporate security officers to stand down, instructing them to simply remain at their posts and not to interfere with their operation.

The second team landed on one of the upper landing pads, setting down next to a cluster of small luxury flyers used by Hypertrans executives. The team quickly moved inside, leaving the exterior surveillance to the drones hovering a hundred meters above. They moved quickly through the offices, their route laid out by agents and techs here in the bullpen; Fischer could hear the instructions at the far end of the room.

Fischer looked away from the live feeds to the list of names still being sorted. There were still hundreds of people to vet, and he'd already watched half a dozen takedowns. He tapped on one of the names and started scrolling through the information. He rubbed his forehead, feeling the tension headache from the day before coming back.

"Seriously, Fischer," Carter said. "Take a couple of days. I need you at top form, especially in the weeks and months to come. This isn't the end of the line for us, even after we parse all this data out.

"Director Clancy is already setting up the framework for a multi-division working group dedicated to the Cardinal case. He's still working on the taskforce designation, but if you thought the presidential mandate we had before was big, well, don't be surprised if the one coming down the pike doesn't put the first one to shame."

Fischer nodded at the holodisplays. "This needs to be done right."

"It will be. But overseeing this"—Carter motioned around them—"isn't your responsibility anymore."

"What are you talking about? This is my case."

"And it always will be," Carter said. "Unfortunately, Director Clancy doesn't believe it's a job for a deputy chief."

"Not a job for…" Fischer trailed off, registering what Carter had said. He frowned. "Deputy… what are you talking about?"

Carter tapped his link. "This came through about twenty minutes ago."

"What did?"

Eliwood laughed.

Fischer's frown deepened. "Carter, what did?"

Carter swiped a finger across his link, sending something to Fischer. His link activated automatically, displaying a message Fischer had to read twice. He looked up at his boss, still not believing. "You're kidding."

"Not in the slightest, Deputy Chief Fischer," Carter said, grinning.

"I don't understand. I'm not due for a promotional board for another two years."

"Yeah, well, Director Clancy didn't believe a special agent could run the new task force." Eliwood slapped him on the back. "Congrats, Fish!"

Fischer read over his new ASI credentials, the title of deputy chief spelled out under the agency crest, his name underneath that. It didn't make any sense, but there it was, plain as day.

"The task force will be assigned to the division, so technically you'll still be under my command, but you'll report directly to the director. You'll have your own offices, be able to pick staff and, best of all, no red tape. You'll be able to run this case the way it needs to be run without having to worry about any oversight, except for the director, of course. To be honest, I'm more than a little bit jealous."

"Has this ever happened before?" Fischer asked.

Carter shook his head. "Not that I can recall, not on this scale at least. Which is why, Chief Fischer, you need to be at the top of your game. This isn't the kind of thing you want to mess up."

"I want Eliwood with me."

"Figured that," Carter said. "Already got the transfer lined up."

Carissa's Hideout
Mist Water Resort, Vernog
28 August 2607

The sun was just dipping behind the horizon when the *Doris*
settled down onto her assigned pad, marker lights flashing. Flood-
lights at the corners threw dancing shadows from overgrown trees
surrounding the pad, *Doris*'s engines kicking up water and leaves.
The night air was warm and damp.

"You sure you don't want to come with me?" Fischer asked,
walking down *Doris*'s still-opening ramp.

Jones laughed. "Are you kidding me? She's already going to
want to kill you. I'm not trying to get in the middle of that. I like
breathing."

"Smart man," Fischer said.

"You know where you're going?"

Fischer motioned to his link. "Got it. Shouldn't be any
surprises, right?"

"You think I'd put her here if I thought that? Come on, man,
that hurts my feelings."

"Sure it does. Give me a couple of hours, would ya."

"Anything you need, man," Jones said. "I'm here for you."

The resort grew out of the jungle as Fischer made his way through, following the directions Jones had sent to his link. Beautifully manicured ferns and flowers lined the stone pathways that crisscrossed each other, leading to various sections. Floating illumination orbs lit the place in a warm yellow glow, as much to relax as to light. Occasionally he passed a couple holding hands and smiling, enjoying their getaway from the chaos of the galaxy. Servers weaved through the guests, bringing everything from drinks and food to clothes and other, more controversial items. In the Greater Alliance, drug use was still largely illegal, but in places like Vernog, the rules were more or less ignored.

Fischer checked his link again as he came to a row of bungalows, counting the small huts, finding the correct one and stopping just outside. He wasn't exactly sure how this was going to go down, and he knew it largely depended on Carissa's mood at the time. Though, regardless of how it began, he was hopeful his news would help smooth this whole thing over.

He took a long breath, then tapped in the code Jones had given him.

The door slid open, revealing a small entryway and bare tile floors. Ahead was a small living area, just large enough to hold the L-shaped sectional, a coffee table and a single recliner. Clothes were tossed over the back of the couch, and toys were scattered across the tan carpet. The holodisplay on the far wall was muted, but Fischer didn't need to hear what the anchor was saying; the headline scrolling across the bottom of the screen told him everything he needed to know.

"Alistair Holdings Incorporated board dissolved. Assets across the Alliance seized."

After receiving Director Clancy's briefing on Cardinal and everything related to the investigation so far, the Holloman Senate had voted unanimously to sanction the company, seize all their assets, and detain the majority of their executives. Every employee, whose names hadn't been included in the data from Saccora, had been placed on a watchlist and were given notice to appear before investigators to give full statements as to their work at Alistair.

Teams of technicians were now working around the clock to find the malicious code left by Alistair and either delete it completely or partition it off from the rest of the system. The news that every single one of the Alliance's systems had been affected by this unprecedented project rocked many of the senators, and for the first time that Fischer could remember, they were all united against the Cardinal threat.

"Hello?" Fischer said, stepping in, allowing the door to slide shut behind him.

A clipped scream echoed out from a back room, and a moment later Carissa appeared, her light blue shirt covered in wet spots, hair disheveled, washrag in hand, a shocked expression on her face. She straightened, shock giving way to surprise as she realized who it was.

"Jackson?"

"Hey, babe," he said, immediately feeling silly. He'd spent hours thinking about what he would say when he finally saw her, and "hey, babe" hadn't been anywhere on the list of good choices.

"Hold on." She disappeared through a door to Fischer's left. "Hey, little girl, guess who came to see us?"

Fischer crossed the room to the door Carissa had gone through and saw her picking their daughter out of the bath, dripping water everywhere.

Maddie's face lit up at the sight of Fischer and she reached out for him. "Dah Dah!"

Fischer smiled and took her in his arms, ignoring the wetness and pulling her in to him. He looked at Carissa over Maddie's shoulder; his wife smiled at him. His heart ached. Over the last few weeks, he'd been too busy to really miss them, but as his daughter squeezed him with her little arms, he felt the onslaught of emotions coming and knew he couldn't stop them.

He put his arm out and Carissa stepped into his embrace, and he held both of them for several moments, grateful.

"Come on," Carissa said, stepping back, taking Maddie with her. "Let's get you dry and in jammies."

Fischer stepped back, allowing her to squeeze through the door. She set Maddie down on the couch, finished toweling her off, then struggled to get her diaper on. Maddie pushed her hands away as she tried to pull her shirt down over her head, and rolled off the couch, laughing and running around the back of the couch to hide.

"Oh, whatever, fine, be naked. I don't care," Carissa told her, tossing the shirt down in surrender. She turned to Fischer, shaking her head. "This has been our life."

He laughed. "I'm jealous."

Carissa rolled her eyes. "Oh, I'm sure you are."

"Come here." He pulled her close again and wrapped his arms around her. "I missed you."

"I missed you," Carissa said. She stepped back. "Does this mean it's over?"

Fischer laughed. "I don't know that it's ever going to be over." Her expression seemed to harden at that, and he held his hands out, palms up. "What?"

"I mean us living in hiding, Jackson," Carissa said. "I don't know how much longer I can do this. Not to mention Maddie. We're both going stir-crazy."

"I can tell." He immediately regretted saying it.

She glared at him. "Hey, you try being locked away with a crazy little gremlin baby twenty hours a day for two weeks and see how you come out on the other side."

"You're right, I didn't mean it like that. I'm sorry. Yes, this part is over."

Carissa's body visibly relaxed, shoulders slumping slightly as she let out a long breath. "Thank God."

"We still have a lot of work to do," Fischer said, "but the worst of it is over. This case isn't like anything else I've ever worked on. There are so many moving parts. The director's working under instructions straight from the president."

"What happened?" Carissa asked. "I mean, did you find Young? Figure out what this thing is all about?"

Fischer nodded. "Yeah, we found him. Sheridan... well, we don't have to worry about Marcus Young anymore."

"He killed him? Is he okay?"

"Sheridan? Yeah, he's fine."

They sat on the couch, and Fischer explained everything that had happened over the last two weeks, from their investigation of Davis to the Cardinal base on Saccora. He left out the gorier details of Young's demise.

"I can't believe that about Davis," Carissa said after he'd finished.

Fischer rubbed his beard. "Yeah, I had a hard time with it, too."

"Do you think you're going to be able to track them all down?"

"The majority of them, yes. There might be some who slip through the cracks, but I'm sure we'll catch them eventually. From the lists we've generated so far, our strike teams are going to be busy for the foreseeable future."

"And let me guess, you're going to be right out there with them? Still neck deep in the shit?"

Fischer chuckled. "Well, actually, no."

She frowned. "What do you mean? That's where you operate.

I've never known you to take a back seat to anyone when there was work that needed to be done."

"Oh, I'm definitely not taking a back seat," Fischer said. "In fact, I'm going to pretty much be as deep as you can be."

"I don't understand."

"Yeah, I didn't either." Fischer tapped his link and pulled up his new ASI credentials, holding them out for his wife to see.

Her eyebrows went up as she read, a wide grin spreading across her face. "Deputy chief, huh? Look at you! But what does that mean?"

"I'll be heading up the Cardinal taskforce," Fischer explained. "Running everything from case presentation to evidence collection to interviewing, pretty much anything and everything that has to do with the case. The director didn't think a regular special agent could manage, so…" He held up the link, showing off the badge again.

"Oh god," Carissa said, rolling her eyes. "How long are you going to be flashing that thing around?"

Fischer grinned. "As often as I need to."

"Deputy chief," she said again. "Running a task force—"

"A new division, actually," Fischer corrected, "adjacent to the New Tuscany field office. Technically I'll still be under Carter, but I'll be reporting to the director."

"So no more running into the fray like some kind of superhero?"

Fischer shook his head. "I'll be home every night to bug you."

"But…" She trailed off. "But that's your whole thing, getting in the shit. Has been since I met you. In fact, it was one of the things that attracted me to you. You aren't going to be able to sit behind a desk all day; you're going to go crazy. And let me just tell you"—she motioned around the apartment—"I've got enough crazy in my life right now."

"It'll be an adjustment, sure. But it'll be good. For me and us." She gave him a look that suggested she didn't quite believe him, and he smiled. "It's true. I want to be here with you guys. I mean, not here, but you know. Not here." He motioned to the apartment.

"What?" Carissa looked around. "I kind of like this place. Full room service, maids come every couple of days to replace the linen and turn down the bed. Hell, they've even offered to do the laundry. It's kind of growing on me."

"Oh, yeah?"

"To hell with that," she said. "I want to sleep in my own bed. That thing in there kills my back."

"Try sleeping on a warship in a space the size of a closet. I don't—oh!" Maddie flopped against his legs, pulling herself up onto Fischer's lap. He picked her up, holding her so her face was level with his. "What about you? Are you ready to go home, you little baby terrorist?"

Maddie laughed and reached out for his face. He kissed her forehead and set her back down on the carpet. She laughed, turned, and took off, almost running right into the coffee table.

"Careful, sweetheart!" Fischer said, reaching out to help her stay on her feet as she angled around the corner.

"Oh, it wouldn't be the first time," Carissa said. "But yeah, she's definitely ready."

Fischer stood and moved around the back of the couch. "Come on, I'll help you pack. Jones is waiting on us."

Carissa pushed herself up and followed. "Oh, you're so helpful."

"You're not ever going to let me live this down, are you?"

"Are you kidding?"

"Yeah, that's what I thought."

"No, but I can tell you one thing you *are* going to do when we get home."

Fischer raised an eyebrow. "Oh, what's that?"

"You're going to do what you promised me you were going to do before all this shit hit the fan. You're going to take me on a vacation."

Fischer laughed and moved to give his wife another hug. "That, my love, I can do."

ACKNOWLEDGMENTS

This book marks the end of a project I started almost seven years ago. When I had the original idea for *Edge of Valor*, I had no clue it would become the trilogy it is today. The story itself has changed quite a bit since its inception, but definitely for the better.

Enemy of Valor would definitely not have been finished at all if not for my wife's constant support and understanding. Despite a crazy work schedule of her own, she managed to wrangle the kids when I needed to work, and without that I doubt I would not have made it past page one, chapter one.

As always, I have to thank my publishers, Steve and Rhett, for putting up with my tardiness and being flexible in this volume's delivery. It's been a crazy six months, and truth be told, there was a time when I wasn't sure this book would ever be finished.

To Scott Moon, Walt Robillard, and Chuck Manley, thanks for allowing me to pester you with questions, read early versions of chapters, and provide some of the most invaluable feedback I've ever received. Always most appreciated!

And to my readers, thank you so much for reading these

books and leaving reviews! It's been a pleasure writing them, but it means so much more that you've taken the time to read them and I think that's awesome!

"Eyes up."

Josh

Thank you for reading *Enemy of Valor,* the final book in the *Valor* series.

We hope you enjoyed it as much as we enjoyed bringing it to you. We just wanted to take a moment to encourage you to review the book on Amazon and Goodreads. Every review helps further the author's reach and, ultimately, helps them continue writing fantastic books for us all to enjoy.

If you liked this book, check out the rest of our catalogue at www.aethonbooks.com. To sign up to receive a FREE collection from some of our best authors as well as updates regarding all new releases, visit www.subscribepage.com/AethonReadersGroup.

JOSH HAYES is a USAF veteran and retired police officer turned author. In addition to the Valor series, his work includes Stryker's War (Galaxy's Edge) and The Terra Nova Chronicles with Richard Fox, as well as numerous short stories.

His love of military science fiction can be traced all the way back when he picked up his first Honor Harrington novel, as well as a healthy portion of Tom Clancy and Michael Crichton.

He is the President and host of Keystroke Medium, a popular community for writers of all levels, which produces weekly content including live YouTube broadcasts, craft discussions, and author interviews. www.keystrokemedium.com

When he's not writing or podcasting, Josh spends time with his wife Jamie and his four children. You can find out more about his books at www.joshhayeswriter.com.

Join his Facebook Fan Club: www.facebook.com/groups/joshhayes/

Receive his newsletter: www.joshhayeswriter.com/free-books--more.html

Made in the USA
Coppell, TX
09 August 2021

60208796R00224